PENGUIN CLASSICS

DRACULA'S GUEST AND
OTHER WEIRD STORIES

BRAM STOKER was born in Dublin in 1847, the son of a civil servant. He overcame a long childhood illness to attend Trinity College Dublin, where he distinguished himself in athletics, became president of both Philosophical and Historical Societies, and graduated in science. From 1870 to 1877 he worked as a civil servant in Dublin Castle, publishing *The Duties of Clerks of Petty Sessions in Ireland* in 1879. During this period he also wrote dramatic criticism, and in 1878 his strong admiration for, and burgeoning friendship with, Henry Irving led the actor to appoint him acting (business) manager at London's Lyceum Theatre, an experience that produced *Personal Reminiscences of Henry Irving* (1906). Apart from *Dracula* (1897), Stoker's other novels and stories have declined in popularity since their original publication, an *oeuvre* which includes *The Mystery of the Sea* (1902), *The Jewel of Seven Stars* (1903), *The Man* (1905) and *The Lair of the White Worm* (1911). A collection of Stoker's short stories, *Dracula's Guest and Other Weird Stories* was published post-humously in 1914 by his widow, Florence Stoker.

KATE HEBBLETHWAITE is a Research Fellow at Trinity College, Dublin. She was educated at the University of St Andrews and Trinity College Dublin, gaining a Ph.D. from Trinity in 2005. She has published a number of articles on popular fiction authors of the nineteenth and twentieth centuries and is currently working on the popular literature and culture of this period, with an especial interest in the relationship between science and the novel.

D1385612

BRAM STOKER

Dracula's Guest and Other Weird Stories
with *The Lair of the White Worm*

Edited with an Introduction and Notes by
KATE HEBBLETHWAITE

PENGUIN BOOKS

PENGUIN BOOKS

Published by the Penguin Group
Penguin Books Ltd, 80 Strand, London WC2R ORL, England
Penguin Group (USA) Inc., 375 Hudson Street, New York, New York 10014, USA
Penguin Group (Canada), 90 Eglinton Avenue East, Suite 700, Toronto, Ontario, Canada M4P 2Y3
(a division of Pearson Penguin Canada Inc.)
Penguin Ireland, 25 St Stephen's Green, Dublin 2, Ireland (a division of Penguin Books Ltd)
Penguin Group (Australia), 250 Camberwell Road, Camberwell, Victoria 3124, Australia
(a division of Pearson Australia Group Pty Ltd)
Penguin Books India Pvt Ltd, 11 Community Centre, Panchsheel Park, New Delhi – 110 017, India
Penguin Group (NZ), cnr Airborne and Rosedale Roads, Albany, Auckland 1310,
New Zealand (a division of Pearson New Zealand Ltd)
Penguin Books (South Africa) (Pty) Ltd, 24 Sturdee Avenue,
Rosebank, Johannesburg 2196, South Africa

Penguin Books Ltd, Registered Offices: 80 Strand, London WC2R ORL, England

www.penguin.com

Dracula's Guest and Other Weird Stories published by George Routledge & Sons Ltd 1914
The Lair of the White Worm first published in 1911 by William Rider and Son Ltd
This collection published in Penguin Classics 2006

3

Editorial matter copyright © Kate Hebblethwaite, 2006
All rights reserved

The moral right of the editor has been asserted

Set in 10.25/12.25pt PostScript Adobe Sabon
Typeset by Rowland Phototypesetting Ltd, Bury St Edmunds, Suffolk
Printed in England by Clays Ltd, St Ives plc

ISBN-13: 978-0-141-44171-9

Contents

Acknowledgements

Thanks are due to the Trinity College Dublin Association and Trust for their allocation of a research grant to enable me to undertake this venture. I also have special debts to the editors at Penguin; particularly to Laura Barber, for commissioning the edition, to Marcella Edwards for seeing it through to its conclusion, and to Lindeth Vasey and Claire Peligry for their limitless patience.

My gratitude is similarly owed to the staff of Trinity's library, in particular Charles Benson and the Department of Early Printed Books, and to my colleagues at the School of English, especially Ian Campbell Ross for his invaluable advice and Elizabeth McCarthy for her knowledge of the French Revolution. Without the practical support and generous friendship of Darryl Jones, however, this project would never have been started, much less completed, and it is to him that this edition is dedicated.

Chronology

1847 8 November: Abraham Stoker (Bram) born in Dublin, to Charlotte and Abraham Stoker, the third of seven children.

1854–64 After long incapacitating childhood illness, attends private day school of Rev. William Woods in Dublin.

1864–70 Successful career at Trinity College Dublin: becomes University athletics champion, unbeatable road walker and capped footballer; speaker at the Philosophical Society, of which he becomes President in 1867; graduates as a Batchelor of Arts in 1870.

1867 28 August: sees Henry Irving acting for the first time at Theatre Royal, Dublin. Develops a passion for theatre.

1868 Deeply impressed by Walt Whitman's *Leaves of Grass* (1855).

1870 Enters the Civil Service as a clerk in Dublin Castle.

1871 May: sees Irving again at the Vaudeville Theatre, Dublin. Accepts unpaid position as theatre critic for middle-class Protestant newspaper the *Dublin Evening Mail*. Becomes regular guest of Sir William Wilde and his family.

1872 18 February: writes long, admiring and confessional letter to Whitman (does not send). Elected Auditor of Trinity College Historical Society. September: short story 'The Crystal Cup' published. 13 November: delivers address 'The Necessity for Political Honesty' in the Dining Hall of Trinity College, later published in Dublin.

1873–4 November–March: becomes (part-time) editor of the short-lived *Halfpenny Press*.

1875 February–May: 'The Primrose Path', 'Buried Treasure' and 'The Chain of Destiny' published.

1876 14 February: writes again to Whitman enclosing his first letter; Whitman replies on 6 March. Irving plays Hamlet at Theatre Royal, Dublin. After Stoker's momentous meeting with Irving on 3 December they become friends. Stoker is promoted to Inspector of Petty Sessions.

1877 June: Irving gives reading at Trinity College; thirteen days later Stoker spends annual holiday seeing Irving at Lyceum Theatre, London.

1878 June: visits and assists Irving at Lyceum in rewriting W. G. Wills's play *Vanderdecken*. Mid November: accepts Irving's invitation to become his acting (business) manager at the Lyceum Theatre. Marries Florence Balcombe on 4 December and joins Irving on tour in Birmingham on 9 December. Ellen Terry joins Irving Company as Ophelia for opening of *Hamlet* on 30 December.

1879 *The Duties of Clerks of Petty Sessions in Ireland* published. March: meets Alfred, Lord Tennyson. 29 December: Florence gives birth to Irving Noel Thornley Stoker.

1881 Autumn: organizes the first provincial tour of Irving and Ellen Terry. November: collection of children's stories, *Under the Sunset*, published.

1883 October: manages the first (of six) of Irving's tours of America.

1884 20 March: meets Whitman in Philadelphia. Becomes friends with Mark Twain.

1885 19 December: *Faust* opens at the Lyceum Theatre with Irving in the role of Mephistopheles: it is the company's greatest commercial success. December: gives lecture at the Royal Institution, 'A Glimpse of America'.

1886 October: visits USA to arrange tour of *Faust* for 1887. Visits Whitman at Camden, New Jersey. 'A Glimpse of America' published.

1889 *The Snake's Pass* appears as a serial story in the *People* and several other provincial papers.

1890 8 March: makes first notes for what will become *Dracula*. 30 April: called to the Bar of the Inner Temple. November: *The Snake's Pass* published.

1892 Death of Walt Whitman.

1895 January: *The Watter's Mou* published as companion volume to Arthur Conan Doyle's *The Parasite*. 18 July: Henry Irving knighted. October: *The Shoulder of Shasta* published.

1897 18 May: the first and only performance of Stoker's play *Dracula, or The Un-Dead* performed at the Lyceum Theatre. 26 May: *Dracula* published.

1898 February: *Miss Betty* published; the Lyceum Storage burns down, destroying all the company's scenes and props.

1901 April: sixpenny paperback edition of *Dracula* published, abridged by Stoker.

1902 July: Lyceum Theatre closes and put into receivership. *The Mystery of the Sea* published, found to be 'admirable' in a congratulatory note sent by Conan Doyle. December: Ellen Terry leaves Irving's company.

1903 November: *The Jewel of Seven Stars* published.

1905 September: *The Man* published. October: while on his farewell tour at Sheffield, Irving collapses and dies; he is buried in Westminster Abbey.

1906 October: *Personal Reminiscences of Henry Irving* (2 vols.) published. Stoker suffers a stroke which leaves his walking and sight impaired.

1908 15 January: interview with Winston Churchill published in the *Daily Chronicle*. June: *Lady Athlyne* published. *Snowbound: The Record of a Theatrical Touring Party* also published.

1909 July: *The Lady of the Shroud* published.

1910 December: *Famous Impostors* published.

1911 November: *The Lair of the White Worm* published.

1912 20 April: dies at 26 St George's Square, London; later cremated at Golders Green Crematorium, where his ashes remain.

1914 *Dracula's Guest and Other Weird Stories* published.

Introduction

(Readers new to this collection are advised that this Introduction discusses the stories' plots in detail.)

To many, Bram Stoker's name has become synonymous with a single piece of work that, since its publication in 1897, has grown to typify the Victorian Gothic genre. *Dracula*, with its smorgasbord of sexual fantasies and social anxieties, has so far eclipsed anything else that he has written that, to the reader unaccustomed to Stoker's oeuvre outside it, the extent and range of work that he produced will be somewhat surprising. Thirteen novels, two biographies, one play, one civil service manual and numerous lectures and short stories have all been overshadowed by a single vampire narrative. For a man who wrote so much, that so much should in turn be written about such a small section of his work is a paradox; *Dracula* remains at the forefront and the focus of both academic and popular interest.

This concept of paradox is actually wholly appropriate to Stoker's work. Despite *Dracula*'s longstanding popularity, its literary merits are less assured, Maud Ellmann arguing that 'the novel wouldn't be so good if it weren't so very bad', whilst of his other works, 'most of them [were] execrable'.[1] In turn, in his introduction to the 1983 Oxford World Classics edition of *Dracula*, A. N. Wilson scoffed that, 'No one in their right mind would think of Stoker as "a great writer".'[2] Popular yet pulp, enduring yet unendurable – the sense of discrepancy inherent in Stoker's work is also applicable to the author himself; the volume of literature that has been produced about Stoker since the revival of his reputation in the early 1970s testifying, ironically, to his indecipherability. Since 1962 four full-length biographies have been written which, whilst illuminating the *facts* about Stoker's life, nevertheless fail to get to grips with the man himself. There is very little material extant in which Stoker bares his innermost thoughts. As enigmatic as his most renowned creation, Stoker himself confessed in a letter to Walt Whitman in 1872 that, 'I . . . am naturally secretive to the world.'[3]

The bare facts about Stoker's life have provided rich pickings for literary detective work, and critics have tended to read his works as much for the potential biographical insight they can offer as for the stories they tell. The most manifestly persistent of these critical interpretations has been speculation about his sexual proclivities. Claims have been equally stringently made for Stoker's rampant heterosexual carnality, his closet homosexuality, his anal fixations, oral fixations, Oedipus complex, fear of assertive women (especially mothers) and domination fetishes. The most enduring mystery surrounding Bram Stoker's life in this respect has been his death. Locomotor Ataxia, a stated cause of death on Stoker's Death Certificate, was hailed as proof of the author's contraction of syphilis and thus womanizing reputation by Daniel Farson.[4] Whilst this was rejected by Stoker's third biographer, Barbara Belford, and similarly dismissed by Haining and Tremayne as 'unproven',[5] Stoker's most recent biographer, Paul Murray, has once more taken up the argument for his 'likely' syphilitic condition, citing the author's stroke in 1906, his prescription for arsenic medication in 1910 and his stamping way of walking as evidence.[6]

The virtual impenetrability of Stoker himself and the excesses contained within his fiction lend themselves to this outpouring of biographical conjecture. William Hughes and Andrew Smith argue that *Dracula* has become '*the* Freudian text *par excellence*',[7] revealing a wide range of repressed sexual desires and concerns. Among other interpretations, the syphilitic condition here too has been raised, the novel's preoccupation with insanity, pestilence and implicitly sexual contamination being cited as evidence of Stoker's own sexual ill-health.

To read novels solely for a glimpse of their biographical signposts, however, is to do both text and author a great disservice. Whilst fascinating in their own right as the last published works of Bram Stoker, the two books that comprise this volume, *Dracula's Guest and Other Weird Stories* and *The Lair of the White Worm* also demonstrate that ultimately Stoker was a master of the Gothic genre, fully justifying his reputation alongside late-nineteenth-century 'greats' such as Robert Louis Stevenson, H. G. Wells, Sheridan Le Fanu, Oscar Wilde and Arthur Conan Doyle.

Aside from the spine-chilling excellence of such stories as 'The Burial of the Rats', 'The Squaw' and 'The Judge's House', Stoker offset his tales of the weird and uncanny with an experimental outlook that not only responded to the social conscience of the late nineteenth and early twentieth centuries, but also tapped into contemporaneous experimental movements in art and literature. Far from the rather slapdash image that Stoker's fiction beyond *Dracula* has generated, such works can be seen to be the product of deep thought, research and a profound understanding of the society in which he lived.[8] *The Lair of the White Worm*, for example, widely dismissed as 'clearly the work of a man sick in mind if not in body',[9] is, in reality, an intensely intriguing novel, working on mythic, historical, social and sexual levels, whilst also responding to nineteenth- and early twentieth-century shifts in artistic expression. In short, Stoker was a popular fiction writer of significant aptitude, in tune with the undercurrents of the social thought and creative articulation of his time.

'Dracula's Guest'

Considerable debate surrounds the relationship between 'Dracula's Guest' and its namesake, *Dracula*. First appearing in *Dracula's Guest and Other Weird Stories* (1914), a volume of short stories collected and published by Bram Stoker's widow after his death, it was claimed by Florence Stoker to be 'an hitherto unpublished episode from *Dracula* ... originally excised owing to the length of the book'. For this reason, the story as it now stands has often been accepted as the 'original' first chapter of *Dracula*, subsequently deleted by Stoker's editors.[10]

However, the relationship between the two stories is rather

more complicated than at first appears. *Dracula* is written as a series of diary entries, letters and newspaper reports; 'Dracula's Guest', on the other hand, is a first-person account written by an *anonymous* author. Dissimilarities in tone and style further separate the two to such an extent that, whilst 'Dracula's Guest' certainly displays strong links with the novel, it is unlikely that the story as it now stands was precisely that which was initially planned for publication with *Dracula*. Much more probable is the notion that the story is a self-contained episode, reworked from Stoker's original ideas for the novel's opening. Certainly, the final published version of *Dracula* itself is a much better work *without* such an opening: it is tighter and more immediate, and the reader is instantly drawn into the physical and psychological journey towards the Transylvanian Count.

Despite its apparently simple plot – a man goes for a walk, gets lost, has an adventure and is rescued – 'Dracula's Guest' is skilfully ambiguous. The identities of both the 'tall and thin' figure that causes the carriage horses to 'jump and kick about' and the wolf that ultimately saves the narrator, and their own relationship to the Boyar Dracula whose telegram ends the story, are never fully stated. Yet similarities to the Count's physiognomy and manner in *Dracula* itself can certainly be drawn; his height, his effect on carriage horses, his ability to metamorphose into 'an immense dog' when disembarking at Whitby, and his 'peculiarly sharp white teeth' and 'red, gleaming eyes',[11] would indeed suggest the two characters are one and the same. Likewise, the narrator's description of the wolf's 'fierce and acrid' breath and his instinctive 'loathing, like the first stage of sea-sickness' when in contact with it are analogous to Harker's reaction to Dracula's touch:

> As the Count leaned over me and his hands touched me, I could not repress a shudder. It may have been that his breath was rank, but a horrible feeling of nausea came over me, which, do what I would, I could not conceal.[12]

That Stoker keeps his readers guessing to the end of the story – and beyond – is testimony to his skill as a writer of the

Gothic tale. His close attention to detail and the progressive intensification of atmosphere and tension are characteristics of all the narratives in this collection. The violent storms at the stories' zenith, in particular, are a familiar feature in Stoker's work.

Such dramatic events and visually evocative scenes have made Stoker's work a goldmine for cinematographic adaptation. From the many and various versions of *Dracula* that have been made subsequent to F. W. Murnau's *Nosferatu* (1922)[13] to Seth Holt's *Blood from the Mummy's Tomb* (1972), Mike Newell's *The Awakening* (1980) and Jeffrey Obrow's *Bram Stoker's The Mummy* (1997), which all drew their source from Stoker's *The Jewel of Seven Stars* (1903), the keen eye for melodramatic detail and imaginative impact that Stoker acquired from his years at the theatre translated perfectly on to the silver screen. From this collection alone, 'Dracula's Guest' and *The Lair of the White Worm* were, respectively, adapted into *Dracula's Daughter* (1936, directed by Lambert Hillyer) and Ken Russell's *tour de force* of satirical camp *The Lair of the White Worm* (1988). Far from being a one-book wonder, then, Stoker has influenced the changing trends in modern cinema.

The undercurrent of sexual tension that critics have been quick to detect in Stoker's work is certainly apparent in 'Dracula's Guest'. The homoerotic nature of Dracula's claim over Harker's prostrate body – 'This man belongs to me!'[14] – is mirrored in this story in the proprietorial guarding of the narrator's body by the wolf. If the wolf is indeed also Dracula, then both its intimate action of licking the narrator's throat and the feeling of 'semi-lethargy' that this prompts in the narrator – which recalls the state of languorous ecstasy induced in Harker by the three female vampires – undoubtedly lend a degree of support to those who have argued for a 'queer' reading of the Count. Certainly, as in *Dracula* the image of the undead female is a source of horror: sexually alluring but deadly, the Countess Dolingen is finally destroyed by a (phallic) iron stake, through which lightning is conducted. Like Lucy Westenra (*Dracula*), similarly pinioned, and Lady Arabella March (*The Lair of the White Worm*) who is also destroyed by lightning, in her death the Countess Dolingen symbolizes both the final triumph of the male over the female and her purgation from Nature itself – punishment perhaps for her beauty, her allure or quite simply for her femininity.

In his depiction of fearsome women and atmospheric excess, parallels have been drawn between Stoker's stories and those of another Irish writer of the Gothic, Joseph Sheridan Le Fanu (1814–73). The possibility of a direct connection between Stoker and Le Fanu is tantalizing: Stoker started working as an unpaid drama critic for the Le Fanu-owned *Dublin Evening Mail* in 1871; during this time he was also a regular visitor to the Wildes' house in Merrion Square, Le Fanu being their close neighbour. Many of Le Fanu's stories were published in the *Dublin University Magazine* (at one time also owned by him), which Stoker would undoubtedly have had access to during his period at Trinity, and Le Fanu's *The Watcher and Other Weird Stories* (1894) was in Stoker's library. Whether the two actually met is unclear, although it seems likely that they must have been aware of one another. Certainly, the influence of Le Fanu upon Stoker's writing is widely acknowledged, most especially in the case of 'Dracula's Guest' and *Carmilla* (1872).

Set in Styria and framed as a case from the file of Le Fanu's psychic doctor, Martin Hesslius, the novella centres on the beautiful young Carmilla, who arrives at the castle of an aristocratic family. Uncannily, Carmilla is the very image of a figure that had appeared, many years before, in a dream of the family's daughter, Laura. Whilst the two girls are forming an unusually close attachment bordering on the sexual, the surrounding villages are beset by a series of mysterious deaths. Laura soon falls victim to this 'plague' but is saved by a family friend, the uncle of one of Carmilla's previous victims, who reveals their mysterious guest's true vampiric identity. Carmilla's tomb is subsequently discovered and, in her lifelike death-state, she is decapitated and staked. Stoker borrowed much from Le Fanu's story, not least his technique of building a story on the shaky foundations of both doubt and fear, leaving the supernatural or unexplainable elements unexplained and indefinitely powerful. In the end we are left with only half a rationalization for the events that take place in both Styria and Munich – and enjoy the stories all the more for it.

Both Stoker's and Le Fanu's Gothic stories deal with the violation of boundaries: between the worlds of the natural and the supernatural, dreams and reality, human and animal, life and death. Carmilla herself violates all four of these, adding sexual ambiguity (akin to Dracula's) to her list of misdemeanours. She woos Laura like a predatory lover with 'gloating eyes' and 'hot lips', female sexuality displaying itself in all its guilty wantonness: 'she would whisper, almost in sobs, "You are mine, you shall be mine, and you and I are one forever."'[15] Whilst homosocial desire may be aberrant for Le Fanu, for Stoker, it is a source of sanctuary from dangerous female sexuality. Men tend to falter when strong women abound, as *Dracula*'s Professor Abraham Van Helsing's words encapsulate:

> Then the beautiful eyes of the fair woman open and look love, and the voluptuous mouth present to a kiss – and man is weak.[16]

Stoker's Short Stories and the Gothic Tradition

Le Fanu's influence on Stoker can be similarly traced in a number of other stories in this volume. Apparitions and dreams, for example, fuelled the momentum of both authors' stories,[17] whilst the tale of the mental breakdown and death of a student under the malign influence of a long-dead judge in Stoker's 'The Judge's House' (1891) bears more than a passing resemblance to Le Fanu's own 'Mr Justice Harbottle' (1872), itself a drastically rewritten version of his 'An Account of Some Strange Disturbances in Aungier Street', published in the *Dublin University Magazine* in 1853. Both of Le Fanu's stories climax with the discovery of the cruel judge suspended by his own hanging rope, whilst in 'The Judge's House' it is the innocent lodger who is the victim of the judge's toxic apparition.

However, it would be misleading to imply that, in displaying similarities with Le Fanu's work, Stoker was merely plagiarizing his ideas. Many of the plot devices that both authors used were longstanding staples of the Gothic tradition. The pictorial image that comes to life and steps out of its frame, substituting itself for its original in 'The Judge's House', is a concept that can be traced from Horace Walpole's *The Castle of Otranto* (1764) to Oscar Wilde's *The Picture of Dorian Gray* (1890), via Charles Maturin's *Melmoth the Wanderer* (1820) and Edgar Allan Poe's 'The Oval Portrait' (1850). In addition, inclement weather, spooky houses, local superstitions, disturbed dreams, vampires, doubles, second sight and malevolent beasts appeared frequently in the Gothic novels and stories of John Polidori, Mary Shelley, Matthew Lewis, Robert Louis Stevenson, Oscar Wilde and Arthur Conan Doyle, among others. Gothic, while imaginative, is certainly not an innovative genre as far as fictional plot mechanisms are concerned. Sets are recycled, plots rehashed and atmosphere remains invariably hyperbolic. Where the very best writers of the Gothic *are* original is in reworking these potentially formulaic devices and indulgence in uncanny excess into relevant, incisive and captivatingly unique tales in their own right. Oscar Wilde's *The Picture of Dorian Gray*, for example, is not merely a pictorial dramatization of the Faustian pact for the *fin de siècle* audience; it is also a direct challenge to society's superficiality, revealing the complex duality of the human condition.

Stoker understood the need for this balancing act between high fancy and deep focus, and his ability to weave such seemingly hackneyed elements seamlessly – and vividly – into his fiction without incurring accusations of belaboured cliché stands as evidence of his considerable abilities as a writer of the Gothic story. The weather may be preternaturally rough at times of high drama; pictures may come to life; animals may stalk humans; dreams and visions may foretell doom; and men may fight for, die for, kill for – and kill – women, yet joining these extreme events lies an overarching unease about the transgression of boundaries. Life and death, known and unknown, animal and human, man and woman, dream and reality, good and evil: each duality is in conflict in the stories, and each remains largely unresolved at their closure. For Stoker, life on the boundaries signified intense anxiety, the human spirit displaying itself at its most dangerous, and most resolute.

Transgression of borders socially or morally imposed results in the disruption of the imperceptible balance of power, and descent into chaos. For death to impose itself on life, for animal to impose itself on human, or for woman to impose herself on man meant a fundamental questioning of the divide separating each from the other, and the ultimate need for a reassessment of the 'acceptable' status quo.

'The Squaw' (1893), for example, reflects the deep unease expressed in much later nineteenth-century popular literature about the need for the reassessment of the boundaries that separate human and animal. The tale of a cat's revenge upon Elias P. Hutcheson of Nebraska for his accidental killing of her kitten is so effectively chilling precisely because the cat expresses very human emotions. Its initial cry of distress upon the death of its litter, 'such as a human being might give', soon gives way to a display of keen intelligence and calculated revenge that results in the American's gruesome death in the Iron Virgin, a formidable cabinet inlaid with sharp spikes that, when closed, pierced the eyes, heart and vitals of the victim enclosed within. The cat's calm satisfaction in its act and the narrator's choice of weapon – a sword for the execution of *humans* – enforces this confusion of the boundaries between man and animal:

> And sitting on the head of the poor American was the cat, purring loudly as she licked the blood which trickled through the gashed socket of his eyes. I think no one will call me cruel because I seized one of the old executioner's swords and shore her in two as she sat.

The certainties of what it meant to be human became increasingly unstable as the nineteenth century drew to a close, as man was forced to re-identify himself in animal rather than divine terms. Following evolution theory's unwelcome suggestion that both man and ape had evolved from a single lineage, and Darwin's later contention, in *The Expression of the Emotions in Man and Animals* (1872), for the essential cross-species universality of emotional expression, a definable body of fiction emerged which confronted the potentials of this narrowing gap between man and beast. When Robert Louis Stevenson's Dr Jekyll creates an alter ego for himself in order that he may indulge his baser desires undetected, his creation, the troglodytic Mr Hyde, is similarly 'ape-like'.[18] H. G. Wells's *The Time Machine* (1895), meanwhile, depicts a future world in which the human species has diverged into two distinct races: the delicate human-like yet mentally degenerate Eloi and their masters, the subterranean Morlocks, who have evolved *back* into 'ape-like' creatures and breed the human Eloi as 'fatted cattle'[19] for their consumption.

Stoker returned to this theme of the humanized animal in a number of his stories and novels. 'The Burial of the Rats' (1914) makes indistinct the line that separates the rats that infest the rubbish heaps, picking clean the bones of the dead, and the human rats, 'more animals than men', who hunt the story's narrator through the streets of Paris. A malevolent rat also terrorizes the doomed student in 'The Judge's House', the inference being that the creature is in some way the transmogrified soul of the judge himself, whilst in *Dracula* the Count displays the ability not only to command rats and wolves, but also to morph into a bat, a large dog and, in 'Dracula's Guest', a werewolf.

This apprehension about the transgression of *physical* boundaries is compounded in Stoker's stories by an overarching concern about the permeability of the boundaries between the rational and the irrational, the known and the unknown. 'The Gipsy Prophecy' (1914) overthrows the comfortable, safe world of middle class self-assurance, symbolized by fat cigars and college chums, with the Gipsy Queen's visionary warning that Joshua Considine will murder his wife. Although ridiculed, her prophecies nevertheless disturb their recipients. At the story's close the prediction of blood flowing 'through the broken circle of a severed ring' certainly comes true, and although Mary Considine takes comfort in the logical rationalization that 'The gipsy was wonderfully near the truth; too near for the real thing ever to occur now, dear', the reader is left wondering whether a worse fate awaits the young bride.

The defiance of logic by the uncanny is particularly palpable in 'The Judge's House', where a student of the reasoned science of mathematics is overwhelmed by the mysterious transmogrification of a portrait, despite his avowed protestations to the contrary:

> A man who is reading for the Mathematical Tripos has too much to think of to be disturbed by any of these mysterious 'somethings,' and his work is of too exact and prosaic a kind to allow of his having any corner in his mind for mysteries of any kind.

Exemplifying this overturning of the world of sense, the giant rat with baleful eyes is unperturbed by a book of logarithms that is used as a missile against it, yet baulks at the Bible – a symbolic triumph of faith over logic. There indeed turn out to be more things in heaven and earth than are dreamt of in Malcolmson's philosophy, the cultured and reasoned scientific defences of his mathematical library proving useless against the uncanny forces which threaten the fundamentals of reason itself.

In deference to the Gothic tradition, Malcolmson's attempt to shore up the fragments of logic against rationality's ruination is strongly reminiscent of the third chapter of Emily Brontë's *Wuthering Heights* (1848), where Lockwood piles a pyramid of books in front of his window in order to prevent Catherine Linton's apparition from entering the room. Himself a town-dweller and therefore a stranger to the elemental effects of the wilderness, Lockwood cannot – and will not – comprehend an explanation for his 'dream' as anything other than the 'effects of bad tea and bad temper'.[20] In like manner, the ideological deconstruction of rigid confines between good and evil that takes place in 'The Judge's House' (a supposedly righteous judge is in fact an envoy of evil) connects the story with the Gothic genre's long-established subversion of 'conventional' powers of right and wrong, for instance in William Godwin's *Caleb Williams* (1794) and Mary Shelley's *Frankenstein* (1818; 1831).

The last two stories in *Dracula's Guest and Other Weird Stories* have a rather different tone to the rest of the collection.

The pietism of the Christian morality tale 'A Dream of Red Hands' (1894) and the acerbic ridiculing of Celtic sentimentality in 'Crooken Sands' (1894) initially seem at odds with the other, dourer, Gothic tales. However, the stories' concerns about Jacob Settle's immortal soul or the comic lingering over the absurdity of Arthur Markam's tartan costume do not irrevocably set them apart. Prophecy, nightmares and the recurrent Gothic motif of the doppelgänger soon offset the reverence and humour with darker revelations about the ability of the mind to react forcibly to the power of suggestion. Furthermore, whilst absolution certainly marks the apogee of each – Settle's hands are wiped clean and Markam learns the 'fatal force' of his vanity – as with the other stories, resolution and satisfaction remain at variance. For Settle to conquer eternal damnation, he must paradoxically give up his life. Markam, meanwhile, learns 'what a vain old fool I was' at the expense of the drowned haberdasher Mr Roderick MacDhu who, it is ultimately revealed, is the apparition that has haunted the London merchant. Contradiction once more dominates the tales of this most enigmatic of writers.

'So much for the fortified heights; but the hollows too have their own story': History, Myth and Stoker's Evil Women

This notion of contradiction is especially pertinent to *The Lair of the White Worm*, originally published by William Rider and Son Ltd in 1911. Often dismissed as the confused ramblings of a dying man, the novel's critical place as the culmination of Stoker's output has been unfairly overshadowed by the assumption that its conception and construction was undertaken in a haze of opium and syphilis.[21] A bizarre novel, certainly, which seems defined more by its collection of inconsistent subplots than by any coherent driving narrative, *The Lair of the White Worm* has languished in obscurity, heavily abridged, since its initial publication. Indeed, subsequent editions were significantly edited or amended in an attempt to extract a degree of coherence from its pages.

Although this story was written between 3 March and 12 June 1911, its hasty composition belies a text that embodies all the concerns and contradictions of Stoker's work. In thrall to the abiding power of myth and legend, yet also attuned to contemporary scientific ideas, the novel crosses borders between the logical and the illogical, the old and the new, the impulsive and the considered, whilst also being thematically engaged in the transgression of boundaries between male and female, human and animal, right and wrong. Simultaneously displaying both irrational flights of imagination and careful research, unconscious impulses and measured ideas, it is Stoker's most inaccessible yet his most revealing work. Like the man himself, *The Lair of the White Worm* is a complex amalgam of self-possession and passion that defies any ready definition.

Set in the ancient lands of Mercia, a kingdom dominant in Anglo-Saxon England from the seventh to the ninth centuries which, at its height, stretched from the River Thames to Yorkshire and from Lincolnshire to Wales, as Seed maintains, 'the action of [*The Lair of the White Worm*] is constantly being displaced from turn-of-the-century England into a legendary past which, Stoker implies, is not anywhere near as remote as we imagined'.[22] Early twentieth-century concerns are framed within a context of historical fact and legendary fable and within the traditional narrative format of a central battle leading to a victorious hero and a displaced villain. As such the heroes and villains of the novel transcend their temporal location and attain a mythic status of universality – 'the history of the Caswall family is coeval with that of England' says Sir Nathaniel (Chapter II). The moral judgements that are made are therefore simultaneously accorded the weight of universal Truth: and in *The Lair of the White Worm* the strongest moral judgement is that held against women.

Bram Stoker's uneasy relationship with the women of his texts has been a matter of considerable debate. In depicting a world of male camaraderie and homosocial salvation, his stories consistently work to demonize the oversexed independent female, whilst praising and advancing the meek woman who displays deference to her male overlords. In *Dracula*, the ultimately biddable Mina Harker is saved from the vampire's kiss whilst Lucy Westenra, desirous of three husbands in life, is transformed into a noxious sexual predator in death, finally finding 'salvation' through the phallic penetration of a wooden stake through her heart. In *The Man* (1905) the female protagonist Stephen Norman, who has been given a man's name, recognizes what she regards as the 'defects' of her femininity and decides that she will base her life, not on 'woman's weakness' but on 'man's strength'.[23] Having taken it upon herself to propose marriage to a man, Stephen is brutally rejected by him, and experiences loneliness and despair, her decline ending happily when she accepts a proposal from the man she herself initially spurned for his assumptions of masculine superiority: 'She was all woman now; all-patient, and all-submissive. She waited for the man; and the man was coming!'[24]

Stoker's penultimate book, *Famous Impostors* (1910), elucidates many of the concerns embedded in his fiction, most conspicuously that of the relationship between the sexes. A curious incursion into cases of historical imposture, the work devotes an entire section to women who disguise themselves as men and another, entitled 'The Bisley Boy', to the attestation that Queen Elizabeth I was in fact a man, the original child having died in infancy and been replaced by a male infant. The inference that a successful woman of power must in fact be a man says much for Stoker's attitude towards the dominant female, whilst the direct relevance of this book's theme of gender inversion to *The Lair of the White Worm* is demonstrable by the latter's dedication to Bertha Nicoll, a friend of Stoker's who first made him aware of the conspiracy theory attached to the young Queen Elizabeth.

Throughout this collection, the driving force of many of the plots is the instability of women, or the evils that women do. Even scorned female animals are to be treated with the utmost caution, as 'The Squaw' amply demonstrates: both this story and 'The Secret of the Growing Gold' (1892) are propelled by the power of female vengeance. The tragedies of 'A Gipsy Prophecy' and 'The Coming of Abel Behenna' (1914), meanwhile, are provoked by their female characters' unnatural command of Second Sight or their inconsistency, vanity and greed, whilst it is discernibly the withered old crone in 'The Burial of the Rats' who synchronizes the deadly assault upon its narrator. The sole female character in 'Dracula's Guest' is likewise an unnatural object of fear and loathing – a suicide-turned-vampire whose seductive 'life in death' trance conjoins the twin pillars of sex and death in horrific association:

> In the instant, as I am a living man, I saw, as my eyes were turned into the darkness of the tomb, a beautiful woman, with rounded cheeks and red lips, seemingly sleeping on a bier.

The incompatible polarization of women as either submissive angels or sexual demons is a particularly unequivocal feature of *The Lair of the White Worm*. Whilst Mimi and Lilla Watford are the embodiment of virtuous, meek womanhood, content to be sustained by their menfolk, Lady Arabella March, the social, sexual and financial independent, is the novel's antagonist, terrifying, in part, precisely because of her overpowering femininity. Flaunting her womanliness in 'tightly fitting white [clothes], which showed off her extraordinarily slim figure' (Chapter X), Lady Arabella uses feminine wiles to lure Edgar Caswall into a promise of matrimony for her own financial ends. However, Lady Arabella is also the white worm of the novel's title, a grotesque prehistoric survival that preys on humans and animals alike. In this way, dynamic femininity translates itself into an overriding animality, in turn transforming active female sexuality into a dangerous and noxious thing. In fact, throughout Stoker's works, female sexual proximity of any kind is to be regarded with the utmost caution. In 'The Squaw', for example, the narrator notes his relief at having Elias P. Hutcheson join him in the second week of his honeymoon, whilst in *The Lair of the White Worm* Adam Salton treats his proposal of marriage to Mimi as a 'painful duty' (Chapter XXVI) that Nathaniel finally agrees to undertake.

The intense anxiety pertaining to strong women in *The Lair of the White Worm* is nowhere more palpable than in Diana's

Grove. Reference to Diana calls to mind the goddess's association with women and childbirth, yet the grove of the novel is reminiscent only of 'many great deaths' (Chapter X). As such, traditional roles of woman as life-giver and nurturer are reversed and the grove's inhabitant is linked instead with death and destruction. Lady Arabella personifies this perversion of the female role, calmly pouring 'shot after shot' (Chapter VIII) into Adam Salton's mongoose, whilst her rancid well-hole at the centre of Diana's Grove perpetuates the image of a monstrous vagina:

> It was like . . . the drainage of war hospitals, of slaughter-houses, the refuse of dissecting rooms. None of these was like it, though it had something of them all, with, added, the sourness of chemical waste and the poisonous effluvium of the bilge of a waterlogged ship whereon a multitude of rats had been drowned. (Chapter XXI)

Its 'Queer smell' (Chapter XIX) characterizes Arabella's perverted womanhood, the rank 'primeval ooze' (Chapter XXI) emanating from it being a harbinger of death rather than life. In her own death, furthermore, Lady Arabella herself is reduced to a putrid slime, unrecognizable in either form or species, the 'great red masses of rent and torn flesh and fat' (Chapter XXXIX) to which she is reduced invoking images of toxic menstrual blood and genital secretions, in turn implying that Lady Arabella has dissolved into her own rancid femininity.

Born not of any union between man and woman but existing since the dawn of history, Lady Arabella is thus the physical manifestation of intrinsic and unbridled woman. Challenging the bounds of gender prescription, however, is not only the prerogative of the women of Stoker's novels. Just as women consistently overstep their feminine margins, men are continually called to live up to their masculinity. Although the 'male' does ultimately triumph in The Lair of the White Worm, it requires a band of men to counteract the threat of a single woman. Furthermore, maleness is repeatedly associated with images of familial, mental or physical degeneration. Both Adam

Salton and Edgar Caswall are the last in their respective family lines, whilst Caswall himself descends into insanity as the novel progresses. In turn, Mimi and Lilla's grandfather is rarely involved in the narrative; Richard Salton all but disappears after the opening chapters, and Arabella's father is but a shadow character, talked about yet never seen. Moreover, the male triumvirate, although vociferous in avowing their willingness 'to risk whatever is to be risked' (Chapter XXVIII), remain a passive force, Sir Nathaniel resolving to 'postpone decisive action until the circumstances depended' (Chapter XXV). Women are the inciters of action whilst men are content to let that action take its course: even Lady Arabella's death is, technically, by her own hand as she removes back to her own lair the kite cable along which the final, deadly, bolt of electricity travels.[25]

The concern about aggressive femininity is augmented in *The Lair of the White Worm* by the species boundaries Lady Arabella straddles between human and snake. Aside from the palpable biblical links with the serpent that identify Arabella with the role of God's nemesis and the augury of Original Sin, the symbolic snake also places *The Lair of the White Worm* within the context of legendary tales of dragon-slaying in England and their own related associations with moral triumphs of good over evil. References to both the 'Lambton Worm' and the 'Laidly Worm of Spindleston Heugh' (1890) (see Appendix II) connect the novel with such folk fables, whilst the specific significance of the symbol of the dragon, or *wyrm*, to the kingdom of Mercia is evident from the place names that have survived into the modern age.[26] The battle between man and worm/woman is thus elevated to a level of universality that encompasses both religion and folklore and accords judgement not only against Lady Arabella but also her ophidian species and her female sex.

This association between serpent and woman at the turn of the twentieth century was not Stoker's alone. Bram Dijkstra's *Idols of Perversity* (1986) makes much of the iconography of misogyny against feminine evil in the late nineteenth and early twentieth centuries, in particular highlighting the recurring image of the serpent in association with women in a large number of works of art produced at this time.[27] Pictures such as Jean Delville's *The Idol of Perversity* (1891) and Franz von Stuck's *Sin* (1893) depicted sexual women and sinuous snakes locked in mutual embrace – an unholy alliance of moral and physical corruption that prompted association with biblical sin and the physical usurpation of the male penis. A direct challenge to the rising force of the New Woman, that new breed of independent female who challenged male prerogatives and refused to be defined by the traditional roles of wife and mother, such works pilloried women both for their 'natural' sinfulness and for their adoption of the male role. In spite of her veneer of female respectability, Lady Arabella's ruthlessness and ambition are revealed when she assumes her true form: a 'tall white shaft' that rises from the bushy tangle of the 'trees which lay between' (Chapter XXVIII). Just as she confuses the male/female divide in her forward conduct, the enormous white penis that Lady Arabella effectively becomes in her ophidian form is the physical representation of her departure from received and acceptable womanhood. .

The physical borderland that Lady Arabella March embodies, between human and animal, and male and female, is similarly reflected in her very name, which also makes a connection with the historical feminine. The name 'Mercia' itself means 'the land of the boundary people', from the Anglo-Saxon word *Mierce* for boundary, whilst the heart of the kingdom of Mercia once covered that area which is now known as the Welsh Marches. Stoker may have also drawn inspiration for his fictional dominatrix from the historical chronicles of Mercia's own commanding female, Queen Æthelflaed. Æthelflaed's reign (911–18) was unique not only because she stood almost alone in early medieval Europe as a female ruler in her own right, or because she was a woman in command of a kingdom dominated by warfare and the needs of warfare, but because her reign was remarkably successful personally, politically and militarily. Mercia prospered under her guidance, successfully defending itself against outside aggression, but also securing a series of victorious military campaigns against the

Welsh and the Danes.[28] Clearly a strong character able to wield power and command respect, Æthelflaed, like Queen Elizabeth I, stepped outside the gender expectations of later historians and chroniclers.

Despite accusations of a hasty pen or an unwieldy imagination, then, the rationality of Stoker's mind in creating *The Lair of the White Worm* cannot be questioned. His knowledge and consideration of historical and thematic material and the story's measured construction within a *fin de siècle* framework of fear of the dominant female reveal an imagination thoroughly in tune with the cultural zeitgeist. Moreover, and as the next section will show, the composition of *The Lair of the White Worm* displays an originality which places the novel at the vanguard of early twentieth-century literary expression.

Twin Pillars of Wisdom: Art and Science

The 1911 edition of *The Lair of the White Worm* included six colour plates by the artist and clairvoyant Pamela Coleman Smith. Illustrating scenes from the novel, the pictures variously depicted: Edgar Caswall mesmerizing Lilla, Caswall's hawk-shaped red kite, Oolanga with an armful of snakes, and Lady Arabella dancing in the wood, descending the turret steps of Castra Regis, and as the White Worm. By virtue of the difficulty of their reproduction, however, these images have been left out of subsequent reprints. This is unfortunate as they draw attention to Stoker's preoccupation with the visual as well as the textual narrative. Coleman Smith had accompanied the Lyceum Theatre Company on its sixth tour of America in 1899 and is probably now best remembered for her illustrations of the classic Rider-Waite tarot deck. The strikingly bold use of block colour combined with an almost cartoon-like simplicity of line and structure that characterizes Coleman Smith's illustrations (as well as her tarot designs) elevates Stoker's narrative beyond formal, definable realism. Indeed, in the hallucinatory game with reality that the novel itself engages in, in its destabilization of rationality and even in the very pace at which it was written, *The Lair of the White Worm* itself displays artistic elements that would be at the heart of the Surrealist movement that emerged six years after its publication.

Surrealism itself was inspired in part by the English Gothic novel's philosophy of immediacy, non-rational emotional excess and exploitation of subconscious desires and fears. The hyperbolic immoderation of novels such as Horace Walpole's *The Castle of Otranto* and Matthew Lewis's *The Monk* (1796) particularly appealed to the Surrealists in their rebellion against propriety and convention, typified in much of the movement's painting by the deliberate displacement of external object for internal meaning. In seeking to put human nature back in touch with the forces of the imaginative unconscious, it also sought inspiration from the non-rational forces of myth, madness and dreams. In 1924 André Breton's First Surrealist Manifesto contended that, 'If the depths of our minds conceal strange forces capable of augmenting or conquering those on the surface, it is in our greatest interest to capture them.'[29] Undermining nineteenth-century naturalism, Surrealism however did not try to transcend realism; rather it sought to dissolve the foundations of stability upon which realism depended and, in the process, to question the basis upon which it claimed to be able to represent reality. In short, Surrealism refused to recognize the existence of a divide between 'real' and 'unreal'.

Abandoning the critical mind to its imaginative faculty, the Surrealists' practice of 'automatic' writing was predicated on the suppression of rational consciousness. For the Surrealists, to write with no predetermined thought as quickly as one could on a blank sheet of paper revealed the infinite powers of imagination, the total surrender of oneself to the impulse of chance illuminating the depths of human consciousness and capturing the immediacy of thought. This quest for a reality beyond logic characterized much of Stoker's writing. Its relevance, however, is particularly apposite to *The Lair of the White Worm*, which, composed in a mere three months, displays the emotional excesses and subversion of logic which were the hallmarks of Surrealism. Demonstrating his own avowal that 'No one has the power to stop the workings of imagination',[30] and emancipating imagination itself from the formal world of logic, Stoker's

Mercia amalgamates dreams, hypnosis, madness and halluci-
nations with the recognized conventions of social propriety.
The novel's hasty production may in turn be seen as a precursor
to the 'automatism' of the Surrealists, the baggy narrative and
disjointed chronology merely by-products of a far more interesting experimentation in the art of subconscious creativity.
Inhabiting a borderland where distinctions between what has
tangible reality and what is imaginary are unclear, Stoker's final
novel encapsulates André Breton's summation of Surrealism's
goal:

> ... there exists a certain point in the mind at which life and
> death, real and imaginary, past and future, communicable and
> incommunicable, high and low, cease to be perceived in terms of
> contradiction.[31]

Rejecting any sense of human identity as serious, stable or
continuous, *The Lair of the White Worm* is therefore both
reflective and progressive in its outlook. Blurring apparent differences between reality and imagination whilst simultaneously
acknowledging an adherence to late-nineteenth-century social
conventions, the novel is an intriguing amalgamation of avant-
garde vision and traditionalist sentiment.

This keen awareness of the artistic atmosphere in which he
was writing may well have been a natural consequence of working in theatreland. There, Stoker met a large number of fellow
artists, from Mark Twain to W. B. Yeats, Ford Maddox Ford
to Walt Whitman. Of all the literary figures with whom Stoker
came into contact at the Lyceum, however, he respected none
more than the Poet Laureate, Alfred, Lord Tennyson (1809–
92), whom he met in March 1879 and whose plays *The Cup*
and *Becket* were produced by the Lyceum Company in January
1881 and February 1893 respectively. Stoker's admiration
for Tennyson reveals itself in *The Lair of the White Worm*,
where allusion is made to the poet's *In Memoriam* (1850), Sir
Nathaniel's observation that 'We are going back to the origin
of superstition – to the age when dragons of the prime tore each
other in their slime' (Chapter XXIV) being a close citation of:

No more? A monster then, a dream,
A discord. Dragons of the prime,
That tare each other in their slime,
Were mellow music matched with him.[32]

Tennyson's and Stoker's consciousness of the potential of
unbridled Nature red in both tooth and claw was similarly
shared by another of Stoker's close acquaintances, Sir Arthur
Conan Doyle. The Lyceum had staged Doyle's play *Waterloo*
to great critical and popular acclaim in September 1894, Doyle
in turn praising *Dracula* as 'the very best story of diablerie
which I have read for many years'.[33] Discreet allusions to Conan
Doyle's works pepper the stories in this collection, from the
overarching horror of strong women that is the hallmark of
The Parasite (1894), the story of a female mesmerist and her
powers of sexual manipulation, to 'The Terror of the Blue John
Gap' (1910) in which a huge subterranean antediluvian beast
terrorizes the inhabitants of the Peak District countryside. 'It is
only the natural process of evolution,' Nathaniel de Salis tells
Adam Salton (Chapter XXV); however, Conan Doyle's and
Stoker's stories reveal an anxiety about the potentials of evolution, both biological *and* social, which has the equal possibility of undermining their species and their sex. In stating that
'We are in a quagmire, my boy, as vast and as deep as that in
which the monsters of the geologic age found shelter and perhaps
advance', de Salis concertinas the millennial process of evolution,
effectively questioning both man and mankind on present, past
and future planes (Chapter XXXVIII). Conan Doyle was to
undertake a very similar approach in his 1912 novel, *The Lost
World*, in which the discovery of a colony of dinosaurs and
ape-men on a remote plateau in South America leads to a
fundamental questioning of both hegemony and humanity.

An anxiety over species transgression and hereditary robust-
ness is further compounded in Stoker's texts by a central concern over racial autonomy. Throughout these stories, frequent
references are made to the might and resilience of Englishness,
from the narrator's exclamation in 'Dracula's Guest' that 'All
my English blood rose' when challenged by the German coach-

driver, to the self-affirmatory 'I was an Englishman and would make a fight for it' by the narrator of 'The Burial of the Rats'. In *The Lair of the White Worm*, likewise, the whiteness of the white worm, whilst certainly relatable to the beds of valuable china clay that lie beneath Diana's Grove, also introduce a racial theme to the narrative that makes contact with the many 'Invasion of England' novels such as Richard Marsh's *The Beetle* (1897), Arthur Conan Doyle's 'Lot 249' (1892) and even Stoker's own *Dracula*, which were popular during the last decades of the nineteenth century. Written in the wake of Sir George Chesney's *The Battle of Dorking* (1871), such narratives played with the conjecture of an assault upon the country from a foreign power and the potential colonization of England's shores that would result. The chief threat against the foundations of England and Englishness in *The Lair of the White Worm*, however, comes from one of its own inhabitants and is manifestly concealed beneath a surface of respectability and assumed propriety: traditional boundaries between native and invading foreigner are thus destabilized whilst, paradoxically, the associations between whiteness and value are reinforced. These opposing (and permeable) worlds of civilization and barbarity are further highlighted by the figure of Edgar Caswall's African servant, Oolanga. Depicted as belonging to an even more primitive evolutionary system than the white worm, he is a 'negroid of the lowest type; hideously ugly, with the animal instincts developed as in the lowest brutes . . . so brutal as to be hardly human' (Chapter V). Adverse stereotyping of the racial 'Other' is similarly prevalent in *Dracula* where the 'Hebrew of rather the Adelphi Theatre type, with a nose like a sheep, and a fez',[34] who is responsible for removing the Count's boxes of earth at Galatz, is but a more defined version of Dracula's own implied Jewishness: a tall black pillar of a man with a hooked nose and an abundance of curly hair. This portrayal of 'primitive' societies as morally under-evolved taps into prevailing anthropological notions about racial and criminological 'underdevelopment': the native and the criminal being regarded as retarded in both their moral and physical bearing, and hence evolutionarily closer to children and the beasts. Dracula is said to have a criminal's 'child-brain',[35] whilst Oolanga is a 'devil-ridden child of the forest and the swamp' (Chapter IV).

The consequences of this less-than-fully-evolved status would, it was believed, manifest themselves physically. *L'Uomo Delinquente* (1876), by Cesare Lombroso (1835–1909), argued that crime was caused almost entirely by the anthropological characteristics of the criminal who was essentially 'an atavistic being who reproduces in his person the ferocious instincts of primitive humanity and the inferior animals'.[36] The criminal type was thus in effect a 'throwback' to humanity's savage past and displayed moral degeneracy through concurrent physical symptoms. Heavily influencing the late nineteenth-century exponents of Degeneration theory such as Max Nordau (1849–1923) and Henry Maudsley (1835–1918), physiological evaluation effectively achieved the deliberate marginalization of certain strata of society, objectifying and – riding on the crest of the evolutionary-degeneration wave – bestializing their 'otherness'.[37] Stoker himself regarded physiognomy as an eminently practical form of knowledge, and there are countless references to it scattered throughout his work.[38] At its most basic, good men are handsome, wicked men hideous: the face of the judge in 'The Judge's House', for example, is 'strong and merciless, evil, crafty, and vindictive, with a sensual mouth, hooked nose of ruddy colour, and shaped like the beak of a bird of prey'. In this collection, physiognomical judgement is also taken one step further, corporeal features often being heralded as connoting origin, whilst characters' temperaments personify the perceived characteristics of their ethnicity. Thus the African Oolanga displays the 'grossest animal passions' that he himself physically embodies (Chapter XV), whilst Edgar Caswall typifies his Roman ancestry:

The aquiline features which masked them seemed to justify every personal harshness. The pictures and effigies of them all show their adherence to the early Roman type. Their eyes were full; their hair, of raven blackness, grew thick and close and curly. Their figures were massive and typical of strength. (Chapter II)

Similar judgements are also made about Mimi and Lilla Watford, and Abel Behenna and Eric Sanson in 'The Coming of Abel Behenna'.

Aside from concerns raised over the potential destabilization of the physical self, Stoker's stories also display an intense anxiety about the capitulation of mental autonomy. Count Dracula, for example, launches a two-fold attack upon his victims, subjecting them to both a corporeal and psychological transformation. Hypnotism as a means of control likewise infuses *The Lair of the White Worm* in both Edgar Caswall's attempts to overpower Lilla through mesmeric manipulation and, ironically, in his own surrender to insanity following the discovery of Mesmer's chest. Overawed by this assault on multiple levels, at one point in the novel Adam Salton asks, 'of what sort is the mystery – physical, mental, moral, historical, scientific, occult?' (Chapter XIX). Dramatizing the vulnerability of the mind as well as the body, Stoker's narratives highlight the potential transgression of *all* barriers of perception. What Stoker himself called the 'strife of living'[39] necessitated a precarious negotiation through those malignant forces which seek to overwhelm life itself, and the durability of his stories' popularity may be attributed to this very awareness of the fundamental anxieties of human existence.

NOTES

1. Maud Ellmann, 'Introduction'. Bram Stoker, *Dracula*, ed. Maud Ellmann (Oxford: Oxford University Press, 1998), pp. viii, xiii.

2. A. N. Wilson, 'Introduction'. Bram Stoker, *Dracula*, ed. A. N. Wilson (Oxford: Oxford University Press, 1983), p. xiv.

3. From letter to Walt Whitman. Barbara Belford, *Bram Stoker: A Biography of the Author of Dracula* (London: Phoenix; Orion Books Ltd, 1997), p. 43.

4. Daniel Farson, *The Man Who Wrote 'Dracula'. A Biography of Bram Stoker* (London: Michael Joseph, 1975), pp. 212, 233–5.

5. Peter Haining and Peter Tremayne, *The Undead: The Legend of Bram Stoker and 'Dracula'* (London: Constable & Company Ltd, 1997), p. 182.

6.   Paul Murray, *From the Shadow of 'Dracula': A Life of Bram Stoker* (London: Jonathan Cape, 2004), pp. 254, 267–9.

7.   William Hughes and Andrew Smith, 'Bram Stoker, the Gothic and the Development of Cultural Studies'. William Hughes and Andrew Smith (ed.), *Bram Stoker: History, Psychoanalysis and the Gothic* (London: Macmillan Press Ltd, 1998), p. 3.

8.   Harry Ludlum claimed that *The Lair of the White Worm* is Stoker's least successful novel because of the speed at which it was written, 'the writing terse, bare, jerky, hurrying on to the next contrived scene, compressing great strides into sentences of convenience'. Harry Ludlum, *A Biography of Dracula. The Life of Bram Stoker* (London: W. Foulsham & Co. Ltd, 1962), p. 148.

9.   Clive Leatherdale, *Dracula the Novel & the Legend. A Study of Bram Stoker's Gothic Masterpiece*. Revised edition (Brighton: Desert Island Books, 1993), p. 72.

10. The tale of a young man who encounters both werewolves and the living dead on Walpurgis Nacht (30 April) whilst in Munich, en route to visiting Count Dracula, would certainly tend to suggest a strong link with *Dracula*, which opens with Jonathan Harker's first diary entry three days later on 3 May, noting that he 'Left Munich at 8.35 p.m.' Furthermore, during Harker's later encounter with the three female vampires in Dracula's castle, he recalls of the fair-haired one, 'I seemed somehow to know her face, and to know it in connection with some dreamy fear': he recognizes her because she was originally intended as the Countess Dolingen. This irregularity was never caught by the original editors, although a subsequently deleted line makes it clear. 'As she spoke I was looking at the fair woman and it suddenly dawned on me that she was the woman – or the image – that I had seen in the tomb on Walpurgis Night.' Cited in Belford, *Bram Stoker*, p. 265.

11. Stoker, *Dracula* (London: Penguin Books Ltd, 2003), pp. 89, 24, 101. The connection between the vampire and the werewolf is certainly one that Stoker would have known about in researching *Dracula*, through his reading of Sabine Baring-Gould's *The Book of Were-Wolves* (1865), which detailed the belief that 'After death lycanthropists become vampires.' Sabine Baring-Gould, *The Book of Were-Wolves: Being an Account of a Terrible Superstition* (London: Senate; Studio Editions Ltd, 1995), p. 115.

12. Stoker, *Dracula*, p. 25.

13. For a complete rundown of *Dracula*-inspired films and plays, see

David J. Skal, *Hollywood Gothic: The Tangled Web of Dracula from Stage to Screen* (London: Andre Deutsch, 1990).

14. Stoker, *Dracula*, p. 46. In his first brief outline of the scene in March 1890 Stoker jotted 'This man belongs to me. I want him'; this was later emended into the final version now published. Maurice Hindle, 'Introduction', Stoker, *Dracula*, p. xxxiv.

15. Sheridan Le Fanu, *Carmilla*, in *In a Glass Darkly*, ed. Robert Tracy (Oxford: Oxford University Press, 1993), p. 264.

16. Stoker, *Dracula*, p. 393.

17. In Le Fanu's *Carmilla*, for example, Laura claims to have 'seen' her mysterious guest in a dream many years before their meeting, while Carmilla avers to having experienced a similar epiphany. Jacob Settle is haunted by dreams of being barred from heaven in Stoker's 'A Dream of Red Hands', whilst Arthur Markam is similarly disturbed by dreams of seeing his own death in 'Crooken Sands'; and in *The Lady of the Shroud* (1909) Rupert Sent Leger's adventures in the Blue Mountains are dreamt about, weeks beforehand, by his aunt in Scotland.

18. Robert Louis Stevenson, *The Strange Case of Doctor Jekyll and Mr Hyde and Other Tales of Terror*, ed. Robert Mighall (London: Penguin Books Ltd, 2002), p. 22.

19. H. G. Wells, *The Time Machine* (London: Victor Gollancz, 1999), pp. 45, 63.

20. Emily Brontë, *Wuthering Heights*, ed. Pauline Nestor (London: Penguin Books Ltd, 2003), p. 22.

21. See Daniel Farson, *The Man Who Wrote 'Dracula'*, p. 217.

22. David Seed, 'Eruptions of the Primitive into the Present: *The Jewel of Seven Stars* and *The Lair of the White Worm*', in *Bram Stoker*, eds. Hughes and Smith, p. 197.

23. Stoker, *The Man* (London: William Heinemann, 1905), pp. 79–80.

24. Ibid., p. 434.

25. Concern over a transient, easily displaced masculinity is evident throughout Stoker's works. The necessity for multiple men to counteract the threat of a single woman is manifest in 'Dracula's Guest' where a male wolf and a entire brigade of dragoons come to the rescue of the narrator who himself admits to feeling 'unmanned' (Chapter II) in the presence of the Countess's tomb. Similarly, in *Dracula* it takes the four-strong 'Crew of Light' to overcome the Count and his group of female revenants.

26. For example: Drakelow ('the dragon's mound'), three miles north of Kidderminster; 'Drakeholes' ('dragon's valley'), four miles

south-east of Bawtry in Nottinghamshire; Wormwood Hill in Stapleford, south-east of Cambridge; and Wormhill and Wormsley, respectively about five miles west and six miles north-west of Hereford. Sarah Zaluckyj, *Mercia: The Anglo-Saxon Kingdom of Central England* (Almley: Logaston Press, 2001), p. 57.

27. Bram Dijkstra, *Idols of Perversity: Fantasies of Feminine Evil in Fin-de-Siècle Culture* (Oxford: Oxford University Press, 1986), pp. 305–15.

28. Ian W. Walker, *Mercia and the Making of England* (Stroud: Sutton Publishing, 2000), pp. 113–21.

29. Cited in Waldberg, *Surrealism* (London: Thames and Hudson, 1965), p. 66.

30. Bram Stoker, 'The Censorship of Fiction'. Cited in *A Glimpse of America and Other Lectures, Interviews and Essays*, ed. Richard Dalby (Essex: Desert Island Books Ltd, 2002), p. 157.

31. From *Le Second Manifeste du Surréalisme* (1929). Cited in Waldberg, *Surrealism*, p. 76.

32. Alfred, Lord Tennyson, *In Memoriam*, 2nd edition, ed. Erik Gray (New York: W. W. Norton & Company Inc., 2004), p. 41.

33. Cited in Murray, *From the Shadow of Dracula*, p. 204.

34. Stoker, *Dracula*, p. 371.

35. Ibid., p. 362.

36. Gina Lombroso-Ferrero, *Criminal Man According to the Classifications of Cesare Lombroso* (London and New York: G. P. Putnam's Sons, 1911), p. xv.

37. In the last decades of the nineteenth century the prospect of what H. G. Wells called 'downward modification' haunted the European imagination. Degeneration theory essentially reversed and compressed the narrative of evolutionary progress, arguing for the latent potential of mankind to physically and morally regress. The works of men such as Benedict Augustin Morel, Cesare Lombroso, Max Nordau and Henry Maudsley proposed a theory of retrograde evolution which appeared to provide a scientific explanation for the ills of society, attributing them to individuals who had been born with mental, moral or physical degenerative symptoms. Indeed, as both a branch of biology and a form of cultural criticism, 'degeneration' became a highly portable term to apply to anything that appeared to deviate from the status quo, from physics to social science to literature and art. As Daniel Pick argues, 'Degeneration involved at once a scenario of racial decline (potentially implicating everyone in the

society) and an explanation of "otherness", securing the identity of, variously, the scientist, (white) man, bourgeoisie against superstition, fiction, darkness, femininity, the masses, effete aristocracy.' Daniel Pick, *Faces of Degeneration: A European Disorder 1848–1918* (Cambridge: Cambridge University Press, 1993), pp. 230–31.

38. At the time of his death Stoker owned a five-volume quarto edition of Johann Caspar Lavater's *Essays on Physiognomy* (1789). David Glover, *Vampires, Mummies and Liberals: Bram Stoker and the Politics of Popular Fiction* (Durham and London: Duke University Press, 1996), p. 72.

39. Stoker, 'The Censorship of Fiction', p. 156.

Further Reading

Although an enormous number of books have been written about *Dracula*, there is a remarkable dearth of critical literature on Bram Stoker's other novels and stories. For a comprehensive list of *Dracula* criticism, readers should consult Maurice Hindle's 'Further Reading' in the Penguin Classics edition of *Dracula*. The list that follows concentrates on criticism that looks beyond Stoker's most renowned work.

BIOGRAPHY

Barbara Belford, *Bram Stoker: A Biography of the Author of 'Dracula'* (New York: Alfred Knopf, and London: Weidenfeld and Nicolson, 1996). The author describes her book as 'the first Stoker biography to make use of unpublished letters and manuscripts from private collections and university archives in Britain, Ireland and the United States'.

Daniel Farson, *The Man Who Wrote 'Dracula': A Biography of Bram Stoker* (London: Michael Joseph, 1975). The first of Stoker's biographers to argue for the author's contraction of syphilis.

Harry Ludlum, *A Biography of Dracula: The Life Story of Bram Stoker* (London: W. Foulsham & Co. Ltd, 1962). Ludlum worked in close collaboration with Stoker's son, Noel, to write the first biography of the author.

Paul Murray, *From the Shadow of 'Dracula': A Life of Bram Stoker* (London: Jonathan Cape, 2004). The most recent biography of Stoker, in which the author's life, rather than his work, is the primary focus.

BIBLIOGRAPHY

Richard Dalby and William Hughes, *Bram Stoker: A Bibliography* (Westcliff-on-Sea, Essex: Desert Island Books, 2004).

ESSAYS AND ARTICLES

Antonio Ballesteros González, 'Portraits, Rats and Other Dangerous Things: Bram Stoker's "The Judge's House", in *That Other World: The Supernatural and the Fantastic in Irish Literature and its Contexts*, ed. Bruce Stewart, vol. 2 (Gerrards Cross: Colin Smyth Ltd, 1998).

William Hughes, '"The Fighting Quality": Physiognomy, Masculinity and Degeneration in Bram Stoker's Later Fiction', in *Fictions of Unease: The Gothic from Otranto to The X-Files*, eds. Andrew Smith, Diane Mason and William Hughes (Bath: Sulis Press, 2002).

Lillian Nayder, 'Virgin Territory and the Iron Virgin: Engendering the Empire in Bram Stoker's "The Squaw"', in *Visions of Motherhood and Sexuality in Britain, 1875–1925*, eds. Claudia Nelson and Ann Sumner Holmes (Basingstoke: Macmillan, 1997).

David Punter, 'Echoes in the Animal House: *The Lair of the White Worm*', in *Bram Stoker: History, Psychoanalysis and the Gothic*, eds. William Hughes and Andrew Smith (Basingstoke: Macmillan, 1998).

David Seed, 'Eruptions of the Primitive into the Present: *The Jewel of Seven Stars* and *The Lair of the White Worm*', in *Bram Stoker: History, Psychoanalysis and the Gothic*, eds. Hughes and Smith.

Carol Senf, '*Dracula* and *The Lair of the White Worm*'. Bram Stoker's Commentary on Victorian Science', *Gothic Studies*, 2/2 (2000): 218–31.

RELATED TEXTS AND STUDIES

Joseph Andriano, *Our Ladies of Darkness: Feminine Dae-monology in Male Gothic Fiction* (University Park: Pennsylvania State University Press, 1993).

Fred Botting, *Gothic* (London: Routledge, 1996).

Richard Davenport-Hines, *Gothic: Four Hundred Years of Excess, Horror, Evil and Ruin* (London: Fourth Estate, 1998).

Bram Dijkstra, *Idols of Perversity: Fantasies of Feminine Evil in Fin-de-Siècle Culture* (Oxford and New York: Oxford University Press, 1986).

Markman Ellis, *The History of Gothic Fiction* (Edinburgh: Edinburgh University Press, 2001).

Christopher Frayling, *Nightmare: The Birth of Horror* (London: BBC Books, 1996).

David Glover, *Vampires, Mummies and Liberals: Bram Stoker and the Politics of Popular Fiction* (Durham: Duke University Press, 1996).

Lucy Hartley, *Physiognomy and the Meaning of Expression in Nineteenth-Century Culture* (Oxford: Oxford University Press, 2001).

William Hughes, *Beyond Dracula: Bram Stoker's Fiction and its Cultural Context* (Basingstoke: Macmillan/Palgrave, 2000).

— and Andrew Smith, eds., *Bram Stoker: History, Psycho-analysis and the Gothic* (Basingstoke: Macmillan, 1998).

Kelly Hurley, *The Gothic Body: Sexuality, Materialism, and Degeneration at the 'Fin de Siècle'* (Cambridge: Cambridge University Press, 1996).

Darryl Jones, *Horror: A Thematic History in Fiction and Film* (London: Arnold Publishers, 2002).

Sally Ledger, *The New Woman: Fiction and Feminism at the Fin de Siècle* (Manchester: Manchester University Press, 1997).

David Punter, *The Literature of Terror: A History of Gothic Fiction from 1765 to the Present Day*, 2 vols. (London: Longman, 1996).

Elaine Showalter, *Sexual Anarchy: Gender and Culture at the 'Fin de Siècle'* (London: Virago Press, 1992).

A Note on the Texts

The text follows that of both the first edition of *Dracula's Guest and Other Weird Stories*, collated by Florence Stoker and published in London in April 1914 by George Routledge & Sons Ltd (price 1s.) and the first edition of *The Lair of the White Worm*, published in London in November 1911 by William Rider and Son Ltd (price 6s.).

The Routledge edition of *Dracula's Guest and Other Weird Stories* went through three impressions in 1914, and ten more in the next twenty years. A souvenir edition limited to 1,000 copies was published in 1927 to mark the occasion of the 250th London performance of *Dracula* at the Prince of Wales's Theatre in London. Given away to members of the audience, when the book was opened, a black bat (separately enclosed in the front cover), powered by elastic, flew out. In 1966 Jarrolds and Arrow simultaneously published the stories under the title *Dracula's Guest* (price 15s., and 3s. 6d. respectively), and in 1974 Arrow published a reprinted edition with identical pagination. An American edition of *Dracula's Guest and Other Weird Stories* was published in New York by Hillman-Curl Inc. in 1937 (price $1.50).

Following its initial publication in 1911, *The Lair of the White Worm* was subsequently published by W. Foulsham & Co. Ltd in 1925 (price 2s.); this edition was heavily abridged and partly rewritten (with the deletion of both the illustrations and several important passages), condensed to only twenty-eight chapters and 182 pages of text. The modern reprints from Arrow (1960), Jarrolds (1966) and Brandon (1991) used this condensed version instead of the original. An American edition of *The Lair of the White Worm* was published by The Paper-back Library (New York) in May 1966 under the title *The Garden of Evil*. This edition contained the complete text of the original edition of *The Lair of the White Worm*.

Minor alterations in typography and punctuation (the length of dashes, single quotation marks for doubles and no full stop after personal titles or monarch's numbers, e.g. Mr, Mrs, William IV) have been silently made throughout the text printed here to conform to house style. The majority of other inconsistencies of spelling and punctuation such as Stoker's fickle use of the oxford comma, variant spellings (e.g. 'realise'/ 'realize', 'Walpurgis Nacht'/'Walpurgis-Nacht'/'Walpurgis night', 'to-day'/'today') and instances of double punctuation (:– and –,) have been left as they originally occurred in the first edition. The exception to this is in 'The Judge's House' where the first edition's interchangeable use of 'Malcolmson' and 'Malcomson' has been regularized to 'Malcolmson'. Obvious misspellings have also been silently corrected, for example 'artistocratic' has been amended to read 'aristocratic'.

In a very few cases punctuation has been added where grammatically required, and very slight textual changes have been made where meaning would otherwise have been compromised. A list of such changes is given below:

page: line	1st edition	Penguin
10:12	cypress	cypress,
18:13–14	took ticket	took a ticket
30:8–9	she added. Dr Thornhill replied.	she added. [new para.] Dr Thornhill replied.
41:7	cat missing . . . face had	cat, missing . . . face, had
50:5	Brent's Rock,	Brent's Rock
52:10	close home	close to home
52:11	feelings	feeling
52:30	Wykham overcome	Wykham, overcome
56:22	eyes seemed	eyes, seemed
59:37	his object	his object,

61:13–14	Geoffrey in the torrent	Geoffrey, in the torrent
62:25	golden-hair	golden hair
66:21–2	to-night.' The gipsy	to-night.' [new para.] The gipsy
67:23	then said.	then said:
72:31	close quarters with	close quarters, with
75:4	calmly for	calmly, for
77:36	She went on.	She went on:
79:22	Both men	Both men,
82:35	hopes which	hopes, which
87:29	Abel encumbered	Abel, encumbered
96:37	each shelf of which	each shelf, of which
109:31	grim, persistency	grim persistency
112:10–11	island for such	island, for such
112:16	I suppose half a	I suppose, half a
115:20	efforts to destroy the bridge was	efforts to destroy the bridge were
123:31	seek for him	seek for him,
125:21	to the uprightness	to uprightness
129:10	Scotch song.	Scotch song,
131:12	sporran that	sporran, that
148:37	evening prayers.	evening prayers:
164:22	moved the previous	moved from the previous
204:11	duties truth	duties, truth
223:29	was, that	was that
226:17	birds, beast, fishes	birds, beasts, fishes
240:18	Watford as a key	Watford a key
256:30	With the outside	The outside
260:12	such as mark	such as marks
283:10	metals, has	metals has
303:10	Adam held him	Adam held out to him
308:6	fast;	fast,
311:2–3	alone by the ship canal	along by the ship canal
315:17–18	had no fears	had fears

316:7	time, soon passes	time soon passes
318:21-2	ordeal, braced him	ordeal braced him
323:6-7	great truth,' Sir Nathaniel went on cheerfully	great truth.' [new para] Sir Nathaniel went on cheerfully
328:13	any disagreeable	anything disagreeable
331:33-4	herself and	herself, and
362:23	and that as	and as
363:9	last, that	last that

DRACULA'S GUEST
and Other Weird Stories

CONTENTS

DRACULA'S GUEST

When we started for our drive the sun was shining brightly on Munich,[1] and the air was full of the joyousness of early summer. Just as we were about to depart, Herr Delbrück (the maître d'hôtel of the Quatre Saisons, where I was staying) came down, bareheaded, to the carriage and, after wishing me a pleasant drive, said to the coachman, still holding his hand on the handle of the carriage door:

'Remember you are back by nightfall. The sky looks bright but there is a shiver in the north wind that says there may be a sudden storm. But I am sure you will not be late.' Here he smiled, and added, 'for you know what night it is.'

Johann answered with an emphatic, 'Ja, mein Herr,' and, touching his hat, drove off quickly. When we had cleared the town, I said, after signalling to him to stop:

'Tell me, Johann, what is to-night?'

He crossed himself, as he answered laconically: 'Walpurgis nacht.'[2] Then he took out his watch, a great, old-fashioned German silver thing as big as a turnip, and looked at it, with his eyebrows gathered together and a little impatient shrug of his shoulders. I realised that this was his way of respectfully protesting against the unnecessary delay, and sank back in the carriage, merely motioning him to proceed. He started off rapidly, as if to make up for lost time. Every now and then the horses seemed to throw up their heads and sniffed the air suspiciously.[3] On such occasions I often looked round in alarm. The road was pretty bleak, for we were traversing a sort of high, wind-swept plateau. As we drove, I saw a road that looked but little used, and which seemed to dip through a little, winding valley. It looked so inviting that, even at the risk of offending him, I called Johann to stop – and when he had pulled up, I told him I would like to drive down that road. He made all sorts of excuses, and frequently crossed himself as he spoke. This somewhat piqued my curiosity, so I asked him various questions. He answered fencingly, and repeatedly looked at his watch in protest. Finally I said:

'Well, Johann, I want to go down this road. I shall not ask you to come unless you like; but tell me why you do not like to go, that is all I ask.' For answer he seemed to throw himself off the box, so quickly did he reach the ground. Then he stretched out his hands appealingly to me, and implored me not to go. There was just enough of English mixed with the German for me to understand the drift of his talk. He seemed always just about to tell me something – the very idea of which evidently frightened him; but each time he pulled himself up, saying, as he crossed himself: 'Walpurgis-Nacht!'

I tried to argue with him, but it was difficult to argue with a man when I did not know his language. The advantage certainly rested with him, for although he began to speak in English, of a very crude and broken kind, he always got excited and broke into his native tongue – and every time he did so, he looked at his watch. Then the horses became restless and sniffed the air. At this he grew very pale, and, looking around in a frightened way, he suddenly jumped forward, took them by the bridles and led them on some twenty feet. I followed, and asked why he had done this. For answer he crossed himself, pointed to the spot we had left and drew his carriage in the direction of the other road, indicating a cross, and said, first in German, then in English: 'Buried him – him what killed themselves.'

I remembered the old custom of burying suicides at cross-roads:[4] 'Ah! I see, a suicide. How interesting!' But for the life of me I could not make out why the horses were frightened.

Whilst we were talking, we heard a sort of sound between a yelp and a bark. It was far away; but the horses got very restless, and it took Johann all his time to quiet them. He was pale, and said: 'It sounds like a wolf – but yet there are no wolves here now.'

'No?' I said, questioning him; 'isn't it long since the wolves were so near the city?'

'Long, long,' he answered, 'in the spring and summer; but with the snow the wolves have been here not so long.'

Whilst he was petting the horses and trying to quiet them, dark clouds drifted rapidly across the sky. The sunshine passed away, and a breath of cold wind seemed to drift past us. It was only a breath, however, and more in the nature of a warning than a fact, for the sun came out brightly again. Johann looked under his lifted hand at the horizon and said:

'The storm of snow, he comes before long time.' Then he looked at his watch again, and, straightway holding his reins firmly – for the horses were still pawing the ground restlessly and shaking their heads – he climbed to his box as though the time had come for proceeding on our journey.

I felt a little obstinate and did not at once get into the carriage.

'Tell me,' I said, 'about this place where the road leads,' and I pointed down.

Again he crossed himself and mumbled a prayer, before he answered: 'It is unholy.'

'What is unholy?' I enquired.

'The village.'

'Then there is a village?'

'No, no. No one lives there hundreds of years.' My curiosity was piqued: 'But you said there was a village.'

'There was.'

'Where is it now?'

Whereupon he burst out into a long story in German and English, so mixed up that I could not quite understand exactly what he said, but roughly I gathered that long ago, hundreds of years, men had died there and been buried in their graves; and sounds were heard under the clay, and when the graves were opened, men and women were found rosy with life, and their mouths red with blood.[5] And so, in haste to save their lives (aye, and their souls! – and here he crossed himself) those who were left fled away to other places, where the living lived, and the dead were dead and not – not something. He was evidently afraid to speak the last words. As he proceeded with his narration, he grew more and more excited. It seemed as if his imagination had got hold of him, and he ended in a perfect paroxysm of fear – white-faced, perspiring, trembling and looking round him, as if expecting that some dreadful presence would manifest itself there in the bright sunshine on the open plain. Finally, in an agony of desperation, he cried:

'Walpurgis nacht!' and pointed to the carriage for me to get in. All my English blood rose at this, and, standing back, I said:

'You are afraid, Johann – you are afraid. Go home; I shall return alone; the walk will do me good.' The carriage door was open. I took from the seat my oak walking-stick – which I always carry on my holiday excursions – and closed the door, pointing back to Munich, and said, 'Go home, Johann – Walpurgis-nacht doesn't concern Englishmen.'

The horses were now more restive than ever, and Johann was trying to hold them in, while excitedly imploring me not to do anything so foolish. I pitied the poor fellow, he was so deeply in earnest; but all the same I could not help laughing. His English was quite gone now. In his anxiety he had forgotten that his only means of making me understand was to talk my language, so he jabbered away in his native German. It began to be a little tedious. After giving the direction, 'Home!' I turned to go down the cross-road into the valley.

With a despairing gesture, Johann turned his horses towards Munich. I leaned on my stick and looked after him. He went slowly along the road for a while: then there came over the crest of the hill a man tall and thin. I could see so much in the distance. When he drew near the horses, they began to jump and kick about, then to scream with terror. Johann could not hold them in; they bolted down the road, running away madly. I watched them out of sight, then looked for the stranger, but I found that he, too, was gone.

With a light heart I turned down the side road through the deepening valley to which Johann had objected. There was not the slightest reason, that I could see, for his objection; and I daresay I tramped for a couple of hours without thinking of time or distance, and certainly without seeing a person or a house. So far as the place was concerned, it was desolation itself. But I did not notice this particularly till, on turning a bend in the road, I came upon a scattered fringe of wood; then I recognised that I had been impressed unconsciously by the desolation of the region through which I had passed.

I sat down to rest myself, and began to look around. It struck me that it was considerably colder than it had been at the commencement of my walk – a sort of sighing sound seemed to be around me, with, now and then, high overhead, a sort of muffled roar. Looking upwards I noticed that great thick clouds were drifting rapidly across the sky from North to South at a great height. There were signs of coming storm in some lofty stratum of the air. I was a little chilly, and, thinking that it was the sitting still after the exercise of walking, I resumed my journey.

The ground I passed over was now much more picturesque. There were no striking objects that the eye might single out; but in all there was a charm of beauty. I took little heed of time and it was only when the deepening twilight forced itself upon me that I began to think of how I should find my way home. The brightness of the day had gone. The air was cold, and the drifting of clouds high overhead was more marked. They were accompanied by a sort of far-away rushing sound, through which seemed to come at intervals that mysterious cry which the driver had said came from a wolf. For a while I hesitated. I had said I would see the deserted village, so on I went, and presently came on a wide stretch of open country, shut in by hills all around. Their sides were covered with trees which spread down to the plain, dotting, in clumps, the gentler slopes and hollows which showed here and there. I followed with my eye the winding of the road, and saw that it curved close to one of the densest of these clumps and was lost behind it.

As I looked there came a cold shiver in the air, and the snow began to fall. I thought of the miles and miles of bleak country I had passed, and then hurried on to seek the shelter of the wood in front. Darker and darker grew the sky, and faster and heavier fell the snow, till the earth before and around me was a glistening white carpet the further edge of which was lost in misty vagueness. The road was here but crude, and when on the level its boundaries were not so marked, as when it passed through the cuttings; and in a little while I found that I must have strayed from it, for I missed underfoot the hard surface, and my feet sank deeper in the grass and moss. Then the wind grew stronger and blew with ever increasing force, till I was fain to run before it. The air became icy-cold, and in spite of my exercise I began to suffer. The snow was now falling so thickly and whirling around me in such rapid eddies that I could hardly keep my eyes open. Every now and then the heavens were torn asunder by vivid lightning, and in the flashes I could see ahead of me a great mass of trees, chiefly yew and cypress,[6] all heavily coated with snow.

I was soon amongst the shelter of the trees, and there, in comparative silence, I could hear the rush of the wind high overhead. Presently the blackness of the storm had become merged in the darkness of the night. By-and-by the storm seemed to be passing away: it now only came in fierce puffs or blasts. At such moments the weird sound of the wolf appeared to be echoed by many similar sounds around me.

Now and again, through the black mass of drifting cloud, came a straggling ray of moonlight, which lit up the expanse, and showed me that I was at the edge of a dense mass of cypress and yew trees. As the snow had ceased to fall, I walked out from the shelter and began to investigate more closely. It appeared to me that, amongst so many old foundations as I had passed, there might be still standing a house in which, though in ruins, I could find some sort of shelter for a while. As I skirted the edge of the copse, I found that a low wall encircled it, and following this I presently found an opening. Here the cypresses formed an alley leading up to a square mass of some kind of building. Just as I caught sight of this, however, the drifting clouds obscured the moon, and I passed up the path in darkness. The wind must have grown colder, for I felt myself shiver as I walked; but there was hope of shelter, and I groped my way blindly on.

I stopped, for there was a sudden stillness. The storm had passed; and, perhaps in sympathy with nature's silence, my heart seemed to cease to beat. But this was only momentarily;

for suddenly the moonlight broke through the clouds, showing me that I was in a graveyard, and that the square object before me was a great massive tomb of marble, as white as the snow that lay on and all around it. With the moonlight there came a fierce sigh of the storm, which appeared to resume its course with a long, low howl, as of many dogs or wolves. I was awed and shocked, and felt the cold perceptibly grow upon me till it seemed to grip me by the heart. Then while the flood of moonlight still fell on the marble tomb, the storm gave further evidence of renewing, as though it was returning on its track. Impelled by some sort of fascination, I approached the sepulchre to see what it was, and why such a thing stood alone in such a place. I walked around it, and read, over the Doric door, in German –

COUNTESS DOLINGEN OF GRATZ
IN STYRIA
SOUGHT AND FOUND DEATH.
1801.

On the top of the tomb, seemingly driven through the solid marble – for the structure was composed of a few vast blocks of stone – was a great iron spike or stake. On going to the back I saw, graven in great Russian letters:

'The dead travel fast.'

There was something so weird and uncanny about the whole thing that it gave me a turn and made me feel quite faint. I began to wish, for the first time, that I had taken Johann's advice. Here a thought struck me, which came under almost mysterious circumstances and with a terrible shock. This was Walpurgis Night!

Walpurgis Night, when, according to the belief of millions of people, the devil was abroad – when the graves were opened and the dead came forth and walked. When all evil things of earth and air and water held revel. This very place the driver had specially shunned. This was the depopulated village of centuries ago. This was where the suicide lay; and this was the place where I was alone – unmanned, shivering with cold in a shroud of snow with a wild storm gathering again upon me! It took all my philosophy, all the religion I had been taught, all my courage, not to collapse in a paroxysm of fright.

And now a perfect tornado burst upon me. The ground shook as though thousands of horses thundered across it; and this time the storm bore on its icy wings, not snow, but great hailstones which drove with such violence that they might have come from the thongs of Balearic slingers – hailstones that beat down leaf and branch and made the shelter of the cypresses of no more avail than though their stems were standing-corn. At the first I had rushed to the nearest tree; but I was soon fain to leave it and seek the only spot that seemed to afford refuge, the deep Doric doorway of the marble tomb. There, crouching against the massive bronze-door, I gained a certain amount of protection from the beating of the hail-stones, for now they only drove against me as they ricochetted from the ground and the side of the marble.

As I leaned against the door, it moved slightly and opened inwards. The shelter of even a tomb was welcome in that pitiless tempest, and I was about to enter it when there came a flash of forked-lightning that lit up the whole expanse of the heavens. In the instant, as I am a living man, I saw, as my eyes were turned into the darkness of the tomb, a beautiful woman, with rounded cheeks and red lips, seemingly sleeping on a bier.[7] As the thunder broke overhead, I was grasped as by the hand of a giant and hurled out into the storm. The whole thing was so sudden that, before I could realize the shock, moral as well as physical, I found the hailstones beating me down. At the same time I had a strange, dominating feeling that I was not alone. I looked towards the tomb. Just then there came another blinding flash, which seemed to strike the iron stake that surmounted the tomb and to pour through to the earth, blasting and crumbling the marble, as in a burst of flame. The dead woman rose for a moment of agony, while she was lapped in the flame, and her bitter scream of pain was drowned in the thundercrash. The last thing I heard was this mingling of dreadful sound, as again

I was seized in the giant-grasp and dragged away, while the hailstones beat on me, and the air around seemed reverberant with the howling of wolves. The last sight that I remembered was a vague, white, moving mass, as if all the graves around me had sent out the phantoms of their sheeted-dead, and that they were closing in on me through the white cloudiness of the driving hail.

Gradually there came a sort of vague beginning of consciousness; then a sense of weariness that was dreadful. For a time I remembered nothing; but slowly my senses returned. My feet seemed positively racked with pain, yet I could not move them. They seemed to be numbed. There was an icy feeling at the back of my neck and all down my spine, and my ears, like my feet, were dead, yet in torment; but there was in my breast a sense of warmth which was, by comparison, delicious. It was as a nightmare – a physical nightmare, if one may use such an expression; for some heavy weight on my chest made it difficult for me to breathe.

This period of semi-lethargy seemed to remain a long time, and as it faded away I must have slept or swooned. Then came a sort of loathing, like the first stage of sea-sickness, and a wild desire to be free from something – I knew not what. A vast stillness enveloped me, as though all the world were asleep or dead – only broken by the low panting as of some animal close to me. I felt a warm rasping at my throat, then came a consciousness of the awful truth, which chilled me to the heart and sent the blood surging up through my brain. Some great animal was lying on me and now licking my throat. I feared to stir, for some instinct of prudence bade me lie still; but the brute seemed to realize that there was now some change in me, for it raised its head. Through my eyelashes I saw above me the two great flaming eyes of a gigantic wolf. Its sharp white teeth gleamed in the gaping red mouth, and I could feel its hot breath fierce and acrid upon me.

For another spell of time I remembered no more. Then I became conscious of a low growl, followed by a yelp, renewed again and again. Then, seemingly very far away, I heard a

'Holloa! holloa!' as of many voices calling in unison. Cautiously I raised my head and looked in the direction whence the sound came; but the cemetery blocked my view. The wolf still continued to yelp in a strange way, and a red glare began to move round the grove of cypresses, as though following the sound. As the voices drew closer, the wolf yelped faster and louder. I feared to make either sound or motion. Nearer came the red glow, over the white pall which stretched into the darkness around me. Then all at once from beyond the trees there came at a trot a troop of horsemen bearing torches. The wolf rose from my breast and made for the cemetery. I saw one of the horsemen (soldiers by their caps and their long military cloaks) raise his carbine and take aim. A companion knocked up his arm, and I heard the ball whizz over my head. He had evidently taken my body for that of the wolf. Another sighted the animal as it slunk away, and a shot followed. Then, at a gallop, the troop rode forward – some towards me, others following the wolf as it disappeared amongst the snow-clad cypresses.

As they drew nearer I tried to move, but was powerless, although I could see and hear all that went on around me. Two or three of the soldiers jumped from their horses and knelt beside me. One of them raised my head, and placed his hand over my heart.

'Good news, comrades!' he cried. 'His heart still beats!'

Then some brandy was poured down my throat; it put vigour into me, and I was able to open my eyes fully and look around. Lights and shadows were moving among the trees, and I heard men call to one another. They drew together, uttering frightened exclamations; and the lights flashed as the others came pouring out of the cemetery pell-mell, like men possessed. When the further ones came close to us, those who were around me asked them eagerly:

'Well, have you found him?'

The reply rang out hurriedly:

'No! no! Come away quick – quick! This is no place to stay, and on this of all nights!'

'What was it?' was the question, asked in all manner of keys. The answer came variously and all indefinitely as though the men were moved by some common impulse to speak, yet were restrained by some common fear from giving their thoughts.

'It – it – indeed!' gibbered one, whose wits had plainly given out for the moment.

'A wolf – and yet not a wolf!' another put in shudderingly.

'No use trying for him without the sacred bullet,'[8] a third remarked in a more ordinary manner.

'Serve us right for coming out on this night! Truly we have earned our thousand marks!' were the ejaculations of a fourth.

'There was blood on the broken marble,' another said after a pause – 'the lightning never brought that there. And for him – is he safe? Look at his throat! See, comrades, the wolf has been lying on him and keeping his blood warm.'

The officer looked at my throat and replied:

'He is all right; the skin is not pierced. What does it all mean? We should never have found him but for the yelping of the wolf.'

'What became of it?' asked the man who was holding up my head, and who seemed the least panic-stricken of the party, for his hands were steady and without tremor. On his sleeve was the chevron of a petty officer.

'It went to its home,' answered the man, whose long face was pallid, and who actually shook with terror as he glanced around him fearfully. 'There are graves enough there in which it may lie. Come, comrades – come quickly! Let us leave this cursed spot.'

The officer raised me to a sitting posture, as he uttered a word of command; then several men placed me upon a horse. He sprang to the saddle behind me, took me in his arms, gave the word to advance; and, turning our faces away from the cypresses, we rode away in swift, military order.

As yet my tongue refused its office, and I was perforce silent. I must have fallen asleep; for the next thing I remembered was finding myself standing up, supported by a soldier on each side of me. It was almost broad daylight, and to the north a red streak of sunlight was reflected, like a path of blood, over the waste of snow. The officer was telling the men to say nothing of what they had seen, except that they found an English stranger, guarded by a large dog.

'Dog! that was no dog,' cut in the man who had exhibited such fear. 'I think I know a wolf when I see one.'

The young officer answered calmly: 'I said a dog.'

'Dog!' reiterated the other ironically. It was evident that his courage was rising with the sun; and, pointing to me, he said, 'Look at his throat. Is that the work of a dog, master?'

Instinctively I raised my hand to my throat, and as I touched it I cried out in pain. The men crowded round to look, some stooping down from their saddles; and again there came the calm voice of the young officer:

'A dog, as I said. If aught else were said we should only be laughed at.'

I was then mounted behind a trooper, and we rode on into the suburbs of Munich. Here we came across a stray carriage, into which I was lifted, and it was driven off to the Quatre Saisons – the young officer accompanying me, whilst a trooper followed with his horse, and the others rode off to their barracks.

When we arrived, Herr Delbrück rushed so quickly down the steps to meet me, that it was apparent he had been watching within. Taking me by both hands he solicitously led me in. The officer saluted me and was turning to withdraw, when I recognized his purpose, and insisted that he should come to my rooms. Over a glass of wine I warmly thanked him and his brave comrades for saving me. He replied simply that he was more than glad, and that Herr Delbrück had at the first taken steps to make all the searching party pleased; at which ambiguous utterance the maître d'hotel smiled, while the officer pleaded duty and withdrew.

'But Herr Delbrück,' I enquired, 'how and why was it that the soldiers searched for me?'

He shrugged his shoulders, as if in depreciation of his own deed, as he replied:

'I was so fortunate as to obtain leave from the commander of the regiment in which I served, to ask for volunteers.'

'But how did you know I was lost?' I asked.

'The driver came hither with the remains of his carriage, which had been upset when the horses ran away.'

'But surely you would not send a search-party of soldiers merely on this account?'

'Oh, no!' he answered; 'but even before the coachman arrived, I had this telegram from the Boyar whose guest you are,' and he took from his pocket a telegram which he handed to me, and I read:

BISTRITZ

'Be careful of my guest – his safety is most precious to me. Should aught happen to him, or if he be missed, spare nothing to find him and ensure his safety. He is English and therefore adventurous. There are often dangers from snow and wolves and night. Lose not a moment if you suspect harm to him. I answer your zeal with my fortune. – Dracula.'

As I held the telegram in my hand, the room seemed to whirl around me; and, if the attentive maître d'hotel had not caught me, I think I should have fallen. There was something so strange in all this, something so weird and impossible to imagine, that there grew on me a sense of my being in some way the sport of opposite forces – the mere vague idea of which seemed in a way to paralyse me. I was certainly under some form of mysterious protection. From a distant country had come, in the very nick of time, a message that took me out of the danger of the snow-sleep and the jaws of the wolf.

THE JUDGE'S HOUSE

When the time for his examination drew near Malcolm Malcolmson made up his mind to go somewhere to read by himself. He feared the attractions of the seaside, and also he feared completely rural isolation, for of old he knew its charms, and so he determined to find some unpretentious little town where there would be nothing to distract him. He refrained from asking suggestions from any of his friends, for he argued that each would recommend some place of which he had knowledge, and where he had already acquaintances. As Malcolmson wished to avoid friends he had no wish to encumber himself with the attention of friends' friends, and so he determined to look out for a place for himself. He packed a portmanteau with some clothes and all the books he required, and then took a ticket for the first name on the local time-table which he did not know.

When at the end of three hours' journey he alighted at Benchurch, he felt satisfied that he had so far obliterated his tracks as to be sure of having a peaceful opportunity of pursuing his studies. He went straight to the one inn which the sleepy little place contained, and put up for the night. Benchurch was a market town, and once in three weeks was crowded to excess, but for the remainder of the twenty-one days it was as attractive as a desert. Malcolmson looked around the day after his arrival to try to find quarters more isolated than even so quiet an inn as 'The Good Traveller' afforded. There was only one place which took his fancy, and it certainly satisfied his wildest ideas regarding quiet; in fact, quiet was not the proper word to apply to it – desolation was the only term conveying any suitable idea of its isolation. It was an old rambling, heavy-built house of the Jacobean style,[1] with heavy gables and windows, unusually small, and set higher than was customary in such houses, and was surrounded with a high brick wall massively built. Indeed, on examination, it looked more like a fortified house than an ordinary dwelling. But all these things pleased Malcolmson. 'Here,' he thought, 'is the very spot I have been looking for, and if I can only get opportunity of using it I shall be happy.' His joy was increased when he realised beyond doubt that it was not at present inhabited.

From the post-office he got the name of the agent, who was rarely surprised at the application to rent a part of the old house. Mr Carnford, the local lawyer and agent, was a genial old gentleman, and frankly confessed his delight at anyone being willing to live in the house.

'To tell you the truth,' said he, 'I should be only too happy, on behalf of the owners, to let anyone have the house rent free for a term of years if only to accustom the people here to see it inhabited. It has been so long empty that some kind of absurd prejudice has grown up about it, and this can be best put down by its occupation – if only,' he added with a sly glance at Malcolmson, 'by a scholar like yourself, who wants its quiet for a time.'

Malcolmson thought it needless to ask the agent about the 'absurd prejudice'; he knew he would get more information, if he should require it, on that subject from other quarters. He paid his three months' rent, got a receipt, and the name of an old woman who would probably undertake to 'do' for him, and came away with the keys in his pocket. He then went to the landlady of the inn, who was a cheerful and most kindly person, and asked her advice as to such stores and provisions as he would be likely to require. She threw up her hands in amazement when he told her where he was going to settle himself.

'Not in the Judge's House!' she said, and grew pale as she spoke. He explained the locality of the house, saying that he did not know its name. When he had finished she answered:

'Aye, sure enough – sure enough the very place! It is the

Judge's House sure enough.' He asked her to tell him about the place, why so called, and what there was against it. She told him that it was so called locally because it had been many years before – how long she could not say, as she was herself from another part of the country, but she thought it must have been a hundred years or more – the abode of a judge who was held in great terror on account of his harsh sentences and his hostility to prisoners at Assizes.[2] As to what there was against the house itself she could not tell. She had often asked, but no one could inform her; but there was a general feeling that there was *something*, and for her own part she would not take all the money in Drinkwater's Bank and stay in the house an hour by herself. Then she apologised to Malcolmson for her disturbing talk.

'It is too bad of me, sir, and you – and a young gentleman, too – if you will pardon me saying it, going to live there all alone. If you were my boy – and you'll excuse me for saying it – you wouldn't sleep there a night, not if I had to go there myself and pull the big alarm bell that's on the roof!' The good creature was so manifestly in earnest, and was so kindly in her intentions, that Malcomson, although amused, was touched. He told her kindly how much he appreciated her interest in him, and added:

'But, my dear Mrs Witham, indeed you need not be concerned about me! A man who is reading for the Mathematical Tripos[3] has too much to think of to be disturbed by any of these mysterious 'somethings,' and his work is of too exact and prosaic a kind to allow of his having any corner in his mind for mysteries of any kind. Harmonical Progression, Permutations and Combinations, and Elliptic Functions[4] have sufficient mysteries for me!' Mrs Witham kindly undertook to see after his commissions, and he went himself to look for the old woman who had been recommended to him. When he returned to the Judge's House with her, after an interval of a couple of hours, he found Mrs Witham herself waiting with several men and boys carrying parcels, and an upholsterer's man with a bed in a cart, for she said, though tables and chairs might be all very well, a bed that hadn't been aired for mayhap fifty years was not proper for young bones to lie on. She was evidently curious to see the inside of the house; and though manifestly so afraid of the 'somethings' that at the slightest sound she clutched on to Malcolmson, whom she never left for a moment, went over the whole place.

After his examination of the house, Malcolmson decided to take up his abode in the great dining-room, which was big enough to serve for all his requirements; and Mrs Witham, with the aid of the charwoman, Mrs Dempster, proceeded to arrange matters. When the hampers were brought in and unpacked, Malcolmson saw that with much kind forethought she had sent from her own kitchen sufficient provisions to last for a few days. Before going she expressed all sorts of kind wishes; and at the door turned and said:

'And perhaps, sir, as the room is big and draughty it might be well to have one of those big screens put round your bed at night – though, truth to tell, I would die myself if I were to be so shut in with all kinds of – of "things," that put their heads round the sides, or over the top, and look on me!' The image which she had called up was too much for her nerves, and she fled incontinently.

Mrs Dempster sniffed in a superior manner as the landlady disappeared, and remarked that for her own part she wasn't afraid of all the bogies in the kingdom.

'I'll tell you what it is, sir,' she said; 'bogies is all kinds and sorts of things – except bogies! Rats and mice, and beetles; and creaky doors, and loose slates, and broken panes, and stiff drawer handles, that stay out when you pull them and then fall down in the middle of the night. Look at the wainscot of the room! It is old – hundreds of years old! Do you think there's no rats and beetles there! And do you imagine, sir, that you won't see none of them! Rats is bogies, I tell you, and bogies is rats; and don't you get to think anything else!'

'Mrs Dempster,' said Malcolmson gravely, making her a polite bow, 'you know more than a Senior Wrangler![5] And let me say, that, as a mark of esteem for your indubitable soundness of head and heart, I shall, when I go, give you possession of this house, and let you stay here by yourself for the last two months of my tenancy, for four weeks will serve my purpose.'

'Thank you kindly, sir!' she answered, 'but I couldn't sleep away from home a night. I am in Greenhow's Charity,[6] and if I slept a night away from my rooms I should lose all I have got to live on. The rules is very strict; and there's too many watching for a vacancy for me to run any risks in the matter. Only for that, sir, I'd gladly come here and attend on you altogether during your stay.'

'My good woman,' said Malcolmson hastily, 'I have come here on purpose to obtain solitude; and believe me that I am grateful to the late Greenhow for having so organised his admirable charity – whatever it is – that I am perforce denied the opportunity of suffering from such a form of temptation! Saint Anthony himself could not be more rigid on the point!'[7]

The old woman laughed harshly. 'Ah, you young gentlemen,' she said, 'you don't fear for naught; and belike you'll get all the solitude you want here.' She set to work with her cleaning; and by nightfall, when Malcolmson returned from his walk – he always had one of his books to study as he walked – he found the room swept and tidied, a fire burning in the old hearth, the lamp lit, and the table spread for supper with Mrs Witham's excellent fare. 'This is comfort, indeed,' he said, as he rubbed his hands.

When he had finished his supper, and lifted the tray to the other end of the great oak dining-table, he got out his books again, put fresh wood on the fire, trimmed his lamp, and set himself down to a spell of real hard work. He went on without pause till about eleven o'clock, when he knocked off for a bit to fix his fire and lamp, and to make himself a cup of tea. He had always been a tea-drinker, and during his college life had sat late at work and had taken tea late. The rest was a great luxury to him, and he enjoyed it with a sense of delicious, voluptuous ease. The renewed fire leaped and sparkled, and threw quaint shadows through the great old room; and as he sipped his hot tea he revelled in the sense of isolation from his kind. Then it was that he began to notice for the first time what a noise the rats were making.

'Surely,' he thought, 'they cannot have been at it all the time I was reading. Had they been, I must have noticed it!' Presently, when the noise increased, he satisfied himself that it was really new. It was evident that at first the rats had been frightened at the presence of a stranger, and the light of fire and lamp; but that as the time went on they had grown bolder and were now disporting themselves as was their wont.

How busy they were! and hark to the strange noises! Up and down behind the old wainscot, over the ceiling and under the floor they raced, and gnawed, and scratched! Malcolmson smiled to himself as he recalled to mind the saying of Mrs Dempster, 'Bogies is rats, and rats is bogies!' The tea began to have its effect of intellectual and nervous stimulus, he saw with joy another long spell of work to be done before the night was past, and in the sense of security which it gave him, he allowed himself the luxury of a good look round the room. He took his lamp in one hand, and went all around, wondering that so quaint and beautiful an old house had been so long neglected. The carving of the oak on the panels of the wainscot was fine, and on and round the doors and windows it was beautiful and of rare merit. There were some old pictures on the walls, but they were coated so thick with dust and dirt that he could not distinguish any detail of them, though he held his lamp as high as he could over his head. Here and there as he went round he saw some crack or hole blocked for a moment by the face of a rat with its bright eyes glittering in the light, but in an instant it was gone, and a squeak and a scamper followed. The thing that most struck him, however, was the rope of the great alarm bell on the roof, which hung down in a corner of the room on the right-hand side of the fire-place. He pulled up close to the hearth a great high-backed carved oak chair, and sat down to his last cup of tea. When this was done he made up the fire, and went back to his work, sitting at the corner of the table, having the fire to his left. For a little while the rats disturbed him somewhat with their perpetual scampering, but he got accustomed to the noise as one does to the ticking of a clock or to the roar of moving water; and he became so immersed in his work that everything in the world, except the problem which he was trying to solve, passed away from him.

He suddenly looked up, his problem was still unsolved, and

there was in the air that sense of the hour before the dawn, which is so dread to doubtful life. The noise of the rats had ceased. Indeed it seemed to him that it must have ceased but lately and that it was the sudden cessation which had disturbed him. The fire had fallen low, but still it threw out a deep red glow. As he looked he started in spite of his *sang froid*.

There on the great high-backed carved oak chair by the right side of the fire-place sat an enormous rat, steadily glaring at him with baleful eyes. He made a motion to it as though to hunt it away, but it did not stir. Then he made the motion of throwing something. Still it did not stir, but showed its great white teeth angrily, and its cruel eyes shone in the lamplight with an added vindictiveness.

Malcolmson felt amazed, and seizing the poker from the hearth ran at it to kill it. Before, however, he could strike it, the rat, with a squeak that sounded like the concentration of hate, jumped upon the floor, and, running up the rope of the alarm bell, disappeared in the darkness beyond the range of the green-shaded lamp. Instantly, strange to say, the noisy scampering of the rats in the wainscot began again.

By this time Malcolmson's mind was quite off the problem; and as a shrill cock-crow outside told him of the approach of morning, he went to bed and to sleep.

He slept so sound that he was not even waked by Mrs Dempster coming in to make up his room. It was only when she had tidied up the place and got his breakfast ready and tapped on the screen which closed in his bed that he woke. He was a little tired still after his night's hard work, but a strong cup of tea soon freshened him up and, taking his book, he went out for his morning walk, bringing with him a few sandwiches lest he should not care to return till dinner time. He found a quiet walk between high elms some way outside the town, and here he spent the greater part of the day studying his Laplace.[8] On his return he looked in to see Mrs Witham and to thank her for her kindness. When she saw him coming through the diamond-paned bay window[9] of her sanctum she came out to meet him and asked him in. She looked at him searchingly and shook her head as she said:

'You must not overdo it, sir. You are paler this morning than you should be. Too late hours and too hard work on the brain isn't good for any man! But tell me, sir, how did you pass the night? Well, I hope? But, my heart! sir, I was glad when Mrs Dempster told me this morning that you were all right and sleeping sound when she went in.'

'Oh, I was all right,' he answered smiling, 'the "somethings" didn't worry me, as yet. Only the rats; and they had a circus, I tell you, all over the place. There was one wicked looking old devil that sat up on my own chair by the fire, and wouldn't go till I took the poker to him, and then he ran up the rope of the alarm bell and got to somewhere up the wall or the ceiling – I couldn't see where, it was so dark.'

'Mercy on us,' said Mrs Witham, 'an old devil, and sitting on a chair by the fireside! Take care, sir! take care! There's many a true word spoken in jest.'

'How do you mean? 'Pon my word I don't understand.'

'An old devil! The old devil, perhaps. There! sir, you needn't laugh,' for Malcolmson had broken into a hearty peal. 'You young folks thinks it easy to laugh at things that makes older ones shudder. Never mind, sir! never mind! Please God, you'll laugh all the time. It's what I wish you myself!' and the good lady beamed all over in sympathy with his enjoyment, her fears gone for a moment.

'Oh, forgive me!' said Malcolmson presently. 'Don't think me rude; but the idea was too much for me – that the old devil himself was on the chair last night!' And at the thought he laughed again. Then he went home to dinner.

This evening the scampering of the rats began earlier; indeed it had been going on before his arrival, and only ceased whilst his presence by its freshness disturbed them. After dinner he sat by the fire for a while and had a smoke; and then, having cleared his table, began to work as before. To-night the rats disturbed him more than they had done on the previous night. How they scampered up and down and under and over! How they squeaked, and scratched, and gnawed! How they, getting bolder by degrees, came to the mouths of their holes and to the chinks and cracks and crannies in the wainscoting till their eyes shone like tiny lamps as the firelight rose and fell. But to him, now doubtless accustomed to them, their eyes were not wicked; only their playfulness touched him. Sometimes the boldest of them made sallies out on the floor or along the mouldings of the wainscot. Now and again as they disturbed him Malcolmson made a sound to frighten them, smiting the table with his hand or giving a fierce 'Hsh, hsh,' so that they fled straightway to their holes.

And so the early part of the night wore on; and despite the noise Malcolmson got more and more immersed in his work.

All at once he stopped, as on the previous night, being overcome by a sudden sense of silence. There was not the faintest sound of gnaw, or scratch, or squeak. The silence was as of the grave. He remembered the odd occurrence of the previous night, and instinctively he looked at the chair standing close by the fireside. And then a very odd sensation thrilled through him.

There, on the great old high-backed carved oak chair beside the fireplace sat the same enormous rat, steadily glaring at him with baleful eyes.

Instinctively he took the nearest thing to his hand, a book of logarithms, and flung it at it. The book was badly aimed and the rat did not stir, so again the poker performance of the previous night was repeated; and again the rat, being closely pursued, fled up the rope of the alarm bell. Strangely too, the departure of this rat was instantly followed by the renewal of the noise made by the general rat community. On this occasion, as on the previous one, Malcolmson could not see at what part of the room the rat disappeared, for the green shade of his lamp left the upper part of the room in darkness, and the fire had burned low.

On looking at his watch he found it was close on midnight; and, not sorry for the *divertissement*, he made up his fire and made himself his nightly pot of tea. He had got through a good spell of work, and thought himself entitled to a cigarette; and so he sat on the great carved oak chair before the fire and enjoyed it. Whilst smoking he began to think that he would like to know where the rat disappeared to, for he had certain ideas for the morrow not entirely disconnected with a rat-trap.

Accordingly he lit another lamp and placed it so that it would shine well into the right-hand corner of the wall by the fireplace. Then he got all the books he had with him, and placed them handy to throw at the vermin. Finally he lifted the rope of the alarm bell and placed the end of it on the table, fixing the extreme end under the lamp. As he handled it he could not help noticing how pliable it was, especially for so strong a rope, and one not in use. 'You could hang a man with it,' he thought to himself. When his preparations were made he looked around, and said complacently:

'There now, my friend, I think we shall learn something of you this time!' He began his work again, and though as before somewhat disturbed at first by the noise of the rats, soon lost himself in his propositions and problems.

Again he was called to his immediate surroundings suddenly. This time it might not have been the sudden silence only which took his attention; there was a slight movement of the rope, and the lamp moved. Without stirring, he looked to see if his pile of books was within range, and then cast his eye along the rope. As he looked he saw the great rat drop from the rope on the oak armchair and sit there glaring at him. He raised a book in his right hand, and taking careful aim, flung it at the rat. The latter, with a quick movement, sprang aside and dodged the missile. He then took another book, and a third, and flung them one after another at the rat, but each time unsuccessfully. At last, as he stood with a book poised in his hand to throw, the rat squeaked and seemed afraid. This made Malcolmson more than ever eager to strike, and the book flew and struck the rat a resounding blow. It gave a terrified squeak, and turning on his pursuer a look of terrible malevolence, ran up the chair-back and made a great jump to the rope of the alarm bell and ran up it like lightning. The lamp rocked under the sudden strain, but it was a heavy one and did not topple over. Malcolmson kept his eyes on the rat, and saw it by the light of the second lamp leap to a moulding of the wainscot and disappear through a hole in one of the great pictures which hung on the wall, obscured and invisible through its coating of dirt and dust.

'I shall look up my friend's habitation in the morning,' said the student, as he went over to collect his books. The third picture from the fireplace; I shall not forget.' He picked up the books one by one, commenting on them as he lifted them. '*Conic Sections* he does not mind, nor *Cycloidal Oscillations*, nor the *Principia*, nor *Quaternions*, nor *Thermodynamics*. Now for the book that fetched him!' Malcolmson took it up and looked at it. As he did so he started, and a sudden pallor overspread his face. He looked round uneasily and shivered slightly, as he murmured to himself:

'The Bible my mother gave me! What an odd coincidence.' He sat down to work again, and the rats in the wainscot renewed their gambols. They did not disturb him, however; somehow their presence gave him a sense of companionship. But he could not attend to his work, and after striving to master the subject on which he was engaged gave it up in despair, and went to bed as the first streak of dawn stole in through the eastern window.

He slept heavily but uneasily, and dreamed much; and when Mrs Dempster woke him late in the morning he seemed ill at ease, and for a few minutes did not seem to realise exactly where he was. His first request rather surprised the servant.

'Mrs Dempster, when I am out to-day I wish you would get the steps and dust or wash those pictures – specially that one the third from the fireplace – I want to see what they are.'

Late in the afternoon Malcolmson worked at his books in the shaded walk, and the cheerfulness of the previous day came back to him as the day wore on, and he found that his reading was progressing well. He had worked out to a satisfactory conclusion all the problems which had as yet baffled him, and it was in a state of jubilation that he paid a visit to Mrs Witham at 'The Good Traveller.' He found a stranger in the cosy sitting-room with the landlady, who was introduced to him as Dr Thornhill. She was not quite at ease, and this, combined with the doctor's plunging at once into a series of questions, made Malcolmson come to the conclusion that his presence was not an accident, so without preliminary he said:

'Dr Thornhill, I shall with pleasure answer you any question you may choose to ask me if you will answer me one question first.'

The doctor seemed surprised, but he smiled and answered at once, 'Done! What is it?'

'Did Mrs Witham ask you to come here and see me and advise me?'

Dr Thornhill for a moment was taken aback, and Mrs Witham got fiery red and turned away; but the doctor was a frank and ready man, and he answered at once and openly:

'She did: but she didn't intend you to know it. I suppose it was my clumsy haste that made you suspect. She told me that she did not like the idea of your being in that house all by yourself, and that she thought you took too much strong tea. In fact, she wants me to advise you if possible to give up the tea and the very late hours. I was a keen student in my time, so I suppose I may take the liberty of a college man, and without offence, advise you not quite as a stranger.'

Malcolmson with a bright smile held out his hand. 'Shake! as they say in America,'[10] he said. 'I must thank you for your kindness and Mrs Witham too, and your kindness deserves a return on my part. I promise to take no more strong tea – no tea at all till you let me – and I shall go to bed to-night at one o'clock at latest. Will that do?'

'Capital,' said the doctor. 'Now tell us all that you noticed in the old house,' and so Malcolmson then and there told in minute detail all that had happened in the last two nights. He was interrupted every now and then by some exclamation from Mrs Witham, till finally when he told of the episode of the Bible the landlady's pent-up emotions found vent in a shriek; and it was not till a stiff glass of brandy and water had been administered that she grew composed again. Dr Thornhill listened with a face of growing gravity, and when the narrative was complete and Mrs Witham had been restored he asked:

'The rat always went up the rope of the alarm bell?'

'Always.'

'I suppose you know,' said the Doctor after a pause, 'what the rope is?'

'No!'

'It is,' said the Doctor slowly, 'the very rope which the hangman used for all the victims of the Judge's judicial rancour!'

Here he was interrupted by another scream from Mrs Witham, and steps had to be taken for her recovery. Malcolmson having looked at his watch, and found that it was close to his dinner hour, had gone home before her complete recovery.

When Mrs Witham was herself again she almost assailed the Doctor with angry questions as to what he meant by putting such horrible ideas into the poor young man's mind. 'He has quite enough there already to upset him,' she added.

Dr Thornhill replied:

'My dear madam, I had a distinct purpose in it! I wanted to draw his attention to the bell rope, and to fix it there. It may be that he is in a highly over-wrought state, and has been studying too much, although I am bound to say that he seems as sound and healthy a young man, mentally and bodily, as ever I saw – but then the rats – and that suggestion of the devil.' The doctor shook his head and went on. 'I would have offered to go and stay the first night with him but that I felt sure it would have been a cause of offence. He may get in the night some strange fright or hallucination; and if he does I want him to pull that rope. All alone as he is it will give us warning, and we may reach him in time to be of service. I shall be sitting up pretty late to-night and shall keep my ears open. Do not be alarmed if Benchurch gets a surprise before morning.'

'Oh, Doctor, what do you mean? What do you mean?'

'I mean this; that possibly – nay, more probably – we shall hear the great alarm bell from the Judge's House to-night,' and the Doctor made about as effective an exit as could be thought of.

When Malcolmson arrived home he found that it was a little after his usual time, and Mrs Dempster had gone away – the rules of Greenhow's Charity were not to be neglected. He was glad to see that the place was bright and tidy with a cheerful fire and a well-trimmed lamp. The evening was colder than might have been expected in April, and a heavy wind was blowing with such rapidly-increasing strength that there was every promise of a storm during the night. For a few minutes after his entrance the noise of the rats ceased; but so soon as they became accustomed to his presence they began again. He was glad to hear them, for he felt once more the feeling of companionship in their noise, and his mind ran back to the strange fact that they only ceased to manifest themselves when that other – the great rat with the baleful eyes – came upon the scene. The reading-lamp only was lit and its green shade kept the ceiling and the upper part of the room in darkness, so that the cheerful light from the hearth spreading over the floor and shining on the white cloth laid over the end of the table was warm and cheery. Malcolmson sat down to his dinner with a good appetite and a buoyant spirit. After his dinner and a cigarette he sat steadily down to work, determined not to let anything disturb him, for he remembered his promise to the doctor, and made up his mind to make the best of the time at his disposal.

For an hour or so he worked all right, and then his thoughts began to wander from his books. The actual circumstances around him, the calls on his physical attention, and his nervous susceptibility were not to be denied. By this time the wind had become a gale, and the gale a storm. The old house, solid though it was, seemed to shake to its foundations, and the storm roared and raged through its many chimneys and its queer old gables, producing strange, unearthly sounds in the empty rooms and corridors. Even the great alarm bell on the roof must have felt the force of the wind, for the rope rose and fell slightly, as though the bell were moved a little from time to time, and the limber rope fell on the oak floor with a hard and hollow sound.

As Malcolmson listened to it he bethought himself of the doctor's words, 'It is the rope which the hangman used for the victims of the Judge's judicial rancour,' and he went over to the corner of the fireplace and took it in his hand to look at it. There seemed a sort of deadly interest in it, and as he stood there he lost himself for a moment in speculation as to who these victims were; and the grim wish of the Judge to have such a ghastly relic ever under his eyes. As he stood there the swaying of the bell on the roof still lifted the rope now and again; but presently there came a new sensation – a sort of tremor in the rope, as though something was moving along it.

Looking up instinctively Malcolmson saw the great rat

coming slowly down towards him, glaring at him steadily. He dropped the rope and started back with a muttered curse, and the rat turning ran up the rope again and disappeared, and at the same instant Malcolmson became conscious that the noise of the rats, which had ceased for a while, began again.

All this set him thinking, and it occurred to him that he had not investigated the lair of the rat or looked at the pictures, as he had intended. He lit the other lamp without the shade, and, holding it up, went and stood opposite the third picture from the fireplace on the right-hand side where he had seen the rat disappear on the previous night.

At the first glance he started back so suddenly that he almost dropped the lamp, and a deadly pallor overspread his face. His knees shook, and heavy drops of sweat came on his forehead, and he trembled like an aspen.[11] But he was young and plucky, and pulled himself together, and after the pause of a few seconds stepped forward again, raised the lamp, and examined the picture which had been dusted and washed, and now stood out clearly.

It was of a judge dressed in his robes of scarlet and ermine. His face was strong and merciless, evil, crafty, and vindictive, with a sensual mouth, hooked nose of ruddy colour, and shaped like the beak of a bird of prey. The rest of the face was of a cadaverous colour. The eyes were of peculiar brilliance and with a terribly malignant expression. As he looked at them, Malcolmson grew cold, for he saw there the very counterpart of the eyes of the great rat. The lamp almost fell from his hand, he saw the rat with its baleful eyes peering out through the hole in the corner of the picture, and noted the sudden cessation of the noise of the other rats. However, he pulled himself together, and went on with his examination of the picture.

The Judge was seated in a great high-backed carved oak chair, on the right-hand side of a great stone fireplace where, in the corner, a rope hung down from the ceiling, its end lying coiled on the floor. With a feeling of something like horror, Malcolmson recognised the scene of the room as it stood, and gazed around him in an awestruck manner as though he expected to find some strange presence behind him. Then he looked over to the corner of the fireplace – and with a loud cry he let the lamp fall from his hand.

There, in the judge's arm-chair, with the rope hanging behind, sat the rat with the Judge's baleful eyes, now intensified and with a fiendish leer. Save for the howling of the storm without there was silence.

The fallen lamp recalled Malcolmson to himself. Fortunately it was of metal, and so the oil was not spilt. However, the practical need of attending to it settled at once his nervous apprehensions. When he had turned it out, he wiped his brow and thought for a moment.

'This will not do,' he said to himself. 'If I go on like this I shall become a crazy fool. This must stop! I promised the doctor I would not take tea. Faith, he was pretty right! My nerves must have been getting into a queer state. Funny I did not notice it. I never felt better in my life. However, it is all right now, and I shall not be such a fool again.'

Then he mixed himself a good stiff glass of brandy and water and resolutely sat down to his work.

It was nearly an hour when he looked up from his book, disturbed by the sudden stillness. Without, the wind howled and roared louder than ever, and the rain drove in sheets against the windows, beating like hail on the glass; but within there was no sound whatever save the echo of the wind as it roared in the great chimney, and now and then a hiss as a few raindrops found their way down the chimney in a lull of the storm. The fire had fallen low and had ceased to flame, though it threw out a red glow. Malcolmson listened attentively, and presently heard a thin, squeaking noise, very faint. It came from the corner of the room where the rope hung down, and he thought it was the creaking of the rope on the floor as the swaying of the bell raised and lowered it. Looking up, however, he saw in the dim light the great rat clinging to the rope and gnawing it. The rope was already nearly gnawed through – he could see the lighter colour where the strands were laid bare. As he looked the job was completed, and the severed end of the rope fell clattering on the oaken floor, whilst for an instant the great rat remained like a knob or tassel at the end of the rope, which now began to sway to and fro. Malcolmson felt for a moment another pang of terror as he thought that now the possibility of calling the outer world to his assistance was cut off, but an intense anger took its place, and seizing the book he was reading he hurled it at the rat. The blow was well aimed, but before the missile could reach him the rat dropped off and struck the floor with a soft thud. Malcolmson instantly rushed over towards him, but it darted away and disappeared in the darkness of the shadows of the room. Malcolmson felt that his work was over for the night, and determined then and there to vary the monotony of the proceedings by a hunt for the rat, and took off the green shade of the lamp so as to insure a wider spreading light. As he did so the gloom of the upper part of the room was relieved, and in the new flood of light, great by comparison with the previous darkness, the pictures on the wall stood out boldly. From where he stood, Malcolmson saw right opposite to him the third picture on the wall from the right of the fireplace. He rubbed his eyes in surprise, and then a great fear began to come upon him.

In the centre of the picture was a great irregular patch of brown canvas, as fresh as when it was stretched on the frame. The background was as before, with chair and chimney-corner and rope, but the figure of the Judge had disappeared.

Malcolmson, almost in a chill of horror, turned slowly round, and then he began to shake and tremble like a man in a palsy. His strength seemed to have left him, and he was incapable of action or movement, hardly even of thought. He could only see and hear.

There, on the great high-backed carved oak chair sat the judge in his robes of scarlet and ermine, with his baleful eyes glaring vindictively, and a smile of triumph on the resolute, cruel mouth, as he lifted with his hands a *black cap*.[12] Malcolmson felt as if the blood was running from his heart, as one does in moments of prolonged suspense. There was a singing in his ears. Without, he could hear the roar and howl of the tempest, and through it, swept on the storm, came the striking of midnight by the great chimes in the market place. He stood for a space of time that seemed to him endless still as a statue, and with wide-open, horror-struck eyes, breathless. As the clock struck, so the smile of triumph on the Judge's face intensified, and at the last stroke of midnight he placed the black cap on his head.

Slowly and deliberately the Judge rose from his chair and picked up the piece of the rope of the alarm bell which lay on the floor, drew it through his hands as if he enjoyed its touch, and then deliberately began to knot one end of it, fashioning it into a noose. This he tightened and tested with his foot, pulling hard at it till he was satisfied and then making a running noose of it, which he held in his hand. Then he began to move along the table on the opposite side to Malcolmson keeping his eyes on him until he had passed him, when with a quick movement he stood in front of the door. Malcolmson then began to feel that he was trapped, and tried to think of what he should do. There was some fascination in the Judge's eyes, which he never took off him, and he had, perforce, to look. He saw the Judge approach – still keeping between him and the door – and raise the noose and throw it towards him as if to entangle him. With a great effort he made a quick movement to one side, and saw the rope fall beside him, and heard it strike the oaken floor. Again the Judge raised the noose and tried to ensnare him, ever keeping his baleful eyes fixed on him, and each time by a mighty effort the student just managed to evade it. So this went on for many times, the Judge seeming never discouraged nor discomposed at failure, but playing as a cat does with a mouse. At last in despair, which had reached its climax, Malcolmson cast a quick glance round him. The lamp seemed to have blazed up, and there was a fairly good light in the room. At the many rat-holes and in the chinks and crannies of the wainscot he saw the rats' eyes; and this aspect, that was purely physical, gave him a gleam of comfort. He looked around and saw that the rope of the great alarm bell was laden with rats. Every inch of it was covered with them, and more and more were pouring through the small circular hole in the ceiling whence it emerged, so that with their weight the bell was beginning to sway.

Hark! it had swayed till the clapper had touched the bell. The sound was but a tiny one, but the bell was only beginning to sway, and it would increase.

At the sound the Judge, who had been keeping his eyes fixed on Malcolmson, looked up, and a scowl of diabolical anger overspread his face. His eyes fairly glowed like hot coals, and he stamped his foot with a sound that seemed to make the house shake. A dreadful peal of thunder broke overhead as he raised the rope again, whilst the rats kept running up and down the rope as though working against time. This time, instead of throwing it, he drew close to his victim, and held open the noose as he approached. As he came closer there seemed something paralysing in his very presence, and Malcolmson stood rigid as a corpse. He felt the Judge's icy fingers touch his throat as he adjusted the rope. The noose tightened – tightened. Then the Judge, taking the rigid form of the student in his arms, carried him over and placed him standing in the oak chair, and stepping up beside him, put his hand up and caught the end of the swaying rope of the alarm bell. As he raised his hand the rats fled squeaking, and disappeared through the hole in the ceiling. Taking the end of the noose which was round Malcolmson's neck he tied it to the hanging-bell rope, and then descending pulled away the chair.

When the alarm bell of the Judge's House began to sound a crowd soon assembled. Lights and torches of various kinds appeared, and soon a silent crowd was hurrying to the spot. They knocked loudly at the door, but there was no reply. Then they burst in the door, and poured into the great dining-room, the doctor at the head.

There at the end of the rope of the great alarm bell hung the body of the student, and on the face of the Judge in the picture was a malignant smile.

THE SQUAW

Nurnberg at the time was not so much exploited as it has been since then. Irving had not been playing *Faust*,[1] and the very name of the old town was hardly known to the great bulk of the travelling public. My wife and I being in the second week of our honeymoon, naturally wanted someone else to join our party, so that when the cheery stranger, Elias P. Hutcheson, hailing from Isthmian City, Bleeding Gulch, Maple Tree County, Neb., turned up at the station at Frankfort, and casually remarked that he was going on to see the most all-fired old Methusaleh of a town in Yurrup,[2] and that he guessed that so much travelling alone was enough to send an intelligent, active citizen into the melancholy ward of a daft house, we took the pretty broad hint and suggested that we should join forces. We found, on comparing notes afterwards, that we had each intended to speak with some diffidence or hesitation so as not to appear too eager, such not being a good compliment to the success of our married life; but the effect was entirely marred by our both beginning to speak at the same instant – stopping simultaneously and then going on together again. Anyhow, no matter how, it was done; and Elias P. Hutcheson became one of our party. Straightway Amelia and I found the pleasant benefit; instead of quarrelling, as we had been doing, we found that the restraining influence of a third party was such that we now took every opportunity of spooning in odd corners. Amelia declares that ever since she has, as the result of that experience, advised all her friends to take a friend on the honeymoon. Well, we 'did' Nurnberg together, and much enjoyed the racy remarks of our Transatlantic friend, who, from his quaint speech and his wonderful stock of adventures, might have stepped out of a novel. We kept for the last object of interest in the city to be visited the Burg,[3] and on the day appointed for the visit strolled round the outer wall of the city by the eastern side.

The Burg is seated on a rock dominating the town, and an immensely deep fosse guards it on the northern side. Nurnberg has been happy in that it was never sacked; had it been it would certainly not be so spick and span perfect as it is at present. The ditch has not been used for centuries, and now its base is spread with tea-gardens and orchards, of which some of the trees are of quite respectable growth. As we wandered round the wall, dawdling in the hot July sunshine, we often paused to admire the views spread before us, and in especial the great plain covered with towns and villages and bounded with a blue line of hills, like a landscape of Claude Lorraine.[4] From this we always turned with new delight to the city itself, with its myriad of quaint old gables and acre-wide red roofs dotted with dormer windows, tier upon tier. A little to our right rose the towers of the Burg, and nearer still, standing grim, the Torture Tower,[5] which was, and is, perhaps, the most interesting place in the city. For centuries the tradition of the Iron Virgin of Nurnberg has been handed down as an instance of the horrors of cruelty of which man is capable; we had long looked forward to seeing it; and here at last was its home.

In one of our pauses we leaned over the wall of the moat and looked down. The garden seemed quite fifty or sixty feet below us, and the sun pouring into it with an intense, moveless heat like that of an oven. Beyond rose the grey, grim wall seemingly of endless height, and losing itself right and left in the angles of bastion and counterscarp. Trees and bushes crowned the wall, and above again towered the lofty houses on whose massive beauty Time has only set the hand of approval. The sun was hot and we were lazy; time was our own, and we lingered, leaning on the wall. Just below us was a pretty sight – a great black cat lying stretched in the sun, whilst round her gambolled prettily a tiny black kitten. The mother would wave her tail for the kitten to play with, or would raise her feet and push away the little one as an encouragement to further play. They were just at the foot of the wall, and Elias P. Hutcheson, in order to help the play, stooped and took from the walk a moderate sized pebble.

'See!' he said, 'I will drop it near the kitten, and they will both wonder where it came from.'

'Oh, be careful,' said my wife; 'you might hit the dear little thing!'

'Not me, ma'am,' said Elias P. 'Why, I'm as tender as a Maine cherry-tree.[6] Lor, bless ye, I wouldn't hurt the poor pooty little critter more'n I'd scalp a baby. An' you may bet your variegated socks on that! See, I'll drop it fur away on the outside so's not to go near her!' Thus saying, he leaned over and held his arm out at full length and dropped the stone. It may be that there is some attractive force which draws lesser matters to greater; or more probably that the wall was not plumb but sloped to its base – we not noticing the inclination from above; but the stone fell with a sickening thud that came up to us through the hot air, right on the kitten's head, and shattered out its little brains then and there. The black cat cast a swift upward glance, and we saw her eyes like green fire fixed an instant on Elias P. Hutcheson; and then her attention was given to the kitten, which lay still with just a quiver of her tiny limbs, whilst a thin red stream trickled from a gaping wound. With a muffled cry, such as a human being might give, she bent over the kitten, licking its wound and moaning. Suddenly she seemed to realise that it was dead, and again threw her eyes up at us. I shall never forget the sight, for she looked the perfect incarnation of hate. Her green eyes blazed with lurid fire, and the white, sharp teeth seemed to almost shine through the blood which dabbled her mouth and whiskers. She gnashed her teeth, and her claws stood out stark and at full length on every paw. Then she made a wild rush up the wall as if to reach us, but when the momentum ended fell back, and further added to her horrible appearance for she fell on the kitten, and rose with her black fur smeared with its brains and blood. Amelia turned quite faint, and I had to lift her back from the wall. There was a seat close by in shade of a spreading plane-tree, and here I placed her whilst she composed herself. Then I went back to Hutcheson, who stood without moving, looking down on the angry cat below.

As I joined him, he said:

'Wall, I guess that air the savagest beast I ever see – 'cept once when an Apache squaw had an edge on a half-breed what they nicknamed "Splinters" 'cos of the way he fixed up her papoose which he stole on a raid just to show that he appreciated the way they had given his mother the fire torture. She got that kinder look so set on her face that it jest seemed to grow there. She followed Splinters more'n three year till at last the braves got him and handed him over to her. They did say that no man, white or Injun, had ever been so long a-dying under the tortures of the Apaches. The only time I ever see her smile was when I wiped her out. I kem on the camp just in time to see Splinters pass in his checks, and he wasn't sorry to go either. He was a hard citizen, and though I never could shake with him after that papoose business – for it was bitter bad, and he should have been a white man, for he looked like one – I see he had got paid out in full. Durn me, but I took a piece of his hide from one of his skinnin' posts an' had it made into a pocket-book. It's here now!' and he slapped the breast pocket of his coat.

Whilst he was speaking the cat was continuing her frantic efforts to get up the wall. She would take a run back and then charge up, sometimes reaching an incredible height. She did not seem to mind the heavy fall which she got each time but started with renewed vigour; and at every tumble her appearance became more horrible. Hutcheson was a kind-hearted man – my wife and I had both noticed little acts of kindness to animals as well as to persons – and he seemed concerned at the state of fury to which the cat had wrought herself.

'Wall, now!' he said, 'I du declare that that poor critter seems quite desperate. There! there! poor thing, it was all an accident – though that won't bring back your little one to you. Say! I wouldn't have had such a thing happen for a thousand! Just shows what a clumsy fool of a man can do when he tries to play! Seems I'm too darned slipperhanded to even play with a cat. Say Colonel!' it was a pleasant way he had to bestow titles freely – 'I hope your wife don't hold no grudge against me on account of this unpleasantness? Why, I wouldn't have had it occur on no account.'

He came over to Amelia and apologised profusely, and she with her usual kindness of heart hastened to assure him that she quite understood that it was an accident. Then we all went again to the wall and looked over.

The cat, missing Hutcheson's face, had drawn back across the moat, and was sitting on her haunches as though ready to spring. Indeed, the very instant she saw him she did spring, and with a blind unreasoning fury, which would have been grotesque, only that it was so frightfully real. She did not try to run up the wall, but simply launched herself at him as though hate and fury could lend her wings to pass straight through the great distance between them. Amelia, womanlike, got quite concerned, and said to Elias P. in a warning voice:

'Oh! you must be very careful. That animal would try to kill you if she were here; her eyes look like positive murder.'

He laughed out jovially. 'Excuse me, ma'am,' he said, 'but I can't help laughin'. Fancy a man that has fought grizzlies an' Injuns bein' careful of bein' murdered by a cat!'

When the cat heard him laugh, her whole demeanour seemed to change. She no longer tried to jump or run up the wall, but went quietly over, and sitting again beside the dead kitten began to lick and fondle it as though it were alive.

'See!' said I, 'the effect of a really strong man. Even that animal in the midst of her fury recognises the voice of a master, and bows to him!'

'Like a squaw!' was the only comment of Elias P. Hutcheson, as we moved on our way round the city fosse. Every now and then we looked over the wall and each time saw the cat following us. At first she had kept going back to the dead kitten, and then as the distance grew greater took it in her mouth and so followed. After a while, however, she abandoned this, for we saw her following all alone; she had evidently hidden the body somewhere. Amelia's alarm grew at the cat's persistence, and more than once she repeated her warning; but the American always laughed with amusement, till finally, seeing that she was beginning to be worried, he said:

'I say, ma'am, you needn't be skeered over that cat. I go heeled, I du!' Here he slapped his pistol pocket at the back of his lumbar region. 'Why sooner'n have you worried, I'll shoot the critter, right here, an' risk the police interferin' with a citizen of the United States for carryin' arms contrairy to reg'lations!' As he spoke he looked over the wall, but the cat, on seeing him, retreated, with a growl, into a bed of tall flowers, and was hidden. He went on: 'Blest if that ar critter ain't got more sense of what's good for her than most Christians. I guess we've seen the last of her! You bet, she'll go back now to that busted kitten and have a private funeral of it, all to herself!'

Amelia did not like to say more, lest he might, in mistaken kindness to her, fulfil his threat of shooting the cat: and so we went on and crossed the little wooden bridge leading to the gateway whence ran the steep paved roadway between the Burg and the pentagonal Torture Tower. As we crossed the bridge we saw the cat again down below us. When she saw us her fury seemed to return, and she made frantic efforts to get up the steep wall. Hutcheson laughed as he looked down at her, and said:

'Good-bye, old girl. Sorry I in-jured your feelin's, but you'll get over it in time! So long!' And then we passed through the long, dim archway and came to the gate of the Burg.

When we came out again after our survey of this most beautiful old place which not even the well-intentioned efforts of the Gothic restorers of forty years[7] ago have been able to spoil – though their restoration was then glaring white – we seemed to have quite forgotten the unpleasant episode of the morning. The old lime tree with its great trunk gnarled with the passing of nearly nine centuries, the deep well cut through the heart of the rock by those captives of old, and the lovely view from the city wall whence we heard, spread over almost a full quarter of an hour, the multitudinous chimes of the city, had all helped to wipe out from our minds the incident of the slain kitten.

We were the only visitors who had entered the Torture Tower that morning – so at least said the old custodian – and as we had the place all to ourselves were able to make a minute and more satisfactory survey than would have otherwise been possible. The custodian, looking to us as the sole source of his gains for the day, was willing to meet our wishes in any way. The Torture Tower is truly a grim place, even now when many thousands of visitors have sent a stream of life, and the joy that follows life, into the place; but at the time I mention it wore its grimmest and most gruesome aspect. The dust of ages seemed to have settled on it, and the darkness and the horror of its memories seem to have become sentient in a way that would have satisfied the Pantheistic souls of Philo or Spinoza.[8] The lower chamber where we entered was seemingly, in its normal state, filled with incarnate darkness; even the hot sunlight streaming in through the door seemed to be lost in the vast thickness of the walls, and only showed the masonry rough as when the builder's scaffolding had come down, but coated with dust and marked here and there with patches of dark stain which, if walls could speak, could have given their own dread memories of fear and pain. We were glad to pass up the dusty wooden staircase, the custodian leaving the outer door open to light us somewhat on our way; for to our eyes the one long-wick'd, evil-smelling candle stuck in a sconce on the wall gave an inadequate light. When we came up through the open trap in the corner of the chamber overhead, Amelia held on to me so tightly that I could actually feel her heart beat. I must say for my own part that I was not surprised at her fear, for this room was even more gruesome than that below. Here there was certainly more light, but only just sufficient to realise the horrible surroundings of the place. The builders of the tower had evidently intended that only they who should gain the top should have any of the joys of light and prospect. There, as we had noticed from below, were ranges of windows, albeit of mediæval smallness, but elsewhere in the tower were only a very few narrow slits such as were habitual in places of mediæval defence. A few of these only lit the chamber, and these so high up in the wall that from no part could the sky be seen through the thickness of the walls. In racks, and leaning in disorder against the walls, were a number of headsmen's swords, great double-handed weapons with broad blade and keen edge. Hard by were several blocks whereon the necks of the victims had lain, with here and there deep notches where the steel had bitten through the guard of flesh and shored into the wood. Round the chamber, placed in all sorts of irregular ways, were many implements of torture which made one's heart ache to see – chairs full of spikes which gave instant and excruciating pain; chairs and couches with dull knobs whose torture was seemingly less, but which, though slower, were equally efficacious; racks, belts, boots, gloves, collars, all made for compressing at will; steel baskets in which the head could be slowly crushed into a pulp if necessary; watchmen's hooks with long handle and knife that cut at resistance – this a specialty of the old Nurnberg police system; and many, many other devices for man's injury to man.[9] Amelia grew quite pale with the horror of the things, but fortunately did not faint, for being a little overcome she sat down on a torture chair, but jumped up again with a shriek, all tendency to faint gone. We both pretended that it was the injury done to her dress by the dust of the chair, and the rusty spikes which had upset her, and Mr Hutcheson acquiesced in accepting the explanation with a kind-hearted laugh.

But the central object in the whole of this chamber of horrors was the engine known as the Iron Virgin, which stood near the centre of the room. It was a rudely-shaped figure of a woman, something of the bell order, or, to make a closer comparison, of the figure of Mrs Noah in the children's Ark, but without that slimness of waist and perfect *rondeur* of hip which marks the æsthetic type of the Noah family. One would hardly have recognised it as intended for a human figure at all had not the founder shaped on the forehead a rude semblance of a woman's face. This machine was coated with rust without, and covered with dust; a rope was fastened to a ring in the front of the figure, about where the waist should have been, and was drawn through a pulley, fastened on the wooden pillar which sustained the flooring above. The custodian pulling this rope showed that a section of the front was hinged like a door at one side; we then saw that the engine was of considerable thickness, leaving just room enough inside for a man to be placed. The door was of equal thickness and of great weight, for it took the custodian all his strength, aided though he was by the contrivance of the pulley, to open it. This weight was partly due to the fact that the door was of manifest purpose hung so as to throw its weight downwards, so that it might shut of its own accord when the strain was released. The inside was honeycombed with rust – nay more, the rust alone that comes through time would hardly have eaten so deep into the iron walls; the rust of the cruel stains was deep indeed! It was only, however, when we came to look at the inside of the door that the diabolical intention was manifest to the full. Here were several long spikes, square and massive, broad at the base and sharp at the points, placed in such a position that when the door should close the upper ones would pierce the eyes of the victim, and the lower ones his heart and vitals. The sight was too much for poor Amelia, and this time she fainted dead off, and I had to carry her down the stairs, and place her on a bench outside till she recovered. That she felt it to the quick was afterwards shown by the fact that my eldest son bears to this day a rude birthmark on his breast, which has, by family consent, been accepted as representing the Nurnberg Virgin.[10]

When we got back to the chamber we found Hutcheson still opposite the Iron Virgin; he had been evidently philosophising, and now gave us the benefit of his thought in the shape of a sort of exordium.

'Wall, I guess I've been learnin' somethin' here while madam has been gettin' over her faint. 'Pears to me that we're a long way behind the times on our side of the big drink. We uster think out on the plains that the Injun could give us points in tryin' to make a man oncomfortable; but I guess your old mediæval law-and-order party could raise him every time. Splinters was pretty good in his bluff on the squaw, but this here young miss held a straight flush all high on him. The points of them spikes air sharp enough still, though even the edges air eaten out by what uster be on them. It'd be a good thing for our Indian section to get some specimens of this here play-toy to send round to the Reservations jest to knock the stuffin' out of the bucks, and the squaws too, by showing them as how old civilisation lays over them at their best. Guess but I'll get in that box a minute jest to see how it feels!'

'Oh no! no!' said Amelia. 'It is too terrible!'

'Guess, ma'am, nothin's too terrible to the explorin' mind. I've been in some queer places in my time. Spent a night inside a dead horse while a prairie fire swept over me in Montana Territory[11] – an' another time slept inside a dead buffler when the Comanches was on the war path an' I didn't keer to leave my kyard on them. I've been two days in a caved-in tunnel in the Billy Broncho gold mine in New Mexico, an' was one of the four shut up for three parts of a day in the caisson what slid over on her side when we was settin' the foundations of the Buffalo Bridge. I've not funked an odd experience yet, an' I don't propose to begin now!'

We saw that he was set on the experiment, so I said: 'Well, hurry up, old man, and get through it quick?'

'All right, General,' said he, 'but I calculate we ain't quite ready yet. The gentlemen, my predecessors, what stood in that thar canister, didn't volunteer for the office – not much! And I guess there was some ornamental tyin' up before the big stroke was made. I want to go into this thing fair and square, so I must get fixed up proper first. I dare say this old galoot can rise some string and tie me up accordin' to sample?'

This was said interrogatively to the old custodian, but the latter, who understood the drift of his speech, though perhaps not appreciating to the full the niceties of dialect and imagery, shook his head. His protest was, however, only formal and made to be overcome. The American thrust a gold piece into his hand, saying, 'Take it, pard! it's your pot; and don't be skeer'd. This ain't no necktie party that you're asked to assist in!' He produced some thin frayed rope and proceeded to bind our companion with sufficient strictness for the purpose. When the upper part of his body was bound, Hutcheson said:

'Hold on a moment, Judge. Guess I'm too heavy for you to tote into the canister. You jest let me walk in, and then you can wash up regardin' my legs!'

Whilst speaking he had backed himself into the opening which was just enough to hold him. It was a close fit and no mistake. Amelia looked on with fear in her eyes, but she evidently did not like to say anything. Then the custodian completed his task by tying the American's feet together so that he was now absolutely helpless and fixed in his voluntary prison. He seemed to really enjoy it, and the incipient smile which was habitual to his face blossomed into actuality as he said:

'Guess this here Eve was made out of the rib of a dwarf! There ain't much room for a full-grown citizen of the United States to hustle. We uster make our coffins more roomier in Idaho territory.[12] Now, Judge, you jest begin to let this door down, slow, on to me. I want to feel the same pleasure as the other jays had when those spikes began to move toward their eyes!'

'Oh no! no! no!' broke in Amelia hysterically. 'It is too terrible! I can't bear to see it! – I can't! I can't!'

But the American was obdurate. 'Say, Colonel,' said he, 'Why not take Madame for a little promenade? I wouldn't hurt her feelin's for the world; but now that I am here, havin' kem eight thousand miles, wouldn't it be too hard to give up the very experience I've been pinin' an' pantin' fur? A man can't get to feel like canned goods every time! Me and the Judge here'll fix up this thing in no time, an' then you'll come back, an' we'll all laugh together!'

Once more the resolution that is born of curiosity triumphed, and Amelia stayed holding tight to my arm and shivering whilst the custodian began to slacken slowly inch by inch the rope that held back the iron door. Hutcheson's face was positively radiant as his eyes followed the first movement of the spikes.

'Wall!' he said, 'I guess I've not had enjoyment like this since I left Noo York. Bar a scrap with a French sailor at Wapping[13] – an' that warn't much of a picnic neither – I've not had a show fur real pleasure in this dod-rotted Continent, where there ain't no b'ars nor no Injuns, an' wheer nary man goes heeled. Slow there, Judge! Don't you rush this business! I want a show for my money this game – I du!'

The custodian must have had in him some of the blood of his predecessors in that ghastly tower, for he worked the engine with a deliberate and excruciating slowness which after five minutes, in which the outer edge of the door had not moved half as many inches, began to overcome Amelia. I saw her lips whiten, and felt her hold upon my arm relax. I looked around an instant for a place whereon to lay her, and when I looked at her again found that her eye had become fixed on the side of the Virgin. Following its direction I saw the black cat crouching out of sight. Her green eyes shone like danger lamps in the gloom of the place, and their colour was heightened by the blood which still smeared her coat and reddened her mouth. I cried out:

'The cat! look out for the cat!' for even then she sprang out before the engine. At this moment she looked like a triumphant demon. Her eyes blazed with ferocity, her hair bristled out till she seemed twice her normal size, and her tail lashed about as does a tiger's when the quarry is before it. Elias P. Hutcheson when he saw her was amused, and his eyes positively sparkled with fun as he said:

'Darned if the squaw hain't got on all her war paint! Jest give her a shove off if she comes any of her tricks on me, for I'm so fixed everlastingly by the boss, that durn my skin if I can keep my eyes from her if she wants them! Easy there, Judge! don't you slack that ar rope or I'm euchered!'[14]

At this moment Amelia completed her faint, and I had to clutch hold of her round the waist or she would have fallen to the floor. Whilst attending to her I saw the black cat crouching for a spring, and jumped up to turn the creature out.

But at that instant, with a sort of hellish scream, she hurled herself, not as we expected at Hutcheson, but straight at the face of the custodian. Her claws seemed to be tearing wildly as one sees in the Chinese drawings of the dragon rampant, and as I looked I saw one of them light on the poor man's eye, and actually tear through it and down his cheek, leaving a wide band of red where the blood seemed to spurt from every vein.

With a yell of sheer terror which came quicker than even his sense of pain, the man leaped back, dropping as he did so the rope which held back the iron door. I jumped for it, but was too late, for the cord ran like lightning through the pulley-block, and the heavy mass fell forward from its own weight.

As the door closed I caught a glimpse of our poor companion's face. He seemed frozen with terror. His eyes stared with a horrible anguish as if dazed, and no sound came from his lips.

And then the spikes did their work. Happily the end was quick, for when I wrenched open the door they had pierced so deep that they had locked in the bones of the skull through which they had crushed, and actually tore him – it – out of his iron prison till, bound as he was, he fell at full length with a sickly thud upon the floor, the face turning upward as he fell.

I rushed to my wife, lifted her up and carried her out, for I feared for her very reason if she should wake from her faint to such a scene. I laid her on the bench outside and ran back. Leaning against the wooden column was the custodian moaning in pain whilst he held his reddening handkerchief to his eyes. And sitting on the head of the poor American was the cat, purring loudly as she licked the blood which trickled through the gashed socket of his eyes.

I think no one will call me cruel because I seized one of the old executioner's swords and shore her in two as she sat.

THE SECRET OF THE
GROWING GOLD

When Margaret Dalandre went to live at Brent's Rock the whole neighbourhood awoke to the pleasure of an entirely new scandal. Scandals in connection with either the Delandre family or the Brents of Brent's Rock were not few; and if the secret history of the county had been written in full both names would have been found well represented. It is true that the status of each was so different that they might have belonged to different continents – or to different worlds for the matter of that – for hitherto their orbits had never crossed. The Brents were accorded by the whole section of the country an unique social dominance, and had ever held themselves as high above the yeoman class to which Margaret Delandre belonged, as a blue-blooded Spanish hidalgo out-tops his peasant tenantry.

The Delandres had an ancient record and were proud of it in their way as the Brents were of theirs. But the family had never risen above yeomanry; and although they had been once well-to-do in the good old times of foreign wars and protection, their fortunes had withered under the scorching of the free trade sun and the 'piping times of peace.' They had, as the elder members used to assert, 'stuck to the land,' with the result that they had taken root in it, body and soul. In fact, they, having chosen the life of vegetables, had flourished as vegetation does – blossomed and thrived in the good season and suffered in the bad. Their holding, Dander's Croft, seemed to have been worked out, and to be typical of the family which had inhabited it. The latter had declined generation after generation, sending out now and again some abortive shoot of unsatisfied energy in the shape of a soldier or sailor, who had worked his way to the minor grades of the services and had there stopped, cut short either from unheeding gallantry in action or from that destroying cause to men without breeding or youthful care – the recognition of a position above them which they feel unfitted to fill. So, little by little, the family dropped lower and lower, the men brooding and dissatisfied, and drinking themselves into the grave, the women drudging at home, or marrying beneath them – or worse. In process of time all disappeared, leaving only two in the Croft, Wykham Delandre and his sister Margaret. The man and woman seemed to have inherited in masculine and feminine form respectively the evil tendency of their race, sharing in common the principles, though manifesting them in different ways, of sullen passion, voluptuousness and recklessness.

The history of the Brents had been something similar, but showing the causes of decadence in their aristocratic and not their plebeian forms.[1] They, too, had sent their shoots to the wars; but their positions had been different, and they had often attained honour – for without flaw they were gallant, and brave deeds were done by them before the selfish dissipation which marked them had sapped their vigour.

The present head of the family – if family it could now be called when one remained of the direct line – was Geoffrey Brent. He was almost a type of a worn-out race, manifesting in some ways its most brilliant qualities, and in others its utter degradation. He might be fairly compared with some of those antique Italian nobles whom the painters have preserved to us with their courage, their unscrupulousness, their refinement of lust and cruelty – the voluptuary actual with the fiend potential. He was certainly handsome, with that dark, aquiline, commanding beauty which women so generally recognise as dominant. With men he was distant and cold; but such a bearing never deters womankind. The inscrutable laws of sex have so arranged that even a timid woman is not afraid of a fierce and haughty man. And so it was that there was hardly a woman of any kind or degree, who lived within view of Brent's Rock, who did not cherish some form of secret admiration for the handsome wastrel. The category was a wide one, for Brent's

Rock rose up steeply from the midst of a level region and for a circuit of a hundred miles it lay on the horizon, with its high old towers and steep roofs cutting the level edge of wood and hamlet, and far-scattered mansions.

So long as Geoffrey Brent confined his dissipations to London and Paris and Vienna – anywhere out of sight and sound of his home – opinion was silent. It is easy to listen to far off echoes unmoved, and we can treat them with disbelief, or scorn, or disdain, or whatever attitude of coldness may suit our purpose. But when the scandal came close to home it was another matter; and the feeling of independence and integrity which is in people of every community which is not utterly spoiled, asserted itself and demanded that condemnation should be expressed. Still there was a certain reticence in all, and no more notice was taken of the existing facts than was absolutely necessary. Margaret Delandre bore herself so fearlessly and so openly – she accepted her position as the justified companion of Geoffrey Brent so naturally that people came to believe that she was secretly married to him, and therefore thought it wiser to hold their tongues lest time should justify her and also make her an active enemy.

The one person who, by his interference, could have settled all doubts was debarred by circumstances from interfering in the matter. Wykham Delandre had quarrelled with his sister – or perhaps it was that she had quarrelled with him – and they were on terms not merely of armed neutrality but of bitter hatred. The quarrel had been antecedent to Margaret going to Brent's Rock. She and Wykham had almost come to blows. There had certainly been threats on one side and on the other; and in the end Wykham, overcome with passion, had ordered his sister to leave his house. She had risen straightway, and, without waiting to pack up even her own personal belongings, had walked out of the house. On the threshold she had paused for a moment to hurl a bitter threat at Wykham that he would rue in shame and despair to the last hour of his life his act of that day. Some weeks had since passed; and it was understood in the neighbourhood that Margaret had gone to London, when she suddenly appeared driving out with Geoffrey Brent, and the entire neighbourhood knew before nightfall that she had taken up her abode at the Rock. It was no subject of surprise that Brent had come back unexpectedly, for such was his usual custom. Even his own servants never knew when to expect him, for there was a private door, of which he alone had the key, by which he sometimes entered without anyone in the house being aware of his coming. This was his usual method of appearing after a long absence.

Wykham Delandre was furious at the news. He vowed vengeance – and to keep his mind level with his passion drank deeper than ever. He tried several times to see his sister, but she contemptuously refused to meet him. He tried to have an interview with Brent and was refused by him also. Then he tried to stop him in the road, but without avail, for Geoffrey was not a man to be stopped against his will. Several actual encounters took place between the two men, and many more were threatened and avoided. At last Wykham Delandre settled down to a morose, vengeful acceptance of the situation.

Neither Margaret nor Geoffrey was of a pacific temperament, and it was not long before there began to be quarrels between them. One thing would lead to another, and wine flowed freely at Brent's Rock. Now and again the quarrels would assume a bitter aspect, and threats would be exchanged in uncompromising language that fairly awed the listening servants. But such quarrels generally ended where domestic altercations do, in reconciliation, and in a mutual respect for the fighting qualities proportionate to their manifestation. Fighting for its own sake is found by a certain class of persons, all the world over, to be a matter of absorbing interest, and there is no reason to believe that domestic conditions minimise its potency. Geoffrey and Margaret made occasional absences from Brent's Rock, and on each of these occasions Wykham Delandre also absented himself; but as he generally heard of the absence too late to be of any service, he returned home each time in a more bitter and discontented frame of mind than before.

At last there came a time when the absence from Brent's Rock became longer than before. Only a few days earlier there had been a quarrel, exceeding in bitterness anything which had gone before; but this, too, had been made up, and a trip on the Continent had been mentioned before the servants. After a few days Wykham Delandre also went away, and it was some weeks before he returned. It was noticed that he was full of some new importance – satisfaction, exaltation – they hardly knew how to call it. He went straightway to Brent's Rock, and demanded to see Geoffrey Brent, and on being told that he had not yet returned, said, with a grim decision which the servants noted:

'I shall come again. My news is solid – it can wait!' and turned away. Week after week went by, and month after month; and then there came a rumour, certified later on, that an accident had occurred in the Zermatt valley. Whilst crossing a dangerous pass the carriage containing an English lady and the driver had fallen over a precipice, the gentleman of the party, Mr Geoffrey Brent, having been fortunately saved as he had been walking up the hill to ease the horses. He gave information, and search was made. The broken rail, the excoriated roadway, the marks where the horses had struggled on the decline before finally pitching over into the torrent – all told the sad tale. It was a wet season, and there had been much snow in the winter, so that the river was swollen beyond its usual volume, and the eddies of the stream were packed with ice. All search was made, and finally the wreck of the carriage and the body of one horse were found in an eddy of the river. Later on the body of the driver was found on the sandy, torrent-swept waste near Täsch; but the body of the lady, like that of the other horse, had quite disappeared, and was – what was left of it by that time – whirling amongst the eddies of the Rhone on its way down to the Lake of Geneva.

Wykham Delandre made all the enquiries possible, but could not find any trace of the missing woman. He found, however, in the books of the various hotels the name of 'Mr and Mrs Geoffrey Brent.' And he had a stone erected at Zermatt to his sister's memory, under her married name, and a tablet put up in the church at Bretten, the parish in which both Brent's Rock and Dander's Croft were situated.

There was a lapse of nearly a year, after the excitement of the matter had worn away, and the whole neighbourhood had gone on its accustomed way. Brent was still absent, and Delandre more drunken, more morose, and more revengeful than before.

Then there was a new excitement. Brent's Rock was being made ready for a new mistress. It was officially announced by Geoffrey himself in a letter to the Vicar, that he had been married some months before to an Italian lady, and that they were then on their way home. Then a small army of workmen invaded the house; and hammer and plane sounded, and a general air of size and paint pervaded the atmosphere. One wing of the old house, the south, was entirely re-done; and then the great body of the workmen departed, leaving only materials for the doing of the old hall when Geoffrey Brent should have returned, for he had directed that the decoration was only to be done under his own eyes. He had brought with him accurate drawings of a hall in the house of his bride's father, for he wished to reproduce for her the place to which she had been accustomed. As the moulding had all to be re-done, some scaffolding poles and boards were brought in and laid on one side of the great hall, and also a great wooden tank or box for mixing the lime, which was laid in bags beside it.

When the new mistress of Brent's Rock arrived the bells of the church rang out, and there was a general jubilation. She was a beautiful creature, full of the poetry and fire and passion of the South; and the few English words which she had learned were spoken in such a sweet and pretty broken way that she won the hearts of the people almost as much by the music of her voice as by the melting beauty of her dark eyes.

Geoffrey Brent seemed more happy than he had ever before appeared; but there was a dark, anxious look on his face that was new to those who knew him of old, and he started at times as though at some noise that was unheard by others.

And so months passed and the whisper grew that at last Brent's Rock was to have an heir. Geoffrey was very tender to his wife, and the new bond between them seemed to soften him. He took more interest in his tenants and their needs than he had ever done; and works of charity on his part as well as on his sweet young wife's were not lacking. He seemed to have set all his hopes on the child that was coming, and as he looked deeper into the future the dark shadow that had come over his face seemed to die gradually away.

All the time Wykham Delandre nursed his revenge. Deep in his heart had grown up a purpose of vengeance which only waited an opportunity to crystallise and take a definite shape. His vague idea was somehow centred in the wife of Brent, for he knew that he could strike him best through those he loved, and the coming time seemed to hold in its womb the opportunity for which he longed. One night he sat alone in the living-room of his house. It had once been a handsome room in its way, but time and neglect had done their work and it was now little better than a ruin, without dignity or picturesqueness of any kind. He had been drinking heavily for some time and was more than half stupefied. He thought he heard a noise as of someone at the door and looked up. Then he called half savagely to come in; but there was no response. With a muttered blasphemy he renewed his potations. Presently he forgot all around him, sank into a daze, but suddenly awoke to see standing before him someone or something like a battered, ghostly edition of his sister. For a few moments there came upon him a sort of fear. The woman before him, with distorted features and burning eyes, seemed hardly human, and the only thing that seemed a reality of his sister, as she had been, was her wealth of golden hair, and this was now streaked with grey. She eyed her brother with a long, cold stare; and he, too, as he looked and began to realise the actuality of her presence, found the hatred of her which he had had, once again surging up in his heart. All the brooding passion of the past year seemed to find a voice at once as he asked her: –

'Why are you here? You're dead and buried.'

'I am here, Wykham Delandre, for no love of you, but because I hate another even more than I do you!' A great passion blazed in her eyes.

'Him?' he asked, in so fierce a whisper that even the woman was for an instant startled till she regained her calm.

'Yes, him!' she answered. 'But make no mistake, my revenge is my own; and I merely use you to help me to it.' Wykham asked suddenly:

'Did he marry you?'

The woman's distorted face broadened out in a ghastly attempt at a smile. It was a hideous mockery, for the broken features and seamed scars took strange shapes and strange colours, and queer lines of white showed out as the straining muscles pressed on the old cicatrices.

'So you would like to know! It would please your pride to feel that your sister was truly married! Well, you shall not know. That was my revenge on you, and I do not mean to change it by a hair's breadth. I have come here to-night simply to let you know that I am alive, so that if any violence be done me where I am going there may be a witness.'

'Where are you going?' demanded her brother.

'That is my affair! and I have not the least intention of letting you know!' Wykham stood up, but the drink was on him and he reeled and fell. As he lay on the floor he announced his intention of following his sister; and with an outburst of splenetic humour[2] told her that he would follow her through the darkness by the light of her hair, and of her beauty. At this she turned on him, and said that there were others beside him that would rue her hair and her beauty too. 'As he will,' she hissed; 'for the hair remains though the beauty be gone. When he withdrew the lynch-pin and sent us over the precipice into the torrent, he had little thought of my beauty. Perhaps his beauty would be scarred like mine were he whirled, as I was, among the rocks of the Visp, and frozen on the ice pack in the drift of the river. But let him beware! His time is coming!' and with a fierce gesture she flung open the door and passed out into the night.

Later on that night, Mrs Brent, who was but half-asleep, became suddenly awake and spoke to her husband:

'Geoffrey, was not that the click of a lock somewhere below our window?'

But Geoffrey – though she thought that he, too, had started at the noise – seemed sound asleep, and breathed heavily. Again Mrs Brent dozed; but this time awoke to the fact that her husband had arisen and was partially dressed. He was deadly pale, and when the light of the lamp which he had in his hand fell on his face, she was frightened at the look in his eyes.

'What is it, Geoffrey? What dost thou?' she asked.

'Hush! little one,' he answered, in a strange, hoarse voice. 'Go to sleep. I am restless, and wish to finish some work I left undone.'

'Bring it here, my husband,' she said; 'I am lonely and I fear when thou art away.'

For reply he merely kissed her and went out, closing the door behind him. She lay awake for awhile, and then nature asserted itself, and she slept.

Suddenly she started broad awake with the memory in her ears of a smothered cry from somewhere not far off. She jumped up and ran to the door and listened, but there was no sound. She grew alarmed for her husband, and called out: 'Geoffrey! Geoffrey!'

After a few moments the door of the great hall opened, and Geoffrey appeared at it, but without his lamp.

'Hush!' he said, in a sort of whisper, and his voice was harsh and stern. 'Hush! Get to bed! I am working, and must not be disturbed. Go to sleep, and do not wake the house!'

With a chill in her heart – for the harshness of her husband's voice was new to her – she crept back to bed and lay there trembling, too frightened to cry, and listened to every sound. There was a long pause of silence, and then the sound of some iron implement striking muffled blows! Then there came a clang of a heavy stone falling, followed by a muffled curse. Then a dragging sound, and then more noise of stone on stone. She lay all the while in an agony of fear, and her heart beat dreadfully. She heard a curious sort of scraping sound; and then there was silence. Presently the door opened gently, and Geoffrey appeared. His wife pretended to be asleep; but through her eyelashes she saw him wash from his hands something white that looked like lime.[3]

In the morning he made no allusion to the previous night, and she was afraid to ask any question.

From that day there seemed some shadow over Geoffrey Brent. He neither ate nor slept as he had been accustomed, and his former habit of turning suddenly as though someone were speaking from behind him revived. The old hall seemed to have some kind of fascination for him. He used to go there many times in the day, but grew impatient if anyone, even his wife, entered it. When the builder's foreman came to inquire about continuing his work Geoffrey was out driving; the man went into the hall, and when Geoffrey returned the servant told him of his arrival and where he was. With a frightful oath he pushed the servant aside and hurried up to the old hall. The workman met him almost at the door; and as Geoffrey burst into the room he ran against him. The man apologised:

'Beg pardon, sir, but I was just going out to make some enquiries. I directed twelve sacks of lime to be sent here, but I see there are only ten.'

'Damn the ten sacks and the twelve too!' was the ungracious and incomprehensible rejoinder.

The workman looked surprised, and tried to turn the conversation.

'I see, sir, there is a little matter which our people must have done; but the governor will of course see it set right at his own cost.'

'What do you mean?'

'That 'ere 'arth-stone, sir: Some idiot must have put a scaffold pole on it and cracked it right down the middle, and it's thick enough you'd think to stand hanythink.' Geoffrey was silent for quite a minute, and then said in a constrained voice and with much gentler manner:

'Tell your people that I am not going on with the work in the hall at present. I want to leave it as it is for a while longer.'

'All right sir. I'll send up a few of our chaps to take away these poles and lime bags and tidy the place up a bit.'

'No! No!' said Geoffrey, 'leave them where they are. I shall send and tell you when you are to get on with the work.' So the foreman went away, and his comment to his master was:

'I'd send in the bill, sir, for the work already done. 'Pears to me that money's a little shaky in that quarter.'

Once or twice Delandre tried to stop Brent on the road, and, at last, finding that he could not attain his object, rode after the carriage, calling out:

'What has become of my sister, your wife.' Geoffrey lashed his horses into a gallop, and the other, seeing from his white face and from his wife's collapse almost into a faint that his object was attained, rode away with a scowl and a laugh.

That night when Geoffrey went into the hall he passed over to the great fireplace, and all at once started back with a smothered cry. Then with an effort he pulled himself together and went away, returning with a light. He bent down over the broken hearth-stone to see if the moonlight falling through the storied window had in any way deceived him. Then with a groan of anguish he sank to his knees.

There, sure enough, through the crack in the broken stone were protruding a multitude of threads of golden hair just tinged with grey!

He was disturbed by a noise at the door, and looking round, saw his wife standing in the doorway. In the desperation of the moment he took action to prevent discovery, and lighting a match at the lamp, stooped down and burned away the hair that rose through the broken stone. Then rising nonchalantly as he could, he pretended surprise at seeing his wife beside him.

For the next week he lived in an agony; for, whether by accident or design, he could not find himself alone in the hall for any length of time. At each visit the hair had grown afresh through the crack, and he had to watch it carefully lest his terrible secret should be discovered. He tried to find a receptacle for the body of the murdered woman outside the house, but someone always interrupted him; and once, when he was coming out of the private doorway, he was met by his wife, who began to question him about it, and manifested surprise that she should not have before noticed the key which he now reluctantly showed her. Geoffrey dearly and passionately loved his wife, so that any possibility of her discovering his dread secrets, or even of doubting him, filled him with anguish; and after a couple of days had passed, he could not help coming to the conclusion that, at least, she suspected something.

That very evening she came into the hall after her drive and found him there sitting moodily by the deserted fireplace. She spoke to him directly.

'Geoffrey, I have been spoken to by that fellow Delandre, and he says horrible things. He tells to me that a week ago his sister returned to his house, the wreck and ruin of her former self, with only her golden hair as of old, and announced some fell intention. He asked me where she is – and oh, Geoffrey, she is dead, she is dead! So how can she have returned? Oh! I am in dread, and I know not where to turn!'

For answer, Geoffrey burst into a torrent of blasphemy which made her shudder. He cursed Delandre and his sister and all their kind, and in especial he hurled curse after curse on her golden hair.

'Oh, hush! hush!' she said, and was then silent, for she feared her husband when she saw the evil effect of his humour. Geoffrey, in the torrent of his anger, stood up and moved away from the hearth; but suddenly stopped as he saw a new look of terror in his wife's eyes. He followed their glance, and then he, too, shuddered – for there on the broken hearth-stone lay a golden streak as the points of the hair rose through the crack.

'Look, look!' she shrieked. 'Is it some ghost of the dead! Come away – come away!' and seizing her husband by the wrist with the frenzy of madness, she pulled him from the room.

That night she was in a raging fever. The doctor of the district attended her at once, and special aid was telegraphed for to London. Geoffrey was in despair, and in his anguish at the danger of his young wife almost forgot his own crime and its consequences. In the evening the doctor had to leave to attend to others; but he left Geoffrey in charge of his wife. His last words were:

'Remember, you must humour her till I come in the morning, or till some other doctor has her case in hand. What you have to dread is another attack of emotion. See that she is kept warm. Nothing more can be done.'

Late in the evening, when the rest of the household had retired, Geoffrey's wife got up from her bed and called to her husband.

'Come!' she said. 'Come to the old hall! I know where the gold comes from! I want to see it grow!'

Geoffrey would fain have stopped her, but he feared for her

life or reason on the one hand, and lest in a paroxysm she should shriek out her terrible suspicion, and seeing that it was useless to try to prevent her, wrapped a warm rug around her and went with her to the old hall. When they entered, she turned and shut the door and locked it.

'We want no strangers amongst us three to-night!' she whispered with a wan smile.

'We three! nay we are but two,' said Geoffrey with a shudder; he feared to say more.

'Sit here,' said his wife as she put out the light. 'Sit here by the hearth and watch the gold growing. The silver moonlight is jealous! See it steals along the floor towards the gold – our gold!' Geoffrey looked with growing horror, and saw that during the hours that had passed the golden hair had protruded further through the broken hearth-stone. He tried to hide it by placing his feet over the broken place; and his wife, drawing her chair beside him, leant over and laid her head on his shoulder.

'Now do not stir, dear,' she said; 'let us sit still and watch. We shall find the secret of the growing gold!' He passed his arm round her and sat silent; and as the moonlight stole along the floor she sank to sleep.

He feared to wake her; and so sat silent and miserable as the hours stole away.

Before his horror-struck eyes the golden hair from the broken stone grew and grew; and as it increased, so his heart got colder and colder, till at last he had not power to stir, and sat with eyes full of terror watching his doom.

In the morning when the London doctor came, neither Geoffrey nor his wife could be found. Search was made in all the rooms, but without avail. As a last resource the great door of the old hall was broken open, and those who entered saw a grim and sorry sight.

There by the deserted hearth Geoffrey Brent and his young wife sat cold and white and dead. Her face was peaceful, and her eyes were closed in sleep; but his face was a sight that made all who saw it shudder, for there was on it a look of unutterable horror. The eyes were open and stared glassily at his feet, which were twined with tresses of golden hair, streaked with grey, which came through the broken hearth-stone.

A GIPSY PROPHECY

'I really think,' said the Doctor, 'that, at any rate, one of us should go and try whether or not the thing is an imposture.'

'Good!' said Considine. 'After dinner we will take our cigars and stroll over to the camp.'

Accordingly, when the dinner was over, and the *La Tour*[1] finished, Joshua Considine and his friend, Dr Burleigh, went over to the east side of the moor, where the gipsy encampment lay. As they were leaving, Mary Considine, who had walked as far as the end of the garden where it opened into the laneway, called after her husband:

'Mind, Joshua, you are to give them a fair chance, but don't give them any clue to a fortune – and don't you get flirting with any of the gipsy maidens – and take care to keep Gerald out of harm.'

For answer Considine held up his hand, as if taking a stage oath, and whistled the air of the old song, 'The Gipsy Countess.' Gerald joined in the strain, and then, breaking into merry laughter, the two men passed along the laneway to the common, turning now and then to wave their hands to Mary, who leaned over the gate, in the twilight, looking after them.

It was a lovely evening in the summer; the very air was full of rest and quiet happiness, as though an outward type of the peacefulness and joy which made a heaven of the home of the young married folk. Considine's life had not been an eventful one. The only disturbing element which he had ever known was in his wooing of Mary Winston, and the long-continued objection of her ambitious parents, who expected a brilliant match for their only daughter. When Mr and Mrs Winston had discovered the attachment of the young barrister,[2] they had tried to keep the young people apart by sending their daughter away for a long round of visits, having made her promise not to correspond with her lover during her absence. Love, however, had stood the test. Neither absence nor neglect seemed to cool the passion of the young man, and jealousy seemed a thing unknown to his sanguine nature; so, after a long period of waiting, the parents had given in, and the young folk were married.

They had been living in the cottage a few months, and were just beginning to feel at home. Gerald Burleigh, Joshua's old college chum, and himself a sometime victim of Mary's beauty, had arrived a week before, to stay with them for as long a time as he could tear himself away from his work in London.

When her husband had quite disappeared Mary went into the house, and, sitting down at the piano, gave an hour to Mendelssohn.[3]

It was but a short walk across the common, and before the cigars required renewing the two men had reached the gipsy camp. The place was as picturesque as gipsy camps – when in villages and when business is good – usually are. There were some few persons round the fire, investing their money in prophecy, and a large number of others, poorer or more parsimonious, who stayed just outside the bounds, but near enough to see all that went on.

As the two gentlemen approached, the villagers, who knew Joshua, made way a little, and a pretty, keen-eyed gipsy girl tripped up and asked to tell their fortunes. Joshua held out his hand, but the girl, without seeming to see it, stared at his face in a very odd manner. Gerald nudged him:

'You must cross her hand with silver,' he said. 'It is one of the most important parts of the mystery.' Joshua took from his pocket a half-crown and held it out to her, but, without looking at it, she answered:

'You must cross the gipsy's hand with gold.'

Gerald laughed. 'You are at a premium as a subject,' he said. Joshua was of the kind of man – the universal kind – who can tolerate being stared at by a pretty girl; so, with some little deliberation, he answered:

'All right; here you are, my pretty girl; but you must give me a real good fortune for it,' and he handed her a half sovereign, which she took, saying:

'It is not for me to give good fortune or bad, but only to read what the Stars have said.' She took his right hand and turned it palm upward; but the instant her eyes met it she dropped it as though it had been red hot, and, with a startled look, glided swiftly away. Lifting the curtain of the large tent, which occupied the centre of the camp, she disappeared within.

'Sold again!' said the cynical Gerald. Joshua stood a little amazed, and not altogether satisfied. They both watched the large tent. In a few moments there emerged from the opening not the young girl, but a stately looking woman of middle age and commanding presence.

The instant she appeared the whole camp seemed to stand still. The clamour of tongues, the laughter and noise of the work were, for a second or two, arrested, and every man or woman who sat, or crouched, or lay, stood up and faced the imperial looking gipsy.

'The Queen, of course,' murmured Gerald. 'We are in luck to-night.'

The gipsy Queen threw a searching glance around the camp, and then, without hesitating an instant, came straight over and stood before Joshua.

'Hold out your hand,' she said in a commanding tone.

Again Gerald spoke, *sotto voce*: 'I have not been spoken to in that way since I was at school.'

'Your hand must be crossed with gold.'

'A hundred per cent at this game,' whispered Gerald, as Joshua laid another half sovereign on his upturned palm.

The gipsy looked at the hand with knitted brows; then suddenly looking up into his face, said:

'Have you a strong will – have you a true heart that can be brave for one you love?'

'I hope so; but I am afraid I have not vanity enough to say "yes."'

'Then I will answer for you; for I read resolution in your face – resolution desperate and determined if need be. You have a wife you love?'

'Yes,' emphatically.

'Then leave her at once – never see her face again. Go from her now, while love is fresh and your heart is free from wicked intent. Go quick – go far, and never see her face again!'

Joshua drew away his hand quickly, and said: 'Thank you!' stiffly but sarcastically, as he began to move away.

'I say!' said Gerald, 'you're not going like that, old man; no use in being indignant with the Stars or their prophet – and, moreover, your sovereign – what of it? At least, hear the matter out.'

'Silence, ribald!' commanded the Queen, 'you know not what you do. Let him go – and go ignorant, if he will not be warned.'

Joshua immediately turned back. 'At all events, we will see this thing out,' he said. 'Now, madam, you have given me advice, but I paid for a fortune.'

'Be warned!' said the gipsy. 'The Stars have been silent for long; let the mystery still wrap them round.'

'My dear madam, I do not get within touch of a mystery every day, and I prefer for my money knowledge rather than ignorance. I can get the latter commodity for nothing when I want any of it.'

Gerald echoed the sentiment. 'As for me I have a large and unsaleable stock on hand.'

The gipsy Queen eyed the two men sternly, and then said: 'As you wish. You have chosen for yourself, and have met warning with scorn, and appeal with levity. On your own heads be the doom!'

'Amen!' said Gerald.

With an imperious gesture the Queen took Joshua's hand again, and began to tell his fortune.

'I see here the flowing of blood; it will flow before long; it is running in my sight. It flows through the broken circle of a severed ring.'

'Go on!' said Joshua, smiling. Gerald was silent.

'Must I speak plainer?'

'Certainly; we commonplace mortals want something definite. The Stars are a long way off, and their words get somewhat dulled in the message.'

The gipsy shuddered, and then spoke impressively. 'This is

the hand of a murderer – the murderer of his wife!' She dropped the hand and turned away.

Joshua laughed. 'Do you know,' said he, 'I think if I were you I should prophesy some jurisprudence into my system. For instance, you say "this hand is the hand of a murderer." Well, whatever it may be in the future – or potentially – it is at present not one. You ought to give your prophecy in such terms as "the hand which will be a murderer's," or, rather, "the hand of one who will be the murderer of his wife." The Stars are really not good on technical questions.'

The gipsy made no reply of any kind, but, with drooping head and despondent mien, walked slowly to her tent, and, lifting the curtain, disappeared.

Without speaking the two men turned homewards, and walked across the moor. Presently, after some little hesitation, Gerald spoke.

'Of course, old man, this is all a joke; a ghastly one, but still a joke. But would it not be well to keep it to ourselves?'

'How do you mean?'

'Well, not to tell your wife. It might alarm her.'

'Alarm her! My dear Gerald, what are you thinking of? Why, she would not be alarmed or afraid of me if all the gipsies that ever didn't come from Bohemia[4] agreed that I was to murder her, or even to have a hard thought of her, whilst so long as she was saying "Jack Robinson."'

Gerald remonstrated. 'Old fellow, women are superstitious – far more than we men are; and, also, they are blessed – or cursed – with a nervous system to which we are strangers. I see too much of it in my work not to realise it. Take my advice and do not let her know, or you will frighten her.'

Joshua's lips unconsciously hardened as he answered: 'My dear fellow, I would not have a secret from my wife. Why, it would be the beginning of a new order of things between us. We have no secrets from each other. If we ever have, then you may begin to look out for something odd between us.'

'Still,' said Gerald, 'at the risk of unwelcome interference, I say again be warned in time.'

'The gipsy's very words,' said Joshua. 'You and she seem

quite of one accord. Tell me, old man, is this a put-up thing? You told me of the gipsy camp – did you arrange it all with Her Majesty?' This was said with an air of bantering earnestness. Gerald assured him that he only heard of the camp that morning; but he made fun of every answer of his friend, and, in the process of this raillery, the time passed, and they entered the cottage.

Mary was sitting by the piano but not playing. The dim twilight had waked some very tender feelings in her breast, and her eyes were full of gentle tears. When the men came in she stole over to her husband's side and kissed him. Joshua struck a tragic attitude.

'Mary,' he said in a deep voice, 'before you approach me, listen to the words of Fate. The Stars have spoken and the doom is sealed.'

'What is it, dear? Tell me the fortune, but do not frighten me.'

'Not at all, my dear; but there is a truth which it is well that you should know. Nay, it is necessary so that all your arrangements can be made beforehand, and everything be decently done and in order.'

'Go on, dear; I am listening.'

'Mary Considine, your effigy may yet be seen at Madame Tussaud's.[5] The juris-imprudent stars have announced their fell tidings that this hand is red with blood – your blood. Mary! Mary! my God!' He sprang forward, but too late to catch her as she fell fainting on the floor.

'I told you,' said Gerald. 'You don't know them as well as I do.'

After a little while Mary recovered from her swoon, but only to fall into strong hysterics, in which she laughed and wept and raved and cried, 'Keep him from me – from me, Joshua, my husband,' and many other words of entreaty and of fear.

Joshua Considine was in a state of mind bordering on agony, and when at last Mary became calm he knelt by her and kissed her feet and hands and hair and called her all the sweet names and said all the tender things his lips could frame. All that night he sat by her bedside and held her hand. Far through the night and up to the early morning she kept waking from sleep and

crying out as if in fear, till she was comforted by the consciousness that her husband was watching beside her.

Breakfast was late the next morning, but during it Joshua
received a telegram which required him to drive over to Wither-
ing, nearly twenty miles. He was loth to go; but Mary would
not hear of his remaining, and so before noon he drove off in
his dog-cart alone.

When he was gone Mary retired to her room. She did not
appear at lunch, but when afternoon tea was served on the
lawn, under the great weeping willow, she came to join her
guest. She was looking quite recovered from her illness of the
evening before. After some casual remarks, she said to Gerald:
'Of course it was very silly about last night, but I could not help
feeling frightened. Indeed I would feel so still if I let myself
think of it. But, after all, these people may only imagine things,
and I have got a test that can hardly fail to show that the
prediction is false – if indeed it be false,' she added sadly.

'What is your plan?' asked Gerald.

'I shall go myself to the gipsy camp, and have my fortune
told by the Queen.'

'Capital. May I go with you?'

'Oh, no! That would spoil it. She might know you and guess
at me, and suit her utterance accordingly. I shall go alone this
afternoon.'

When the afternoon was gone Mary Considine took her way
to the gipsy encampment. Gerald went with her as far as the
near edge of the common, and returned alone.

Half-an-hour had hardly elapsed when Mary entered the
drawing-room, where he lay on a sofa reading. She was ghastly
pale and was in a state of extreme excitement. Hardly had she
passed over the threshold when she collapsed and sank moaning
on the carpet. Gerald rushed to aid her, but by a great effort
she controlled herself and motioned him to be silent. He waited,
and his ready attention to her wish seemed to be her best help,
for, in a few minutes, she had somewhat recovered, and was
able to tell him what had passed.

'When I got to the camp,' she said, 'there did not seem to be
a soul about. I went into the centre and stood there. Suddenly

a tall woman stood beside me. "Something told me I was wanted!" she said. I held out my hand and laid a piece of silver on it. She took from her neck a small golden trinket and laid it there also; and then, seizing the two, threw them into the stream that ran by. Then she took my hand in hers and spoke: "Naught but blood in this guilty place," and turned away. I caught hold of her and asked her to tell me more. After some hesitation, she said: "Alas! alas! I see you lying at your husband's feet, and his hands are red with blood."'

Gerald did not feel at all at ease, and tried to laugh it off. 'Surely,' he said, 'this woman has a craze about murder.'

'Do not laugh,' said Mary, 'I cannot bear it,' and then, as if with a sudden impulse, she left the room.

Not long after Joshua returned, bright and cheery, and as hungry as a hunter after his long drive. His presence cheered his wife, who seemed much brighter, but she did not mention the episode of the visit to the gipsy camp, so Gerald did not mention it either. As if by tacit consent the subject was not alluded to during the evening. But there was a strange, settled look on Mary's face, which Gerald could not but observe.

In the morning Joshua came down to breakfast later than usual. Mary had been up and about the house from an early hour; but as the time drew on she seemed to get a little nervous, and now and again threw around an anxious look.

Gerald could not help noticing that none of those at breakfast could get on satisfactorily with their food. It was not altogether that the chops were tough, but that the knives were all so blunt. Being a guest, he, of course, made no sign; but presently saw Joshua draw his thumb across the edge of his knife in an unconscious sort of way. At the action Mary turned pale and almost fainted.

After breakfast they all went out on the lawn. Mary was making up a bouquet, and said to her husband, 'Get me a few of the tea-roses, dear.'

Joshua pulled down a cluster from the front of the house. The stem bent, but was too tough to break. He put his hand in his pocket to get his knife; but in vain. 'Lend me your knife, Gerald,' he said. But Gerald had not got one, so he went into the breakfast-room and took one from the table. He came out feeling its edge and grumbling. 'What on earth has happened to all the knives – the edges seem all ground off?' Mary turned away hurriedly and entered the house.

Joshua tried to sever the stalk with the blunt knife as country cooks sever the necks of fowl – as schoolboys cut twine. With a little effort he finished the task. The cluster of roses grew thick, so he determined to gather a great bunch.

He could not find a single sharp knife in the sideboard where the cutlery was kept, so he called Mary, and when she came, told her the state of things. She looked so agitated and so miserable that he could not help knowing the truth, and, as if astounded and hurt, asked her:

'Do you mean to say that *you* have done it?'

She broke in, 'Oh, Joshua, I was so afraid.'

He paused, and a set, white look came over his face. 'Mary!' said he, 'is this all the trust you have in me? I would not have believed it.'

'Oh, Joshua! Joshua!' she cried entreatingly, 'forgive me,' and wept bitterly.

Joshua thought a moment and then said: 'I see how it is. We shall better end this or we shall all go mad.'

He ran into the drawing-room.

'Where are you going?' almost screamed Mary.

Gerald saw what he meant – that he would not be tied to blunt instruments by the force of a superstition, and was not surprised when he saw him come out through the French window, bearing in his hand a large Ghourka knife, which usually lay on the centre table, and which his brother had sent him from Northern India. It was one of those great hunting-knives which worked such havoc, at close quarters, with the enemies of the loyal Ghourkas during the mutiny,[6] of great weight but so evenly balanced in the hand as to seem light, and with an edge like a razor. With one of these knives a Ghourka can cut a sheep in two.

When Mary saw him come out of the room with the weapon in his hand she screamed in an agony of fright, and the hysterics of last night were promptly renewed.

Joshua ran toward her, and, seeing her falling, threw down the knife and tried to catch her.

However, he was just a second too late, and the two men cried out in horror simultaneously as they saw her fall upon the naked blade.

When Gerald rushed over he found that in falling her left hand had struck the blade, which lay partly upwards on the grass. Some of the small veins were cut through, and the blood gushed freely from the wound. As he was tying it up he pointed out to Joshua that the wedding ring was severed by the steel.

They carried her fainting to the house. When, after a while, she came out, with her arm in a sling, she was peaceful in her mind and happy. She said to her husband:

'The gipsy was wonderfully near the truth; too near for the real thing ever to occur now, dear.'

Joshua bent over and kissed the wounded hand.

THE COMING OF
ABEL BEHENNA

The little Cornish port of Pencastle was bright in the early April, when the sun had seemingly come to stay after a long and bitter winter. Boldly and blackly the rock stood out against a background of shaded blue, where the sky fading into mist met the far horizon. The sea was of true Cornish hue – sapphire, save where it became deep emerald green in the fathomless depths under the cliffs, where the seal caves opened their grim jaws. On the slopes the grass was parched and brown. The spikes of furze bushes were ashy grey, but the golden yellow of their flowers streamed along the hillside, dipping out in lines as the rock cropped up, and lessening into patches and dots till finally it died away all together where the sea winds swept round the jutting cliffs and cut short the vegetation as though with an ever-working aerial shears. The whole hillside, with its body of brown and flashes of yellow, was just like a colossal yellow-hammer.[1]

The little harbour opened from the sea between towering cliffs, and behind a lonely rock, pierced with many caves and blow-holes through which the sea in storm time sent its thunderous voice, together with a fountain of drifting spume. Hence, it wound westwards in a serpentine course, guarded at its entrance by two little curving piers to left and right. These were roughly built of dark slates placed endways and held together with great beams bound with iron bands. Thence, it flowed up the rocky bed of the stream whose winter torrents had of old cut out its way amongst the hills. This stream was deep at first, with here and there, where it widened, patches of broken rock exposed at low water, full of holes where crabs and lobsters were to be found at the ebb of the tide. From amongst the rocks rose sturdy posts, used for warping in the little coasting vessels which frequented the port. Higher up, the stream still flowed deeply, for the tide ran far inland, but always calmly, for all the force of the wildest storm was broken below. Some quarter mile inland the stream was deep at high water, but at low tide there were at each side patches of the same broken rock as lower down, through the chinks of which the sweet water of the natural stream trickled and murmured after the tide had ebbed away. Here, too, rose mooring posts for the fishermen's boats. At either side of the river was a row of cottages down almost on the level of high tide. They were pretty cottages, strongly and snugly built, with trim narrow gardens in front, full of old-fashioned plants, flowering currants, coloured primroses, wallflower, and stonecrop.[2] Over the fronts of many of them climbed clematis and wisteria. The window sides and door posts of all were as white as snow, and the little pathway to each was paved with light coloured stones. At some of the doors were tiny porches, whilst at others were rustic seats cut from tree trunks or from old barrels; in nearly every case the window ledges were filled with boxes or pots of flowers or foliage plants.

Two men lived in cottages exactly opposite each other across the stream. Two men, both young, both good-looking, both prosperous, and who had been companions and rivals from their boyhood. Abel Behenna was dark with the gypsy darkness which the Phœnician mining wanderers left in their track; Eric Sanson – which the local antiquarian said was a corruption of Sagamanson – was fair, with the ruddy hue which marked the path of the wild Norseman.[3] These two seemed to have singled out each other from the very beginning to work and strive together, to fight for each other and to stand back to back in all endeavours. They had now put the coping-stone on their Temple of Unity by falling in love with the same girl. Sarah Trefusis was certainly the prettiest girl in Pencastle, and there was many a young man who would gladly have tried his fortune with her, but that there were two to contend against, and each of these the strongest and most resolute man in the port –

except the other. The average young man thought that this was very hard, and on account of it bore no good will to either of the three principals: whilst the average young woman who had, lest worse should befall, to put up with the grumbling of her sweetheart, and the sense of being only second best which it implied, did not either, be sure, regard Sarah with friendly eye. Thus it came, in the course of a year or so, for rustic courtship is a slow process, that the two men and the woman found themselves thrown much together. They were all satisfied, so it did not matter, and Sarah, who was vain and something frivolous, took care to have her revenge on both men and women in a quiet way. When a young woman in her 'walking out' can only boast one not-quite-satisfied young man, it is no particular pleasure to her to see her escort cast sheep's eyes[4] at a better-looking girl supported by two devoted swains.

At length there came a time which Sarah dreaded, and which she had tried to keep distant – the time when she had to make her choice between the two men. She liked them both, and, indeed, either of them might have satisfied the ideas of even a more exacting girl. But her mind was so constituted that she thought more of what she might lose, than of what she might gain; and whenever she thought she had made up her mind she became instantly assailed with doubts as to the wisdom of her choice. Always the man whom she had presumably lost became endowed afresh with a newer and more bountiful crop of advantages than had ever arisen from the possibility of his acceptance. She promised each man that on her birthday she would give him his answer, and that day, the 11th of April, had now arrived. The promises had been given singly and confidentially, but each was given to a man who was not likely to forget. Early in the morning she found both men hovering round her door. Neither had taken the other into his confidence, and each was simply seeking an early opportunity of getting his answer, and advancing his suit if necessary. Damon, as a rule, does not take Pythias[5] with him when making a proposal; and in the heart of each man his own affairs had a claim far above any requirements of friendship. So, throughout the day, they kept seeing each other out. The position was doubtless somewhat embarrassing to Sarah, and though the satisfaction of her vanity that she should be thus adored was very pleasing, yet there were moments when she was annoyed with both men for being so persistent. Her only consolation at such moments was that she saw, through the elaborate smiles of the other girls when in passing they noticed her door thus doubly guarded, the jealousy which filled their hearts. Sarah's mother was a person of commonplace and sordid ideas, and, seeing all along the state of affairs, her one intention, persistently expressed to her daughter in the plainest of words, was to so arrange matters that Sarah should get all that was possible out of both men. With this purpose she had cunningly kept herself as far as possible in the background in the matter of her daughter's wooings, and watched in silence. At first Sarah had been indignant with her for her sordid views; but, as usual, her weak nature gave way before persistence, and she had now got to the stage of passive acceptance. She was not surprised when her mother whispered to her in the little yard behind the house:—

'Go up the hill-side for a while; I want to talk to these two. They're both red-hot for ye, and now's the time to get things fixed!' Sarah began a feeble remonstrance, but her mother cut her short.

'I tell ye, girl, that my mind is made up! Both these men want ye, and only one can have ye, but before ye choose it'll be so arranged that ye'll have all that both have got! Don't argy, child! Go up the hill-side, and when ye come back I'll have it fixed – I see a way quite easy!' So Sarah went up the hill-side through the narrow paths between the golden furze, and Mrs Trefusis joined the two men in the living-room of the little house.

She opened the attack with the desperate courage which is in all mothers when they think for their children, howsoever mean the thoughts may be.

'Ye two men, ye're both in love with my Sarah!'

Their bashful silence gave consent to the barefaced proposition. She went on:

'Neither of ye has much!' Again they tacitly acquiesced in the soft impeachment.

'I don't know that either of ye could keep a wife!' Though neither said a word their looks and bearing expressed distinct dissent. Mrs Trefusis went on:

'But if ye'd put what ye both have together ye'd make a comfortable home for one of ye – and Sarah!' She eyed the men keenly, with her cunning eyes half shut, as she spoke; then satisfied from her scrutiny that the idea was accepted she went on quickly, as if to prevent argument:

'The girl likes ye both, and mayhap it's hard for her to choose. Why don't ye toss up for her? First put your money together – ye've each got a bit put by, I know. Let the lucky man take the lot and trade with it a bit, and then come home and marry her. Neither of ye's afraid, I suppose! And neither of ye'll say that he won't do that much for the girl that ye both say ye love!'

Abel broke the silence:

'It don't seem the square thing to toss for the girl! She wouldn't like it herself, and it doesn't seem – seem respectful like to her –' Eric interrupted. He was conscious that his chance was not so good as Abel's, in case Sarah should wish to choose between them:

'Are ye afraid of the hazard?'

'Not me!' said Abel, boldly. Mrs Trefusis, seeing that her idea was beginning to work, followed up the advantage.

'It is settled that ye put yer money together to make a home for her, whether ye toss for her or leave it for her to choose?'

'Yes,' said Eric quickly, and Abel agreed with equal sturdiness. Mrs Trefusis' little cunning eyes twinkled. She heard Sarah's step in the yard, and said:

'Well! here she comes, and I leave it to her.' And she went out.

During her brief walk on the hillside Sarah had been trying to make up her mind. She was feeling almost angry with both men for being the cause of her difficulty, and as she came into the room said shortly:

'I want to have a word with you both – come to the Flagstaff Rock, where we can be alone.' She took her hat and went out of the house up the winding path to the steep rock crowned with a high flagstaff, where once the wreckers' fire basket[6] used to burn. This was the rock which formed the northern jaw of the little harbour. There was only room on the path for two abreast, and it marked the state of things pretty well when, by a sort of implied arrangement, Sarah went first, and the two men followed, walking abreast and keeping step. By this time, each man's heart was boiling with jealousy. When they came to the top of of the rock, Sarah stood against the flagstaff, and the two young men stood opposite her. She had chosen her position with knowledge and intention, for there was no room for anyone to stand beside her. They were all silent for a while; then Sarah began to laugh and said:–

'I promised the both of you to give you an answer to-day. I've been thinking and thinking and thinking, till I began to get angry with you both for plaguing me so; and even now I don't seem any nearer than ever I was to making up my mind.' Eric said suddenly:

'Let us toss for it, lass!' Sarah showed no indignation whatever at the proposition; her mother's eternal suggestion had schooled her to the acceptance of something of the kind, and her weak nature made it easy to her to grasp at any way out of the difficulty. She stood with downcast eyes idly picking at the sleeve of her dress, seeming to have tacitly acquiesced in the proposal. Both men, instinctively realising this, pulled each a coin from his pocket, spun it in the air, and dropped his other hand over the palm on which it lay. For a few seconds they remained thus, all silent; then Abel, who was the more thoughtful of the men, spoke:

'Sarah! is this good?' As he spoke he removed the upper hand from the coin and placed the latter back in his pocket. Sarah was nettled.

'Good or bad, it's good enough for me! Take it or leave it as you like,' she said, to which he replied quickly:

'Nay lass! Aught that concerns you is good enow for me. I did but think of you lest you might have pain or disappointment hereafter. If you love Eric better nor me, in God's name say so, and I think I'm man enow to stand aside. Likewise, if I'm the one, don't make us both miserable for life!' Face to face with a difficulty, Sarah's weak nature proclaimed itself; she put her hands before her face and began to cry, saying –

'It was my mother. She keeps telling me!' The silence which followed was broken by Eric, who said hotly to Abel:

'Let the lass alone, can't you? If she wants to choose this way, let her. It's good enough for me – and for you, too! She's said it now, and must abide by it!' Hereupon Sarah turned upon him in sudden fury, and cried:

'Hold your tongue! What is it to you, at any-rate?' and she resumed her crying. Eric was so flabbergasted that he had not a word to say, but stood looking particularly foolish, with his mouth open and his hands held out with the coin still between them. All were silent till Sarah, taking her hands from her face, laughed hysterically and said:

'As you two can't make up your minds, I'm going home!' and she turned to go.

'Stop,' said Abel, in an authoritative voice. 'Eric, you hold the coin, and I'll cry. Now, before we settle it, let us clearly understand: the man who wins takes all the money that we both have got, brings it to Bristol and ships on a voyage and trades with it. Then he comes back and marries Sarah, and they two keep all, whatever there may be, as the result of the trading. Is this what we understand?'

'Yes,' said Eric.

'I'll marry him on my next birthday,' said Sarah. Having said it the intolerably mercenary spirit of her action seemed to strike her, and impulsively she turned away with a bright blush. Fire seemed to sparkle in the eyes of both the men. Said Eric: 'A year so be! The man that wins is to have one year.'

'Toss!' cried Abel, and the coin spun in the air. Eric caught it, and again held it between his outstretched hands.

'Heads!' cried Abel, a pallor sweeping over his face as he spoke. As he leaned forward to look Sarah leaned forward too, and their heads almost touched. He could feel her hair blowing on his cheek, and it thrilled through him like fire. Eric lifted his upper hand; the coin lay with its head up. Abel stepped forward and took Sarah in his arms. With a curse Eric hurled the coin far into the sea. Then he leaned against the flagstaff and scowled at the others with his hands thrust deep in his pockets. Abel whispered wild words of passion and delight into Sarah's ears, and as she listened she began to believe that fortune had rightly interpreted the wishes of her secret heart, and that she loved Abel best.

Presently Abel looked up and caught sight of Eric's face as the last ray of sunset struck it. The red light intensified the natural ruddiness of his complexion, and he looked as though he were steeped in blood. Abel did not mind his scowl, for now that his own heart was at rest he could feel unalloyed pity for his friend. He stepped over, meaning to comfort him, and held out his hand, saying:

'It was my chance, old lad. Don't grudge it me. I'll try to make Sarah a happy woman, and you shall be a brother to us both!'

'Brother be damned!' was all the answer Eric made, as he turned away. When he had gone a few steps down the rocky path he turned and came back. Standing before Abel and Sarah, who had their arms round each other, he said:

'You have a year. Make the most of it! And be sure you're in time to claim your wife! Be back to have your banns up in time to be married on the 11th April. If you're not, I tell you I shall have my banns up, and you may get back too late.'

'What do you mean, Eric? You are mad!'

'No more mad than you are, Abel Behenna. You go, that's your chance! I stay, that's mine! I don't mean to let the grass grow under my feet. Sarah cared no more for you than for me five minutes ago, and she may come back to that five minutes after you're gone! You won by a point only – the game may change.'

'The game won't change!' said Abel shortly. 'Sarah, you'll be true to me? You won't marry till I return?'

'For a year!' added Eric, quickly, 'that's the bargain.'

'I promise for the year,' said Sarah. A dark look came over Abel's face, and he was about to speak, but he mastered himself and smiled.

'I mustn't be too hard or get angry to-night! Come, Eric! we played and fought together. I won fairly. I played fairly all the game of our wooing! You know that as well as I do; and now when I am going away, I shall look to my old and true comrade to help me when I am gone!'

'I'll help you none,' said Eric, 'so help me God!'

'It was God helped me,' said Abel, simply.

'Then let Him go on helping you,' said Eric angrily. 'The Devil is good enough for me!' and without another word he rushed down the steep path and disappeared behind the rocks.

When he had gone Abel hoped for some tender passage with Sarah, but the first remark she made chilled him.

'How lonely it all seems without Eric!' and this note sounded till he had left her at home – and after.

Early on the next morning Abel heard a noise at his door, and on going out saw Eric walking rapidly away: a small canvas bag full of gold and silver lay on the threshold; on a small slip of paper pinned to it was written:

'Take the money and go. I stay. God for you! The Devil for me! Remember the 11th of April. – ERIC SANSON.' That afternoon Abel went off to Bristol, and a week later sailed on the *Star of the Sea* bound for Pahang. His money – including that which had been Eric's – was on board in the shape of a venture of cheap toys. He had been advised by a shrewd old mariner of Bristol whom he knew, and who knew the ways of the Chersonese,[7] who predicted that every penny invested would be returned with a shilling to boot.

As the year wore on Sarah became more and more disturbed in her mind. Eric was always at hand to make love to her in his own persistent, masterful manner, and to this she did not object. Only one letter came from Abel, to say that his venture had proved successful, and that he had sent some two hundred pounds to the bank at Bristol, and was trading with fifty pounds still remaining in goods for China, whither the *Star of the Sea* was bound and whence she would return to Bristol. He suggested that Eric's share of the venture should be returned to him with his share of the profits. This proposition was treated with anger by Eric, and as simply childish by Sarah's mother.

More than six months had since then elapsed, but no other letter had come, and Eric's hopes, which had been dashed down by the letter from Pahang, began to rise again. He perpetually assailed Sarah with an 'if!' If Abel did not return, would she then marry him? If the 11th April went by without Abel being in the port, would she give him over? If Abel had taken his fortune, and married another girl on the head of it, would she marry him, Eric, as soon as the truth were known? And so on in an endless variety of possibilities. The power of the strong will and the determined purpose over the woman's weaker nature became in time manifest. Sarah began to lose her faith in Abel and to regard Eric as a possible husband; and a possible husband is in a woman's eye different to all other men. A new affection for him began to arise in her breast, and the daily familiarities of permitted courtship furthered the growing affection. Sarah began to regard Abel as rather a rock in the road of her life, and had it not been for her mother's constantly reminding her of the good fortune already laid by in the Bristol Bank she would have tried to have shut her eyes altogether to the fact of Abel's existence.

The 11th April was Saturday, so that in order to have the marriage on that day it would be necessary that the banns should be called on Sunday, 22nd March. From the beginning of that month Eric kept perpetually on the subject of Abel's absence, and his outspoken opinion that the latter was either dead or married began to become a reality to the woman's mind. As the first half of the month wore on Eric became more jubilant, and after church on the 15th he took Sarah for a walk to the Flagstaff Rock. There he asserted himself strongly:

'I told Abel, and you too, that if he was not here to put up his banns in time for the eleventh, I would put up mine for the twelfth. Now the time has come when I mean to do it. He hasn't kept his word' – here Sarah struck in out of her weakness and indecision:

'He hasn't broken it yet!' Eric ground his teeth with anger.

'If you mean to stick up for him,' he said, as he smote his hands savagely on the flagstaff, which sent forth a shivering murmur, 'well and good. I'll keep my part of the bargain. On Sunday I shall give notice of the banns, and you can deny them in the church if you will. If Abel is in Pencastle on the eleventh, he can have them cancelled, and his own put up; but till then, I take my course, and woe to anyone who stands in my way!' With that he flung himself down the rocky pathway, and Sarah could not but admire his Viking strength and spirit, as, crossing the hill, he strode away along the cliffs towards Bude.

During the week no news was heard of Abel, and on Saturday Eric gave notice of the banns of marriage between himself and Sarah Trefusis. The clergyman would have remonstrated with him, for although nothing formal had been told to the neighbours, it had been understood since Abel's departure that on his return he was to marry Sarah; but Eric would not discuss the question.

'It is a painful subject, sir,' he said with a firmness which the parson, who was a very young man, could not but be swayed by. 'Surely there is nothing against Sarah or me. Why should there be any bones made about the matter?' The parson said no more, and on the next day he read out the banns for the first time amidst an audible buzz from the congregation. Sarah was present, contrary to custom, and though she blushed furiously enjoyed her triumph over the other girls whose banns had not yet come. Before the week was over she began to make her wedding dress. Eric used to come and look at her at work and the sight thrilled through him. He used to say all sorts of pretty things to her at such times, and there were to both delicious moments of love-making.

The banns were read a second time on the 29th, and Eric's hope grew more and more fixed, though there were to him moments of acute despair when he realised that the cup of happiness might be dashed from his lips at any moment, right up to the last. At such times he was full of passion – desperate and remorseless – and he ground his teeth and clenched his hands in a wild way as though some taint of the old Berserker fury[8] of his ancestors still lingered in his blood. On the Thursday of that week he looked in on Sarah and found her, amid a flood of sunshine, putting finishing touches to her white wedding gown. His own heart was full of gaiety, and the sight of the woman who was so soon to be his own so occupied, filled him with a joy unspeakable, and he felt faint with a languorous ecstasy. Bending over he kissed Sarah on the mouth, and then whispered in her rosy ear –

'Your wedding dress, Sarah! And for me!' As he drew back to admire her she looked up saucily, and said to him –

'Perhaps not for you. There is more than a week yet for Abel!' and then cried out in dismay, for with a wild gesture and a fierce oath Eric dashed out of the house, banging the door behind him. The incident disturbed Sarah more than she could have thought possible, for it awoke all her fears and doubts and indecision afresh. She cried a little, and put by her dress, and to soothe herself went out to sit for a while on the summit of the Flagstaff Rock. When she arrived she found there a little group anxiously discussing the weather. The sea was calm and the sun bright, but across the sea were strange lines of darkness and light, and close in to shore the rocks were fringed with foam, which spread out in great white curves and circles as the currents drifted. The wind had backed, and came in sharp, cold puffs. The blowhole, which ran under the Flagstaff Rock, from the rocky bay without to the harbour within, was booming at intervals, and the seagulls were screaming ceaselessly as they wheeled about the entrance of the port.

'It looks bad,' she heard an old fisherman say to the coast-guard. 'I seen it just like this once before, when the East Indiaman *Coromandel* went to pieces in Dizzard Bay!' Sarah did not wait to hear more. She was of a timid nature where danger was concerned, and could not bear to hear of wrecks and disasters. She went home and resumed the completion of her dress, secretly determined to appease Eric when she should meet him with a sweet apology – and to take the earliest opportunity of being even with him after her marriage.

The old fisherman's weather prophecy was justified. That night at dusk a wild storm came on. The sea rose and lashed the western coasts from Skye to Scilly and left a tale of disaster everywhere. The sailors and fishermen of Pencastle all turned out on the rocks and cliffs and watched eagerly. Presently, by a flash of lightning, a 'ketch' was seen drifting under only a jib[9] about half-a-mile outside the port. All eyes and all glasses were concentrated on her, waiting for the next flash, and when it came a chorus went up that it was the *Lovely Alice*, trading between Bristol and Penzance, and touching at all the little ports between. 'God help them!' said the harbour-master, 'for nothing in this world can save them when they are between

Bude and Tintagel and the wind on shore!' The coastguards exerted themselves, and, aided by brave hearts and willing hands, they brought the rocket apparatus up on the summit of the Flagstaff Rock. Then they burned blue lights so that those on board might see the harbour opening in case they could make any effort to reach it. They worked gallantly enough on board; but no skill or strength of man could avail. Before many minutes were over the *Lovely Alice* rushed to her doom on the great island rock that guarded the mouth of the port. The screams of those on board were fairly borne on the tempest as they flung themselves into the sea in a last chance for life. The blue lights were kept burning, and eager eyes peered into the depths of the waters in case any face could be seen; and ropes were held ready to fling out in aid. But never a face was seen, and the willing arms rested idle. Eric was there amongst his fellows. His old Icelandic origin was never more apparent than in that wild hour. He took a rope, and shouted in the ear of the harbour-master:

'I shall go down on the rock over the seal cave. The tide is running up, and someone may drift in there!'

'Keep back, man!' came the answer. 'Are you mad? One slip on that rock and you are lost: and no man could keep his feet in the dark on such a place in such a tempest!'

'Not a bit,' came the reply. 'You remember how Abel Behenna saved me there on a night like this when my boat went on the Gull Rock. He dragged me up from the deep water in the seal cave, and now someone may drift in there again as I did,' and he was gone into the darkness. The projecting rock hid the light on the Flagstaff Rock, but he knew his way too well to miss it. His boldness and sureness of foot standing to him, he shortly stood on the great round-topped rock cut away beneath by the action of the waves over the entrance of the seal cave, where the water was fathomless. There he stood in comparative safety, for the concave shape of the rock beat back the waves with their own force, and though the water below him seemed to boil like a seething cauldron, just beyond the spot there was a space of almost calm. The rock, too, seemed here to shut off the sound of the gale, and he listened as well as watched. As he stood there ready, with his coil of rope poised to throw, he thought he heard below him, just beyond the whirl of the water, a faint, despairing cry. He echoed it with a shout that rang out into the night. Then he waited for the flash of lightning, and as it passed flung his rope out into the darkness where he had seen a face rising through the swirl of the foam. The rope was caught, for he felt a pull on it, and he shouted again in his mighty voice:

'Tie it round your waist, and I shall pull you up.' Then when he felt that it was fast he moved along the rock to the far side of the sea cave, where the deep water was something stiller, and where he could get foothold secure enough to drag the rescued man on the overhanging rock. He began to pull, and shortly he knew from the rope taken in that the man he was now rescuing must soon be close to the top of the rock. He steadied himself for a moment, and drew a long breath, that he might at the next effort complete the rescue. He had just bent his back to the work when a flash of lightning revealed to each other the two men – the rescuer and the rescued.

Eric Sanson and Abel Behenna were face to face – and none knew of the meeting save themselves; and God.

On the instant a wave of passion swept through Eric's heart. All his hopes were shattered, and with the hatred of Cain[10] his eyes looked out. He saw in the instant of recognition the joy in Abel's face that his was the hand to succour him, and this intensified his hate. Whilst the passion was on him he started back, and the rope ran out between his hands. His moment of hate was followed by an impulse of his better manhood, but it was too late.

Before he could recover himself, Abel, encumbered with the rope that should have aided him, was plunged with a despairing cry back into the darkness of the devouring sea.

Then, feeling all the madness and the doom of Cain upon him, Eric rushed back over the rocks, heedless of the danger and eager only for one thing – to be amongst other people whose living noises would shut out that last cry which seemed to ring still in his ears. When he regained the Flagstaff Rock the men surrounded him, and through the fury of the storm he heard the harbour-master say: –

'We feared you were lost when we heard a cry! How white you are! Where is your rope? Was there anyone drifted in?'

'No one,' he shouted in answer, for he felt that he could never explain that he had let his old comrade slip back into the sea, and at the very place and under the very circumstances in which that comrade had saved his own life. He hoped by one bold lie to set the matter at rest for ever. There was no one to bear witness – and if he should have to carry that still white face in his eyes and that despairing cry in his ears for evermore – at least none should know of it. 'No one,' he cried, more loudly still. 'I slipped on the rock, and the rope fell into the sea!' So saying he left them, and, rushing down the steep path, gained his own cottage and locked himself within.

The remainder of that night he passed lying on his bed – dressed and motionless – staring upwards, and seeming to see through the darkness a pale face gleaming wet in the lightning, with its glad recognition turning to ghastly despair, and to hear a cry which never ceased to echo in his soul.

In the morning the storm was over and all was smiling again, except that the sea was still boisterous with its unspent fury. Great pieces of wreck drifted into the port, and the sea around the island rock was strewn with others. Two bodies also drifted into the harbour – one the master of the wrecked ketch, the other a strange seaman whom no one knew.

Sarah saw nothing of Eric till the evening, and then he only looked in for a minute. He did not come into the house, but simply put his head in through the open window.

'Well, Sarah,' he called out in a loud voice, though to her it did not ring truly, 'is the wedding dress done? Sunday week, mind! Sunday week!'

Sarah was glad to have the reconciliation so easy; but, womanlike, when she saw the storm was over and her own fears groundless, she at once repeated the cause of offence.

'Sunday so be it,' she said, without looking up, 'if Abel isn't there on Saturday!' Then she looked up saucily, though her heart was full of fear of another outburst on the part of her impetuous lover. But the window was empty; Eric had taken himself off, and with a pout she resumed her work. She saw

Eric no more till Sunday afternoon, after the banns had been
called the third time, when he came up to her before all the
people with an air of proprietorship which half-pleased and
half-annoyed her.

'Not yet, mister!' she said, pushing him away, as the other
girls giggled. 'Wait till Sunday next, if you please – the day after
Saturday!' she added, looking at him saucily. The girls giggled
again, and the young men guffawed. They thought it was the
snub that touched him so that he became as white as a sheet as
he turned away. But Sarah, who knew more than they did,
laughed, for she saw triumph through the spasm of pain that
overspread his face.

The week passed uneventfully; however, as Saturday drew
nigh Sarah had occasional moments of anxiety, and as to Eric
he went about at night-time like a man possessed. He restrained
himself when others were by, but now and again he went down
amongst the rocks and caves and shouted aloud. This seemed
to relieve him somewhat, and he was better able to restrain
himself for some time after. All Saturday he stayed in his own
house and never left it. As he was to be married on the morrow,
the neighbours thought it was shyness on his part, and did not
trouble or notice him. Only once was he disturbed, and that
was when the chief boatman came to him and sat down, and
after a pause said:

'Eric, I was over in Bristol yesterday. I was in the ropemaker's
getting a coil to replace the one you lost the night of the storm,
and there I saw Michael Heavens of this place, who is salesman
there. He told me that Abel Behenna had come home the week
ere last on the *Star of the Sea* from Canton,[11] and that he had
lodged a sight of money in the Bristol Bank in the name of
Sarah Behenna. He told Michael so himself – and that he had
taken a passage on the *Lovely Alice* to Pencastle. Bear up, man,'
for Eric had with a groan dropped his head on his knees, with
his face between his hands. 'He was your old comrade, I know,
but you couldn't help him. He must have gone down with the
rest that awful night. I thought I'd better tell you, lest it might
come some other way, and you might keep Sarah Trefusis from
being frightened. They were good friends once, and women

take these things to heart. It would not do to let her be pained with such a thing on her wedding-day!' Then he rose and went away, leaving Eric still sitting disconsolately with his head on his knees.

'Poor fellow!' murmured the chief boatman to himself; 'he takes it to heart. Well, well! right enough! They were true comrades once, and Abel saved him!'

The afternoon of that day, when the children had left school, they strayed as usual on half-holidays along the quay and the paths by the cliffs. Presently some of them came running in a state of great excitement to the harbour, where a few men were unloading a coal ketch, and a great many were superintending the operation. One of the children called out:

'There is a porpoise in the harbour mouth! We saw it come through the blow hole! It had a long tail, and was deep under the water!'

'It was no porpoise,' said another; 'it was a seal; but it had a long tail! It came out of the seal cave!' The other children bore various testimony, but on two points they were unanimous – it, whatever 'it' was, had come through the blow-hole deep under the water, and had a long, thin tail – a tail so long that they could not see the end of it. There was much unmerciful chaffing of the children by the men on this point, but as it was evident that they had seen something, quite a number of persons, young and old, male and female, went along the high paths on either side of the harbour-mouth to catch a glimpse of this new addition to the fauna of the sea, a long-tailed porpoise or seal. The tide was now coming in. There was a slight breeze, and the surface of the water was rippled so that it was only at moments that anyone could see clearly into the deep water. After a spell of watching a woman called out that she saw something moving up the channel, just below where she was standing. There was a stampede to the spot, but by the time the crowd had gathered the breeze had freshened, and it was impossible to see with any distinctness below the surface of the water. On being questioned the woman described what she had seen, but in such an incoherent way that the whole thing was put down as an effect of imagination; had it not been for the children's report she would not have been credited at all. Her semi-hysterical statement that what she saw was 'like a pig with the entrails out' was only thought anything of by an old coastguard, who shook his head but did not make any remark. For the remainder of the daylight this man was seen always on the bank, looking into the water, but always with disappointment manifest on his face.

Eric arose early on the next morning – he had not slept all night, and it was a relief to him to move about in the light. He shaved himself with a hand that did not tremble, and dressed himself in his wedding clothes. There was a haggard look on his face, and he seemed as though he had grown years older in the last few days. Still there was a wild, uneasy light of triumph in his eyes, and he kept murmuring to himself over and over again:

'This is my wedding-day! Abel cannot claim her now – living or dead! – living or dead! Living or dead!' He sat in his arm-chair, waiting with an uncanny quietness for the church hour to arrive. When the bell began to ring he arose and passed out of his house, closing the door behind him. He looked at the river and saw that the tide had just turned. In the church he sat with Sarah and her mother, holding Sarah's hand tightly in his all the time, as though he feared to lose her. When the service was over they stood up together, and were married in the presence of the entire congregation; for no one left the church. Both made the responses clearly – Eric's being even on the defiant side. When the wedding was over Sarah took her husband's arm, and they walked away together, the boys and younger girls being cuffed by their elders into a decorous behaviour, for they would fain have followed close behind their heels.

The way from the church led down to the back of Eric's cottage, a narrow passage being between it and that of his next neighbour. When the bridal couple had passed through this the remainder of the congregation, who had followed them at a little distance, were startled by a long, shrill scream from the bride. They rushed through the passage and found her on the bank with wild eyes, pointing to the river bed opposite Eric Sanson's door.

The falling tide had deposited there the body of Abel Behenna stark upon the broken rocks. The rope trailing from its waist had been twisted by the current round the mooring post, and had held it back whilst the tide had ebbed away from it. The right elbow had fallen in a chink in the rock, leaving the hand outstretched toward Sarah, with the open palm upward as though it were extended to receive hers, the pale drooping fingers open to the clasp.

All that happened afterwards was never quite known to Sarah Sanson. Whenever she would try to recollect there would come a buzzing in her ears and a dimness in her eyes, and all would pass away. The only thing that she could remember of it at all – and this she never forgot – was Eric's breathing heavily, with his face whiter than that of the dead man, as he muttered under his breath:

'Devil's help! Devil's faith! Devil's price!'

THE BURIAL OF THE RATS

Leaving Paris by the Orleans road, cross the Enceinte,[1] and, turning to the right, you find yourself in a somewhat wild and not at all savoury district. Right and left, before and behind, on every side rise great heaps of dust and waste accumulated by the process of time.

Paris has its night as well as its day life, and the sojourner who enters his hotel in the Rue de Rivoli or the Rue St Honoré late at night or leaves it early in the morning, can guess, in coming near Montrouge – if he has not done so already – the purpose of those great waggons that look like boilers on wheels which he finds halting everywhere as he passes.

Every city has its peculiar institutions created out of its own needs; and one of the most notable institutions of Paris is its rag-picking population. In the early morning – and Parisian life commences at an early hour – may be seen in most streets standing on the pathway opposite every court and alley and between every few houses, as still in some American cities, even in parts of New York, large wooden boxes into which the domestics or tenement-holders empty the accumulated dust of the past day. Round these boxes gather and pass on, when the work is done, to fresh fields of labour and pastures new, squalid, hungry-looking men and women, the implements of whose craft consist of a coarse bag or basket slung over the shoulder and a little rake with which they turn over and probe and examine in the minutest manner the dustbins. They pick up and deposit in their baskets, by aid of their rakes, whatever they may find, with the same facility as a Chinaman uses his chopsticks.

Paris is a city of centralisation – and centralisation and

classification are closely allied. In the early times, when centralisation is becoming a fact, its forerunner is classification. All things which are similar or analogous become grouped together, and from the grouping of groups rises one whole or central point. We see radiating many long arms with innumerable tentaculæ, and in the centre rises a gigantic head with a comprehensive brain and keen eyes to look on every side and ears sensitive to hear – and a voracious mouth to swallow.

Other cities resemble all the birds and beasts and fishes whose appetites and digestions are normal. Paris alone is the analogical apotheosis of the octopus. Product of centralisation carried to an *ad absurdum*, it fairly represents the devil fish;[2] and in no respects is the resemblance more curious than in the similarity of the digestive apparatus.

Those intelligent tourists who, having surrendered their individuality into the hands of Messrs Cook or Gaze,[3] 'do' Paris in three days, are often puzzled to know how it is that the dinner which in London would cost about six shillings, can be had for three francs in a café in the Palais Royal. They need have no more wonder if they will but consider the classification which is a theoretic speciality of Parisian life, and adopt all round the fact from which the chiffonier[4] has his genesis.

The Paris of 1850 was not like the Paris of to-day, and those who see the Paris of Napoleon and Baron Hausseman[5] can hardly realise the existence of the state of things forty-five years ago.

Amongst other things, however, which have not changed are those districts where the waste is gathered. Dust is dust all the world over, in every age, and the family likeness of dust-heaps is perfect. The traveller, therefore, who visits the environs of Montrouge can go back in fancy without difficulty to the year 1850.

In this year I was making a prolonged stay in Paris. I was very much in love with a young lady who, though she returned my passion, so far yielded to the wishes of her parents that she had promised not to see me or to correspond with me for a year. I, too, had been compelled to accede to these conditions under a vague hope of parental approval. During the term of probation I had promised to remain out of the country and not to write to my dear one until the expiration of the year.

Naturally the time went heavily with me. There was no one of my own family or circle who could tell me of Alice, and none of her own folk had, I am sorry to say, sufficient generosity to send me even an occasional word of comfort regarding her health and well-being. I spent six months wandering about Europe, but as I could find no satisfactory distraction in travel, I determined to come to Paris, where, at least, I would be within easy hail of London in case any good fortune should call me thither before the appointed time. That 'hope deferred maketh the heart sick'[6] was never better exemplified than in my case, for in addition to the perpetual longing to see the face I loved there was always with me a harrowing anxiety lest some accident should prevent me showing Alice in due time that I had, throughout the long period of probation, been faithful to her trust and my own love. Thus, every adventure which I undertook had a fierce pleasure of its own, for it was fraught with possible consequences greater than it would have ordinarily borne.

Like all travellers I exhausted the places of most interest in the first month of my stay, and was driven in the second month to look for amusement whithersoever I might. Having made sundry journeys to the better-known suburbs, I began to see that there was a *terra incognita*, in so far as the guide book was concerned, in the social wilderness lying between these attractive points. Accordingly I began to systematise my researches, and each day took up the thread of my exploration at the place where I had on the previous day dropped it.

In process of time my wanderings led me near Montrouge, and I saw that hereabouts lay the Ultima Thule[7] of social exploration – a country as little known as that round the source of the White Nile. And so I determined to investigate philosophically the chiffonier – his habitat, his life, and his means of life.

The job was an unsavoury one, difficult of accomplishment, and with little hope of adequate reward. However, despite reason, obstinacy prevailed, and I entered into my new investigation with a keener energy than I could have summoned to aid me in any investigation leading to any end, valuable or worthy.

One day, late in a fine afternoon, toward the end of September, I entered the holy of holies of the city of dust. The place was evidently the recognised abode of a number of chiffoniers, for some sort of arrangement was manifested in the formation of the dust heaps near the road. I passed amongst these heaps, which stood like orderly sentries, determined to penetrate further and trace dust to its ultimate location.

As I passed along I saw behind the dust heaps a few forms that flitted to and fro, evidently watching with interest the advent of any stranger to such a place. The district was like a small Switzerland, and as I went forward my tortuous course shut out the path behind me.

Presently I got into what seemed a small city or community of chiffoniers. There were a number of shanties or huts, such as may be met with in the remote parts of the Bog of Allan[8] – rude places with wattled walls, plastered with mud and roofs of rude thatch made from stable refuse – such places as one would not like to enter for any consideration, and which even in water-colour could only look picturesque if judiciously treated. In the midst of these huts was one of the strangest adaptations – I cannot say habitations – I had ever seen. An immense old wardrobe, the colossal remnant of some boudoir of Charles VII or Henry II,[9] had been converted into a dwelling-house. The double doors lay open, so that the entire menage was open to public view. In the open half of the wardrobe was a common sitting-room of some four feet by six, in which sat, smoking their pipes round a charcoal brazier, no fewer than six old soldiers of the First Republic,[10] with their uniforms torn and worn threadbare. Evidently they were of the *mauvais sujet* class; their blear eyes and limp jaws told plainly of a common love of absinthe;[11] and their eyes had that haggard, worn look which stamps the drunkard at his worst, and that look of slumbering ferocity which follows hard in the wake of drink. The other side stood as of old, with its shelves intact, save that they were cut to half their depth, and in each shelf, of which there were six, was a bed made with rags and straw. The half-dozen of worthies who inhabited this structure looked at me curiously as I passed; and when I looked back after going a little way I saw their heads together in a whispered conference. I did not like the look of this at all, for the place was very lonely, and the men looked very, very villainous. However, I did not see any cause for fear, and went on my way, penetrating further and further into the Sahara. The way was tortuous to a degree, and from going round in a series of semi-circles, as one goes in skating with the Dutch roll,[12] I got rather confused with regard to the points of the compass.

When I had penetrated a little way I saw, as I turned the corner of a half-made heap, sitting on a heap of straw an old soldier with threadbare coat.

'Hallo!' said I to myself; 'the First Republic is well represented here in its soldiery.'

As I passed him the old man never even looked up at me, but gazed on the ground with stolid persistency. Again I remarked to myself: 'See what a life of rude warfare can do! This old man's curiosity is a thing of the past.'

When I had gone a few steps, however, I looked back suddenly, and saw that curiosity was not dead, for the veteran had raised his head and was regarding me with a very queer expression. He seemed to me to look very like one of the six worthies in the press. When he saw me looking he dropped his head; and without thinking further of him I went on my way, satisfied that there was a strange likeness between these old warriors.

Presently I met another old soldier in a similar manner. He, too, did not notice me whilst I was passing.

By this time it was getting late in the afternoon, and I began to think of retracing my steps. Accordingly I turned to go back, but could see a number of tracks leading between different mounds and could not ascertain which of them I should take. In my perplexity I wanted to see someone of whom to ask the way, but could see no one. I determined to go on a few mounds further and so try to see someone – not a veteran.

I gained my object, for after going a couple of hundred yards I saw before me a single shanty such as I had seen before –

with, however, the difference that this was not one for living in, but merely a roof with three walls open in front. From the evidences which the neighbourhood exhibited I took it to be a place for sorting. Within it was an old woman wrinkled and bent with age; I approached her to ask the way.

She rose as I came close and I asked her my way. She immediately commenced a conversation; and it occurred to me that here in the very centre of the Kingdom of Dust was the place to gather details of the history of Parisian rag-picking – particularly as I could do so from the lips of one who looked like the oldest inhabitant.

I began my inquiries, and the old woman gave me most interesting answers – she had been one of the ceteuces who sat daily before the guillotine and had taken an active part among the women who signalised themselves by their violence in the revolution.[13] While we were talking she said suddenly: 'But m'sieur must be tired standing,' and dusted a rickety old stool for me to sit down. I hardly liked to do so for many reasons; but the poor old woman was so civil that I did not like to run the risk of hurting her by refusing, and moreover the conversation of one who had been at the taking of the Bastille was so interesting that I sat down and so our conversation went on.

While we were talking an old man – older and more bent and wrinkled even than the woman – appeared from behind the shanty. 'Here is Pierre,' said she. 'M'sieur can hear stories now if he wishes, for Pierre was in everything, from the Bastille to Waterloo.' The old man took another stool at my request and we plunged into a sea of revolutionary reminiscences. This old man, albeit clothed like a scare-crow, was like any one of the six veterans.

I was now sitting in the centre of the low hut with the woman on my left hand and the man on my right, each of them being somewhat in front of me. The place was full of all sorts of curious objects of lumber, and of many things that I wished far away. In one corner was a heap of rags which seemed to move from the number of vermin it contained, and in the other a heap of bones whose odour was something shocking. Every now and then, glancing at the heaps, I could see the gleaming

eyes of some of the rats which infested the place. These loathsome objects were bad enough, but what looked even more
dreadful was an old butcher's axe with an iron handle stained
with clots of blood leaning up against the wall on the right
hand side. Still these things did not give me much concern. The
talk of the two old people was so fascinating that I stayed on
and on, till the evening came and the dust heaps threw dark
shadows over the vales between them.

After a time I began to grow uneasy, I could not tell how or
why, but somehow I did not feel satisfied. Uneasiness is an
instinct and means warning. The psychic faculties are often the
sentries of the intellect; and when they sound alarm the reason
begins to act, although perhaps not consciously.

This was so with me. I began to bethink me where I was and
by what surrounded, and to wonder how I should fare in case
I should be attacked; and then the thought suddenly burst upon
me, although without any overt cause, that I was in danger.
Prudence whispered: 'Be still and make no sign,' and so I was
still and made no sign, for I knew that four cunning eyes were
on me. 'Four eyes – if not more.' My God, what a horrible
thought! The whole shanty might be surrounded on three sides
with villains! I might be in the midst of a band of such desper-
adoes as only half a century of periodic revolution can produce.

With a sense of danger my intellect and observation quick-
ened, and I grew more watchful than was my wont. I noticed
that the old woman's eyes were constantly wandering toward
my hands. I looked at them too, and saw the cause – my rings.
On my left little finger I had a large signet and on the right a
good diamond.

I thought that if there was any danger my first care was to
avert suspicion. Accordingly I began to work the conversation
round to rag-picking – to the drains – of the things found there;
and so by easy stages to jewels. Then, seizing a favourable
opportunity, I asked the old woman if she knew anything of
such things. She answered that she did, a little. I held out my
right hand, and, showing her the diamond, asked her what she
thought of that. She answered that her eyes were bad, and
stooped over my hand. I said as nonchalantly as I could: 'Pardon

me! You will see better thus!' and taking it off handed it to her. An unholy light came into her withered old face, as she touched it. She stole one glance at me swift and keen as a flash of lightning.

She bent over the ring for a moment, her face quite concealed as though examining it. The old man looked straight out of the front of the shanty before him, at the same time fumbling in his pockets and producing a screw of tobacco in a paper and a pipe, which he proceeded to fill. I took advantage of the pause and the momentary rest from the searching eyes on my face to look carefully round the place, now dim and shadowy in the gloaming. There still lay all the heaps of varied reeking foulness; there the terrible blood-stained axe leaning against the wall in the right hand corner, and everywhere, despite the gloom, the baleful glitter of the eyes of the rats. I could see them even through some of the chinks of the boards at the back low down close to the ground. But stay! these latter eyes seemed more than usually large and bright and baleful!

For an instant my heart stood still, and I felt in that whirling condition of mind in which one feels a sort of spiritual drunkenness, and as though the body is only maintained erect in that there is no time for it to fall before recovery. Then, in another second, I was calm – coldly calm, with all my energies in full vigour, with a self-control which I felt to be perfect and with all my feeling and instincts alert.

Now I knew the full extent of my danger: I was watched and surrounded by desperate people! I could not even guess at how many of them were lying there on the ground behind the shanty, waiting for the moment to strike. I knew that I was big and strong, and they knew it, too. They knew also, as I did, that I was an Englishman and would make a fight for it; and so we waited. I had, I felt, gained an advantage in the last few seconds, for I knew my danger and understood the situation. Now, I thought, is the test of my courage – the enduring test: the fighting test may come later!

The old woman raised her head and said to me in a satisfied kind of way:

'A very fine ring, indeed – a beautiful ring! Oh, me! I once had such rings, plenty of them, and bracelets and earrings! Oh! for in those fine days I led the town a dance! But they've forgotten me now! They've forgotten me! They? Why they never heard of me! Perhaps their grandfathers remember me, some of them!' and she laughed a harsh, croaking laugh. And then I am bound to say that she astonished me, for she handed me back the ring with a certain suggestion of old-fashioned grace which was not without its pathos.

The old man eyed her with a sort of sudden ferocity, half rising from his stool, and said to me suddenly and hoarsely:

'Let me see!'

I was about to hand the ring when the old woman said:

'No! no, do not give it to Pierre! Pierre is eccentric. He loses things; and such a pretty ring!'

'Cat!' said the old man, savagely. Suddenly the old woman said, rather more loudly than was necessary:

'Wait! I shall tell you something about a ring.' There was something in the sound of her voice that jarred upon me. Perhaps it was my hyper-sensitiveness, wrought up as I was to such a pitch of nervous excitement, but I seemed to think that she was not addressing me. As I stole a glance round the place I saw the eyes of the rats in the bone heaps, but missed the eyes along the back. But even as I looked I saw them again appear. The old woman's 'Wait!' had given me a respite from attack, and the men had sunk back to their reclining posture.

'I once lost a ring – a beautiful diamond hoop that had belonged to a queen, and which was given to me by a farmer of the taxes, who afterwards cut his throat because I sent him away. I thought it must have been stolen, and taxed my people; but I could get no trace. The police came and suggested that it had found its way to the drain. We descended – I in my fine clothes, for I would not trust them with my beautiful ring! I know more of the drains since then, and of rats, too! but I shall never forget the horror of that place – alive with blazing eyes, a wall of them just outside the light of our torches. Well, we got beneath my house. We searched the outlet of the drain, and there in the filth found my ring, and we came out.

'But we found something else also before we came! As we

were coming toward the opening a lot of sewer rats – human ones this time – came toward us. They told the police that one of their number had gone into the drain, but had not returned. He had gone in only shortly before we had, and, if lost, could hardly be far off. They asked help to seek him, so we turned back. They tried to prevent me going, but I insisted. It was a new excitement, and had I not recovered my ring? Not far did we go till we came on something. There was but little water, and the bottom of the drain was raised with brick, rubbish, and much matter of the kind. He had made a fight for it, even when his torch had gone out. But they were too many for him! They had not been long about it! The bones were still warm; but they were picked clean. They had even eaten their own dead ones and there were bones of rats as well as of the man. They took it cool enough those other – the human ones – and joked of their comrade when they found him dead, though they would have helped him living. Bah! what matters it – life or death?'

'And had you no fear?' I asked her.

'Fear!' she said with a laugh. 'Me have fear? Ask Pierre! But I was younger then, and, as I came through that horrible drain with its wall of greedy eyes, always moving with the circle of the light from the torches, I did not feel easy. I kept on before the men, though! It is a way I have! I never let the men get it before me. All I want is a chance and a means! And they ate him up – took every trace away except the bones; and no one knew it, nor no sound of him was ever heard!' Here she broke into a chuckling fit of the ghastliest merriment which it was ever my lot to hear and see. A great poetess describes her heroine singing: 'Oh! to see or hear her singing! Scarce I know which is the divinest.'[14]

And I can apply the same idea to the old crone – in all save the divinity, for I scarce could tell which was the most hellish – the harsh, malicious, satisfied, cruel laugh, or the leering grin, and the horrible square opening of the mouth like a tragic mask, and the yellow gleam of the few discoloured teeth in the shapeless gums. In that laugh and with that grin and the chuckling satisfaction I knew as well as if it had been spoken to me in words of thunder that my murder was settled, and the murderers only bided the proper time for its accomplishment. I could read between the lines of her gruesome story the commands to her accomplices. 'Wait,' she seemed to say, 'bide your time. I shall strike the first blow. Find the weapon for me, and I shall make the opportunity! He shall not escape! Keep him quiet, and then no one will be wiser. There will be no outcry, and the rats will do their work!'

It was growing darker and darker; the night was coming. I stole a glance round the shanty, still all the same! The bloody axe in the corner, the heaps of filth, and the eyes on the bone heaps and in the crannies of the floor.

Pierre had been still ostensibly filling his pipe; he now struck a light and began to puff away at it. The old woman said:

'Dear heart, how dark it is! Pierre, like a good lad, light the lamp!'

Pierre got up and with the lighted match in his hand touched the wick of a lamp which hung at one side of the entrance to the shanty, and which had a reflector that threw the light all over the place. It was evidently that which was used for their sorting at night.

'Not that, stupid! Not that! The lantern!' she called out to him.

He immediately blew it out, saying: 'All right, mother, I'll find it,' and he hustled about the left corner of the room – the old woman saying through the darkness:

'The lantern! the lantern! Oh! That is the light that is most useful to us poor folks. The lantern was the friend of the revolution! It is the friend of the chiffonier! It helps us when all else fails.'

Hardly had she said the word when there was a kind of creaking of the whole place, and something was steadily dragged over the roof.

Again I seemed to read between the lines of her words. I knew the lesson of the lantern.

'One of you get on the roof with a noose and strangle him as he passes out if we fail within.'

As I looked out of the opening I saw the loop of a rope outlined black against the lurid sky. I was now, indeed, beset!

Pierre was not long in finding the lantern. I kept my eyes fixed through the darkness on the old woman. Pierre struck his light, and by its flash I saw the old woman raise from the ground beside her where it had mysteriously appeared, and then hide in the folds of her gown, a long sharp knife or dagger. It seemed to be like a butcher's sharpening iron fined to a keen point.

The lantern was lit.

'Bring it here, Pierre,' she said. 'Place it in the doorway where we can see it. See how nice it is! It shuts out the darkness from us; it is just right!'

Just right for her and her purposes! It threw all its light on my face, leaving in gloom the faces of both Pierre and the woman, who sat outside of me on each side.

I felt that the time of action was approaching; but I knew now that the first signal and movement would come from the woman, and so watched her.

I was all unarmed, but I had made up my mind what to do. At the first movement I would seize the butcher's axe in the right-hand corner and fight my way out. At least, I would die hard. I stole a glance round to fix its exact locality so that I could not fail to seize it at the first effort, for then, if ever, time and accuracy would be precious.

Good God! It was gone! All the horror of the situation burst upon me; but the bitterest thought of all was that if the issue of the terrible position should be against me Alice would infallibly suffer. Either she would believe me false – and any lover, or any one who has ever been one, can imagine the bitterness of the thought – or else she would go on loving long after I had been lost to her and to the world, so that her life would be broken and embittered, shattered with disappointment and despair. The very magnitude of the pain braced me up and nerved me to bear the dread scrutiny of the plotters.

I think I did not betray myself. The old woman was watching me as a cat does a mouse; she had her right hand hidden in the folds of her gown, clutching, I knew, that long, cruel-looking dagger. Had she seen any disappointment in my face she would, I felt, have known that the moment had come, and would have sprung on me like a tigress, certain of taking me unprepared.

I looked out into the night, and there I saw new cause for danger. Before and around the hut were at a little distance some shadowy forms; they were quite still, but I knew that they were all alert and on guard. Small chance for me now in that direction.

Again I stole a glance round the place. In moments of great excitement and of great danger, which is excitement, the mind works very quickly, and the keenness of the faculties which depend on the mind grows in proportion. I now felt this. In an instant I took in the whole situation. I saw that the axe had been taken through a small hole made in one of the rotten boards. How rotten they must be to allow of such a thing being done without a particle of noise.

The hut was a regular murder-trap, and was guarded all around. A garrotter lay on the roof ready to entangle me with his noose if I should escape the dagger of the old hag. In front the way was guarded by I know not how many watchers. And at the back was a row of desperate men – I had seen their eyes still through the crack in the boards of the floor, when last I looked – as they lay prone waiting for the signal to start erect. If it was to be ever, now for it!

As nonchalantly as I could I turned slightly on my stool so as to get my right leg well under me. Then with a sudden jump, turning my head, and guarding it with my hands, and with the fighting instinct of the knights of old, I breathed my lady's name, and hurled myself against the back wall of the hut.

Watchful as they were, the suddenness of my movement surprised both Pierre and the old woman. As I crashed through the rotten timbers I saw the old woman rise with a leap like a tiger and heard her low gasp of baffled rage. My feet lit on something that moved, and as I jumped away I knew that I had stepped on the back of one of the row of men lying on their faces outside the hut. I was torn with nails and splinters, but otherwise unhurt. Breathless I rushed up the mound in front of me, hearing as I went the dull crash of the shanty as it collapsed into a mass.

It was a nightmare climb. The mound, though but low, was awfully steep, and with each step I took the mass of dust and cinders tore down with me and gave way under my feet. The dust rose and choked me; it was sickening, foetid, awful; but my climb was, I felt, for life or death, and I struggled on. The seconds seemed hours; but the few moments I had in starting, combined with my youth and strength, gave me a great advantage, and, though several forms struggled after me in deadly silence which was more dreadful than any sound, I easily reached the top. Since then I have climbed the cone of Vesuvius, and as I struggled up that dreary steep amid the sulphurous fumes the memory of that awful night at Montrouge came back to me so vividly that I almost grew faint.

The mound was one of the tallest in the region of dust, and as I struggled to the top, panting for breath and with my heart beating like a sledge-hammer, I saw away to my left the dull red gleam of the sky, and nearer still the flashing of lights. Thank God! I knew where I was now and where lay the road to Paris!

For two or three seconds I paused and looked back. My pursuers were still well behind me, but struggling up resolutely, and in deadly silence. Beyond, the shanty was a wreck – a mass of timber and moving forms. I could see it well, for flames were already bursting out; the rags and straw had evidently caught fire from the lantern. Still silence there! Not a sound! These old wretches could die game, anyhow.

I had no time for more than a passing glance, for as I cast an eye round the mound preparatory to making my descent I saw several dark forms rushing round on either side to cut me off on my way. It was now a race for life. They were trying to head me on my way to Paris, and with the instinct of the moment I dashed down to the right-hand side. I was just in time, for, though I came as it seemed to me down the steep in a few steps, the wary old men who were watching me turned back, and one, as I rushed by into the opening between the two mounds in front, almost struck me a blow with that terrible butcher's axe. There could surely not be two such weapons about!

Then began a really horrible chase. I easily ran ahead of the old men, and even when some younger ones and a few women joined in the hunt I easily distanced them. But I did not know the way, and I could not even guide myself by the light in the sky, for I was running away from it. I had heard that, unless of conscious purpose, hunted men turn always to the left, and so I found it now; and so, I suppose, knew also my pursuers, who were more animals than men, and with cunning or instinct had found out such secrets for themselves: for on finishing a quick spurt, after which I intended to take a moment's breathing space, I suddenly saw ahead of me two or three forms swiftly passing behind a mound to the right.

I was in the spider's web now indeed! But with the thought of this new danger came the resource of the hunted, and so I darted down the next turning to the right. I continued in this direction for some hundred yards, and then, making a turn to the left again, felt certain that I had, at any rate, avoided the danger of being surrounded.

But not of pursuit, for on came the rabble[15] after me, steady, dogged, relentless, and still in grim silence.

In the greater darkness the mounds seemed now to be somewhat smaller than before, although – for the night was closing – they looked bigger in proportion. I was now well ahead of my pursuers, so I made a dart up the mound in front.

Oh joy of joys! I was close to the edge of this inferno of dustheaps. Away behind me the red light of Paris in the sky, and towering up behind rose the heights of Montmartre – a dim light, with here and there brilliant points like stars.

Restored to vigour in a moment, I ran over the few remaining mounds of decreasing size, and found myself on the level land beyond. Even then, however, the prospect was not inviting. All before me was dark and dismal, and I had evidently come on one of those dank, low-lying waste places which are found here and there in the neighbourhood of great cities. Places of waste and desolation, where the space is required for the ultimate agglomeration of all that is noxious, and the ground is so poor as to create no desire of occupancy even in the lowest squatter. With eyes accustomed to the gloom of the evening, and away now from the shadows of those dreadful dustheaps, I could see much more easily than I could a little while ago. It might have been, of course, that the glare in the sky of the lights of Paris, though the city was some miles away, was reflected here. How-soever it was, I saw well enough to take bearings for certainly some little distance around me.

In front was a bleak, flat waste that seemed almost dead level, with here and there the dark shimmering of stagnant pools. Seemingly far off on the right, amid a small cluster of scattered lights, rose a dark mass of Fort Montrouge, and away to the left in the dim distance, pointed with stray gleams from cottage windows, the lights in the sky showed the locality of Bicêtre. A moment's thought decided me to take to the right and try to reach Montrouge. There at least would be some sort of safety, and I might possibly long before come on some of the cross roads which I knew. Somewhere, not far off, must lie the stra-tegic road made to connect the outlying chain of forts circling the city.

Then I looked back. Coming over the mounds, and outlined black against the glare of the Parisian horizon, I saw several moving figures, and still a way to the right several more de-ploying out between me and my destination. They evidently meant to cut me off in this direction, and so my choice became constricted; it lay now between going straight ahead or turning to the left. Stooping to the ground, so as to get the advantage of the horizon as a line of sight, I looked carefully in this direction, but could detect no sign of my enemies. I argued that as they had not guarded or were not trying to guard that point, there was evidently danger to me there already. So I made up my mind to go straight on before me.

It was not an inviting prospect, and as I went on the reality grew worse. The ground became soft and oozy, and now and again gave way beneath me in a sickening kind of way. I seemed somehow to be going down, for I saw round me places seem-ingly more elevated than where I was, and this in a place which from a little way back seemed dead level. I looked around, but could see none of my pursuers. This was strange, for all along these birds of the night had followed me through the darkness as well as though it was broad daylight. How I blamed myself for coming out in my light-coloured tourist suit of tweed. The silence, and my not being able to see my enemies, whilst I felt that they were watching me, grew appalling, and in the hope of some one not of this ghastly crew hearing me I raised my voice and shouted several times. There was not the slightest response; not even an echo rewarded my efforts. For a while I stood stock still and kept my eyes in one direction. On one of the rising places around me I saw something dark move along, then another, and another. This was to my left, and seemingly moving to head me off.

I thought that again I might with my skill as a runner elude my enemies at this game, and so with all my speed darted forward.

Splash!

My feet had given way in a mass of slimy rubbish, and I had fallen headlong into a reeking, stagnant pool. The water and the mud in which my arms sank up to the elbows was filthy and nauseous beyond description, and in the suddenness of my fall I had actually swallowed some of the filthy stuff, which nearly choked me, and made me gasp for breath. Never shall I forget the moments during which I stood trying to recover myself almost fainting from the fœtid odour of the filthy pool, whose white mist rose ghostlike around. Worst of all, with the acute despair of the hunted animal when he sees the pursuing pack closing on him, I saw before my eyes whilst I stood helpless the dark forms of my pursuers moving swiftly to surround me.

It is curious how our minds work on odd matters even when the energies of thought are seemingly concentrated on some terrible and pressing need. I was in momentary peril of my life: my safety depended on my action, and my choice of alternatives coming now with almost every step I took, and yet I could not but think of the strange dogged persistency of these old men. Their silent resolution, their steadfast, grim persistency even in such a cause commanded, as well as fear, even a measure of respect. What must they have been in the vigour of their youth. I could understand now that whirlwind rush on the bridge of Arcola, that scornful exclamation of the Old Guard at Waterloo![16] Unconscious cerebration has its own pleasures, even at such moments; but fortunately it does not in any way clash with the thought from which action springs.

I realised at a glance that so far I was defeated in my object, my enemies as yet had won. They had succeeded in surrounding me on three sides, and were bent on driving me off to the left-hand, where there was already some danger for me, for they had left no guard. I accepted the alternative – it was a case of Hobson's choice[17] and run. I had to keep the lower ground, for my pursuers were on the higher places. However, though the ooze and broken ground impeded me my youth and training made me able to hold my ground, and by keeping a diagonal line I not only kept them from gaining on me but even began to distance them. This gave me new heart and strength, and by this time habitual training was beginning to tell and my second wind had come. Before me the ground rose slightly. I rushed up the slope and found before me a waste of watery slime, with a low dyke or bank looking black and grim beyond. I felt that if I could but reach that dyke in safety I could there, with solid ground under my feet and some kind of path to guide me, find with comparative ease a way out of my troubles. After a glance right and left and seeing no one near, I kept my eyes for a few minutes to their rightful work of aiding my feet whilst I crossed the swamp. It was rough, hard work, but there was little danger, merely toil; and a short time took me to the dyke. I rushed up the slope exulting; but here again I met a new shock. On either side of me rose a number of crouching figures. From right and left they rushed at me. Each body held a rope.

The cordon was nearly complete. I could pass on neither side, and the end was near.

There was only one chance, and I took it. I hurled myself across the dyke, and escaping out of the very clutches of my foes threw myself into the stream.

At any other time I should have thought that water foul and filthy, but now it was as welcome as the most crystal stream to the parched traveller. It was a highway of safety!

My pursuers rushed after me. Had only one of them held the rope it would have been all up with me, for he could have entangled me before I had time to swim a stroke; but the many hands holding it embarrassed and delayed them, and when the rope struck the water I heard the splash well behind me. A few minutes' hard swimming took me across the stream. Refreshed with the immersion and encouraged by the escape, I climbed the dyke in comparative gaiety of spirits.

From the top I looked back. Through the darkness I saw my assailants scattering up and down along the dyke. The pursuit was evidently not ended, and again I had to choose my course. Beyond the dyke where I stood was a wild, swampy space very similar to that which I had crossed. I determined to shun such a place, and thought for a moment whether I would take up or down the dyke. I thought I heard a sound – the muffled sound of oars, so I listened, and then shouted.

No response; but the sound ceased. My enemies had evidently got a boat of some kind. As they were on the up side of me I took the down path and began to run. As I passed to the left of where I had entered the water I heard several splashes, soft and stealthy, like the sound a rat makes as he plunges into the stream, but vastly greater; and as I looked I saw the dark sheen of the water broken by the ripples of several advancing heads. Some of my enemies were swimming the stream also.

And now behind me, up the stream, the silence was broken by the quick rattle and creak of oars; my enemies were in hot pursuit. I put my best leg foremost and ran on. After a break of a couple of minutes I looked back, and by a gleam of light through the ragged clouds I saw several dark forms climbing the bank behind me. The wind had now begun to rise, and the water beside me was ruffled and beginning to break in tiny waves on the bank. I had to keep my eyes pretty well on the ground before me, lest I should stumble, for I knew that to stumble was death. After a few minutes I looked back behind me. On the dyke were only a few dark figures, but crossing the waste, swampy ground were many more. What new danger this portended I did not know – could only guess. Then as I ran it seemed to me that my track kept ever sloping away to the right. I looked up ahead and saw that the river was much wider than before, and that the dyke on which I stood fell quite away, and beyond it was another stream on whose near bank I saw some of the dark forms now across the marsh. I was on an island of some kind.

My situation was now indeed terrible, for my enemies had hemmed me in on every side. Behind came the quickening roll of the oars, as though my pursuers knew that the end was close. Around me on every side was desolation; there was not a roof or light, as far as I could see. Far off to the right rose some dark mass, but what it was I knew not. For a moment I paused to think what I should do, not for more, for my pursuers were drawing closer. Then my mind was made up. I slipped down the bank and took to the water. I struck out straight ahead, so as to gain the current by clearing the backwater of the island, for such I presume it was, when I had passed into the stream. I waited till a cloud came driving across the moon and leaving all in darkness. Then I took off my hat and laid it softly on the water floating with the stream, and a second after dived to the right and struck out under water with all my might. I was, I suppose, half a minute under water, and when I rose came up as softly as I could, and turning, looked back. There went my light brown hat floating merrily away. Close behind it came a rickety old boat, driven furiously by a pair of oars. The moon was still partly obscured by the drifting clouds, but in the partial light I could see a man in the bows holding aloft ready to strike what appeared to me to be that same dreadful pole-axe which I had before escaped. As I looked the boat drew closer, closer, and the man struck savagely. The hat disappeared. The man fell forward, almost out of the boat. His comrades dragged him in but without the axe, and then as I turned with all my energies bent on reaching the further bank, I heard the fierce whirr of the muttered 'Sacre!' which marked the anger of my baffled pursuers.

That was the first sound I had heard from human lips during all this dreadful chase, and full as it was of menace and danger to me it was a welcome sound for it broke that awful silence which shrouded and appalled me. It was as though an overt sign that my opponents were men and not ghosts, and that with them I had, at least, the chance of a man, though but one against many.

But now that the spell of silence was broken the sounds came thick and fast. From boat to shore and back from shore to boat came quick question and answer, all in the fiercest whispers. I looked back – a fatal thing to do – for in the instant someone caught sight of my face, which showed white on the dark water, and shouted. Hands pointed to me, and in a moment or two the boat was under weigh, and following hard after me. I had but a little way to go, but quicker and quicker came the boat after me. A few more strokes and I would be on the shore, but I felt the oncoming of the boat, and expected each second to feel the crash of an oar or other weapon on my head. Had I not seen that dreadful axe disappear in the water I do not think that I could have won the shore. I heard the muttered curses of those not rowing and the laboured breath of the rowers. With one supreme effort for life or liberty I touched the bank and sprang up it. There was not a single second to spare, for hard behind me the boat grounded and several dark forms sprang after me. I gained the top of the dyke, and keeping to the left ran on again. The boat put off and followed down the stream. Seeing this I feared danger in this direction, and quickly turning, ran down the dyke on the other side, and after passing a short stretch of marshy ground gained a wild, open flat country and sped on.

Still behind me came on my relentless pursuers. Far away, below me, I saw the same dark mass as before, but now grown closer and greater. My heart gave a great thrill of delight, for I knew that it must be the fortress of Bicêtre, and with new courage I ran on. I had heard that between each and all of the protecting forts of Paris there are strategic ways, deep sunk roads, where soldiers marching should be sheltered from an enemy. I knew that if I could gain this road I would be safe, but in the darkness I could not see any sign of it, so, in blind hope of striking it, I ran on.

Presently I came to the edge of a deep cut, and found that down below me ran a road guarded on each side by a ditch of water fenced on either side by a straight, high wall.

Getting fainter and dizzier, I ran on; the ground got more broken – more and more still, till I staggered and fell, and rose again, and ran on in the blind anguish of the hunted. Again the thought of Alice nerved me. I would not be lost and wreck her life: I would fight and struggle for life to the bitter end. With a great effort I caught the top of the wall. As, scrambling like a catamount, I drew myself up, I actually felt a hand touch the sole of my foot. I was now on a sort of causeway, and before me I saw a dim light. Blind and dizzy, I ran on, staggered, and fell, rising, covered with dust and blood.

'Halt la!'

The words sounded like a voice from heaven. A blaze of light seemed to enwrap me, and I shouted with joy.

'Qui va la?' The rattle of musketry, the flash of steel before my eyes. Instinctively I stopped, though close behind me came a rush of my pursuers.

Another word or two, and out from a gateway poured, as it seemed to me, a tide of red and blue, as the guard turned out. All around seemed blazing with light, and the flash of steel, the clink and rattle of arms, and the loud, harsh voices of command. As I fell forward, utterly exhausted, a soldier caught me. I looked back in dreadful expectation, and saw the mass of dark forms disappearing into the night. Then I must have fainted. When I recovered my senses I was in the guard room. They gave me brandy, and after a while I was able to tell them something of what had passed. Then a commissary of police appeared, apparently out of the empty air, as is the way of the Parisian police officer. He listened attentively, and then had a moment's consultation with the officer in command. Apparently they were agreed, for they asked me if I were ready now to come with them.

'Where to?' I asked, rising to go.

'Back to the dust heaps. We shall, perhaps, catch them yet!'

'I shall try!' said I.

He eyed me for a moment keenly, and said suddenly:

'Would you like to wait a while or till tomorrow, young Englishman?' This touched me to the quick, as, perhaps, he intended, and I jumped to my feet.

'Come now!' I said; 'now! now! An Englishman is always ready for his duty!'

The commissary was a good fellow, as well as a shrewd one; he slapped my shoulder kindly. 'Brave garçon!' he said. 'Forgive me, but I knew what would do you most good. The guard is ready. Come!'

And so, passing right through the guard room, and through a long vaulted passage, we were out into the night. A few of the men in front had powerful lanterns. Through courtyards and down a sloping way we passed out through a low archway to a sunken road, the same that I had seen in my flight. The order was given to get at the double, and with a quick, springing stride, half run, half walk, the soldiers went swiftly along. I felt my strength renewed again – such is the difference between hunter and hunted. A very short distance took us to a low-lying pontoon bridge across the stream, and evidently very little higher up than I had struck it. Some effort had evidently been made to damage it, for the ropes had all been cut, and one of the chains had been broken. I heard the officer say to the commissary:

'We are just in time! A few more minutes, and they would have destroyed the bridge. Forward, quicker still!' and on we went. Again we reached a pontoon on the winding stream; as we came up we heard the hollow boom of the metal drums as the efforts to destroy the bridge were again renewed. A word of command was given, and several men raised their rifles.

'Fire!' A volley rang out. There was a muffled cry, and the dark forms dispersed. But the evil was done, and we saw the far end of the pontoon swing into the stream. This was a serious delay, and it was nearly an hour before we had renewed ropes and restored the bridge sufficiently to allow us to cross.

We renewed the chase. Quicker, quicker we went towards the dust heaps.

After a time we came to a place that I knew. There were the remains of a fire – a few smouldering wood ashes still cast a red glow, but the bulk of the ashes were cold. I knew the site of the hut and the hill behind it up which I had rushed, and in the flickering glow the eyes of the rats still shone with a sort of phosphorescence. The commissary spoke a word to the officer, and he cried:

'Halt!'

The soldiers were ordered to spread around and watch, and then we commenced to examine the ruins. The commissary himself began to lift away the charred boards and rubbish. These the soldiers took and piled together. Presently he started back, then bent down and rising beckoned me.

'See!' he said.

It was a gruesome sight. There lay a skeleton face downwards, a woman by the lines – an old woman by the coarse fibre of the bone. Between the ribs rose a long spike-like dagger made from a butcher's sharpening knife, its keen point buried in the spine.

'You will observe,' said the commissary to the officer and to me as he took out his note book, 'that the woman must have fallen on her dagger. The rats are many here – see their eyes glistening among that heap of bones – and you will also notice' – I shuddered as he placed his hand on the skeleton – 'that but little time was lost by them, for the bones are scarcely cold!'

There was no other sign of any one near, living or dead; and so deploying again into line the soldiers passed on. Presently we came to the hut made of the old wardrobe. We approached. In five of the six compartments was an old man sleeping – sleeping so soundly that even the glare of the lanterns did not wake them. Old and grim and grizzled they looked, with their gaunt, wrinkled, bronzed faces and their white moustaches.

The officer called out harshly and loudly a word of command, and in an instant each one of them was on his feet before us and standing at 'attention!'

'What do you here?'

'We sleep,' was the answer.

'Where are the other chiffoniers?' asked the commissary.

'Gone to work.'

'And you?'

'We are on guard!'

'Peste!' laughed the officer grimly, as he looked at the old men one after the other in the face and added with cool deliberate cruelty, 'Asleep on duty! Is this the manner of the Old Guard? No wonder, then, a Waterloo!'

By the gleam of the lantern I saw the grim old faces grow deadly pale, and almost shuddered at the look in the eyes of the old men as the laugh of the soldiers echoed the grim pleasantry of the officer.

I felt in that moment that I was in some measure avenged.

For a moment they looked as if they would throw themselves on the taunter, but years of their life had schooled them and they remained still.

'You are but five,' said the commissary; 'where is the sixth?' The answer came with a grim chuckle.

'He is there!' and the speaker pointed to the bottom of the wardrobe. 'He died last night. You won't find much of him. The burial of the rats is quick!'

The commissary stooped and looked in. Then he turned to the officer and said calmly:

'We may as well go back. No trace here now; nothing to prove that man was the one wounded by your soldiers' bullets! Probably they murdered him to cover up the trace. See!' again he stooped and placed his hands on the skeleton. 'The rats work quickly and they are many. These bones are warm!'

I shuddered, and so did many more of those around me.

'Form!' said the officer, and so in marching order, with the lanterns swinging in front and the manacled veterans in the midst, with steady tramp we took ourselves out of the dust-heaps and turned backward to the fortress of Bicêtre.

My year of probation has long since ended, and Alice is my wife. But when I look back upon that trying twelvemonth one of the most vivid incidents that memory recalls is that associated with my visit to the City of Dust.

A DREAM OF RED HANDS

The first opinion given to me regarding Jacob Settle was a simple descriptive statement, 'He's a down-in-the-mouth chap': but I found that it embodied the thoughts and ideas of all his fellow-workmen. There was in the phrase a certain easy tolerance, an absence of positive feeling of any kind, rather than any complete opinion, which marked pretty accurately the man's place in public esteem. Still, there was some dissimilarity between this and his appearance which unconsciously set me thinking, and by degrees, as I saw more of the place and the workmen, I came to have a special interest in him. He was, I found, for ever doing kindnesses, not involving money expenses beyond his humble means, but in the manifold ways of fore-thought and forbearance and self-repression which are of the truer charities of life. Women and children trusted him implicitly, though, strangely enough, he rather shunned them, except when anyone was sick, and then he made his appearance to help if he could, timidly and awkwardly. He led a very solitary life, keeping house by himself in a tiny cottage, or rather hut, of one room, far on the edge of the moorland. His existence seemed so sad and solitary that I wished to cheer it up, and for the purpose took the occasion when we had both been sitting up with a child, injured by me through accident, to offer to lend him books. He gladly accepted, and as we parted in the grey of the dawn I felt that something of mutual confidence had been established between us.

The books were always most carefully and punctually re-turned, and in time Jacob Settle and I became quite friends. Once or twice as I crossed the moorland on Sundays I looked in on him; but on such occasions he was shy and ill at ease so that I felt diffident about calling to see him. He would never under any circumstances come into my own lodgings.

One Sunday afternoon, I was coming back from a long walk beyond the moor, and as I passed Settle's cottage stopped at the door to say 'How do you do?' to him. As the door was shut, I thought that he was out, and merely knocked for form's sake, or through habit, not expecting to get any answer. To my surprise, I heard a feeble voice from within, though what was said I could not hear. I entered at once, and found Jacob lying half-dressed upon his bed. He was as pale as death, and the sweat was simply rolling off his face. His hands were unconsciously gripping the bed-clothes as a drowning man holds on to whatever he may grasp. As I came in he half arose, with a wild, hunted look in his eyes, which were wide open and staring, as though something of horror had come before him; but when he recognised me he sank back on the couch with a smothered sob of relief and closed his eyes. I stood by him for a while, quite a minute or two, while he gasped. Then he opened his eyes and looked at me, but with such a despairing, woeful expression that, as I am a living man, I would have rather seen that frozen look of horror. I sat down beside him and asked after his health. For a while he would not answer me except to say that he was not ill; but then, after scrutinising me closely, he half arose on his elbow and said –

'I thank you kindly, sir, but I'm simply telling you the truth. I am not ill, as men call it, though God knows whether there be not worse sicknesses than doctors know of. I'll tell you, as you are so kind, but I trust that you won't even mention such a thing to a living soul, for it might work me more and greater woe. I am suffering from a bad dream.'

'A bad dream!' I said, hoping to cheer him; 'but dreams pass away with the light – even with waking.' There I stopped, for before he spoke I saw the answer in his desolate look round the little place.

'No! no! that's all well for people that live in comfort and with those they love around them. It is a thousand times worse for those who live alone and have to do so. What cheer is there for me, waking here in the silence of the night, with the wide moor around me full of voices and full of faces that make my waking a worse dream than my sleep? Ah, young sir, you have no past that can send its legions to people the darkness and the empty space, and I pray the good God that you may never have!' As he spoke, there was such an almost irresistible gravity of conviction in his manner that I abandoned my remonstrance about his solitary life. I felt that I was in the presence of some secret influence which I could not fathom. To my relief, for I knew not what to say, he went on –

'Two nights past have I dreamed it. It was hard enough the first night, but I came through it. Last night the expectation was in itself almost worse than the dream – until the dream came, and then it swept away every remembrance of lesser pain. I stayed awake till just before the dawn, and then it came again, and ever since I have been in such an agony as I am sure the dying feel, and with it all the dread of to-night.' Before he had got to the end of the sentence my mind was made up, and I felt that I could speak to him more cheerfully.

'Try and get to sleep early to-night – in fact, before the evening has passed away. The sleep will refresh you, and I promise you there will not be any bad dreams after to-night.' He shook his head hopelessly, so I sat a little longer and then left him.

When I got home I made my arrangements for the night, for I had made up my mind to share Jacob Settle's lonely vigil in his cottage on the moor. I judged that if he got to sleep before sunset he would wake well before midnight, and so, just as the bells of the city were striking eleven, I stood opposite his door armed with a bag, in which were my supper, an extra large flask, a couple of candles, and a book. The moonlight was bright, and flooded the whole moor, till it was almost as light as day; but ever and anon black clouds drove across the sky, and made a darkness which by comparison seemed almost tangible. I opened the door softly, and entered without waking Jacob, who lay asleep with his white face upward. He was still, and again bathed in sweat. I tried to imagine what visions were passing before those closed eyes which could bring with them the misery and woe which were stamped on the face, but fancy failed me, and I waited for the awakening. It came suddenly, and in a fashion which touched me to the quick, for the hollow groan that broke from the man's white lips as he half arose and sank back was manifestly the realisation or completion of some train of thought which had gone before.

'If this be dreaming,' said I to myself, 'then it must be based on some very terrible reality. What can have been that unhappy fact that he spoke of?'

While I thus spoke, he realised that I was with him. It struck me as strange that he had no period of that doubt as to whether dream or reality surrounded him which commonly marks an expected environment of waking men. With a positive cry of joy, he seized my hand and held it in his two wet, trembling hands, as a frightened child clings on to someone whom it loves. I tried to soothe him –

'There, there! it is all right. I have come to stay with you to-night, and together we will try to fight this evil dream.' He let go my hand suddenly, and sank back on his bed and covered his eyes with his hands.

'Fight it? – the evil dream! Ah! no, sir no! No mortal power can fight that dream, for it comes from God – and is burned in here;' and he beat upon his forehead. Then he went on –

'It is the same dream, ever the same, and yet it grows in its power to torture me every time it comes.'

'What is the dream?' I asked, thinking that the speaking of it might give him some relief, but he shrank away from me, and after a long pause said –

'No, I had better not tell it. It may not come again.'

There was manifestly something to conceal from me – something that lay behind the dream, so I answered –

'All right. I hope you have seen the last of it. But if it should come again, you will tell me, will you not? I ask, not out of curiosity, but because I think it may relieve you to speak.' He answered with what I thought was almost an undue amount of solemnity –

'If it comes again, I shall tell you all.'

Then I tried to get his mind away from the subject to more

mundane things, so I produced supper, and made him share it with me, including the contents of the flask. After a little he braced up, and when I lit my cigar, having given him another, we smoked a full hour, and talked of many things. Little by little the comfort of his body stole over his mind, and I could see sleep laying her gentle hands on his eyelids. He felt it, too, and told me that now he felt all right, and I might safely leave him; but I told him that, right or wrong, I was going to see in the daylight. So I lit my other candle, and began to read as he fell asleep.

By degrees I got interested in my book, so interested that presently I was startled by its dropping out of my hands. I looked and saw that Jacob was still asleep, and I was rejoiced to see that there was on his face a look of unwonted happiness, while his lips seemed to move with unspoken words. Then I turned to my work again, and again woke, but this time to feel chilled to my very marrow by hearing the voice from the bed beside me –

'Not with those red hands! Never! never!' On looking at him, I found that he was still asleep. He woke, however, in an instant, and did not seem surprised to see me; there was again that strange apathy as to his surroundings. Then I said:

'Settle, tell me your dream. You may speak freely, for I shall hold your confidence sacred. While we both live I shall never mention what you may choose to tell me.'

'I said I would; but I had better tell you first what goes before the dream, that you may understand. I was a schoolmaster when I was a very young man; it was only a parish school in a little village in the West Country. No need to mention any names. Better not. I was engaged to be married to a young girl whom I loved and almost reverenced. It was the old story. While we were waiting for the time when we could afford to set up house together, another man came along. He was nearly as young as I was, and handsome, and a gentleman, with all a gentleman's attractive ways for a woman of our class. He would go fishing, and she would meet him while I was at my work in school. I reasoned with her and implored her to give him up. I offered to get married at once and go away and begin the world in a strange country; but she would not listen to anything I could say, and I could see that she was infatuated with him. Then I took it on myself to meet the man and ask him to deal well with the girl, for I thought he might mean honestly by her, so that there might be no talk or chance of talk on the part of others. I went where I should meet him with none by, and we met!' Here Jacob Settle had to pause, for something seemed to rise in his throat, and he almost gasped for breath. Then he went on –

'Sir, as God is above us, there was no selfish thought in my heart that day; I loved my pretty Mabel too well to be content with a part of her love, and I had thought of my own unhappiness too often not to have come to realise that, whatever might come to her, my hope was gone. He was insolent to me – you, sir, who are a gentleman, cannot know, perhaps, how galling can be the insolence of one who is above you in station – but I bore with that. I implored him to deal well with the girl, for what might be only a pastime of an idle hour with him might be the breaking of her heart. For I never had a thought of her truth, or that the worst of harm could come to her – it was only the unhappiness to her heart I feared. But when I asked him when he intended to marry her his laughter galled me so that I lost my temper and told him that I would not stand by and see her life made unhappy. Then he grew angry too, and in his anger said such cruel things of her that then and there I swore he should not live to do her harm. God knows how it came about, for in such moments of passion it is hard to remember the steps from a word to a blow, but I found myself standing over his dead body, with my hands crimson with the blood that welled from his torn throat. We were alone and he was a stranger, with none of his kin to seek for him, and murder does not always out – not all at once. His bones may be whitening still, for all I know, in the pool of the river where I left him. No one suspected his absence, or why it was, except my poor Mabel, and she dared not speak. But it was all in vain, for when I came back again after an absence of months – for I could not live in the place – I learned that her shame had come and that she had died in it. Hitherto I had been borne up by the thought that my ill deed had saved her future, but now, when I learned that I had been too late, and that my poor love was smirched with that man's sin, I fled away with the sense of my useless guilt upon me more heavily than I could bear. Ah! sir, you that have not done such a sin don't know what it is to carry it with you. You may think that custom makes it easy to you, but it is not so. It grows and grows with every hour, till it becomes intolerable, and with it growing, too, the feeling that you must for ever stand outside Heaven. You don't know what that means, and I pray God that you never may. Ordinary men, to whom all things are possible, don't often, if ever, think of Heaven. It is a name, and nothing more, and they are content to wait and let things be; but to those who are doomed to be shut out for ever you cannot think what it means; you cannot guess or measure the terrible endless longing to see the gates opened, and to be able to join the white figures within.

'And this brings me to my dream. It seemed that the portal was before me, with great gates of massive steel with bars of the thickness of a mast, rising to the very clouds, and so close that between them was just a glimpse of a crystal grotto, on whose shining walls were figured many white-clad forms with faces radiant with joy. When I stood before the gate my heart and my soul were so full of rapture and longing that I forgot. And there stood at the gate two mighty angels with sweeping wings, and, oh! so stern of countenance. They held each in one hand a flaming sword,[1] and in the other the latchet, which moved to and fro at their lightest touch. Nearer were the figures all draped in black, with heads covered so that only the eyes were seen, and they handed to each who came white garments such as the angels wear. A low murmur came that told that all should put on their own robes, and without soil, or the angels would not pass them in, but would smite them down with flaming swords. I was eager to don my own garment, and hurriedly threw it over me and stepped swiftly to the gate; but it moved not, and the angels, loosing the latchet, pointed to my dress, and I looked down, and was aghast, for the whole robe was smeared with blood. My hands were red; they glittered with blood that dripped from them as on that day by the river bank. And then the angels raised their flaming swords to smite me down, and the horror was complete – I awoke. Again, and again, and again, that awful dream comes to me. I never learn from the experience, I never remember, but at the beginning the hope is ever there to make the end more appalling; and I know that the dream does not come out of the common darkness where the dreams abide, but that it is sent from God as a punishment! Never, never shall I be able to pass the gate, for the soil on the angel garments must ever come from those bloody hands!'

I listened as in a spell as Jacob Settle spoke. There was something so far away in the tone of his voice – something so dreamy and mystic in the eyes that looked as if through me at some spirit beyond – something so lofty in his very diction and in such marked contrast to his workworn clothes and his poor surroundings that I wondered if the whole thing were not a dream.

We were both silent for a long time. I kept looking at the man before me in growing wonderment. Now that his confession had been made, his soul, which had been crushed to the very earth, seemed to leap back again to uprightness with some resilient force. I suppose I ought to have been horrified with his story, but, strange to say, I was not. It certainly is not pleasant to be made the recipient of the confidence of a murderer, but this poor fellow seemed to have had, not only so much provocation, but so much self-denying purpose in his deed of blood that I did not feel called upon to pass judgement upon him. My purpose was to comfort, so I spoke out with what calmness I could, for my heart was beating fast and heavily –

'You need not despair, Jacob Settle. God is very good, and his mercy is great. Live on and work on in the hope that some day you may feel that you have atoned for the past.' Here I paused, for I could see that sleep, natural sleep this time, was creeping upon him. 'Go to sleep,' I said; 'I shall watch with you here, and we shall have no more evil dreams tonight.'

He made an effort to pull himself together and answered –

'I don't know how to thank you for your goodness to me this night, but I think you had best leave me now. I'll try and sleep this out; I feel a weight off my mind since I have told you all. If there's anything of the man left in me, I must try and fight out life alone.'

'I'll go to-night, as you wish it,' I said; 'but take my advice, and do not live in such a solitary way. Go among men and women; live among them. Share their joys and sorrows, and it will help you to forget. This solitude will make you melancholy mad.'

'I will!' he answered, half unconsciously, for sleep was over-mastering him.

I turned to go, and he looked after me. When I had touched the latch I dropped it, and, coming back to the bed, held out my hand. He grasped it with both his as he rose to a sitting posture, and I said my good-night, trying to cheer him –

'Heart, man, heart! There is work in the world for you to do, Jacob Settle. You can wear those white robes yet and pass through that gate of steel!'

Then I left him.

A week after I found his cottage deserted, and on asking at the works was told that he had 'gone north,' no one exactly knew whither.

Two years afterwards, I was staying for a few days with my friend Dr Munro in Glasgow. He was a busy man, and could not spare much time for going about with me, so I spent my days in excursions to the Trossachs and Loch Katrine and down the Clyde. On the second last evening of my stay I came back somewhat later than I had arranged, but found that my host was late too. The maid told me that he had been sent for to the hospital – a case of accident at the gas-works, and the dinner was postponed an hour; so telling her I would stroll down to find her master and walk back with him, I went out. At the hospital I found him washing his hands preparatory to starting for home. Casually, I asked him what his case was.

'Oh, the usual thing! A rotten rope and men's lives of no account. Two men were working in a gasometer, when the rope that held their scaffolding broke. It must have occurred just before the dinner hour, for no one noticed their absence till the men had returned. There was about seven feet of water in the gasometer, so they had a hard fight for it, poor fellows. However, one of them was alive, just alive, but we have had a hard job to pull him through. It seems that he owes his life to his mate, for I have never heard of greater heroism. They swam together while their strength lasted, but at the end they were so done up that even the lights above, and the men slung with ropes, coming down to help them, could not keep them up. But one of them stood on the bottom and held up his comrade over his head, and those few breaths made all the difference between life and death. They were a shocking sight when they were taken out, for that water is like a purple dye with the gas and the tar. The man upstairs looked as if he had been washed in blood. Ugh!'

'And the other?'

'Oh, he's worse still. But he must have been a very noble fellow. That struggle under the water must have been fearful; one can see that by the way the blood has been drawn from the extremities. It makes the idea of the *Stigmata* possible to look at him. Resolution like this could, you would think, do anything in the world. Ay! it might almost unbar the gates of Heaven. Look here, old man, it is not a very pleasant sight, especially just before dinner, but you are a writer, and this is an odd case. Here is something you would not like to miss, for in all human probability you will never see anything like it again.' While he was speaking he had brought me into the mortuary of the hospital.

On the bier lay a body covered with a white sheet, which was wrapped close round it.

'Looks like a chrysalis, don't it? I say, Jack, if there be anything in the old myth that a soul is typified by a butterfly,[2] well, then the one that this chrysalis sent forth was a very noble specimen and took all the sunlight on its wings. See here!' He uncovered the face. Horrible, indeed, it looked, as though stained with blood. But I knew him at once, Jacob Settle! My friend pulled the winding sheet further down.

The hands were crossed on the purple breast as they had been reverently placed by some tenderhearted person. As I saw them, my heart throbbed with a great exultation, for the memory of his harrowing dream rushed across my mind. There was no stain now on those poor, brave hands, for they were blanched white as snow.

And somehow as I looked I felt that the evil dream was all over. That noble soul had won a way through the gate at last. The white robe had now no stain from the hands that had put it on.

CROOKEN SANDS

Mr Arthur Fernlee Markam, who took what was known as the Red House above the Mains of Crooken, was a London merchant, and being essentially a cockney, thought it necessary when he went for the summer holidays to Scotland to provide an entire rig-out as a Highland chieftain, as manifested in chromolithographs and on the music-hall stage. He had once seen in the Empire the Great Prince – 'The Bounder King' – bring down the house by appearing as 'The MacSlogan of that Ilk,' and singing the celebrated Scotch song, 'There's naething like haggis to mak a mon dry!' and he had ever since preserved in his mind a faithful image of the picturesque and warlike appearance which he presented. Indeed, if the true inwardness of Mr Markam's mind on the subject of his selection of Aberdeenshire as a summer resort were known, it would be found that in the foreground of the holiday locality which his fancy painted stalked the many-hued figure of the MacSlogan of that Ilk. However, be this as it may, a very kind fortune – certainly so far as external beauty was concerned – led him to the choice of Crooken Bay. It is a lovely spot, between Aberdeen and Peterhead, just under the rock-bound headland whence the long, dangerous reefs known as The Spurs run out into the North Sea. Between this and the 'Mains of Crooken' – a village sheltered by the northern cliffs – lies the deep bay, backed with a multitude of bent-grown dunes where the rabbits are to be found in thousands. Thus at either end of the bay is a rocky promontory, and when the dawn or the sunset falls on the rocks of red syenite the effect is very lovely. The bay itself is floored with level sand and the tide runs far out, leaving a smooth waste of hard sand on which are dotted here and there the stake nets and bag nets of the salmon fishers. At one end of the bay there is a little group or cluster of rocks whose heads are raised something above high water, except when in rough weather the waves come over them green. At low tide they are exposed down to sand level; and here is perhaps the only little bit of dangerous sand on this part of the the eastern coast. Between the rocks, which are apart about some fifty feet, is a small quicksand, which, like the Goodwins,[1] is dangerous only with the incoming tide. It extends outwards till it is lost in the sea, and inwards till it fades away in the hard sand of the upper beach. On the slope of the hill which rises beyond the dunes, midway between the Spurs and the Port of Crooken, is the Red House. It rises from the midst of a clump of fir-trees which protect it on three sides, leaving the whole sea front open. A trim, old-fashioned garden stretches down to the roadway, on crossing which a grassy path, which can be used for light vehicles, threads a way to the shore, winding amongst the sand hills.

When the Markam family arrived at the Red House after their thirty-six hours of pitching on the Aberdeen steamer *Ban Righ* from Blackwall, with the subsequent train to Yellon and drive of a dozen miles, they all agreed that they had never seen a more delightful spot. The general satisfaction was more marked as at that very time none of the family were, for several reasons, inclined to find favourable anything or any place over the Scottish border. Though the family was a large one, the prosperity of the business allowed them all sorts of personal luxuries, amongst which was a wide latitude in the way of dress. The frequency of the Markam girls' new frocks was a source of envy to their bosom friends and of joy to themselves.

Arthur Fernlee Markam had not taken his family into his confidence regarding his new costume. He was not quite certain that he should be free from ridicule, or at least from sarcasm, and as he was sensitive on the subject, he thought it better to be actually in the suitable environment before he allowed the full splendour to burst on them. He had taken some pains to insure the completeness of the Highland costume. For the purpose he had paid many visits to 'The Scotch All-wool Tartan clothing Mart' which had been lately established in Copthall-court[2] by the Messrs MacCallum More and Roderick MacDhu. He had anxious consultations with the head of the firm – MacCullum as he called himself, resenting any such additions as 'Mr' or 'Esquire.' The known stock of buckles, buttons, straps, brooches and ornaments of all kinds were examined in critical detail; and at last an eagle's feather of sufficiently magnificent proportions was discovered, and the equipment was complete. It was only when he saw the finished costume, with the vivid hues of the tartan seemingly modified into comparative sobriety by the multitude of silver fittings, the cairngorm brooches, the philibeg, dirk and sporran,[3] that he was fully and absolutely satisfied with his choice. At first he had thought of the Royal Stuart dress tartan, but abandoned it on the MacCallum pointing out that if he should happen to be in the neighbourhood of Balmoral[4] it might lead to complications. The MacCullum, who, by the way, spoke with a remarkable cockney accent, suggested other plaids in turn; but now that the other question of accuracy had been raised, Mr Markam foresaw difficulties if he should by chance find himself in the locality of the clan whose colours he had usurped. The Mac-Callum at last undertook to have, at Markam's expense, a special pattern woven which would not be exactly the same as any existing tartan, though partaking of the characteristics of many. It was based on the Royal Stuart, but contained suggestions as to simplicity of pattern from the Macalister and Ogilvie clans, and as to neutrality of colour from the clans of Buchanan, Macbeth, Chief of Macintosh and Macleod. When the specimen had been shown to Markam he had feared somewhat lest it should strike the eye of his domestic circle as gaudy; but as Roderick MacDhu fell into perfect ecstasies over its beauty he did not make any objection to the completion of the piece. He thought, and wisely, that if a genuine Scotchman like MacDhu liked it, it must be right – especially as the junior partner was a man very much of his own build and appearance. When the MacCullum was receiving his cheque – which, by the way, was a pretty stiff one – he remarked:

'I've taken the liberty of having some more of the stuff woven in case you or any of your friends should want it.' Markam was gratified, and told him that he should be only too happy if the beautiful stuff which they had originated between them should become a favourite, as he had no doubt it would in time. He might make and sell as much as he would.

Markam tried the dress on in his office one evening after the clerks had all gone home. He was pleased, though a little frightened, at the result. The MacCullum had done his work thoroughly, and there was nothing omitted that could add to the martial dignity of the wearer.

'I shall not, of course, take the claymore[5] and the pistols with me on ordinary occasions,' said Markam to himself as he began to undress. He determined that he would wear the dress for the first time on landing in Scotland, and accordingly on the morning when the *Ban Righ* was hanging off the Girdle Ness lighthouse,[6] waiting for the tide to enter the port of Aberdeen, he emerged from his cabin in all the gaudy splendour of his new costume. The first comment he heard was from one of his own sons, who did not recognise him at first.

'Here's a guy! Great Scott! It's the governor!' And the boy fled forthwith and tried to bury his laughter under a cushion in the saloon. Markam was a good sailor and had not suffered from the pitching of the boat, so that his naturally rubicund face was even more rosy by the conscious blush which suffused his cheeks when he had found himself at once the cynosure of all eyes. He could have wished that he had not been so bold, for he knew from the cold that there was a big bare spot under one side of his jauntily worn Glengarry cap.[7] However, he faced the group of strangers boldly. He was not, outwardly, upset even when some of their comments reached his ears.

'He's off his bloomin' chump,' said a cockney in a suit of exaggerated plaid.

'There's flies on him,' said a tall thin Yankee, pale with seasickness, who was on his way to take up his residence for a time as close as he could get to the gates of Balmoral.

'Happy thought! Let us fill our mulls;[8] now's the chance!' said a young Oxford man on his way home to Inverness. But presently Mr Markam heard the voice of his eldest daughter.

'Where is he? Where is he?' and she came tearing along the deck with her hat blowing behind her. Her face showed signs of agitation, for her mother had just been telling her of her father's condition; but when she saw him she instantly burst into laughter so violent that it ended in a fit of hysterics. Something of the same kind happened to each of the other children. When they had all had their turn Mr Markam went to his cabin and sent his wife's maid to tell each member of the family that he wanted to see them at once. They all made their appearance, suppressing their feelings as well as they could. He said to them very quietly:

'My dears, don't I provide you all with ample allowances!'

'Yes, father!' they all answered gravely, 'no one could be more generous!'

'Don't I let you dress as you please?'

'Yes, father!' – this a little sheepishly.

'Then, my dears, don't you think it would be nicer and kinder of you not to try and make me feel uncomfortable, even if I do assume a dress which is ridiculous in your eyes, though quite common enough in the country where we are about to sojourn.' There was no answer except that which appeared in their hanging heads. He was a good father and they all knew it. He was quite satisfied and went on:

'There, now, run away and enjoy yourselves! We shan't have another word about it.' Then he went on deck again and stood bravely the fire of ridicule which he recognised around him, though nothing more was said within his hearing.

The astonishment and the amusement which his get-up occasioned on the *Ban Righ* was, however, nothing to that which it created in Aberdeen. The boys and loafers, and women with babies, who waited at the landing shed, followed *en masse* as the Markam party took their way to the railway station; even the porters with their old-fashioned knots and their new-fashioned barrows, who await the traveller at the foot of the gang-plank, followed in wondering delight. Fortunately the Peterhead train was just about to start, so that the martyrdom was not unnecessarily prolonged. In the carriage the glorious Highland costume was unseen, and as there were but few persons at the station at Yellon, all went well there. When, however, the carriage drew near the Mains of Crooken and the fisher folk had run to their doors to see who it was that was passing, the excitement exceeded all bounds. The children with one impulse waved their bonnets and ran shouting behind the carriage; the men forsook their nets and their baiting and followed; the women clutched their babies and followed also. The horses were tired after their long journey to Yellon and back, and the hill was steep, so that there was ample time for the crowd to gather and even to pass on ahead.

Mrs Markam and the elder girls would have liked to make some protest or to do something to relieve their feelings of chagrin at the ridicule which they saw on all faces, but there was a look of fixed determination on the face of the seeming Highlander which awed them a little, and they were silent. It might have been that the eagle's feather, even when rising above the bald head, the cairngorm brooch even on the fat shoulder, and the claymore, dirk and pistols, even when belted round the extensive paunch and protruding from the stocking on the sturdy calf, fulfilled their existence as symbols of martial and terrifying import! When the party arrived at the gate of the Red House there awaited them a crowd of Crooken inhabitants, hatless and respectfully silent; the remainder of the population was painfully toiling up the hill. The silence was broken by only one sound, that of a man with a deep voice.

'Man! but he's forgotten the pipes!'

The servants had arrived some days before, and all things were in readiness. In the glow consequent on a good lunch after a hard journey all the disagreeables of travel and all the chagrin consequent on the adoption of the obnoxious costume were forgotten.

That afternoon Markam, still clad in full array, walked through the Mains of Crooken. He was all alone, for, strange to say, his wife and both daughters had sick headaches, and were, as he was told, lying down to rest after the fatigue of the journey. His eldest son, who claimed to be a young man, had gone out by himself to explore the surroundings of the place, and one of the boys could not be found. The other boy, on being told that his father had sent for him to come for a walk, had managed – by accident, of course – to fall into a water butt, and had to be dried and rigged out afresh. His clothes not having been as yet unpacked this was of course impossible without delay.

Mr Markam was not quite satisfied with his walk. He could not meet any of his neighbours. It was not that there were not enough people about, for every house and cottage seemed to be full; but the people when in the open were either in their doorways some distance behind him, or on the roadway a long distance in front. As he passed he could see the tops of heads and the whites of eyes in the windows or round the corners of doors. The only interview which he had was anything but a pleasant one. This was with an odd sort of old man who was hardly ever heard to speak except to join in the 'Amens' in the meeting-house. His sole occupation seemed to be to wait at the window of the post-office from eight o'clock in the morning till the arrival of the mail at one, when he carried the letter-bag to a neighbouring baronial castle. The remainder of his day was spent on a seat in a draughty part of the port, where the offal of the fish, the refuse of the bait, and the house rubbish was thrown, and where the ducks were accustomed to hold high revel.

When Saft Tammie beheld him coming he raised his eyes, which were generally fixed on the nothing which lay on the roadway opposite his seat, and, seeming dazzled as if by a burst of sunshine, rubbed them and shaded them with his hand. Then he started up and raised his hand aloft in a denunciatory manner as he spoke: –

'"Vanity of vanities, saith the preacher. All is vanity." Mon, be warned in time! "Behold the lilies of the field, they toil not, neither do they spin, yet Solomon in all his glory was not arrayed like one of these."[9] Mon! mon! Thy vanity is as the quicksand which swallows up all which comes within its spell. Beware vanity! Beware the quicksand, which yawneth for thee, and which will swallow thee up! See thyself! Learn thine own vanity! Meet thyself face to face, and then in that moment thou shalt learn the fatal force of thy vanity. Learn it, know it, and repent ere the quicksand swallow thee!' Then without another word he went back to his seat and sat there immovable and expressionless as before.

Markam could not but feel a little upset by this tirade. Only that it was spoken by a seeming madman, he would have put it down to some eccentric exhibition of Scottish humour or impudence; but the gravity of the message – for it seemed nothing else – made such a reading impossible. He was, however, determined not to give in to ridicule, and although he had not as yet seen anything in Scotland to remind him even of a kilt, he determined to wear his Highland dress. When he returned home, in less than half-an-hour, he found that every member of the family was, despite the headaches, out taking a walk. He took the opportunity afforded by their absence of locking himself in his dressing-room, took off the Highland dress, and, putting on a suit of flannels, lit a cigar and had a snooze. He was awakened by the noise of the family coming in, and at once donning his dress made his appearance in the drawing-room for tea.

He did not go out again that afternoon; but after dinner he put on his dress again – he had, of course, dressed for dinner as usual – and went by himself for a walk on the sea-shore. He had by this time come to the conclusion that he would get by degrees accustomed to the Highland dress before making it his ordinary wear. The moon was up and he easily followed the path through the sand-hills, and shortly struck the shore. The tide was out and the beach firm as a rock, so he strolled southwards to nearly the end of the bay. Here he was attracted by two isolated rocks some little way out from the edge of the dunes, so he strolled towards them. When he reached the nearest one he climbed it, and, sitting there elevated some fifteen or twenty feet over the waste of sand, enjoyed the lovely, peaceful prospect. The moon was rising behind the headland of Penny-fold, and its light was just touching the top of the furthermost rock of the Spurs some three-quarters of a mile out; the rest of the rocks were in dark shadow. As the moon rose over the headland, the rocks of the Spurs and then the beach by degrees became flooded with light.

For a good while Mr Markam sat and looked at the rising moon and the growing area of light which followed its rise. Then he turned and faced eastwards, and sat with his chin in his hand looking seawards, and revelling in the peace and beauty and freedom of the scene. The roar of London – the darkness and the strife and weariness of London life – seemed to have passed quite away, and he lived at the moment a freer and higher life. He looked at the glistening water as it stole its way over the flat waste of sand, coming closer and closer insensibly – the tide had turned. Presently he heard a distant shouting along the beach very far off.

'The fishermen calling to each other,' he said to himself and looked around. As he did so he got a horrible shock, for though just then a cloud sailed across the moon he saw, in spite of the sudden darkness around him, his own image. For an instant, on the top of the opposite rock he could see the bald back of the head and the Glengarry cap with the immense eagle's feather. As he staggered back his foot slipped, and he began to slide down towards the sand between the two rocks. He took no concern as to falling, for the sand was really only a few feet below him, and his mind was occupied with the figure or simulacrum of himself, which had already disappeared. As the easiest way of reaching *terra firma* he prepared to jump the remainder of the distance. All this had taken but a second, but the brain works quickly, and even as he gathered himself for the spring he saw the sand below him lying so marbly level shake and shiver in an odd way. A sudden fear overcame him; his knees failed, and instead of jumping he slid miserably down the rock, scratching his bare legs as he went. His feet touched the sand – went through it like water – and he was down below his knees before he realised that he was in a quicksand. Wildly he grasped at the rock to keep himself from sinking further, and fortunately there was a jutting spur or edge which he was able to grasp instinctively. To this he clung in grim desperation. He tried to shout, but his breath would not come, till after a great effort his voice rang out. Again he shouted, and it seemed as if the sound of his own voice gave him new courage, for he was able to hold on to the rock for a longer time than he thought possible

– though he held on only in blind desperation. He was, however, beginning to find his grasp weakening, when, joy of joys! his shout was answered by a rough voice from just above him.

'God be thankit, I'm nae too late!' and a fisherman with great thigh-boots came hurriedly climbing over the rock. In an instant he recognised the gravity of the danger, and with a cheering 'Haud fast, mon! I'm comin'!' scrambled down till he found a firm foothold. Then with one strong hand holding the rock above, he leaned down, and catching Markam's wrist, called out to him, 'Haud to me, mon! Haud to me wi' your ither hond!'

Then he lent his great strength, and with a steady, sturdy pull, dragged him out of the hungry quicksand and placed him safe upon the rock. Hardly giving him time to draw breath, he pulled and pushed him – never letting him go for an instant – over the rock into the firm sand beyond it, and finally deposited him, still shaking from the magnitude of his danger, high up on the beach. Then he began to speak:

'Mon! but I was just in time. If I had no laucht at yon foolish lads and begun to rin at the first you'd a bin sinkin' doon to the bowels o' the airth be the noo! Wully Beagrie thocht you was a ghaist, and Tom MacPhail swore ye was only like a goblin on a puddick-steel! "Na!" said I. "Yon's but the daft Englishman – the loony that has escapit frae the waxwarks." I was thinkin' that bein' strange and silly – if not a whole-made feel – ye'd no ken the ways o' the quicksan'! I shouted till warn ye, and then ran to drag ye aff, if need be. But God be thankit, be ye fule or only half-daft wi' yer vanity, that I was no that late!' and he reverently lifted his cap as he spoke.

Mr Markam was deeply touched and thankful for his escape from a horrible death; but the sting of the charge of vanity thus made once more against him came through his humility. He was about to reply angrily, when suddenly a great awe fell upon him as he remembered the warning words of the half-crazy letter-carrier: 'Meet thyself face to face, and repent ere the quicksand shall swallow thee!'

Here, too, he remembered the image of himself that he had seen and the sudden danger from the deadly quicksand that had followed. He was silent a full minute, and then said:

'My good fellow, I owe you my life!'

The answer came with reverence from the hardy fisherman, 'Na! Na! Ye owe that to God; but, as for me, I'm only too glad till be the humble instrument o' His mercy.'

'But you will let me thank you,' said Mr Markam, taking both the great hands of his deliverer in his and holding them tight. 'My heart is too full as yet, and my nerves are too much shaken to let me say much; but, believe me, I am very, very grateful!' It was quite evident that the poor old fellow was deeply touched, for the tears were running down his cheeks.

The fisherman said, with a rough but true courtesy:

'Ay, sir! thank me and ye will – if it'll do yer poor heart good. An' I'm thinking that if it were me I'd like to be thankful too. But, sir, as for me I need no thanks. I am glad, so I am!'

That Arthur Fernlee Markam was really thankful and grateful was shown practically later on. Within a week's time there sailed into Port Crooken the finest fishing smack that had ever been seen in the harbour of Peterhead. She was fully found with sails and gear of all kinds, and with nets of the best. Her master and men went away by the coach, after having left with the salmon-fisher's wife the papers which made her over to him.

As Mr Markam and the salmon-fisher walked together along the shore the former asked his companion not to mention the fact that he had been in such imminent danger, for that it would only distress his dear wife and children. He said that he would warn them all of the quicksand, and for that purpose he, then and there, asked questions about it till he felt that his information on the subject was complete. Before they parted he asked his companion if he had happened to see a second figure, dressed like himself, on the other rock as he had approached to succour him.

'Na! Na!' came the answer, 'there is nae sic another fule in these parts. Nor has there been since the time o' Jamie Fleeman – him that was fule to the Laird o' Udny. Why, mon! sic a heathenish dress as ye have on till ye has nae been seen in these pairts within the memory o' mon. An' I'm thinkin' that sic a dress never was for sittin' on the cauld rock, as ye done beyont. Mon! but do ye no fear the rheumatism or the lumbagy wi' floppin' doon on to the cauld stanes wi' yer bare flesh! I was thinking that it was daft ye waur when I see ye the mornin' doon be the port, but it's fule or eediot ye maun be for the like o' thot!' Mr Markam did not care to argue the point, and as they were now close to his own home he asked the salmon-fisher to have a glass of whisky – which he did – and they parted for the night. He took good care to warn all his family of the quicksand, telling them that he had himself been in some danger from it.

All that night he never slept. He heard the hours strike one after the other; but try how he would he could not get to sleep. Over and over again he went through the horrible episode of the quicksand, from the time that Saft Tammie had broken his habitual silence to preach to him of the sin of vanity and to warn him. The question kept ever arising in his mind – 'Am I then so vain as to be in the ranks of the foolish?' and the answer ever came in the words of the crazy prophet: ' "Vanity of vanities! All is vanity." Meet thyself face to face, and repent ere the quicksand shall swallow thee!' Somehow a feeling of doom began to shape itself in his mind that he would yet perish in that same quicksand, for there he had already met himself face to face.

In the gray of the morning he dozed off, but it was evident that he continued the subject in his dreams, for he was fully awakened by his wife, who said:

'Do sleep quietly! That blessed Highland suit has got on your brain. Don't talk in your sleep, if you can help it!' He was somehow conscious of a glad feeling, as if some terrible weight had been lifted from him, but he did not know any cause for it. He asked his wife what he had said in his sleep, and she answered:

'You said it often enough, goodness knows, for one to remember it – "Not face to face! I saw the eagle plume over the bald head! There is hope yet! Not face to face!" Go to sleep! Do!' And then he did go to sleep, for he seemed to realize that the prophecy of the crazy man had not yet been fulfilled. He had not met himself face to face – as yet at all events.

He was awakened early by a maid who came to tell him that

there was a fisherman at the door who wanted to see him. He dressed himself as quickly as he could – for he was not yet expert with the Highland dress – and hurried down, not wishing to keep the salmon-fisher waiting. He was surprised and not altogether pleased to find that his visitor was none other than Saft Tammie, who at once opened fire on him:

'I maun gang awa' t' the post; but I thocht that I would waste an hour on ye, and ca' roond just to see if ye waur still that fou wi' vanity as on the nicht gane by. An I see that ye've no learned the lesson. Well! the time is comin', sure eneucht! However I have all the time i' the marnins to my ain sel, so I'll aye look roond jist till see how ye gang yer ain gait to the quicksan', and then to the de'il! I'm aff till ma wark the noo!' And he went straightway, leaving Mr Markam considerably vexed, for the maids within earshot were vainly trying to conceal their giggles. He had fairly made up his mind to wear on that day ordinary clothes, but the visit of Saft Tammie reversed his decision. He would show them all that he was not a coward, and he would go on as he had begun – come what might. When he came to breakfast in full martial panoply the children, one and all, held down their heads and the backs of their necks became very red indeed. As, however, none of them laughed – except Titus, the youngest boy, who was seized with a fit of hysterical choking and was promptly banished from the room – he could not reprove them, but began to break his egg with a sternly determined air. It was unfortunate that as his wife was handing him a cup of tea one of the buttons of his sleeve caught in the lace of her morning wrapper, with the result that the hot tea was spilt over his bare knees. Not unnaturally, he made use of a swear word, whereupon his wife, somewhat nettled, spoke out:

'Well, Arthur, if you will make such an idiot of yourself with that ridiculous costume what else can you expect? You are not accustomed to it – and you never will be!' In answer he began an indignant speech with: 'Madam!' but he got no further, for now that the subject was broached, Mrs Markam intended to have her say out. It was not a pleasant say, and, truth to tell, it was not said in a pleasant manner. A wife's manner seldom is pleasant when she undertakes to tell what she considers 'truths' to her husband. The result was that Arthur Fernlee Markam undertook, then and there, that during his stay in Scotland he would wear no other costume than the one she abused. Woman-like his wife had the last word – given in this case with tears:

'Very well, Arthur! Of course you will do as you choose. Make me as ridiculous as you can, and spoil the poor girls' chances in life. Young men don't seem to care, as a general rule, for an idiot father-in-law! But I warn you that your vanity will some day get a rude shock – if indeed you are not before then in an asylum or dead!'

It was manifest after a few days that Mr Markam would have to take the major part of his outdoor exercise by himself. The girls now and again took a walk with him, chiefly in the early morning or late at night, or on a wet day when there would be no one about; they professed to be willing to go at all times, but somehow something always seemed to occur to prevent it. The boys could never be found at all on such occasions, and as to Mrs Markam she sternly refused to go out with him on any consideration so long as he should continue to make a fool of himself. On the Sunday he dressed himself in his habitual broadcloth, for he rightly felt that church was not a place for angry feelings; but on Monday morning he resumed his Highland garb. By this time he would have given a good deal if he had never thought of the dress, but his British obstinacy was strong, and he would not give in. Saft Tammie called at his house every morning, and, not being able to see him nor to have any message taken to him, used to call back in the afternoon when the letter-bag had been delivered and watched for his going out. On such occasions he never failed to warn him against his vanity in the same words which he had used at the first. Before many days were over Mr Markam had come to look upon him as little short of a scourge.

By the time the week was out the enforced partial solitude, the constant chagrin, and the never-ending brooding which was thus engendered, began to make Mr Markam quite ill. He was too proud to take any of his family into his confidence, since they had in his view treated him very badly. Then he did not sleep well at night, and when he did sleep he had constantly bad dreams. Merely to assure himself that his pluck was not failing him he made it a practice to visit the quicksand at least once every day; he hardly ever failed to go there the last thing at night. It was perhaps this habit that wrought the quicksand with its terrible experience so perpetually into his dreams. More and more vivid these became, till on waking at times he could hardly realise that he had not been actually in the flesh to visit the fatal spot. He sometimes thought that he might have been walking in his sleep.

One night his dream was so vivid that when he awoke he could not believe that it had only been a dream. He shut his eyes again and again, but each time the vision, if it was a vision, or the reality, if it was a reality, would rise before him. The moon was shining full and yellow over the quicksand as he approached it; he could see the expanse of light shaken and disturbed and full of black shadows as the liquid sand quivered and trembled and wrinkled and eddied as was its wont between its pauses of marble calm. As he drew close to it another figure came towards it from the opposite side with equal footsteps. He saw that it was his own figure, his very self, and in silent terror, compelled by what force he knew not, he advanced – charmed as the bird is by the snake, mesmerised or hypnotised, – to meet this other self. As he felt the yielding sand closing over him he awoke in the agony of death, trembling with fear, and, strange to say, with the silly man's prophecy seeming to sound in his ears: ' "Vanity of vanities! All is vanity!" See thyself and repent ere the quicksand swallow thee!'

So convinced was he that was no dream that he arose, early as it was, and dressing himself without disturbing his wife took his way to the shore. His heart fell when he came across a series of footsteps on the sands, which he at once recognised as his own. There was the same wide heel, the same square toe; he had no doubt now that he had actually been there, and half horrified, and half in a state of dreamy stupor, he followed the footsteps, and found them lost in the edge of the yielding quicksand. This gave him a terrible shock, for there were no return steps marked on the sand, and he felt that there was some dread mystery which he could not penetrate, and the penetration of which would, he feared, undo him.

In this state of affairs he took two wrong courses. Firstly he kept his trouble to himself, and, as none of his family had any clue to it, every innocent word or expression which they used supplied fuel to the consuming fire of his imagination. Secondly he began to read books professing to bear upon the mysteries of dreaming and of mental phenomena generally, with the result that every wild imagination of every crank or half-crazy philosopher became a living germ of unrest in the fertilising soil of his disordered brain. Thus negatively and positively all things began to work to a common end. Not the least of his disturbing causes was Saft Tammie, who had now become at certain times of the day a fixture at his gate. After a while, being interested in the previous state of this individual, he made inquiries regarding his past with the following result.

Saft Tammie was popularly believed to be the son of a laird in one of the counties round the Firth of Forth. He had been partially educated for the ministry, but for some cause which no one ever knew threw up his prospects suddenly, and, going to Peterhead in its days of whaling prosperity, had there taken service on a whaler. Here off and on he had remained for some years, getting gradually more and more silent in his habits, till finally his shipmates protested against so taciturn a mate, and he had found service amongst the fishing smacks of the northern fleet. He had worked for many years at the fishing with always the reputation of being 'a wee bit daft,' till at length he had gradually settled down at Crooken, where the laird, doubtless knowing something of his family history, had given him a job which practically made him a pensioner. The minister who gave the information finished thus:–

'It is a very strange thing, but the man seems to have some odd kind of gift. Whether it be that "second sight" which we Scotch people are so prone to believe in, or some other occult form of knowledge, I know not, but nothing of a disastrous tendency ever occurs in this place but the men with whom he lives are able to quote after the event some saying of his which certainly appears to have foretold it. He gets uneasy or excited – wakes up, in fact – when death is in the air!'

This did not in any way tend to lessen Mr Markam's concern, but on the contrary seemed to impress the prophecy more deeply on his mind. Of all the books which he had read on his new subject of study none interested him so much as a German one 'Die Döppleganger,' by Dr Heinrich von Aschenberg, formerly of Bonn. Here he learned for the first time of cases where men had led a double existence – each nature being quite apart from the other – the body being always a reality with one spirit, and a simulacrum with the other. Needless to say that Mr Markam realised this theory as exactly suiting his own case. The glimpse which he had of his own back the night of his escape from the quicksand – his own foot-marks disappearing into the quicksand with no return steps visible – the prophecy of Saft Tammie about his meeting himself and perishing in the quicksand – all lent aid to the conviction that he was in his own person an instance of the döppleganger.[10] Being then conscious of a double life he took steps to prove its existence to his own satisfaction. To this end on one night before going to bed he wrote his name in chalk on the soles of his shoes. That night he dreamed of the quicksand, and of his visiting it – dreamed so vividly that on waking in the gray of the dawn he could not believe that he had not been there. Arising, without disturbing his wife, he sought his shoes.

The chalk signatures were undisturbed! He dressed himself and stole out softly. This time the tide was in, so he crossed the dunes and struck the shore on the further side of the quicksand. There, oh, horror of horrors! he saw his own footprints dying into the abyss!

He went home a desperately sad man. It seemed incredible that he, an elderly commercial man, who had passed a long and uneventful life in the pursuit of business in the midst of roaring, practical London, should thus find himself enmeshed in mystery and horror, and that he should discover that he had two existences. He could not speak of his trouble even to his own wife, for well he knew that she would at once require the fullest particulars of that other life – the one which she did not know;

and that she would at the start not only imagine but charge him with all manner of infidelities on the head of it. And so his brooding grew deeper and deeper still. One evening – the tide then going out and the moon being at the full – he was sitting waiting for dinner when the maid announced that Saft Tammie was making a disturbance outside because he would not be let in to see him. He was very indignant, but did not like the maid to think that he had any fear on the subject, and so told her to bring him in. Tammie entered, walking more briskly than ever with his head up and a look of vigorous decision in the eyes that were so generally cast down. As soon as he entered he said:

'I have come to see ye once again – once again; and there ye sit, still just like a cockatoo on a pairch. Weel, mon, I forgie ye! Mind ye that, I forgie ye!' And without a word more he turned and walked out of the house, leaving the master in speechless indignation.

After dinner he determined to pay another visit to the quick-sand – he would not allow even to himself that he was afraid to go. And so, about nine o'clock, in full array, he marched to the beach, and passing over the sands sat on the skirt of the nearer rock. The full moon was behind him and its light lit up the bay so that its fringe of foam, the dark outline of the headland, and the stakes of the salmon-nets were all empha-sised. In the brilliant yellow glow the lights in the windows of Port Crooken and in those of the distant castle of the laird trembled like stars through the sky. For a long time he sat and drank in the beauty of the scene, and his soul seemed to feel a peace that it had not known for many days. All the pettiness and annoyance and silly fears of the past weeks seemed blotted out, and a new and holy calm took the vacant place. In this sweet and solemn mood he reviewed his late action calmly, and felt ashamed of himself for his vanity and for the obstinacy which had followed it. And then and there he made up his mind that the present would be the last time he would wear the costume which had estranged him from those whom he loved, and which had caused him so many hours and days of chagrin, vexation, and pain.

But almost as soon as he arrived at this conclusion another

voice seemed to speak within him and mockingly to ask him if he should ever get the chance to wear the suit again – that it was too late – he had chosen his course and must now abide the issue.

'It is not too late,' came the quick answer of his better self; and full of the thought, he rose up to go home and divest himself of the now hateful costume right away. He paused for one look at the beautiful scene. The light lay pale and mellow, softening every outline of rock and tree and house-top, and deepening the shadows into velvety-black, and lighting, as with a pale flame, the incoming tide, that now crept fringe-like across the flat waste of sand. Then he left the rock and stepped out for the shore.

But as he did so a frightful spasm of horror shook him, and for an instant the blood rushing to his head shut out all the light of the full moon. Once more he saw that fatal image of himself moving beyond the quicksand from the opposite rock to the shore. The shock was all the greater for the contrast with the spell of peace which he had just enjoyed; and, almost paralysed in every sense, he stood and watched the fatal vision and the wrinkly, crawling quicksand that seemed to writhe and yearn for something that lay between. There could be no mistake this time, for though the moon behind threw the face into shadow he could see there the same shaven cheeks as his own, and the small stubby moustache of a few weeks' growth. The light shone on the brilliant tartan, and on the eagle's plume. Even the bald space at one side of the Glengarry cap glistened, as did the Cairngorm brooch on the shoulder and the tops of the silver buttons. As he looked he felt his feet slightly sinking, for he was still near the edge of the belt of quicksand, and he stepped back. As he did so the other figure stepped forward, so that the space between them was preserved.

So the two stood facing each other, as though in some weird fascination; and in the rushing of the blood through his brain Markam seemed to hear the words of the prophecy: 'See thyself face to face, and repent ere the quicksand swallow thee.' He did stand face to face with himself, he had repented – and now he was sinking in the quicksand! The warning and prophecy were coming true!

Above him the seagulls screamed, circling round the fringe

of the incoming tide, and the sound being entirely mortal recalled him to himself. On the instant he stepped back a few quick steps, for as yet only his feet were merged in the soft sand. As he did so the other figure stepped forward, and coming within the deadly grip of the quicksand began to sink. It seemed to Markam that he was looking at himself going down to his doom, and on the instant the anguish of his soul found vent in a terrible cry. There was at the same instant a terrible cry from the other figure, and as Markam threw up his hands the figure did the same. With horror-struck eyes he saw him sink deeper into the quicksand; and then, impelled by what power he knew not, he advanced again towards the sand to meet his fate. But as his more forward foot began to sink he heard again the cries of the seagulls which seemed to restore his benumbed faculties. With a mighty effort he drew his foot out of the sand which seemed to clutch it, leaving his shoe behind, and then in sheer terror he turned and ran from the place, never stopping till his breath and strength failed him, and he sank half swooning on the grassy path through the sandhills.

Arthur Markam made up his mind not to tell his family of his terrible adventure – until at least such time as he should be complete master of himself. Now that the fatal double – his other self – had been engulfed in the quicksand he felt something like his old peace of mind.

  That night he slept soundly and did not dream at all; and in the morning was quite his old self. It really seemed as though his newer and worser self had disappeared for ever; and strangely enough Saft Tammie was absent from his post that morning and never appeared there again, but sat in his old place watching nothing, as of old, with lack-lustre eye. In accordance with his resolution he did not wear his Highland suit again, but one evening tied it up in a bundle, claymore, dirk and philibeg and all, and bringing it secretly with him threw it into the quicksand. With a feeling of intense pleasure he saw it sucked below the sand, which closed above it into marble smoothness. Then he went home and announced cheerily to his family assembled for evening prayers:

'Well! my dears, you will be glad to hear that I have abandoned my idea of wearing the Highland dress. I see now what a vain old fool I was and how ridiculous I made myself! You shall never see it again!'

'Where is it, father?' asked one of the girls, wishing to say something so that such a self-sacrificing announcement as her father's should not be passed in absolute silence. His answer was so sweetly given that the girl rose from her seat and came and kissed him. It was:

'In the quicksand, my dear! and I hope that my worser self is buried there along with it – for ever.'

The remainder of the summer was passed at Crooken with delight by all the family, and on his return to town Mr Markam had almost forgotten the whole of the incident of the quicksand, and all touching on it, when one day he got a letter from the MacCallum More which caused him much thought, though he said nothing of it to his family, and left it, for certain reasons, unanswered. It ran as follows:–

'The MacCallum More and Roderick MacDhu.
'The Scotch All-Wool Tartan Clothing Mart,
'Copthall Court, E.C.,
'30th September, 1892.

'DEAR SIR, – I trust you will pardon the liberty which I take in writing to you, but I am desirous of making an inquiry, and I am informed that you have been sojourning during the summer in Aberdeenshire (Scotland, NB). My partner, Mr Roderick MacDhu – as he appears for business reasons on our bill heads and in our advertisements, his real name being Emmanuel Moses Marks of London – went early last month to Scotland (NB) for a tour, but as I have only once heard from him, shortly after his departure, I am anxious lest any misfortune may have befallen him. As I have been unable to obtain any news of him on making all inquiries in my power, I venture to appeal to you. His letter was written in deep dejection of spirit, and mentioned that he feared a judgment had come upon him for wishing to appear as a Scotchman on Scottish soil, as he had one moonlight night shortly after his arrival seen his 'wraith.' He evidently alluded to the fact that before his departure he had procured for himself a Highland costume similar to that which we had the honour to supply to you, with which, as perhaps you will remember, he was much struck. He may, however, never have worn it, as he was, to my own knowledge, diffident about putting it on, and even went so far as to tell me that he would at first only venture to wear it late at night or very early in the morning, and then only in remote places, until such time as he should get accustomed to it. Unfortunately he did not advise me of his route, so that I am in complete ignorance of his whereabouts; and I venture to ask if you may have seen or heard of a Highland costume similar to your own having been seen anywhere in the neighbourhood in which I am told you have recently purchased the estate which you temporarily occupied. I shall not expect an answer to this letter unless you can give me some information regarding my friend and partner, so pray do not trouble yourself to reply unless there be cause. I am encouraged to think that he may have been in your neighbourhood as, though his letter is not dated, the envelope is marked with the postmark of 'Yellon,' which I find is in Aberdeenshire, and not far from the Mains of Crooken.

'I have the honour to be, dear sir,
  'Yours very respectfully,
    'JOSHUA SHEENY COHEN BENJAMIN.
     '(The MacCallum More.)'

THE LAIR OF
THE WHITE WORM

TO

MY FRIEND

BERTHA NICOLL[1]

WITH AFFECTIONATE ESTEEM

CONTENTS

CHAPTER I
ADAM SALTON ARRIVES

When Adam Salton arrived at the Great Eastern Hotel[1] he
found awaiting him a letter in the hand-writing of his grand-
uncle, Richard Salton, which he knew so well from the many
kind letters which he had received from him in West Australia.[2]
The first of them had been written less than a year before, in
which the old gentleman, who had in it claimed kinship, stated
that he had been unable to write earlier because until then he
did not know even of his existence, and it had taken him some
time to find out his address. The last, sent after him, had only
just arrived, and conveyed a most cordial invitation to stop
with him at Lesser Hill for as long a time as he could spare.
'Indeed,' his grand-uncle went on, 'I am in hopes that you will
make your permanent home here. You see, my dear boy, that
you and I are all that remain of our race, and it is but fitting
that you should succeed me when the time comes, which cannot
be long now. I am getting close on eighty years of age, and
though we have been a long-lived race, the span of life cannot
be prolonged beyond reasonable bounds. I am prepared to like
you and to make your home with me as happy a one as I can
achieve. So do come at once on receipt of this and find the
welcome I am waiting to give you. I send, in case such may
make matters easy for you, a banker's draft for £500. Come
soon, so that we may both of us have such happy days as are
still possible to us. For me this is all-important, as the sands of
my life are fast running out; but for you I trust there are many
happy years to come. If you are able to give me the pleasure of
seeing you, send me as soon as you can a letter telling me to
expect you. Then when you arrive at Plymouth or Southampton

(or whatever port you are bound for), send me a telegram, and I shall come to meet you at the earliest hour possible.'

On Monday, Adam Salton's letter arrived by the morning post, saying that he hoped to travel by the boat which carried it, and that he would therefore be ready to meet his grand-uncle so soon after the arrival of the letter in Mercia[3] as he should be able to reach London. 'I shall wait your arrival, sir, on the ship. By this means we may avoid any cross purposes.'

Mr Salton took it for granted that, no matter how fast he might travel, his guest would be awaiting him; so he gave instructions to have ready a carriage at seven the next morning to start for Stafford,[4] where he would catch the 11.40 for Euston, arriving at 2.10. Thence, driving to Waterloo, he could catch the 3 P.M., due at Southampton at 5.38. He would that night stay with his grand-nephew, either on the ship, which would be a new experience for him, or, if his guest should prefer it, at a hotel. In either case they would start in the early morning for home. He had given instructions to his bailiff to send the postillion carriage on to Southampton to be ready for their journey home, and to arrange for relays of his own horses to be sent on at once. He intended that his grand-nephew, who had been all his life in Australia, should see something of central England on the drive. He had plenty of young horses of his own breeding and breaking, and could depend on a journey memorable to the young man. The luggage would be sent on by rail the same day to Stafford, where one of his own carts would meet it. Mr Salton, during the journey to Southampton, often wondered if his grand-nephew was as much excited as he was at the idea of meeting so near a relation for the first time; and it was with an effort that he controlled himself. The endless railway lines and switches round the Southampton Docks fired his anxiety afresh.

As the train drew up on the dockside, he was getting his hand traps together, when the carriage door was wrenched open and a young man jumped in, saying as he came:

'How are you, uncle? I wanted to meet you as soon as I could, but everything is so strange to me that I didn't quite know what to do. However, I took chance that the railway people knew something of their own business – and here I am. I am glad to see you, sir. I have been dreaming of the happiness for thousands of miles; and now I find that the reality beats all the dreaming!' As he spoke the old man and the young one were heartily wringing each other's hands. He went on: 'I think I knew you the moment I set eyes on you. I am glad that that dream was only enhanced by the reality!'

The meeting so auspiciously begun proceeded well. Adam, seeing that the old man was interested in the novelty of the ship, suggested timidly that he should stay the night on board, and that he would himself be ready to start at any hour and go anywhere that the other suggested. This affectionate willingness to fall in with his own plans quite won the old man's heart. He warmly accepted the invitation, and at once they became not only on terms of affectionate relationship, but almost as old friends. The heart of the old man, which had been empty for so long, found a new delight. So, too, the young man found on landing in the old country a welcome and a surrounding in full harmony with all his dreams of such matters throughout all his wanderings and solitude, and the promise of a fresh and adventurous life. It was not long before the old man accepted him to full relationship by calling him by his Christian name. The other accepted the proffer with such heartiness that he was soon regarded as the future companion, almost the child, of his old age. After a long talk on affairs of interest, they retired to the cabin, which the elder was to share. Richard Salton, putting his hands affectionately on the boy's shoulders – though Adam was in his twenty-seventh year, he was a boy, and always would be, to his grand-uncle, – said warmly:

'I am so glad to find you as you are, my dear boy – just such a young man as I had always hoped for as a son in the days when I still had such hopes. However, dear boy, that is all past. But thank God there is a new life to begin for both of us. To you must be the larger part – but there is still time for some of it to be shared in common. I have waited till we should have seen each other to enter upon the subject; for I thought it better not to tie up your young life to my old one till we should have both sufficient personal knowledge to justify such a venture.

Now I can (so far as I am concerned) enter into it freely, since from the moment my eyes rested on you I saw my son – as he shall be, God willing – if he chooses such a course himself.'

'Indeed I do, sir – with all my heart!'

'Thank you, Adam, for that.' The old man's eyes filled and his voice trembled. Then, after a long silence between them, he went on: 'When I heard you were coming I made my will. It was well that your interests should be protected from that moment on. Here is the deed – keep it, Adam. All I have shall belong to you; and if love and good wishes or the memory of them can make life sweeter, yours shall be a happy one. And now, my dear boy, let us turn in. We start early in the morning and have a long drive before us. I hope you don't mind carriage driving? I was going to have sent down the old travelling carriage in which my grandfather, your great-grand-uncle, went to Court when William IV[5] was king. It is all right – they built well in those days – and it has been kept in perfect order. But I think I have done better: I have sent the carriage in which I travel myself. The horses are of my own breeding, and relays of them shall take us all the way. I hope you like horses? They have long been one of my greatest interests in life.'

'I love them, sir, and I am happy to say I have many of my own. My father gave me a horse farm for myself when I was sixteen. I devoted myself to it, and it has gone on. Before I came away, my steward gave me a memorandum that we have in my own places more than a thousand, nearly all good.'

'I am glad, my boy. Another link between us.'

'Just fancy what a delight it will be, sir, to see so much of middle England – and with you!'

'Thank you again, my boy. I shall tell you all about your future home and its surroundings as we go. We shall travel in old-fashioned state, I tell you. My grandfather always drove four-in-hand; and so shall we.'

'Oh, thanks, sir, thanks. May I take the ribbons[6] sometimes?'

'Whenever you choose, Adam. The team is your own. Every horse we use to-day is to be your own.'

'You are too generous, uncle!'

'Not at all. Only an old man's selfish pleasure. It is not every day that an heir to the old home comes back. And – oh, by the way . . . No, we had better turn in now – I shall tell you the rest in the morning.'

CHAPTER II
THE CASWALLS OF CASTRA REGIS

Mr Salton had all his life been an early riser, and necessarily an early waker. But early as he woke on the next morning, and although there was an excuse for not prolonging sleep in the constant whirr and rattle of the 'donkey' engine[1] winches of the great ship, when he waked he met the eyes of Adam fixed on him from his berth. His grand-nephew had given him the sofa, occupying the lower berth himself. The old man, despite his great strength and normal activity, was somewhat tired by his long journey of the day before and the prolonged and exciting interview which followed it. So he was glad to lie still and rest his body, whilst his mind was actively exercised in taking in all he could of his strange surroundings. Adam, too, after the pastoral habit to which he had been bred, woke with the dawn, if not before it, and was ready to enter on the experiences of the new day whenever it might suit his elder companion. It was little wonder, then, that, so soon as each realised the other's readiness, they simultaneously jumped up and began to dress. The steward had by previous instructions early breakfast prepared, and it was not long before they went down the gangway on shore in search of the carriage.

They found Mr Salton's bailiff waiting on the dock, and he brought them at once to where the carriage was waiting in the street. Richard Salton pointed out with pride to his young companion the suitability of the trap to every need of travel. It was a sort of double gig, excellently made, and with every appliance adapted for both speed and safety. To it were harnessed four fine, useful horses, with a postillion to each pair.

'See,' said the old man proudly, 'how it has all the luxuries

of useful travel – silence and isolation as well as speed. There
is nothing to obstruct the view of those travelling and no one
to overhear what they may say. I have used that trap for a
quarter of a century, and I never saw one more suitable for
travel. You shall test it shortly. We are going to drive through
the heart of England; and as we go I shall tell you what I was
speaking of last night. Our route is to be by Salisbury, Bath,
Bristol, Cheltenham, Worcester, Stafford;[2] and so home.'

After remaining silent a few minutes, what time he seemed
all eyes, for he perpetually ranged the whole circle of the horizon, Adam said:

'Has our journey to-day, sir, any special relation to what you
said last night that you wanted to tell me?'

'Not directly; but indirectly, everything.'

'Won't you tell me now – I see we cannot be overheard – and
if anything strikes you as we go along, just run it in. I shall
understand.'

So old Salton spoke:

'To begin at the beginning, Adam. That lecture of yours on
"The Romans in Britain" set me thinking – in addition to telling
me where you were. I wrote to you at once and asked you to
come home, for it struck me that if you were fond of historical
research – as seemed a fact – this was exactly the place for you,
in addition to its being the place of your own forbears. If you
could learn so much of the British Romans[3] so far away in West
Australia, where there cannot be even a tradition of them, what
might you not make of the same amount of study on the very
spot. Where we are going is in the real heart of the old kingdom
of Mercia, where there are traces of all the various nationalities
which made up the conglomerate which became Britain.'[4]

After a slight pause Adam said:

'I rather gathered that you had some more definite – more
personal reason for my hurrying. After all, history can keep –
except in the making!'

'Quite right, my boy. I had a reason such as you very wisely
guessed at. I was anxious for you to be here when a rather
important phase of our local history occurred.'

'What is that, if I may ask, sir?'

'Certainly. The great owner of all this part of the county – of several of the counties – is on his way home, and there will be a great home-coming, which you may care to see. The fact is, that for more than a century the various owners in the succession here, with the exception of a short time, lived abroad.'

'How is that, sir, if I may again ask?'

'By all means. That is why I wished you to be here – so that you might learn. We have a good stretch without incident before us till we get in sight of Salisbury, so I had better begin now:

'Our great house and estate in this part of the world is Castra Regis, the family seat of the Caswall family. The last owner who lived here was Edgar Caswall, great-grand-uncle of the man who is coming here – and he was the only man who stayed even the short time. His grandfather, also named Edgar – they keep the tradition of the family Christian name – quarrelled with his family and went to live abroad, not keeping up any relations, good or bad, with his relatives. His son was born and lived and died abroad. His son, the latest inheritor, was also born and lived abroad till he was over thirty, – his present age. This was the second line of absentees. The great-great-grandfather of the present Edgar also cut himself off from his family and went abroad, from which sojourn he never returned. The consequence has been that the great estate of Castra Regis has had no knowledge of its owner for six generations – covering more than a hundred years. It has been well administered, however, and no tenant or other connected with it has had anything to complain of. All the same, there has been much natural anxiety to see the new owner, and we are all excited about the event of his coming. Even I am, though I own my own estate, which, though adjacent, is quite apart from Castra Regis. – Here we are now in new ground for you. That is the spire of Salisbury Cathedral,[5] and when we leave that we shall be getting close to the old Roman county and you will naturally want your eyes. So we shall shortly have to keep our minds on old Mercia. However, you need not be disappointed. My old friend, Sir Nathaniel de Salis, who, like myself, is a freeholder near Castra Regis, though not on it – his estate, Doom Tower, is over the border of Derbyshire, on the Peak – is coming to stay with me for all the festivities to welcome Edgar Caswall. He is just the sort of man you will like. He is devoted to history, and is President of the Mercian Archæological Society. He knows more of our own part of the country, with its history and its people, than anyone else. I expect he will have arrived before us, and we three can have a long chat after dinner. He is also our local geologist and natural historian. So you and he will have many interests in common. Amongst other things he has a special knowledge of the Peak and its caverns, and knows all the old legends of the days when prehistoric times were vital.'

From this on till they came to Stafford, Adam's eyes were in constant employment on matters of the road; and it was not till Salton had declared that they had now entered on the last stage of their journey that he referred back to Sir Nathaniel's coming.

As the dusk was closing down they drove on to Lesser Hill, Mr Salton's house. It was now too dark to see detail of their surrounding. Adam could just see that it was on the top of a hill, not quite so high as that which was covered by the Castle, on whose tower flew the flag, and which was all ablaze with moving lights, manifestly used in the preparations for the festivities on the morrow. So Adam deferred his curiosity till daylight. His grand-uncle was met at the door by a fine old man, who said as he greeted him warmly:

'I came over early as you wished me to. I suppose this is your grand-nephew – I am glad to meet you, Mr Adam Salton. I am Nathaniel de Salis, and your uncle is the oldest of my friends.'

Adam, from the moment of their eyes meeting, felt as if they were already old friends. The meeting was a new note of welcome to those that had already sounded in his ears.

The cordiality with which Sir Nathaniel and Adam met made the imparting of the former's information easy both to speak and to hear. Sir Nathaniel was quite a clever old man of the world, who had travelled much and within a certain area studied deeply. He was a brilliant conversationalist, as was to be expected from a successful diplomatist, even under unstimulating conditions. But he had been touched and to a certain extent fired by the younger man's evident admiration and willingness to learn from him. Accordingly the conversation, which began on the most friendly basis, soon warmed to an interest above proof as the old man spoke of it next day to Richard Salton. He knew already that his old friend wanted his grand-nephew to learn all he could of the subject in hand, and so had during his journey from the Peak put his thoughts in sequence for narration and explanation. Accordingly, Adam had only to listen and he must learn much that he wanted to know. When dinner was over and the servants had withdrawn, leaving the three men at their wine, Sir Nathaniel began:

'I gather from your uncle – by the way, I suppose we had better speak of you as uncle and nephew, instead of going into exact relationship? In fact, your uncle is so old and dear a friend, that, with your permission, I shall drop formality with you altogether and speak of you and to you as Adam, as though you were his son.'

'I would wish, sir,' answered the young man, 'nothing better in the world!'

The answer warmed the hearts of both the old men who heard. All the men felt touched, but, with the usual avoidance of Englishmen of emotional subjects personal to themselves, they instinctively moved from the previous question. Sir Nathaniel took the lead:

'I understand, Adam, that your uncle has posted you regarding the relationships of the Caswall family?'

'Partly, sir; but I understood that I was to hear minuter details from you – if you would be so good.'

'I shall be delighted to tell you anything so far as my knowledge goes. Well, we have to remember, in connection with the events of to-morrow, that not less than ten generations of that family are involved. And I really believe that for a true understanding of the family ramifications you cannot begin better than having the list as a basis. Everything which we may consider as we go along will then take its natural place without extra trouble. The present branch of affairs begins only about something more than a hundred and fifty years ago. Later we may have to go further back, for the history of the Caswall family is coeval with that of England – we need not trouble ourselves with dates; the facts will be more easily grasped in a general way.

'The first Caswall in our immediate record is Edgar, who was head of the family and owner of the estate, who came into his kingdom just about the time that George III did. He had one son of about twenty-four. There was a violent quarrel between the two. No one of this generation has any idea of the cause of it; but, considering the family characteristics, we may take it for granted that though it was deep and violent, it was on the surface trivial.

'The result of the quarrel was that the son left the house without approaching a reconciliation or without even telling his father where he was going. He never came back to the house again. A few years after, he died without having in the meantime exchanged a word or a letter with his father. He married abroad and left one son, who seems to have been brought up in ignorance of all belonging to him. The gulf between them appears to have been unbridgeable; for in time this son married and in turn had a son, but neither joy nor sorrow brought the sundered together. Under such conditions no *rapprochement* was to be looked for, and an utter indifference, founded at best on ignorance, took the place of family affection – even on community of interests. It was only due to the watchfulness of the lawyers that the birth and death of a new heir was ever made known. In time a second son appeared, but without any effect of friendly advance.

'At last there arose a dim hope of some cessation of hostility, for though none of the separated made mention of the fact – knowledge of which was again due to the lawyers – a son was born to this youngest member of the voluntary exiles – the great-grandson of the Edgar whose son had left him. After this the family interest merely rested on heirship of the estate – any outside interest being submerged in the fact of a daughter being born to the grandson of the first Edgar. Some twenty years afterwards, the interest flickered up when it was made known – again through the lawyers – that the last two born had been married, thus shutting off any possibility of disputed heirship. As no other child had been born to any of the newer generations in the intervening twenty years, all hopes of heritage were now centred in the son of this last couple – the heir whose home-coming we are to celebrate to-morrow. The elder generations had all died away, and there were no collaterals, so there was no possibility of the heirship being disputed.

'Now, it will be well for you to bear in mind the prevailing characteristics of this race. These were well preserved and unchanging; one and all they are the same: cold, selfish, dominant, reckless of consequences in pursuit of their own will. It was not that they did not keep faith, though that was a matter which gave them little concern, but that they took care to think beforehand of what they should do in order to gain their ends. If they should make a mistake someone else should bear the burthen of it. This was so perpetually recurrent that it seemed to be a part of a fixed policy. It was no wonder indeed that whatever changes took place they were always ensured in their own possessions. They were absolutely of cold, hard nature. Not one of them – so far as we have any knowledge – was ever known to be touched by the softer sentiments, to swerve from his purpose, or hold his hand in obedience to the dictates of his heart. Part of this was due to their dominant, masterful nature. The aquiline features which marked them seemed to justify every personal harshness. The pictures and effigies of them all show their adherence to the early Roman type. Their eyes were full; their hair, of raven blackness, grew thick and close and curly.[6] Their figures were massive and typical of strength.

'The thick black hair growing low down on the neck told of vast physical strength and endurance. But the most remarkable characteristic is the eyes. Black, piercing, almost unendurable, they seem to contain in themselves a remarkable will power which there is no gainsaying. It is a power that is partly racial and partly individual: a power impregnated with some mysterious quality, partly hypnotic, partly mesmeric,[7] which seems to take away from eyes that meet them all power of resistance, nay, deeper, all power of wishing to resist. With eyes like those set in that aquiline, all-commanding face one would need to be strong indeed to even think of resisting the inflexible will that lay beyond. Even the habit and the exercise of power which they implied was a danger to anyone who was conscious of a weakness on his own part.

'You may think, Adam, that all this is imagination on my part, especially as I have never seen any belonging to the generation I have spoken of. So it is. But imagination based on deep study. I have made use of all I know or can surmise logically regarding this strange race. And with this data, however received, I have thought out logical results, correcting, amending, intensifying accepted conclusions, till at times I see as though various members of the race had always been under my observation – that they are even under it still. With such strange compelling qualities, is it any wonder that there is abroad an idea that in the race there is some demoniac possession, which tends to a more definite belief that certain individuals have in the past sold themselves to the Devil? The Devil, I may say in this connection, is seldom mentioned *in propria persona*,[8] but generally under some accepted guise, "The Powers of Evil," "The Enemy of Mankind," "The Prince of the Air," etc. I don't know what it is in other places; but along this eastern coast it is not considered polite to speak the truth plainly, baldly, in such matters, but to cover up the idea with a veil of obscurity in which safety or security may be hidden.

'But I think we had better go to bed now. We have a lot to go through to-morrow, and I want you to have your brain clear, and all your susceptibilities fresh. Moreover, I want you to come with me in an early walk in which we may notice, whilst the matter is fresh in our minds, the peculiar disposition of this place – not merely your grandfather's estate, but the lie of the country around it. There are many things on which we may seek – and perhaps find – enlightenment. The more we know at the start, the more things which may come into our view will develop themselves.'

So they all went off to bed.

CHAPTER III
DIANA'S GROVE

Curiosity took Adam Salton out of bed in the early morning, but when he had dressed and gone downstairs, he found that, early as he was, Sir Nathaniel de Salis was ahead of him. The old gentleman was quite prepared for a long walk if necessary, and they started at once. Sir Nathaniel, without speaking, led the way a little to the east down the hill. When they had descended and risen again, they found themselves on the eastern brink of a steep hill. It was of lesser height than that on which the Castle was seated; but it was so placed that it commanded the various hills that crowned the ridge. All along the ridge the rock cropped out, bare and bleak, but broken in rough formed natural castellation. The form of the ridge was a segment of a circle, with the higher points inland to the west. In the centre rose the Castle on the highest point of all. Between the various rocky excrescences were groups of trees of various sizes and heights, amongst some of which were what in the early morning light looked like ruins. These – whatever they were – were of massive grey stone, probably limestone rudely cut – if indeed they were not shaped naturally. The largest of these clumps was of oak trees of great age. They crossed the least of the hills, that which lay to the eastward. The fall of the ground was steep all along the ridge, so steep that here and there both trees and rocks and buildings seemed to overhang the level plain far below. Through this level ran many streams, and there was a number of blue pools, where was evidently fairly deep water.

Sir Nathaniel stopped and looked all around him, as though to lose nothing of the effect. The sun had climbed the eastern sky and was making all details clear. Sir Nathaniel pointed all round him with a sweeping gesture, as though calling Adam's attention to the wideness of the view. He did so so rapidly as to suggest that he wished the other to take, in the first survey, rather the *coup d'œil*[1] than any detail. Having done so, he covered the ground in a similar way, but more slowly, as though inviting attention to detail. Adam was a willing and attentive pupil, and followed his motions exactly, missing – or trying to miss – nothing. When they had made the rough survey round the whole sweep of the eastern horizon, Sir Nathaniel spoke:

'I have brought you here, Adam, because it seems to me that this is the spot on which to begin our investigations. You have now in front of you almost the whole of the ancient kingdom of Mercia. In fact, we see, theoretically if not practically, the whole of it except that furthest part which is covered by the Welsh Marches and those parts which are hidden from where we stand by the high ground of the immediate west. We can see – again theoretically if not practically – the whole of the eastern bound of the kingdom which ran south from the Humber to the Wash.[2] I want you to bear in mind the trend of the ground, for some time, sooner or later, we shall do well to have it in our mind's eye when we are considering the ancient traditions and even superstitions and are trying to find the *rationale* of them. I think we had better not try to differentiate between these, but let them naturally take their places as we go on. Each legend, each superstition which we receive will help in the understanding and possible elucidation of the others. And as all such have a local basis, we can come closer to the truth – or the probability – by knowing the local conditions as we go along. It will help us to bring to our aid even such geological truth as we may have between us. For instance, the building materials used in various ages can afford their own lessons to understanding eyes. The very heights and shapes and materials of these hills, nay, even of the wide plain that lies between us and the sea, have in themselves the materials of enlightening books.'

'For instance, sir?' said Adam, venturing a question.

'Well, for instance, look at those hills which surround the main one where the site for the Castle was wisely chosen –

on the highest ground. Take the others. There is something ostensible in each of them, and in all probability something unseen and unproved, but to be imagined, also.'

'For instance?' continued Adam.

'Let us take them *seriatim*.[3] That to the east, where the trees are, lower down. That was once the location of a Roman temple, possibly founded on a pre-existing Druidical[4] one. Its name implies the former, and the grove of ancient oaks suggests the latter.'

'Please explain.'

'The old name translated means "Diana's Grove." Then the next one higher than it, but just beyond it, is called "*Mercy*." In all probability a corruption or perhaps a familiarisation of the word *Mercia* with a Roman pun included. We learn from early manuscripts that the place was called *Vilula Misericordiæ*.[5] It was originally a nunnery founded by Queen Bertha, but done away with by King Penda, the reactionary to Paganism after St Augustine.[6] Then comes your uncle's place – Lesser Hill. Though it is so close to the Castle, it is not connected with it. It is a freehold, and, so far as we know, of equal age. It has always belonged to your family.'

'Then there only remains the Castle!'

'That is all; but its history contains the histories of all the others – in fact, the whole history of early England.'

Sir Nathaniel, seeing the expectant look on Adam's face, went on:

'The history of the Castle has no beginning so far as we know. The furthest records or surmises or inferences simply accept it as existing. Some of these – guesses let us call them – seem to show that there was some sort of structure there when the Romans came, therefore it must have been a place of importance in Druid times – if indeed that was the beginning. Naturally the Romans accepted it, as they did everything of the kind that was, or might be, useful. The change is shown or inferred in the name Castra. It was the highest protected ground, and so naturally became the most important of their camps. A study of the map will show you that it must have been a most important strategic centre. It both protected the advances already made to the north, and it helped to dominate the sea coast to the east. It sheltered the western marches, beyond which lay savage Wales[7] – and danger. It provided a means of getting to the Severn, round which lay the great Roman roads then coming into existence, and made possible the great waterway to the heart of England – through the Severn and its tributaries. And it brought the east and the west together by the swiftest and easiest ways known to those times. And, finally, it provided means of descent on London and all the expanse of country watered by the Thames.

'With such a centre, already known and organised, we can easily see that each fresh wave of invasion – the Angles, the Saxons, the Danes, and the Normans[8] – found it a desirable possession and so ensured its upholding. In the earlier centuries it was merely a vantage ground. But when the victorious Romans brought with them the heavy solid fortifications impregnable to the weapons of the time, its commanding position alone ensured its adequate building and equipment. Then it was that the fortified camp of the Cæsars developed into the castle of the king. As we are as yet entirely ignorant of even the names of the first kings of Mercia, no historian has been able to even guess what king made it his ultimate defence; and I suppose we shall never know now. In process of time, as the arts of war developed, it increased in size and strength, and although recorded details are lacking, the history is written in not merely the stone of its building, but is inferred in the changes of structure. Then the general sweeping changes which followed the Norman Conquest wiped out all lesser records than its own. To-day we must accept it as one of the earliest castles of the Conquest, probably not later than the time of Henry I.[9] Roman and Norman were both wise in their retention of places of approved strength or utility. So it was that these surrounding heights, already established and to a certain extent proved, were retained. Indeed, such characteristics as already pertained to them were preserved and to-day afford to us lessons regarding things which have themselves long since passed away.

'So much for the fortified heights; but the hollows too have their own story. But how the time passes! We must hurry home, or else your uncle will wonder what has become of us.' As he spoke he was hurrying with long steps towards Lesser Hill, and Adam was furtively running to be able to keep up with him. When they had arrived close to the house, Sir Nathaniel said:

'I am sorry to cut short our interesting conversation. But it will be only postponed. I want to tell you, and I am sure you want to know, all that I know of this place. And, if I am not mistaken, our next instalment of history will be even more interesting than the first.'

CHAPTER IV
THE LADY
ARABELLA MARCH

Breakfast had just begun when Mr Salton said:

'Now, there is no hurry, but so soon as you are both ready we shall start. I want to take you first to see a remarkable relic of Mercia, and then we shall go down to Liverpool through what is called "The Great Vale of Cheshire." You may be disappointed, but take care not to prepare your mind' – this to Adam – 'for anything stupendous or heroic. You would not think the place you are going through was a vale at all, unless you were told it beforehand, and had confidence in the veracity of the teller. We should get to the Landing Stage in time to meet the *West African*. We ought to meet Mr Caswall as he comes ashore. We want to do him honour – and, besides, it will be more pleasant to have the introductions over before we go to his *fête* at the Castle.'

The carriage was ready, the same as was used the previous day. The postillions, too, were the same, but there were two pairs of different horses – magnificent animals, and keen for work. Breakfast was soon over, and they shortly took their places. The postillions had their orders, and they were soon on their way at an exhilarating pace.

Presently, in obedience to Mr Salton's signal, the carriage drew up near Stone,[1] opposite a great heap of stones by the wayside. 'Here,' he said, 'is something that you of all men should not pass by unnoticed. That heap of stones brings us at once to the dawn of the Anglian kingdom. It was begun more than a thousand years ago, in the latter part of the seventh century, in memory of a murder. Wulfere, King of Mercia, nephew of Penda, here murdered his two sons for embracing

Christianity.[2] As was the custom of the time, each passer-by added a stone to the memorial heap. Penda represented heathen reaction after St Augustine's mission. Sir Nathaniel can tell you as much as you want about this, and put you, if you wish, on the track of such accurate knowledge as there is.'

Whilst they were looking at the heap of stones, they noticed that another carriage had drawn up beside them, and the passenger – there was only one – was regarding them curiously. The carriage was an old heavy travelling one, with arms blazoned on it gorgeously. The coronet was an earl's, and there were many quarterings. Seeing then the occupant was a lady, the men took off their hats. The occupant spoke:

'How do you do, Sir Nathaniel? How do you do, Mr Salton? I hope none of you has met with any accident. Look at me!'

As she spoke she pointed where one of the heavy springs was broken across, the broken metal showing bright. Adam spoke up at once:

'Oh, that will be soon put right.'

'Soon? I shall have to wait till we get to Wolverhampton. There is no one near who can mend a break like that.'

'I can.'

'You!' She looked incredulously at the dapper young gentleman who spoke. 'You – why, it's a workman's job.'

'All right, I am a workman – though that is not the only sort of work I do. Let me explain. I am an Australian, and, as we have to move about fast, we are all trained to farriery and such mechanics as come into travel – and I am quite at your service.'

She said sweetly: 'I hardly know how to thank you for your kindness, of which I gladly avail myself. I don't know what else I can do. My father is Lord Lieutenant of the County,[3] and he asked me to take his carriage – he is abroad himself – and meet Mr Caswall of Castra Regis, who arrives home from Africa to-day. It is a notable home-coming; his predecessor in the event made his entry more than a century ago, and all the countryside want to do him honour.' She looked at the old men and quickly made up her mind as to the identity of the stranger. 'You must be Mr Salton – Mr Adam Salton of Lesser Hill. I am Lady Arabella March of Diana's Grove.' As she spoke she turned slightly to Mr Salton, who took the hint and made a formal introduction.

So soon as this was done, Adam took some tools from his uncle's carriage, and at once began work on the broken spring. He was an expert workman, and the breach was soon made good. Adam was gathering the tools which he had been using, and which, after the manner of all workmen, had been scattered about, when he noticed that several black snakes[4] had crawled out from the heap of stones and were gathering round him. This naturally occupied his mind, and he was not thinking of anything else when he noticed Lady Arabella, who had opened the door of the carriage, slip from it with a quick gliding motion. She was already among the snakes when he called out to warn her. But there seemed to be no need of warning. The snakes had turned and were wriggling back to the mound as quickly as they could. He laughed to himself behind his teeth as he whispered, 'No need to fear there. They seem much more afraid of her than she of them.' All the same he began to beat on the ground with a stick which was lying close to him, with the instinct of one used to such vermin. In an instant he was alone beside the mound with Lady Arabella, who appeared quite unconcerned at the incident. Then he took a long look at her. She was certainly good to look at in herself, and her dress alone was sufficient to attract attention. She was clad in some kind of soft white stuff, which clung close to her form, showing to the full every movement of her sinuous figure.[5] She was tall and exceedingly thin. Her eyes appeared to be weak, for she wore large spectacles which seemed to be of green glass. Certainly in the centre they had the effect of making her naturally piercing eyes of a vivid green. She wore a close-fitting cap of some fine fur of dazzling white. Coiled round her white throat was a large necklace of emeralds, whose profusion of colour quite outshone the green of her spectacles – even when the sun shone on them. Her voice was very peculiar, very low and sweet, and so soft that the dominant note was of sibilation. Her hands, too, were peculiar – long, flexible, white, with a strange movement as of waving gently to and fro.

She appeared quite at ease, and, after thanking Adam, said

that if any of his uncle's party were going to Liverpool she
would be most happy to join forces. She added cordially:

'Whilst you are staying here, Mr Salton, you must look on
the grounds of Diana's Grove as your own, so that you may
come and go just as you do in Lesser Hill. There are some fine
views and not a few natural curiosities which are sure to interest
you. There are some views in the twilight which are, they say,
unique. And if you are a student of natural history – specially
of an earlier kind, when the world was younger – you shall not
have your labour of discovery in vain.'

The heartiness with which she spoke and warmth of her
words – not of her manner, which was abnormally cold and
distant – repelled him, made him suspicious. He felt as if he
was naturally standing on guard. In the meantime both his
uncle and Sir Nathaniel had thanked her for the invitation – of
which, however, they said they were unable to avail themselves.
Adam had a sort of suspicion that though she answered regret-
fully, she was in reality relieved. When he had got into the
carriage with the two old men and they had driven off, he was
not surprised when Sir Nathaniel said:

'I could not but feel that she was glad to be rid of us. She can
play her game better alone!'

'What is her game, sir?' asked Adam unthinkingly, but the
old man answered without comment:

'All the county knows it, my boy. Caswall is a very rich man.
Her husband was rich when she married him – or seemed to
be. When he committed suicide it was found that he had nothing
at all. Her father has a great position and a great estate – on
paper. But the latter is mortgaged up to the hilt, and is held in
male tail only, so that her only hope is in a rich marriage. I
suppose I need not draw any conclusion. You can do that as
well as I can.'

Adam remained silent nearly all the time they were travelling
through the alleged Vale of Cheshire. He thought much during
that journey and came to several conclusions, though his lips
were unmoved. One of these conclusions was that he would be
very careful about paying any attention to Lady Arabella. He
was himself a rich man, how rich not even his uncle had the

least idea, and would have been surprised had he known. The other resolution was that he would be very careful how he went moonlighting in Diana's Grove, especially if he were un-attended.

At Liverpool they went aboard the *West African*, which had just come to the landing-stage. There his uncle introduced himself to Mr Caswall, and followed this up by introducing Sir Nathaniel and then Adam. The new-comer received them all very graciously, and said what a pleasure it was on coming home after so long an absence of his family from their old seat, and hoped they would see much of each other in the future. Adam was much pleased at the warmth of the reception; but he could not avoid a feeling of repugnance at the man's face. He was trying hard to overcome this when a diversion was caused by the arrival of Lady Arabella. The diversion was welcome to all; the two Saltons and Sir Nathaniel were shocked at Caswall's face – so hard, so ruthless, so selfish, so dominant. 'God help any,' was the common thought, 'who is under the domination of such a one!'

But presently his African servant approached him, and at once their thoughts changed to a larger toleration. For by comparison with this man his face seemed to have a certain nobility hitherto lacking. Caswall looked indeed a savage – but a cultured savage. In him were traces of the softening civilisation of ages – of some of the higher instincts and education of man, no matter how rudimentary these might be. But the face of Oolanga, as his master at once called him, was pure pristine, unreformed, unsoftened savage, with inherent in it all the hideous possibilities of a lost, devil-ridden child of the forest and the swamp – the lowest and most loathsome of all created things which were in some form ostensibly human.

CHAPTER V

HOME-COMING

As Lady Arabella and Oolanga arrived almost simultaneously, Adam began to surmise what effect their appearance would have on each other. They were exactly opposite in every quality of appearance, and, so far as he could judge, of mental or moral gifts or traits. The girl of the Caucasian type, beautiful, Saxon blonde, with a complexion of milk and roses, high-bred, clever, serene of nature. The other negroid of the lowest type; hideously ugly, with the animal instincts developed as in the lowest brutes; cruel, wanting in all the mental and moral faculties – in fact, so brutal as to be hardly human.[1] If Adam expected her to show any repugnance he was disappointed. If anything, her pride heightened into disdain. She seemed as if she would not – could not – condescend to exhibit any concern or interest in such a creature. On the other hand, his bearing was such as in itself to justify her pride. He treated her not merely as a slave treats his master, but as a worshipper would treat a deity.[2] He knelt before her with his hands outstretched and his forehead in the dust. So long as she remained he did not move; it was only when she went over to Caswall and spoke that he relaxed his attitude of devotion and simply stood by respectfully. His dress, which was a grotesque mixture, more than ever seemed absurd. He had on evening dress of an ill cut, an abnormally efflorescent white shirt with exaggerated cuffs and collar, all holding mock jewels of various colours. In his nose was a silver ring, and in his ears large ornaments composed of trophies of teeth. He wore a tall hat, which had once been of a shape of *some* kind, with a band of gold lace. Altogether he looked like a horrible distortion of a gentleman's servant. All those around grinned or openly jeered. One of the stewards, who was carrying some of Mr Caswall's lighter luggage and making himself important, after the manner of stewards to debarking passengers, was attentive even to him.

Adam spoke to his own bailiff, Davenport, who was standing by, having arrived with the bailiff of Lesser Hill, who had followed Mr Salton in his own pony trap. As he spoke he pointed to the attentive ship's steward, and presently the two men were conversing.

After a little time Mr Salton said to Adam:

'I think we ought to be moving. I have some things to do in Liverpool, and I am sure that both Mr Caswall and Lady Arabella would like to get under weigh for Castra Regis.' To which said Adam:

'I too, sir, would like to do something. I want to find out where Ross, the animal merchant, lives – you know, the local Jamrach.[3] I want to take a small animal home with me, if you don't mind. He is only a little thing, and will be no trouble.'

'Of course not, my boy. Whatever you like. What kind of animal is it that you want?'

'A mongoose.'

'A mongoose! What on earth do you want it for?'

'To kill snakes.'

'Good!' The old man remembered the mound at Stone. No explanation was needed.

Ross, the animal merchant, had had dealings with Adam chiefly in the way of mongooses. When he heard what was wanted he asked:

'Do you want something special, or will an ordinary mongoose do?'

'Well, of course I want a good one. But I see no need for anything special. It is for ordinary use.'

'I can let you have a choice of ordinary ones. I only asked because I have in stock a very special one which I got lately from Nepaul. He has a record of his own. He killed a king cobra that had been seen in the Rajah's garden. But I don't suppose we have any snakes of the kind in this cold climate – I daresay an ordinary one will do.'

The bargain was effected. When Adam was coming away with the box under his arm, he said to Ross:

'I don't know anything of the snakes here. I wouldn't have believed there are any at all, only I saw some to-day. I shall try this mongoose, and if he is any good I shall be glad to keep him. But don't part with the other yet. I shall send you word if I want him.'

When Adam got back to the carriage, carefully carrying the box with the mongoose, Sir Nathaniel said:

'Hullo! what have you got there?'

'A mongoose.'

'What for?'

'To kill snakes!'

Sir Nathaniel laughed. 'Well, even as yet, it seems you have come to the right place.'

'How do you mean? Why "as yet"?'

'Remember the snakes yesterday. But that is only a beginning.'

'A beginning! How so?'

'That, my boy, belongs to the second section of our inquiry. It will have a direct bearing on it.'

'You mean about the legends?'

'We shall begin on them.'

'And then?'

'I heard Lady Arabella's invitation to you to come to Diana's Grove in the twilight.'

'Well, what on earth has that got to do with it?'

'Nothing directly that I know of. But we shall see.'

Adam waited, and the old man went on:

'Have you by any chance heard the other name which was given long ago to that place?'

'No, sir.'

'It was called – Look here, this subject wants a lot of talking over and listening. Suppose we wait till after dinner to-night, when we shall be alone and shall have lots of time before us.'

'All right, sir. Let us wait!' Adam was filled with curiosity, but he thought it better not to hurry matters. All would come in good time.

His attention was then claimed by the events of the day. Shortly the Lesser Hill party set out for Castra Regis, and for the time he thought no more of Diana's Grove or of what mysteries it had contained – or might still contain.

The guests were crowding in and special places were marked for important guests. Some little time was occupied in finding their seats. Adam, seeing so many persons of varied degree, looked round for Lady Arabella, but could not locate her. It was only when he saw the old-fashioned travelling carriage approach and heard the sound of cheering which went with it, that he realised that Edgar Caswall had arrived. Then, on looking more closely, he saw that Lady Arabella, dressed as he had seen her last, was seated beside him. When the carriage drew up at the great flight of steps, the host jumped down and gave her his hand and led her up to the great daïs table, and placed her in the seat to the right of that kept for himself.

It was evident to all that she was the chief guest at the festivities. It was not long before the seats on the daïs were filled and the tenants and guests of lesser importance had occupied all the coigns of vantage[4] not reserved. The order of the day had been carefully arranged by the committee. There were some speeches, happily neither many nor long; and then festivities were suspended till the time for feasting had arrived. In the interval Caswall walked among his guests, speaking to all in a friendly manner and expressing a general welcome. The other guests came down from the daïs and followed his example, so there was unceremonious meeting and greeting between gentle and simple. Adam Salton naturally followed with his eyes all that went on within their scope, taking note of all who seemed to afford any interest. He was young and a man and a stranger from a far distance; so on all these accounts he naturally took stock rather of the women than of the men, and of these, those who were young and attractive. There were lots of pretty girls among the crowd who had seemingly no dislike to be looked at; and Adam, who was a handsome young man and well set up, got his full share of admiring glances. These did not concern him much, and he remained unmoved until there came along a group of three, by their dress and bearing, of the farmer class.

One was a sturdy old man; the other two were good-looking girls, one of a little over twenty, the other not quite grown – seventeen at most. So soon as Adam's eyes met those of the younger girl, who stood nearest to him, some sort of electricity flashed – that divine spark which begins by recognition and ends in obedience. Men call it 'Love.'

Both the elders of the party noticed how much Adam was taken by the pretty girl, and both spoke of her to him in a way which made his heart warm to them.

'Did you notice that party that passed? The old man is Michael Watford, one of the tenants of Mr Caswall. He occupies Mercy Farm, which Sir Nathaniel tells me he pointed out to you to-day. The girls are his grand-daughters, the elder, Lilla, being the only child of his eldest son, who died when she was less than a year old. His wife died on the same day – in fact at the same time. She is a good girl – as good as she is pretty. The other is her first cousin, the daughter of Watford's second son. He went for a soldier when he was just over twenty, and was drafted abroad. He was not a good correspondent, though he was a good enough son. A few letters came, and then his father heard from the colonel of his regiment that he had been killed by dacoits in Burmah.[5] He heard from the same source that his boy had been married to a Burmese, and that there was a daughter only a year old. Watford had the child brought home, and she grew up beside Lilla. The only thing that they heard of her birth was that her name was Mimi. The two children adored each other, and do to this day. Strange how different they are! Lilla all fair, like the old Saxon stock she is sprung from; Mimi almost as dark as the darkest of her mother's race.[6] Lilla is as gentle as a dove, but Mimi's black eyes can glow whenever she is upset. The only thing that upsets her is when anything happens to injure or threaten or annoy Lilla. Then her eyes glow as do the eyes of a bird when her young are threatened.'

CHAPTER VI
THE WHITE WORM

Mr Salton introduced Adam to Mr Watford and his grand-daughters, and they all moved on together. Of course people, neighbours, in the position of the Watfords knew all about Adam Salton, his relationship, circumstances, and prospects. So it would have been strange indeed if both girls did not see or dream of possibilities of the future. In agricultural England, eligible men of any class were rare. This particular man was specially eligible, for he did not belong to a class in which barriers of caste were strong. So when it began to be noticed that he walked beside Mimi Watford and seemed to desire her society, all their friends seemed to give the promising affair a helping hand. When the gongs sounded for the banquet, he went with her into the tent where her father had seats. Mr Salton and Sir Nathaniel noticed that the young man did not come to claim his appointed place at the daïs table; but they understood and made no remark, or indeed did not seem to notice his absence. Lady Arabella sat as before at Edgar Caswall's right hand. She was certainly a very beautiful woman, and to all it seemed fitting from her rank and personal qualities that she should be the chosen partner of the heir on his first appearance. Of course nothing was said openly by those of her own class who were present; but words were not necessary when so much could be expressed by nods and smiles. It seemed to be an accepted thing that at last there was to be a mistress of Castra Regis, and that she was present amongst them. There were not lacking some who, whilst admitting all her charm and beauty, placed her in only the second rank of beauty, Lilla Watford being marked as first. There was sufficient divergence of type as well as of individual beauty to allow of fair commenting; Lady Arabella represented the aristocratic type, and Lilla that of the commonalty.

When the dusk began to thicken, Mr Salton and Sir Nathaniel walked home – the trap had been sent away early in the day, leaving Adam to follow in his own time. He came in earlier than was expected, and seemed upset about something. Neither of the elders made any comment. They all lit cigarettes, and, as dinner-time was close at hand, went to their rooms to get ready. Adam had evidently been thinking in the interval. He joined the others in the drawing-room, looking ruffled and impatient – a condition of things seen for the first time. The others, with the patience – or the experience – of age trusted to time to unfold and explain things. They had not long to wait. After sitting down and standing up several times, Adam suddenly burst out:

'That fellow seems to think he owns the earth. Can't he let people alone! He seems to think that he has only to throw his handkerchief to any woman, and be her master.'

This outburst was in itself enlightening. Only thwarted affection in some guise could produce this feeling in an amiable young man. Sir Nathaniel, as an old diplomatist, had a way of understanding, as if by foreknowledge, the true inwardness of things, and asked suddenly, but in a matter-of-fact, indifferent voice:

'Was he after Lilla?'

'Yes. And he didn't lose any time either. Almost as soon as they met he began to butter her up, and to tell her how beautiful she is. Why, before he left her side he had asked himself to tea to-morrow at Mercy Farm. Stupid ass! He might see that the girl isn't his sort! I never saw anything like it. It was just like a hawk and a pigeon.'

As he spoke, Sir Nathaniel turned and looked at Mr Salton – a keen look which implied a full understanding. Then the latter said quietly:

'Tell us all about it, Adam. There are still ten minutes before dinner, and we shall all have better appetites when we have come to some conclusion on this matter.'

Adam spoke with an unwonted diffidence:

'There is nothing to tell, sir; that is the worst of it. I am bound to say that there was not a word said that a human being could object to. He was very civil, and all that was proper – just what a landlord might be to a tenant's daughter ... And yet – and yet – well, I don't know how it was, but it made my blood simply boil.'

'How did the hawk and the pigeon come in?' Sir Nathaniel's voice was soft and soothing, nothing of contradiction or overdone curiosity in it – a tone eminently suited to win confidence.

'I can hardly explain it. I can only say that he looked like a hawk and she like a dove – and, now that I think of it, that is what they each did look like; and do look like in their normal condition.'

'That is so!' came the soft voice of Sir Nathaniel.

Adam went on:

'Perhaps that early Roman look of his set me off. But I wanted to protect her; she seemed in danger.'

'She seems in danger, in a way, from all you young men. I couldn't help noticing the way that even you looked, as if you wished to absorb her.'

Here the kindly, temperate voice of Mr Salton came in:

'I hope both you young men will keep your heads cool. You know, Adam, it won't do to have any quarrel between you, especially so soon after his home-coming and your arrival here. We must think of the feelings and happiness of our neighbours; mustn't we?'

'I hope so, sir. And I assure you that, whatever may happen, or even threaten, I shall obey your wishes in this as in all things.'

'Silence!' whispered Sir Nathaniel, who heard the servants in the passage bringing dinner.

After dinner, over the walnuts and the wine, Sir Nathaniel returned to the subject of the local legends, saying: 'It will perhaps be a less dangerous topic for us to discuss than more recent ones.'

'All right, sir,' said Adam heartily. 'I think you may depend on me now with regard to any topic. I can even discuss with Mr Caswall. Indeed, I may meet him to-morrow. He is going, as I said, to call at Mercy Farm at three o'clock – but I have an appointment at two.'

'I notice,' said Mr Salton, 'that you do not lose any time.'

'No, sir. Perhaps that is the reason why the part I came from has for its motto – "Advance, Australia!" '[1]

'All right, my boy. Advance is good – so long as you take care where you are going and how. There is a line in one of Shakespeare's plays, "They stumble that run fast."[2] It is worth bearing in mind.'

'All right again, sir; but I don't think you need fear me now I have had my kick.'

The two old men once more looked at each other steadily. It was as much as to say, 'Good! The boy has had his lesson. He will be all right!' Then, lest the mood of his listener should change with delay, Sir Nathaniel began at once:

'I don't propose to tell you all the legends of Mercia, or even to make a selection of them. It will be better, I think, for our purpose if we consider a few facts – recorded or unrecorded – about this neighbourhood. I shall try to remember, and you, Adam, shall ask me questions as we go along. We all want stimulation to memory. When we have nothing amongst us to remember it will be time enough to invent. I propose to go on where we left off yesterday morning, about the few places round here that we spoke of. I think we might begin with Diana's Grove. It has roots in the different epochs of our history, and each has, be sure, its special crop of legend. The Druid and the Roman are too far off for matters of detail; but it seems to me the Saxon and the Angles are near enough to yield material for legendary lore. If there were anything well remembered of an earlier period, we may take it that it had some beginning in what was accepted as fact. We find that this particular place had another name or sobriquet besides Diana's Grove. This was manifestly of Roman origin, or of Grecian accepted as Roman. The former is more pregnant of adventure and romance than the Roman name. In Mercian tongue it was "The Lair of the White Worm." This needs a word of explanation at the beginning.

'In the dawn of the language, the word "worm" had a somewhat different meaning from that in use to-day. It was an adaptation of the Anglo-Saxon "wyrm," meaning primarily a dragon or snake; or from the Gothic "waurms," a serpent; or the Icelandic "ormur," or the German "wurm." We gather that it conveyed originally an idea of size and power, not as now in the diminutive of both these meanings. Here legendary history helps us. We have the well-known legend of the "Worm Well" of Lambton Castle, and that of the "Laidly Worm of Spindleston Heugh" near Bamborough.³ In both these legends the "worm" was a monster of vast size and power – a veritable dragon or serpent, such as legend attributes to vast fens or quags where there was illimitable room for expansion. A glance at a geological map will show that whatever truth there may have been of the actuality of such monsters in the early geologic periods, at least there was plenty of possibility. In the eastern section of England there were originally vast plains where the naturally plentiful supply of water could gather. There the streams were deep and slow, and there were holes of abysmal depth, where any kind and size of antediluvian monster could find a habitat. In places, which now we can see from our windows, were mud-holes a hundred or more feet deep. Who can tell us when the age of the monsters which flourished in slime came to an end? If such a time there was indeed, its limits could only apply to the vast number of such dangers. There must have been times and places and conditions which made for greater longevity, greater size, greater strength than was usual. Such overlappings may have come down even to our earlier centuries. Nay, are there not now creatures of a vastness of bulk regarded by the generality of men as impossible? Even in our own day there are here and there seen the traces of animals, if not the animals themselves, of stupendous size – veritable survivals from earlier ages, preserved by some special qualities in their habitats. I remember meeting a distinguished man in India, who had the reputation of being a great shikaree,⁴ who told me that the greatest temptation he had ever had in his life was to shoot a giant snake which he had literally come across in the Terai of Upper India. He was on a tiger-shooting expedition, and as his elephant was crossing a nullah it squealed. He looked down from his howdah and saw that the elephant had stepped across the body of a snake which was dragging itself through the jungle. "So far as I could see," he said, "it must have been eighty or one hundred feet in length. Fully forty or fifty feet was on each side of the track, and though the weight which it dragged had thinned it to its least, it was as thick round as a man's body. I suppose you know that when you are after tiger, it is a point of honour not to shoot at anything else, as life may depend on it. I could easily and with safety have spined this monster, but I felt that I must not – and so with regret I had to let it go."

'Just imagine such a monster anywhere in this country, and at once we could get a sort of idea of the "worms," which possibly did frequent the great morasses which spread round the mouths of any of the great European rivers.'

Adam had been thinking; at last he spoke:

'I haven't the least doubt, sir, that there may have been such monsters as you have spoken of still existing at a much later period than is generally accepted. Also, that if there were such things, that this was the very place for them. I have tried to think over the matter since you pointed out the configuration of the ground. But if you will not be offended by my expressing – not indeed a doubt, but a difficulty – it seems to me that there is a hiatus somewhere.'

'Where? What kind? Tell me frankly, where is your difficulty. You know I am always glad of an honest opinion in any difficulty.'

'Well, sir, all that you say may be, probably is, true. But are there not mechanical difficulties?'

'As how?'

'Well, our antique monster must have been mighty heavy, and the distances he had to travel were long and the ways difficult. From where we are now sitting down to the level of the mud-holes even the top of them is a distance of several hundred feet – I am leaving out of consideration altogether for the present lateral distance. Is it possible that there was a way by which a monster such as you have spoken of could travel up and down, and yet no chance recorder have ever seen him? Of course we have the legends; but is not some more exact evidence necessary in a scientific investigation?'

'My dear Adam, all you say is perfectly right, and, were we starting on just such an investigation, we could not do better than follow your reasoning. But, my dear boy, you must remember that all this took place thousands of years ago. You must remember, too, that all records of the kind that would help us are lacking. Also, that the places to be considered were absolutely desert so far as human habitation or population are considered. In the vast desolation of such a place as complied with the necessary conditions there must have been such profusion of natural growth as would bar the progress of men formed as we are. The lair of such a monster as we have in mind would not have been disturbed for hundreds – or thousands – of years. Moreover, these creatures must have occupied places quite inaccessible to man. A snake who could make himself comfortable in a quagmire a hundred feet deep would be protected even on the outskirts by such stupendous morasses as now no longer exist, or which, if they exist anywhere at all, can be on very few places on the earth's surface. Far be it from me to say, or even to think for a moment, that in more elemental times such things could not have been. The condition of things we speak of belongs to the geologic age – the great birth and growth of the world, when natural forces ran riot, when the struggle for existence was so savage that no vitality which was not founded in a gigantic form could have even a possibility of survival.[5] That such a time was we have evidences in geology, but there only. We can never expect proofs such as this age demands. We can only imagine or surmise such things – or such conditions and such forces as overcame them.'

'Come, let us get to bed,' said Mr Salton. 'Like you both, I enjoy the conversation. But one thing is certain: we cannot settle it before breakfast.'

CHAPTER VII

HAWK AND PIGEON

At breakfast-time next morning Sir Nathaniel and Mr Salton were seated when Adam came hurriedly into the room.

'Any news?' asked his uncle mechanically.

'Four.'

'Four what?' asked Sir Nathaniel.

'Snakes,' said Adam, helping himself to a grilled kidney.

'Four snakes. How? I don't understand.'

'Mongoose,' said Adam, and then added explanatorily: 'I was out with the mongoose just after three.'

'Four snakes in one morning! Why, I didn't know there were so many on the Brow' – the local name for the western cliff. 'I hope that wasn't the consequence of our talk of last night?'

'It was, sir. But not directly.'

'But, God bless my soul, you didn't expect to get a snake like the Lambton worm, did you? Why, a mongoose to tackle a monster like that – if there were one – would have to be bigger than a haystack.'

'These were ordinary snakes, only about as big as a walking-stick.'

'Well, it's well to be rid of them, big or little. That is a good mongoose, I suppose; he'll clear out all such vermin round here,' said Mr Salton.

Adam went quietly on with his breakfast. Killing a few snakes in a morning was no new experience to him. He left the room the moment breakfast was finished and went to the study that his uncle had arranged for him. Both Sir Nathaniel and Mr Salton took it that he wanted to be by himself as so to avoid any questioning or talk of the visit that he was to make that afternoon. He stayed by himself either in the house or walking, till about half an hour before dinner-time. Then he came quietly into the smoking-room, where Mr Salton and Sir Nathaniel were sitting together ready dressed. He too was dressed, and the old diplomatist noticed that his hand was, if possible, more steady than usual. He had actually shaved himself when making his toilet, but there was no sign of a cut or even of a quiver of the hand. Sir Nathaniel smiled to himself quietly as he said under his voice:

'He is all right. That is a sign there is no mistaking – for a man in love. He certainly was in love yesterday; and one way or another, if he can get rid of, or overcome, troubles of the heart like that, I think we needn't have any special apprehension about him.' So he resumed the magazine which he had been reading.

After a few minutes of silence all round, Adam gave further evidence of his *aplomb*. He suddenly said, looking at the others:

'I suppose there is no use waiting. We had better get it over at once.'

His uncle, thinking to make things easier to him, said:

'Get what over?'

There was a sign of shyness about him at this. He stammered a little at first, but his voice became more even as he went on:

'My visit to Mercy Farm.'

Mr Salton waited eagerly. The old diplomatist simply smiled easily.

'I suppose you both know that I was much interested yesterday in the Watfords?' There was no denial or fending off the question. Both the old men smiled acquiescence. Adam went on: 'I meant you to see it – both of you. You, uncle, because you are my uncle and the nearest thing to me on earth – of my own kin, and, moreover, you couldn't have been more kind to me or made me more welcome if you had been my own father.' Mr Salton said nothing. He simply held out his hand, and the other took it and held it for a few seconds. 'And you, sir, because you have shown me something of the same affection which in my wildest dreams of home I had no right to expect.' He stopped for an instant, much moved.

Sir Nathaniel said softly, laying his hand on the boy's shoulder:

'You are right, my boy; quite right. That is the proper way to look at it. And I may tell you that we old men, who have no children of our own, feel our hearts growing warm when we hear words like those.'

Then Adam hurried on, speaking with a rush, as if he wanted to come to the crucial point:

'Mr Watford had not come in, but Lilla and Mimi were at home, and they made me feel very welcome. They have all a great regard for my uncle. I am glad of that any way, for I like them all – much. We were having tea when Mr Caswall came to the door, attended by the Christy Minstrel.'[1]

'The Christy Minstrel!' repeated Sir Nathaniel. His voice sounded simply as an acknowledgment, not as a comment of any kind.

'Lilla opened the door herself. The window of the living-room at the farm, as of course you know, is a large one, and from within you cannot help seeing anyone coming. Mr Caswall said he ventured to call, as he wished to make the acquaintance of all his tenants in a less formal way and more individually than had been possible to him on the previous day. The girls made him very welcome. They are very sweet girls those, sir. Someone will be very happy some day there – with either of them.'

'And that man may be you, Adam,' said Mr Salton heartily.

A sad look came over the young man's eyes, and the fire his uncle had seen there died out. Likewise the timbre had left his voice, making it sound dreadfully lonely as he spoke:

'Such might crown my life. But that happiness, I fear, is not for me, or not without pain and loss and woe.'

'Well, it's early days yet!' said Sir Nathaniel heartily.

The young man turned on him his eyes, which had now grown excessively sad, as he answered:

'Yesterday – a few hours ago – that remark would have given me new hope – new courage; but since then I have learned too much.'

The old man, skilled in the human heart, did not attempt to argue in such a matter. He simply varied the idea and went on:

'Too early to give in, my boy.'

'I am not of a giving-in kind,' said the young man earnestly. 'But, after all, it is wise to realise a truth. And when a man, though he is young, feels as I do – as I have felt ever since yesterday, when I first saw Mimi's eyes – his heart jumps. He does not need to learn things. He knows.'

There was silence in the room, during which the twilight stole on imperceptibly. It was Adam who again broke the silence as he asked his uncle:

'Do you know, uncle, if we have any second sight in our family?'

'Second sight? No, not that I ever heard of. Why?'

'Because,' he answered slowly, 'I have a conviction over me which seems to answer all the conditions of second sight that I have ever heard of.'

'And then?' asked the old man, much perturbed.

'And then the usual inevitable. What in the Hebrides and other places, where the Sight is a cult – a belief – is called "the doom" – the court from which there is no appeal. I have often heard of second sight – you know we have many western Scots in Australia; but I have realised more of its true inwardness in an instant of this afternoon than I did in the whole of my life previously – a granite wall stretching up to the very heavens, so high and so dark that the eye of God Himself cannot see beyond. Well, if the Doom must come, it must. That is all.'

The voice of Sir Nathaniel broke in, smooth and sweet and grave, but very, very stern:

'Can there not be a fight for it? There can for most things.'

'For most things, yes. But for the Doom, no. What a man can do I shall do. There will be – must be – a fight. When and where and how I know not. But a fight there will be. But, after all, what is a man in such a case?'

'A man! Adam, there are three of us.' He looked at his old friend as he spoke, and that old friend's eyes blazed.

'Ay, three of us,' he said, and his voice rang.

There was again a pause, and Sir Nathaniel, anxious to get back to less emotional and more neutral ground, said quietly:

'Tell us of the rest of the meeting. Omit no detail. It may be useful. Remember we are all pledged to this. It is a fight *à l'outrance*,[2] and we can afford to throw away or forgo no chance.'

Adam said quietly, looking at him:

'We shall throw away or lose nothing that we can help. We fight to win, and the stake is a life – perhaps more than one – we shall see.' Then he went on in a conversational tone, such as he had used when he spoke of the coming to the farm of Edgar Caswall: 'When Mr Caswall came in the Christy Minstrel touched his ridiculous hat and went away – at least, he went a short distance and there remained. It gave one the idea that he expected to be called and intended to remain in sight, or within hail. Then Mimi got another cup and made fresh tea, and we all went on together.'

'Was there anything uncommon – were you all quite friendly?' asked Sir Nathaniel quietly.

Adam answered at once:

'Quite friendly. There was nothing that I could notice out of the common – except,' he went on, with a slight hardening of the voice, 'except that he kept his eyes fixed on Lilla in a way which was quite intolerable to any man who might hold her dear.'

'Now, in what way did he look?' asked Sir Nathaniel. 'I am not doubting. I only ask for information.'

'I can hardly say,' was the answer. 'There was nothing in itself offensive; but no one could help noticing it.'

'You did. Miss Watford herself, who was the victim, and Mr Caswall, who was the offender, are out of range as witnesses. Was there anyone else who noticed?'

'Mimi did. I tell you her face flamed with anger as she saw the look.'

'What kind of look was it? Over-ardent or too admiring, or what? Was it the look of a lover or one who fain would be? You understand?'

'Yes, sir, I quite understand. Anything of that sort I should of course notice. It would be part of my preparation for keeping my self-control – to which I am pledged.'

'If it were not amatory, was it threatening? Where was the offence?'

Adam smiled kindly at the old man:

'It was not amatory. Even if it was, such was to be expected. I should be the last man in the world to object, since I am myself an offender in that respect. Moreover, not only have I been taught to fight fair, but by nature I really believe I am just. I would be as tolerant of and as liberal to a rival if he were one as I should expect him to be to me. No, the look I mean was nothing of that kind. And so long as it did not lack proper respect I should not of my own part condescend to notice it. I shall try to describe it to you. Did you ever seriously study the eyes of a hound?'

'At rest?'

'No, when he is following his instincts! Or, better still,' Adam went on, 'the eyes of a bird of prey when he is following his instincts. Not when he is swooping, but merely when he is watching his quarry?'

'No,' said Sir Nathaniel, 'I don't know that I ever did. Why, may I ask?'

'That was the look. Certainly not amatory or anything of that kind – and yet it was, it struck me, more dangerous, if not so deadly as an actual threatening.'

Again there was a silence, which Sir Nathaniel broke as he stood up:

'I think it would be well if we all thought over this by ourselves. Then we can renew the subject.'

CHAPTER VIII
OOLANGA

Mr Salton had an appointment for six o'clock at Walsall. When he had driven off, Sir Nathaniel took Adam by the arm and said to him:

'May I come with you for a while to your study? I want to speak to you privately without your uncle knowing about it, or even what the subject is. You don't mind, do you? It is not any idle curiosity. No, no. It is on the subject to which we are all committed.'

Adam said with some constraint:

'Is it necessary to keep my uncle in the dark about it? He might be offended.'

'It is not necessary; but it is advisable. It is for his sake that I asked. My friend is an old man, and it might concern him unduly – even alarm him. I promise you there shall be nothing that could cause him anxiety in our silence, or at which he could take umbrage.'

'Go on, sir!' said Adam simply.

When they were locked into the study he spoke:

'You see, your uncle is now an old man. I know it, for we were boys together. He has led an uneventful and somewhat self-contained life, so that any such condition of things as has now arisen is apt to perplex him from its very strangeness. In fact, any new matter is trying to old people. It has its own disturbances and its own anxieties, and neither of these things are good for lives that should be restful. Your uncle is a strong man with a very happy and placid nature. Given health and ordinary conditions of life, there is no reason why he should not live to be a hundred. You and I therefore, who both love

him, though in different ways, should make it our business
to protect him from all disturbing influences. Such care shall
undoubtedly add to the magnitude of his span of life and the
happiness of his days. I am sure you will agree with me that
any labour to this end would be well spent. All right, my boy!
I see your answer in your eyes; so we need say no more of that.
And now,' here his voice changed, 'tell me all that took place
at that interview. You cannot be too exhaustive. Nothing is too
trivial. There are strange things in front of us – how strange we
cannot at present even guess. Doubtless some of the difficult
things to understand which lie behind the veil will in time be
shown to us to see and understand. In the meantime, all we can
do is to think and work patiently, fearlessly, and unselfishly to
an end that we think is right. Tell me as well as you can – I
shall try to help you. You had just got so far as where Lilla
opened the door to Mr Caswall, and the Christy Minstrel, who
had followed him, went a little distance away and lurked. You
also observed that Mimi was disturbed in her mind at the way
Mr Caswall looked at her cousin.'

'Certainly – though "disturbed in her mind" is only a poor
way of expressing her objection.'

'Can you remember well enough to describe Caswall's eyes,
and how Lilla looked, and what Mimi said and did? Also of
the Christy Minstrel, who is, I take it, Oolanga, Caswall's West
African servant. When you have said all you know of these
things I want you to tell me what you have heard in any way
about the "Christy Minstrel." I take it this will be the most
humorous way of bringing him in. Though indeed I doubt his
being in any conceivable way a subject of humour. Tragedy
would more probably be a follower in his train.'

'I'll do what I can, sir. All the time Mr Caswall was staring
he kept his eyes fixed and motionless – but not as if he was
dead or in a trance. His forehead was wrinkled up as it is when
one is trying to see through or into something. At the best of
times his face is not of very equable or of gentle expression; but
when it was screwed up like that it was almost diabolical. It
frightened poor Lilla so that she trembled, and after a bit got
so pale that I thought she had fainted. However, she held up

and tried to stare back, but in a feeble kind of way. Then Mimi came close and held her hand. That braced her up, and – still, never ceasing her return stare – she got colour again and seemed more like herself.'

'Did he stare too?'

'More than ever. The weaker Lilla seemed the stronger he seemed to get, just as if he was feeding on her strength. All at once she turned round, threw up her hands, and fell down in a faint. I could not see what else happened just then, for Mimi had thrown herself on her knees beside her and hid her from me. Then there was something like a black shadow between us, and there was the pleasing form of the Christy Minstrel, looking more like a malignant devil than ever. He had better look out. I am not usually a patient man, and the sight of that ugly devil is enough to make an Eskimo's blood boil. When he saw my face he seemed to realise danger – immediate danger – and he slunk out of the room as noiselessly as if he had been blown out. I learned one thing, however. He is an enemy, if ever a man had one.'

'That still leaves us three to two!' – this from Sir Nathaniel.

'Then Caswall slunk out much as the nigger had done. When he had gone, Lilla recovered at once. I hope I won't see Mr Christy look at Lilla again!' As he spoke he took a nickel-plated revolver from his pocket and put it back again with an ominous remark: 'I don't know if he wishes to be buried on English soil. He can have his choice if he likes. Ordinarily speaking, he isn't worth a cartridge; but when there is a lady in the case –' The revolver clicked.

'Now,' said Sir Nathaniel, anxious to restore peace, 'have you found out anything yet regarding your friend the Christy Minstrel? I am anxious to be posted regarding him. I fear there will be, or may be, grave trouble with him.'

'Yes, sir, I've heard a good deal about him – of course it is not official; but then hearsay may guide us at first. You know my man Davenport, I think. He really is my *alter ego* – private secretary, confidential man of business, and general factotum. He came with me in a journey of exploration across the desert. He saved my life many times. He is devoted to me, and has my full confidence. I asked him to go on board the *West African* and have a good look round, and find out what he could about Mr Caswall. Naturally, he was struck with the aboriginal savage. He found one of the ship's stewards who had been on the regular voyages to South Africa. He knew Oolanga and had made a study of him. He is a man who gets on well with niggers, and they opened their hearts to him. It seems that this Oolanga is quite a great person in the nigger world of the African West Coast. He has the two things which men of his own colour respect: he can make them afraid, and he is lavish with money. I don't know whose money – but that does not matter. They are always ready to trumpet his greatness. Evil greatness it is – but neither does that matter. Briefly, this is his history. He was originally a witch-finder – about as low an occupation as exists amongst even aboriginal savages, amongst the mangrove swamps. Then he got up in the world and became an Obi-man, which gives an opportunity to wealth *via* blackmail. Finally, he reached the highest honour in hellish service. He became a user of Voodoo,[1] which seems to be a service of the utmost baseness and cruelty. I was told some of his deeds of cruelty, which are simply sickening. They made me long for an opportunity of helping to drive him back to hell. You might think to look at him that you could measure in some way the extent of his vileness; but it would be a vain hope. Monsters such as he is belong to an earlier and more rudimentary stage of barbarism. Whoever kills him when the time comes will not have to fear punishment, but to expect praise. He is in his way a clever fellow – for a nigger; but is none the less dangerous or the less hateful for that. The men in the ship told me that he was a collector: some of them had seen his collections. Such collections! All that was potent for evil in bird or beast, or even in fish. Beaks that could break and rend and tear. All the birds represented were of a predatory kind. Even the fishes are those which are born to destroy, to wound, to torture. The collection, I assure you, was an object lesson in human malignity. This being has enough evil in his face to frighten even a strong man. It is little wonder that the sight of it unexpectedly put that poor girl into a dead faint! If that other savage intends to keep him round here they may build a new prison at once; for there won't be a decent man or woman in his neighbourhood that won't be a criminal at the very start, if indeed it be a crime to destroy such a thing.'

Adam was up in the early morning and took a smart walk round the Brow. As he was passing Diana's Grove he looked in on the short avenue of trees, and noticed the snakes killed on the previous morning by the mongoose. They all lay in a row, straight and rigid, as if they had been placed by hands. Their skins seemed all damp and sticky, and they were covered all over with ants and all sorts of insects. They looked loathsome, so after a glance he passed on. A little later, when his steps took him, naturally enough, past the entrance to Mercy Farm, he was passed by the Christy Minstrel moving quickly under the trees wherever there was shadow. Laid across one extended arm, and looking like dirty towels across a rail, he had the horrid-looking snakes. He did not seem to see Adam, to the pleasant surprise of the latter. No one was to be seen at Mercy except a few workmen in the farmyard. So, after waiting round on a chance of seeing Mimi, he began to go slowly home. Once more he was passed on the way. This time it was by Lady Arabella, walking hurriedly and so furiously angry that she did not seem to recognise him even to the extent of acknowledging his bow. He wondered, but simply went on his way. When he got to Lesser Hill, he went to the coach-house where the box with the mongoose was kept, and took it with him, intending to finish at the Mound of Stone what he had begun the previous morning with regard to the extermination. He found that the snakes were even more easily attacked than on the previous day; no less than six were killed in the first half-hour. As no more appeared, he took it for granted that the morning's work was over, and went towards home. The mongoose had by this time become accustomed to him, and was willing to let himself be handled freely. Adam lifted him up and put him on his shoulders and walked on. Presently he saw a lady advancing towards him, and as they grew nearer recognised Lady Arabella. Hitherto the mongoose had been quiet, like a playful affection-ate kitten; but when the two got close he was horrified to see the mongoose, in a state of the wildest fury, with every hair standing on end, jump from his shoulder and run towards Lady Arabella. It looked so furious and so intent on attack that he called out:

'Look out – look out! The animal is furious and means to attack.'

She looked more than ever disdainful and was passing on; the mongoose jumped at her in a furious attack. Adam rushed forward with his stick, the only weapon he had. But just as he got within striking distance the lady drew out a revolver and shot the animal, breaking his backbone. Not satisfied with this, she poured shot after shot into him till the magazine was exhausted. There was no coolness or hauteur about her now. She seemed more furious even than the animal, her face transformed with hate, and as determined to kill as he had appeared to be. Adam, not knowing exactly what to do, lifted his hat in apology and hurried on to Lesser Hill.

CHAPTER IX

SURVIVALS

At breakfast Sir Nathaniel noticed that Adam was put out about something. But he said nothing. The lesson of silence is better remembered in age than in youth. When they were both in the study, where Sir Nathaniel had followed him, Adam at once began to tell his companion of what had happened. Sir Nathaniel looked graver and graver as the narration proceeded, and when Adam had stopped he remained silent for several minutes. At last he said:

'This is very grave. I have not formed my thought yet; but it seems to me at first impression that this is worse than anything we had thought of.'

'Why, sir?' said Adam. 'Is the killing of a mongoose – no matter by whom – so serious a thing as all that?'

The other smoked on quietly for quite another few minutes before he spoke.

'When I have properly thought it over I may moderate my opinion. But in the meantime it seems to me that there is something dreadful behind all this – something that may affect all our lives – that may mean the issue of life or death to any of us.'

Adam sat up quickly.

'Do tell me, sir, what is in your mind – if, of course, you have no objection to, or do not think it better not.'

'I have no objection, Adam. In fact, if I had, I should have to overcome it. I fear there can be no more hidden or reserved thoughts between us.'

'Indeed, sir, that sounds serious, worse than serious!'

Again they both resumed their cigars, and presently Sir Nathaniel said gravely:

'Adam, I greatly fear the time has come for us – for you and me, at all events – to speak out plainly to one another. Does not there seem something very mysterious about this?'

'I have thought so, sir, all along. The only difficulty one has is what one is to think and where to begin.'

'Let us begin with what you have told me. First take the conduct of the mongoose.'

Adam waited; the other went on:

'He was quiet, even friendly and affectionate with you. He only attacked the snakes, which is, after all, only his business in life.'

'That is so!'

'Then we must try to find out or imagine some reason why he attacked Lady Arabella.'

'I fear we shall have to imagine; there is no logical answer to that question.'

'Then let us imagine. He had not shown any disposition hitherto to attack strangers?'

'No; the opposite. He made friends at once with everyone he came across.'

'Then even if his action is based on instinct, why does he single out one person in such a way?'

'In that, sir, I see a difficulty, or, if you will permit me, it may be only a flaw in your reasoning.'

'Permit! I shall be glad. Go on.'

'It seems to me that you take "instinct" as a definite fixed thing concerning which there can be only one reading – even by the brute creation.'

'Go on, Adam. This is very interesting.'

'We both may have erred in our idea of "instinct." May it not be that a mongoose may have merely the instinct to attack, that nature does not allow or provide him with the fine reasoning powers to discriminate who he is to attack?'

'Good! Of course that may be so. But then, on the other hand, should we not satisfy ourselves why he does wish to attack anything? If for centuries in all parts of the world this particular animal is known to attack only one kind of other animal, are we not justified in assuming that when a case strange to us comes before us, if one of the first class attacks a hitherto unclassed animal, he recognises in that animal some quality which it has in common with the hitherto classed animal?'

'That is a good argument, sir,' Adam went on, 'but a dangerous one. If we followed it out with pure logic it would lead us to believe that Lady Arabella is a snake. And I doubt if we – either of us – are prepared to go so far.'

'So far as I am concerned I am to follow blindly the lead of logic. But before doing so we have a duty to fulfil.'

'What is that duty, sir?'

'The first of all duties, truth. We must be sure before going to such an end that there is no point as yet unconsidered which would account for the unknown thing which puzzles us.'

'As how?'

'Well, suppose the instinct works on some physical basis – sight, for instance, or smell. If there were anything in recent juxtaposition to the accused which would look like the cause or would carry the scent, surely that would supply the missing cause.'

'Of course!' Adam spoke with conviction.

Sir Nathaniel went on:

'Now, from what you tell me, your Christy Minstrel friend had just come from the direction of Diana's Grove carrying the dead snakes, which the mongoose had killed the previous morning. Might not the scent have been carried that way?'

'Of course it might, probably was. I never thought of that. Look here, sir, I really think it will be prudent of us not to draw final conclusions till we know more. At any rate that episode has a suggestive hint for us – one which we can follow up without saying anything to anybody. Then we shall be in a safer position for going on.'

'Good and sensible!' Sir Nathaniel spoke approvingly; and so it was tacitly arranged between the two to wait.

But whilst they were sitting in silence an idea struck Adam, and he thought it wise to make it known to the elder man.

'Two things I want to ask you, if I may. One is a sort of corollary to the other.' Sir Nathaniel listened. He went on: 'Is there any possible way of even guessing approximately how long a scent will remain? You see, this is a natural scent, and may derive from a place where it has been effective for thousands of years. Then, does a scent of any kind carry with it any form or quality of another kind, either good or evil? I ask you because one ancient name of the house lived in by the lady who was attacked by the mongoose was "The Lair of the White Worm." If any of these things be so, our possibilities of knowledge and our difficulties have multiplied indefinitely. They may even change in kind. We may get into even moral entanglements; before we know it we may be even in the midst of a bedrock struggle between good and evil.'

Sir Nathaniel, after a pause, asked:

'Is that the question you wished to ask me?'

'Yes, sir.'

Sir Nathaniel smiled gravely.

'I don't see on what the corollary rests. With regard to the first question – or the first part, though, so far as I know, there are no fixed periods with which a scent may be active – I think we may take it that that period does not run into thousands of years. As to whether any moral change accompanies a physical one, I can only say that I have met no argument of proof or even no assertion of the fact. At the same time, we must remember that "good" and "evil" are terms so wide as to take in the whole scheme of creation and all that is implied by them and by their mutual action and reaction. Generally, I would say that in the scheme of a First Cause[1] anything is possible. So long as the inherent forces or tendencies of any one thing are veiled from us we must expect mystery. This hides from us more than we at first conceive, and as time goes on and *some* light gets into the darker places, we are able to understand that there are other darknesses. And so on, until the time shall come when the full light of understanding beats upon us.'

'Then I presume, sir,' said Adam, 'that it would be at least wise of us to leave these questions alone till we know more.'

'Most certainly. To listen and remember should be our guiding principle in such an inquiry.'

'There is one other question on which I should like to ask your opinion. It is the last of my general questions – for the present. Suppose that there are any permanent forces appertaining to the past, what we may call "survivals," do these belong to good as well as to evil? For instance, if the scent of the primæval monster can so remain in proportion to the original strength, can the same be true of things of good import?'

Sir Nathaniel thought a while, then he answered:

'We must be careful from the beginning not to confuse the physical and the moral, to differentiate the two and to keep them differentiated. I can see that already you have switched on the moral entirely, so perhaps we had better follow it up first. On the side of the moral we have certain justification for belief in the utterances of revealed religion. For instance, "the effectual fervent prayer of a righteous man availeth much"[2] is altogether for good. We have nothing of a similar kind on the side of evil. But if we accept this dictum we need have no more fear of "mysteries": these become thenceforth merely obstacles.'

Adam waited in silence, which was intended to be, and was, respectful. Then he suddenly changed to another phase of the subject.

'And now, sir, may I turn for a few minutes to purely practical things, or rather to matters of historical fact?'

Sir Nathaniel bowed acquiescence. He went on:

'We have already spoken of the history, so far as it is known, of some of the places round us – "Castra Regis," "Diana's Grove" and "The Lair of the White Worm." I would like to ask if there is anything not necessarily of evil import about any of the places?'

'Which?' asked Sir Nathaniel shrewdly.

'Well, for instance, this house and Mercy Farm?'

'Here we turn,' said Sir Nathaniel, 'to the other side, the light side of things. Let us take Mercy Farm first. You have no objection?'

'Thank you, sir.' The young man's comment was complete and illuminative.

'Perhaps we had better remember the history of that particular place. The details may later on help us in coming to some useful, or at all events interesting, conclusion.

'When Augustine was sent by Pope Gregory to Christianise

England in the time of the Romans, he was received and protected by Ethelbert, King of Kent, whose wife, daughter of Charibert, King of Paris, was a Christian, and did much for Augustine. She founded a nunnery in memory of Columba, which was named *Sedes misericordiæ*, the House of Mercy, and, as the region was Mercian, the two names became inextricably involved. As Columba is the Latin for dove, the dove became a sort of signification of the nunnery.[3] She seized on the idea and made the newly-founded nunnery a house of doves. Someone sent her a freshly-discovered dove, a sort of carrier, but which had in the white feathers of its head and neck the form of a religious cowl. And so in especial the bird became the symbol of the nuns of Mercy. The nunnery flourished for more than a century, when, in the time of Penda,[4] who was the reactionary of heathendom, it fell into decay. In the meantime the doves, which, protected by religious feeling, had increased mightily, were known in all Catholic communities. When King Offa ruled in Mercia about a hundred and fifty years later, he restored Christianity,[5] and under its protection the nunnery of St Columba was restored and its doves flourished again. In process of time this religious house again fell into desuetude; but before it disappeared it had achieved a great name for good works, and in especial for the piety of its members. I think I see now where your argument leads. I do not know if you started it, having thought it out to the full. But in any case I will venture an opinion; that if deeds and prayers and hopes and earnest thinking leave anywhere any moral effect, Mercy Farm and all around it have almost the right to be considered holy ground.'

'Thank you, sir,' said Adam earnestly, and was silent. Again Sir Nathaniel understood.

CHAPTER X
SMELLING DEATH

Adam Salton, though he made little talk, did not let the grass grow under his feet in any matter which he had undertaken, or in which he was interested. He had agreed with Sir Nathaniel that they should not *do* anything with regard to the mystery of Lady Arabella's fear of the mongoose, but he steadily pursued his course in being *prepared* to do whenever the opportunity might come. He was in his own mind perpetually casting about for information or clues which might lead to such. Baffled by the killing of the mongoose, he looked around for another line to follow. He did not intend to give up the idea of there being a link between the woman and the animal, but he was already preparing a second string to his bow. His new idea was to use the faculties of Oolanga, so far as he could, in the service of discovery. His first move was to send Davenport to Liverpool to try to find the steward of the *West African*, who had told him about Oolanga, and then to get him to try to induce (by bribery or other means) the nigger to come to the Brow. So soon as he himself would have speech of the Voodoo-man he would be able to learn from him something useful. Davenport went away in the early morning, and was successful in both his missions, for he had to get Ross to send another mongoose, and also the one reserved for sending when told; he was able to tell Adam that he had seen the steward, who already told him a lot he wanted to know, and had also arranged to have Oolanga brought to Lesser Hill the following day. At this point Adam saw his way sufficiently clear to adumbrate to Davenport with fair exactness what he wished him to find out. He had come to the conclusion that it would be better – certainly at first – not himself to appear in the matter, with which Davenport was fully competent to deal. It would be time for himself to take a personal part when matters had advanced a little further.

That evening, when Davenport arrived, he had a long interview with Adam, in which he told what he had learned, partly from the ship steward, partly from the other Africans in the ship's service, and partly from Oolanga's own boasting. If what the nigger said was in any wise true, the man had a rare gift which might be useful in the quest they were after. He could, as it were, 'smell death.' If any one was dead, if any one had died, or if a place had been used in connection with death, he seemed to know the broad fact by intuition. Adam made up his mind that to test this faculty with regard to several places would be his first task. Naturally he was anxious for this, and the time passed slowly. The only comfort was the arrival the next morning of a strong packing case, locked, from Ross, the key being in the custody of Davenport. In the case were two smaller boxes, both locked. One of them contained a mongoose to replace that killed by Lady Arabella; the other was the reserved mongoose which had already killed the king-cobra in Nepaul. When both the animals had been safely put under lock and key in the place arranged for them, he felt that he might breathe more freely. Of course no one was allowed to know the secret of their existence in the house, except himself and Davenport. He arranged that Davenport should take Oolanga round the neighbourhood for a walk, stopping at each of the places which he designated. Having gone all along the Brow, he was to return the same way and induce him to touch on the same subjects in talking with Adam, who was to meet them as if by chance at the farthest part – that beyond Mercy Farm. Davenport was never to lose sight of him and was to bring him back to Liverpool safely, and leave him on board the ship, where he was to wait till his master should send for him.

The incidents of the day were just what Adam expected. At Mercy Farm, at Diana's Grove, at Castra Regis, and a few other spots, he stopped and, opening his wide nostrils as if to sniff boldly, said that he smelled death. It was not always in the same form. At Mercy Farm he said there were many small deaths. At Diana's Grove his bearing was different. There was a distinct sense of enjoyment about him, especially when he spoke of many great deaths long ago. Here, too, he sniffed in a strange way, like a bloodhound at check, and looked puzzled. He said no word in either praise or disparagement, but in the centre of the Grove where, hidden amongst ancient oak stumps, was a block of granite slightly hollowed on the top, he bent low and placed his forehead on the ground. This was the only place where he showed distinct reverence. At the Castle, though he spoke of much death, he showed no sign of respect. There was evidently something about Diana's Grove which both interested and baffled him. Before leaving he moved all over the place unsatisfied, and in one spot where, close to the edge of the Brow, was a deep hollow, he appeared to be afraid. After returning several times to this place, he suddenly turned and ran in a panic of fear to the higher ground, crossing as he did so the outcropping rock. Then he seemed to breathe more freely, and even recovered some of his jaunty impudence.

All this seemed to satisfy Adam's expectations. He went back to Lesser Hill with a serene and settled calm upon him.

When he went back to the house, Adam met Sir Nathaniel, who followed him into his study, saying as he closed the door behind him:

'By the way, I forgot to ask you details about one thing. When that extraordinary staring episode of Mr Caswall went on, how did Lilla take it – how did she bear herself?'

'She looked frightened, and trembled just as I have seen a pigeon with a hawk, or a bird with a serpent.'

'Thanks. That will do. It is just as I expected. There have been circumstances in the Caswall family which lead one to believe that they have had from the earliest times some extraordinary mesmeric or hypnotic faculty. Indeed, a skilled eye could read so much in their physiognomy. That shot of yours, whether by instinct or intention, of the hawk and the pigeon was peculiarly apposite. I think we may settle on that as a fixed trait to be accepted throughout our investigation.'

When the dusk had fallen, Adam took the new mongoose –

not the one from Nepaul – and, carrying the box slung over his shoulder, strolled towards Diana's Grove. Close to the gateway he met Lady Arabella, clad as usual in tightly fitting white, which showed off her extraordinarily slim figure.

To his intense astonishment the mongoose allowed her to pet him, take him up in her arms and fondle him. As she was coming in his direction he left him with her and walked on.

Round the roadway between the entrances of Diana's Grove and Lesser Hill were many trees with tall thin trunks with not much foliage except at top. In the dusk this place was shadowy, and the view of anyone was hampered by the clustering trunks. In the uncertain, tremulous light which fell through the tree-tops, it was hard to distinguish anything clearly, and as Adam looked back it seemed to him that Lady Arabella was actually dancing in a fantastic sort of way. Her arms were opening and shutting and winding about strangely; the white fur which she wore round her throat was also twisting about, or seemed to be. Not a sound was to be heard. There was something uncanny in all this silent movement which struck Adam as worthy of notice; so he waited, almost stopping his progress altogether, and walked with lingering steps, so as to let her overtake him. But as the dusk was thickening he could distinguish no more than he could at first. At last somehow he lost sight of her altogether, and turned back on his track to find her. Presently he came across her close to her own gate. She was leaning over the paling of split oak branches which formed the paling of the avenue. He could not see the mongoose, so he asked her where he had gone to.

'He slipt out of my arms while I was petting him,' she answered, 'and disappeared under the hedges.'

As she spoke she was walking back with him looking for the little animal. They found him at a place where the avenue widened so as to let carriages pass each other. The little creature seemed quite changed. He had been ebulliently active; now he was dull and spiritless – seemed to be dazed. He allowed himself to be lifted by either of the pair; but when he was alone with Lady Arabella he kept looking round him in a strange way, as though trying to escape. When they had come out on the roadway Adam held the mongoose tight to him, and, lifting his hat to his companion, moved quickly towards Lesser Hill; he and Lady Arabella lost sight of each other in the thickening gloom.

When Adam got home he put the mongoose in his box, which was left in the room where he had been, and locked the door. The other mongoose – the one from Nepaul – was safely locked in his own box, but he lay quiet and did not stir. When he got to his study Sir Nathaniel came in, shutting the door behind him.

'I have come,' he said, 'while we have an opportunity of being alone, to tell you something of the Caswall family which I think will interest you. Somehow we got switched off when we were within touch of the subject this afternoon.'

Adam prepared himself to listen. The other began at once:

'The point I was coming to to-day, when we were diverted from the subject, was this: there is, or used to be, a belief in this part of the world that the Caswall family had some strange power of making the wills of other persons subservient to their own. There are many allusions to the subject in memoirs and other unimportant works, but I only know of one where the subject is spoken of definitely. It is *Mercia and its Worthies*, written by Ezra Toms more than a hundred years ago. The author more than infers that it was a mesmeric power, for he goes into the question of the close association of the then Edgar Caswall with Mesmer in Paris. He speaks of Caswall being a pupil and the fellow worker of Mesmer, and states that though, when the latter left France, he took away with him a vast quantity of philosophical and electric instruments, he was never known to use them again. He once made it known to a friend that he had given them to his old pupil. The term he used was odd, for it was "bequeathed," but no such bequest of Mesmer was ever made known. At any rate the instruments were missing, and never turned up. I just thought I would call your attention to this, as you might want to make a note of it. We have not come, yet at all events, to the mystery of the "hawk and the pigeon."'

Just as he finished speaking, a servant came into the room to tell Adam that there was some strange noise coming from the

locked room into which he had gone when he came in. He
hurried off to the place at once, Sir Nathaniel going with him.
Having locked the door behind him, Adam opened the packing-
case where the boxes of the two mongooses were locked up.
There was no sound from one of them, but from the other a
queer restless struggling. Having opened both boxes, he found
that the noise was from the Nepaul animal, which, however,
became quiet at once. In the other box the new mongoose lay
dead, with every appearance of having been strangled.

There was nothing to be done that night. So Adam locked
the boxes and the room again, taking with him the keys; and
both he and Sir Nathaniel went off to bed.

CHAPTER XI

THE FIRST ENCOUNTER

Adam Salton was up with the dawn, and, taking a fast horse, rode off to Liverpool, bringing with him, slung across his shoulders, the box with the body of the mongoose. He was so early that he had to wake up Mr Ross. From him he, however, got what he wanted, the address of a comparative anatomist,[1] who helped him in dealing with the health of his menagerie. Dr Cleaver lived not far away, and in a very short time Adam was ushered into his study. Unstrapping the box, he took out the body of the mongoose, now as stiff as wood, for the *rigor mortis* had long ago set in. Laying the body on Dr Cleaver's table, he said:

'Last night this was frisky in my arms. Now it is dead. What did it die of?'

The doctor went methodically to work and made a full examination. Then he said gravely:

'It may be necessary to make a more exhaustive examination. But in the meantime, I may say that it has been choked to death. And, considering the nature of its uses and its enemies, I think it was killed by some powerful snake of the constrictor class. Vast pressure must have been exercised, as every bone in its body seems to have been broken.' As the doctor accompanied Adam to the door, he said: 'Of course it is none of my business, but as I am a comparative anatomist, such things are of keen interest to me – I shall be really grateful if some time you will give me details of the death; and if you can possibly do so, supply me with weights and measures of both the animals.'

Adam, on paying his fee, thanked him warmly, gave him his card, and promised that some time later on he would be happy to tell him all he himself knew. Then he rode back to Lesser Hill and got in just as his uncle and Sir Nathaniel were sitting down to breakfast.

When breakfast was over, Sir Nathaniel went with Adam to the study. When he had closed the door, and Adam had told him all up to the previous night, he looked at the young man with a grave, inquiring glance and said:

'Well?'

Adam told him all that occurred at his visit to Dr Cleaver. He finished up with:

'I am at sea, sir. I am looking for your opinion.'

'So am I for yours,' said Sir Nathaniel. 'This gets worse and worse. It seems to me that the mysteries are only beginning. We have now a detective story added. I suppose there is nothing to do but to wait – as we are doing – for the other parts of the mystery.'

'Do you want me specially for anything this afternoon?' asked Adam, adding, 'Of course I am at your command if you do. If not, I thought of calling at Mercy Farm.' He said this with a diffidence which made the old man's stern features relax.

'I suppose you would not wish me to come with you?' he asked playfully.

Adam at once replied:

'I should love it, sir; but to-day I think it would be better not.' Then, seeing the other's inquiring look, he went on: 'The fact is, sir, that Mr Caswall is going to tea to-day, and I think it would be wiser if I were present.'

'Quite so. Of course you will tell me later if there should take place anything which it would be well for me to know.'

'Certainly. I shall try to see you as soon as I get home.'

They said no more, and a little after four o'clock Adam set out for Mercy.

He was home just as the clocks were striking six. He was pale and upset, but otherwise looked strong and alert. The old man summed up his appearance and manner thus: 'Braced up for battle.' Realising that Adam wished to talk with him, he quietly went over and locked the door.

'Now!' said Sir Nathaniel, and settled down to listen, looking at Adam steadily and listening attentively that he might miss nothing – even the inflection of a word.

'I found Miss Watford and Mimi at home. Watford had been detained by business on the farm. Miss Watford received me as kindly as before. Mimi, too, seemed glad to see me. Mr Caswall came so soon after I had arrived, that he or someone on his behalf must have been watching for me. He was followed closely by the Christy Minstrel, who was puffing hard as if he had been running – so it was probably he who watched. Mr Caswall was very cool and collected, but there was a more than usually iron look about his face that I did not like. However, both he and I got on very well. He talked pleasantly on all sorts of questions. The nigger waited a while and then disappeared as on the other occasion. Mr Caswall's eyes were as usual fixed on Lilla. True, they seemed to be very deep and earnest, but there was no offence in them. Had it not been for the drawing down of the brows and the stern set of the jaws, I should not at first have noticed anything. But the stare, when presently it began, increased in intensity. I could see that Lilla began to suffer from nervousness, as on the first occasion; but she carried herself bravely. However, the more nervous she grew, the harder Mr Caswall stared. It was evident to me that he had come prepared for some sort of mesmeric or hypnotic battle. After a while he began to throw glances round him and then raised his hand, without letting either Lilla or Mimi see the action. It was evidently intended to give some sign to the Christy Minstrel, for he came, in his usual stealthy way, quietly in by the hall door, which was open. Then Mr Caswall's efforts at staring became intensified, and poor Lilla's nervousness grew greater. Mimi, seeing that her cousin was distressed, came close to her, as if to comfort or strengthen her with the consciousness of her presence. This evidently made a difficulty for Mr Caswall, for his efforts, without seeming to get feebler, seemed less effective. This continued for a little while, to the gain of both Lilla and Mimi. Then there was a diversion. Without word or apology the door opened and Lady Arabella March entered the room. We had seen her coming through the great window. Without a word she crossed the room and stood beside Mr Caswall. It really was very like a fight of a peculiar kind; and the longer it was sustained the more earnest – the fiercer – it grew. That combination of forces – the over-lord, the white woman, and the black man – would have cost some – probably all of them – their lives in the Southern States of America. To us all it was simply horrible. But all that you can understand. This time, to go on in sporting phrase, it was understood by all to be a "fight to a finish," and the mixed group did not slacken a moment or relax their efforts. On Lilla the strain began to tell disastrously. She grew pale – a patchy pallor, which meant that all her nerves were out of order. She trembled like an aspen, and though she struggled bravely, I noticed that her legs would hardly stiffen. A dozen times she seemed about to collapse in a faint, but each time, on catching sight of Mimi's eyes, she made a fresh struggle and pulled through.

'By now Mr Caswall's face had lost its appearance of passivity. No longer was it immobile. His eyes glowed with a red fiery light. He was still the old Roman in inflexibility of purpose; but grafted on the Roman was a new Berserker fury.[2] The statical force of his nature had entered on a new phase. It had become dynamical. His companions in the baleful work seemed to have taken on something of his feeling. Lady Arabella looked like a soulless, pitiless being, not human unless it revived old legends of transformed human beings who had lost their humanity in some transformation or in the sweep of natural savagery. As for the Christy Minstrel, the only comparison I can suggest was a fiend from hell, engaged in the active pursuit of his natural purpose. I think I have already given you my impression of his lofty natural beauty. That I take back, for then I only spoke of possibilities . . . Now that I have seen his devilry in full blast, such a belief is inadequate. I can only say, that it was solely due to the self-restraint which you impressed on me that I did not wipe him out as he stood – without warning, without fair play – without a single one of the graces of life and death. Lilla was silent in the helpless concentration of deadly fear; Mimi was all resolve and self-forgetfulness, so intent on the soul-struggle in which she was engaged that there was no possibility of any other thought. As for myself, the bonds of will which held me inactive seemed like bands of steel which numbed all my faculties, except sight and hearing. I was limited absolutely to the power of waiting. We seemed fixed in an *impasse*. Something must happen, though the power of guessing what was inactive. As in a dream, I saw Mimi's hand move restlessly, as if groping for something. It was like a hand grown blind. Mechanically it touched that of Lilla, and in that instant she was transformed. It was as if youth and strength entered afresh into something already dead to sensibility and intention. As if by inspiration, she grasped the other's hand with a force which blenched the knuckles. Her face suddenly flamed, as if some divine light shone through it. Her form rose and expanded till it stood out majestically. Lifting her right hand, she stepped forward towards Caswall, and with a bold sweep of her arm seemed to drive some strange force towards him. Again and again was the gesture repeated, the man falling back from her at each movement. Towards the door he retreated, she following. There was a sound as of the cooing sob of doves, which seemed to multiply and intensify with each second. The sound from the unseen source rose and rose as he retreated, till finally it swelled out in a triumphant peal, as she, with a fierce sweep of her arm, seemed to hurl something at her foe, and he, moving his hands blindly before his face, appeared to be swept through the doorway and out into the open sunlight. At the same moment as he went, the light of day became suddenly dimmed, as though a mighty shadow had swept over the face of the earth. The air was full of a fierce continuous sound as of whirring wings.

'All at once my own faculties were fully restored; I could see and hear everything, and be fully conscious of what was going on. Even the figures of the baleful group were there, though dimly seen as through a veil – a shadowy veil. I saw Lilla sink down in a swoon, and Mimi throw up her arms in a gesture of triumph. As I saw her through the great window, the sunshine flooded the landscape, which, however, was momentarily becoming eclipsed by an on-rush of a myriad birds.

'Hark to the rushing of their wings!'

CHAPTER XII

THE KITE

By the next morning, daylight showed the actual danger which threatened the east side of England. From every part of the eastern counties reports were received concerning the enormous immigration of birds. Experts were sending – on their own account, on behalf of learned societies, and through local and imperial governing bodies – reports dealing with the matter, and suggesting remedies. As might have been expected, the latter were mostly worthless. They were either disguised or undisguised advertisements with some personal object, or else merely the babble of persons desirous of notoriety on a quasi-scientific basis. The long-suffering public showed by its indifference to such reports forced upon them that they were not such fools as they were supposed to be. Of course the reports closer to home were more disturbing, even if more monotonous, for Castra Regis was the very centre of the trouble. All day long, and even all night long, it would seem that the birds were coming thicker from all quarters. Doubtless many were going as well as coming, but the mass seemed never to get less. Each bird seemed to sound some note of fear or anger or seeking, and the whirring of wings never ceased nor lessened. The air was full of a muttered throb. No window or barrier could shut out the sound, till the ears of any listening became partly paralysed by the ceaseless sound. So monotonous it was, so cheerless, so disheartening, so melancholy, that all longed, but in vain, for any variety, no matter how terrible it might be.

The second morning the reports from all the districts round were more alarming than ever. Farmers began to dread the

coming of winter as they saw the dwindling of the timely fruit-
fulness of the earth. And as yet it was only warning of evil, not
the evil accomplished; the ground began to look bare whenever
some passing sound temporarily frightened the birds.

Edgar Caswall tortured his brain for a long time unavailingly,
to think of some means of getting rid of what he as well as his
neighbours had come to regard as a plague of birds. At last
he recalled a circumstance which promised a solution of the
difficulty. The experience was of some years ago in China, far
up-country, towards the head-waters of the Yang-tze-kiang,[1]
where the smaller tributaries spread out in a sort of natural
irrigation scheme to supply the wilderness of paddy-fields. It
was at the time of the ripening rice, and the wilderness of birds
which came to feed on the coming crop was a serious menace
not only to the district, but to the country at large. The farmers,
who were more or less afflicted with the same trouble every
season, knew how to deal with it. They made a vast kite, which
they caused to be flown over the centre spot of the incursion.
The kite was shaped like a great hawk; and the moment it rose
into the air the birds began to cower and seek protection and
then to disappear. So long as that kite was flying overhead the
birds lay low. The crop was saved. Accordingly Caswall had
his men construct an immense kite, adhering as well as they
could to the lines of a hawk. Then he and his men, with a
sufficiency of string, began to fly it high overhead. The experience of China was repeated. The moment the kite rose, the
birds hid or sought shelter. The following morning, the kite still
flying high, no bird was to be seen as far as the eye could reach
from Castra Regis. But there followed in turn what proved even
a worse evil. All the birds were cowed; their sounds stopped.
Neither song nor chirp was heard – silence seemed to have
taken the place of the myriad voices of bird life. But that was
not all. The silence spread to all animals.

The fear and restraint which brooded amongst the denizens
of the air began to affect all life. Not only did the birds cease
song or chirp, but the lowing of the cattle ceased in the fields
and the myriad sounds of life died away. In the place of these
things was only a soundless gloom, more dreadful, more dis-

heartening, more soul-killing than any concourse of sounds, no matter how full of fear and dread. Pious individuals and bodies put up constant prayers for relief from the intolerable solitude. After a little there were signs of universal depression which who ran might read.[2] One and all the faces of men and women seemed bereft of vitality, of interest, of thought, and, most of all, of hope. Men seemed to have lost the power of expression of their thoughts. The soundless air seemed to have the same effect as the universal darkness when men gnawed their tongues with pain.[3]

From this infliction of silence there was no relief. Everything was affected; gloom was the predominant note. Joy appeared to have passed away as a factor of life, and this creative impulse had nothing to take its place. That giant spot in high air was a plague of evil influence. It seemed like a new misanthropic belief which had fallen on human beings, carrying with it the negation of all hope. After a few days, men began to grow desperate; their very words as well as their senses seemed to be in chains. Edgar Caswall again tortured his brain to find any antidote or palliative of this greater evil than before. He would gladly have destroyed the kite, or caused its flying to cease; but he dared not. The instant it was pulled down, the birds rose up in even greater numbers; all those who depended in any way on agriculture sent pitiful protests to Castra Regis.

It was strange indeed what influence that kite seemed to exercise. Even human beings were affected by it, as if both it and they were realities. As for the people at Mercy Farm, it was like a taste of actual death. Lilla felt it most. If she had been indeed a real dove, with a real kite hanging over her in the air, she could not have been more frightened or more affected by the fright this created.

Of course, some of those already drawn into the vortex noticed the effect on individuals. Those who were interested took care to compare their information. They felt that it might be of service later on. Strangely enough, as it seemed to the others, the person who took the ghastly silence least to heart was the Christy Minstrel. By nature he was not a man sensitive to, or afflicted by, nerves. This alone would not have produced the seeming indifference, so they set their minds to discover the real cause. Adam came quickly to the conclusion that there was for him some compensation that the others did not share; and he soon believed that that compensation was in one form or another enjoyment of the sufferings of others. Thus, he had a never-failing source of amusement. The birds alone seemed as if they would satisfy even him. He took delight in the oppression by the predatory birds of the others of their kind. And then, even of them he took the occasion to add to his collection of beaks. Lady Arabella's cold nature rendered her immune to anything in the way of pain or trouble to or of others. And Edgar Caswall was far too haughty a person, and too stern of nature, to concern himself about even poor or helpless people, much less the lower order of mere animals. Mr Watford, Mr Salton, and Sir Nathaniel were all concerned in the issue, partly from kindness of heart – for none of them could see suffering, even of wild birds, unmoved – and partly on account of their property, which had to be protected, or ruin would stare them in the face before long. Lilla suffered acutely. As time went on, her face became pinched, and her eyes dull with watching and crying. Mimi suffered too on account of her cousin's suffering. But as she could do nothing, she resolutely made up her mind to self-restraint and patience. The inhabitants of the district around took the matter with indifference. They had been freed from the noises, and the silence did not trouble them. It is often so; people put a different and more lofty name on their own purposes. For instance, these people probably considered their own view founded on common weal, whereas it was merely indifference founded on selfishness.

CHAPTER XIII
MESMER'S CHEST

After a couple of weeks had passed, the kite seemed to give to Edgar Caswall a new zest for life. It appeared to have a satisfying influence on him. He was never tired of looking at its movements. He had a comfortable armchair put out on the tower, wherein he sat sometimes all day long, watching as though the kite was a new toy and he a child lately come into possession of it. He did not seem to have lost interest in Lilla, for he still paid an occasional visit at Mercy Farm.

Indeed, his feeling towards her, whatever it had been at first, had now so far changed that it had become a distinct affection of a purely animal kind. In the change of the kind of affection, the peculiarly impersonal, philosophic, almost platonic, had shed all the finer qualities that had belonged to it. Indeed, it seemed as though the man's nature had become corrupted, and that all the baser and more selfish and more reckless qualities had become more conspicuous. There was not so much sternness apparent in his nature, because there was less self-restraint. Determination had become indifference. Sensitiveness, such as had been, became callousness. Altogether, there did not seem to be in his nature the same singleness of purpose, either in kind or degree. Strangely, as he unconsciously yielded to this demoralising process, he seemed to be achieving a new likeness to Oolanga. Sometimes as Adam – ever on the watch – noticed the growing change, he began to wonder whether the body was answering to the mind or the mind to the body. Accordingly, it was a never-ending thought to him which momentum – the physical or the moral – was antecedent. The thing which puzzled him most was that the forbidding qualities in the African, which had at first evoked his attention and his disgust, remained the same. Had it been that the two men had been affected, one changing with the other by slow degrees – a sort of moral metabolism, – he could have better and more easily understood it. Transmutation of different bodies is, in a way, more under-standable than changes in one body that have no equivalent equipoise in the other. The idea was recurrent to him that perhaps when a nature has reached its lowest point of deca-dence[1] it loses the faculty of change of any kind. However it was, the fact remained. Oolanga preserved all his original brutal decadence, while Caswall slowly deteriorated without any hint of resilience.

The visible change in Edgar was that he grew morbid, sad, silent; the neighbours thought he was mad. He became absorbed in the kite, and watched it not only by day, but often all night long. It became an obsession to him.

Adam kept his eyes and ears open and his mouth shut. He felt that he was learning. And, indeed, he was not mistaken when he acted as if silence was a virtue. He took a certain amount of interest – pleasure would be too smooth a word – in the generally expressed opinions of the neighbours of Castra Regis. It was commonly held regarding Caswall that he was mad. He took a personal interest in the keeping of the great kite flying. He had a vast coil of string efficient for the purpose, which worked on a roller fixed on the parapet of the tower. There was a winch for the pulling in of the slack of the string; the outgoing line was controlled by a racket. There was invariably one man at least, day and night, on the tower to attend to it. At such an elevation there was always a strong wind, and at times the kite rose to an enormous height, as well as travelling for great distances laterally. In fact, the kite became, in a short time, one of the curiosities of Castra Regis and all around it. Edgar began to attribute to it, in his own mind, almost human qualities. It became to him a separate entity, with a mind and a soul of its own. Being idle-handed all day, he began to apply to what he considered the service of the kite some of his spare time, and found a new pleasure – a new object in life – in the old schoolboy game of sending up 'runners' to the kite. The way this is done is to get round pieces of paper so cut that there is a hole in the centre through which the string of the kite passes. The natural action of the wind-pressure takes the paper thus cut along the string, and so up to the kite itself, no matter how high or how far it may have gone. In the early days of this amusement Edgar Caswall spent hours. Hundreds of such messengers flew along the string, until soon he bethought him of writing messages on these papers so that he could make known his ideas to the kite. It may be that his brain gave way under the opportunities given by his foregone illusion of the entity of the toy and its power of separate thought. From sending messages he came to making direct speech to the kite – without, however, ceasing to send the runners. Doubtless, the height of the tower, seated as it was on the hill-top, the rushing of the ceaseless wind, the hypnotic effect of the lofty altitude of the speck in the sky at which he gazed, and the rushing of the paper messengers up the string till sight of them was lost in distance, all helped to further affect his brain, undoubtedly giving way under the strain of a concatenation of beliefs and circumstances which were at once stimulating to the imagination, occupative of his mind, and absorbing.

The next step of intellectual decline was to bring to bear on the main idea of the conscious identity of the kite all sorts of subjects which had imaginative force or tendency of their own. He had, in Castra Regis, a large collection of curious and interesting things formed in the past by his forebears, of similar likes to his own. There were all sorts of strange anthropological specimens, both old and new, which had been collected through various travels in strange places: ancient Egyptian relics from tombs, and mummies;[2] curios from Australia, New Zealand, and the South Seas; idols and images – from Tartar ikons to ancient Egyptian, Persian, and Indian objects of worship; objects of death and torture of American Indians; and, above all, a vast collection of lethal weapons of every kind and from every place – Chinese 'high pinders,' double knives, Afghan double-edged scimitars made to cut a body in two, heavy knives from all the Eastern countries, ghost daggers from Thibet, the terrible kukri of the Ghourka and other hill tribes of India,

assassins' weapons from Italy and Spain, even the knife which
was formerly carried by the slave-drivers of the Mississippi
region. Death and pain of every kind were fully represented in
that gruesome collection. That it had a fascination for Oolanga
goes without saying. He was never tired of visiting the museum
in the tower, and spent endless hours in inspecting the exhibits,
till he was thoroughly familiar with every detail of all of them.
He asked permission to clean and polish and sharpen them – a
favour which was readily granted. In addition to the above
objects, there were many things of a kind to awaken human
fear. Stuffed serpents of the most objectionable and horrid kind;
giant insects from the tropics, fearsome in every detail; fishes
and crustaceans covered with weird spikes; dried octopuses of
great size. Other things, too, there were not less deadly though
seemingly innocuous – dried fungi, the touch of which was
death and whose poison was carried on the air; also traps
intended for birds, beasts, fishes, reptiles, and insects; machines
which could produce pain of any kind and degree, and the only
mercy of which was the power of producing speedy death.
Caswall, who had never seen any of these things, except those
which he had collected himself, found a constant amusement
and interest in them. He studied them, their uses, their mechanism – where there was such, – and their places of origin, until
he had an ample and real knowledge of all belonging to them.
Many were secret and intricate, but he never rested till he found
out all the secrets. When once he had become interested in
strange objects and the way to use them, he began to explore
various likely places for similar finds. He began to inquire of
his household where strange lumber was kept. Several of the
men spoke of old Simon Chester as one who knew everything
in and about the house. Accordingly, he sent for the old man,
who came at once. He was very old, nearly ninety years of age,
and very infirm. He had been born in the Castle, and served its
succession of masters – present or absent – ever since. When
Edgar began to question him on the subject regarding which he
had sent for him, old Simon exhibited much perturbation. In
fact, he became so frightened that his master, fully believing
that he was concealing something, ordered him to tell at once

what remained unseen, and where such was hidden away. Face to face with discovery of his secret, the old man, in a pitiable state of concern, spoke out even more fully than Mr Caswall had expected:

'Indeed, indeed, sir, everything is here in the tower that has ever been imported or put away in my time – except – except' – here he began to shake and tremble – 'except the chest which Mr Edgar – he who was Mr Edgar when I first took service – brought back from France, after he had been with Dr Mesmer. The trunk has been kept in my room for safety; but I shall send it down here now.'

'What is in it?' asked Edgar sharply.

'That I do not know. Moreover, it is a peculiar trunk, without any visible means of opening it.'

'Is there no lock?'

'I suppose so, sir; but I do not know. There is no keyhole.'

'Send it here; and then come to me yourself.'

The trunk, a heavy one with steel bands round it, but no lock or keyhole, was carried in by four men. Shortly afterwards old Simon attended his master. When he came into the room, Mr Caswall himself went and closed the door; then he asked:

'How do you open it?'

'I do not know, sir.'

'Do you mean to say you never opened it?'

With considerable and pathetic dignity, the old man answered:

'Most certainly I do say so, your honour. How could I? It was entrusted to me with the other things by my master. To open it would have been a breach of trust.'

Caswall sneered as he said:

'Quite remarkable! Leave it with me. Close the door behind you. Stay – did no one ever tell you about it – say anything regarding it – make any remark?'

Old Simon turned pale, and put his trembling hands together as though imploring:

'Oh, sir, I entreat you not to touch it. That probably contains secrets which Dr Mesmer told my master. Told them to his ruin!'

'How do you mean? What ruin?'

'Sir, he it was who, men said, sold his soul to the Evil One; I had thought that that time and the evil of it had all passed away.'

'That will do. Go away; but remain in your own room, or within call. I may want you.'

The old man bowed deeply and went out trembling, but without speaking a word.

CHAPTER XIV
THE CHEST OPENED

Left alone in the turret-room, Edgar Caswall carefully locked the door and hung a handkerchief over the keyhole. Next, he inspected the windows, and saw that they were not overlooked from any angle of the main building. Then he carefully examined the trunk, going over it with a magnifying glass. He found it intact: the steel bands were flawless; the whole trunk was compact into unity. After sitting opposite to it for some time, and the shades of evening beginning to melt into darkness, he gave up the task and took himself to his bedroom, after locking the door of the turret-room behind him and taking away the key.

He woke in the morning at daylight, and resumed his patient but unavailing study of the metal trunk. This he continued during the whole day with the same result – humiliating disappointment which overwrought his nerves and made his head ache. The result of the long strain was seen later in the afternoon, when he sat locked within the turret-room before the still baffling trunk, distrait, listless and yet agitated, sunk in a settled gloom. As the dusk was falling he told the steward to send him four men, strong ones. These he told to take the trunk to his bedroom. In that room he then sat on into the night, without pausing even to take any food. His mind was in a whirl, a fever of excitement. The result was that when late in the night he locked himself in his room his brain was full of odd fancies; he was on the high road to mental disturbance. He lay down on his bed in the dark, still brooding over the mystery of the closed trunk.

Gradually he yielded to the influences of silence and darkness.

After lying there quietly for some time his mind became active again. But this time there were round him no disturbing influences; his brain was active and able to work freely and to deal with memory. A thousand forgotten – or only half-known – incidents, fragments of conversations or theories long ago guessed at and long forgotten, crowded in on his mind. He seemed to hear again around him the legions of whirring wings to which he had been so lately accustomed. Even to himself he knew that that was an effort of imagination founded on imperfect memory. But he was content that imagination should work, for out of it might come some solution of the mystery which surrounded him. And in this frame of mind, sleep made another and more successful essay. This time he enjoyed peaceful slumber, restful alike to his wearied body and his overwrought brain.

In his sleep in the darkness he arose, and, as if in obedience to some influence beyond and greater than himself, lifted the great trunk and set it on a strong table at one side of the room, from which he had previously removed a quantity of books. To do this, he had to use an amount of strength which was, he knew, far beyond him in his normal state. As it was, it seemed easy enough; everything yielded before his touch. Then he became conscious that somehow – how, he never could remember – the chest was open. Again another wonder. He unlocked his door, and, taking the chest on his shoulder, carried it up to the turret-room, the door of which also he unlocked. Even at the time he was amazed at his own strength, and wondered unavailingly whence it had come. His mind, lost in conjecture, was too far off to realise more immediate things. He knew that the chest was enormously heavy. He seemed, in a sort of vision which lit up the absolute blackness around, to see the four sturdy servant men staggering under its great weight. He locked himself again in the turret-room and laid the opened chest on a table, and in the darkness began to carefully unpack it, laying out the contents, which were mainly of metal and glass – great pieces in strange forms, – on another table. He was conscious of being still asleep, and of acting rather in obedience to some unseen and unknown command than in accordance with any reasonable plan to be followed by results which he understood and was aiming at. This phase completed, he proceeded to arrange in order the component parts of some large instruments formed mostly of glass. His fingers seemed to have acquired a new and exquisite subtlety and even a volition of their own. Then he brought some force to bear – how or where, he knew not, – and soon the room was filled with the whirr of machinery moving at great speed. Through the darkness, in its vicinity, came irregularly quick intermittent flashes of dazzling light. All else was still. Then weariness of brain came upon him; his head sank down on his breast, and little by little everything became wrapped in gloom.

He awoke in the early morning in his bedroom, and looked around him, now clear-headed, in amazement. In its usual place on the strong table stood the great steel-hooped chest without lock or key. But it was now locked. He arose quietly and stole to the turret-room. There everything was as it had been on the previous evening. He looked out of the window where high in air flew, as usual, the giant kite. He unlocked the wicket gate of the turret stair and went out on the roof. Close to him was the great coil of string on its reel. It was humming in the morning breeze, and when he touched the string it sent a quick thrill through hand and arm. There was no sign anywhere that there had been any disturbance or displacement of anything during the night.

Utterly bewildered, he sat down in his room to think. Now for the first time he *felt* that he was asleep and dreaming. Presently he fell asleep again, and slept for a long time. He awoke hungry and made a hearty meal. Then towards evening, having locked himself in, he fell asleep again. When he awoke he was in darkness, and was quite at sea as to his whereabouts. He began feeling about the dark room, and was recalled to the consequences of his position by the breaking of a large piece of glass. This he, having obtained a light, discovered to be a glass wheel, part of an elaborate piece of mechanism which he must have in his sleep taken from the chest, which was opened. He had once again opened it whilst asleep, but he had no sort of recollection of the circumstances. He came to the conclusion that there had been some sort of dual action of his mind which might lead to some catastrophe or some discovery of his secret plans; so he resolved to forgo for a while the pleasure of making discoveries regarding the chest. To this end, he applied himself to quite another matter – an investigation of the other treasures and rare objects in his collections. He went amongst them in simple, idle curiosity, his main object being to discover some strange item which he might use for experiment with the kite. He had already resolved to try some runners other than those made of paper. He had a vague idea that with such a force as the great kite straining at its leash, this might be used to lift to the altitude of the kite itself heavier articles. His first experiment with articles of little but increasing weight was eminently successful. So he added by degrees more and more weight, until he found out that the lifting power of the kite was considerable. He then determined to take a step still further, and to use for sending to the kite some of the articles which lay in the steel-hooped chest. The last time he had opened it in sleep it had not been shut again, so he had inserted a wedge so that he could open it at will. He made examination of the contents, but came to the conclusion that the glass objects were unsuitable. They were too light for testing weight, and they were so frail as to be dangerous to send to such a height. So he looked around for something more solid with which to experiment. His eye caught sight of an object which at once attracted him. This was a small copy of one of the ancient Egyptian gods – that of Bes, who represented the destructive power of nature.[1] It was so bizarre and mysterious as to commend itself to his humour. In lifting it from the cabinet, he was struck by its great weight in proportion to its size. He made accurate examination of it by the aid of some philosophical instruments, and came to the conclusion that it was carven from a lump of lodestone. He remembered that he had read somewhere of an ancient Egyptian god cut from a similar substance, and, thinking it over, he came to the conclusion that he must have read it in Sir Thomas Brown's *Popular Errors*,[2] a book of the seventeenth century. He got the book from the library, and looked out the passage:

   'A great example we have from the observation of our learned friend Mr *Graves*,[3] in an Ægyptian idol cut out of Loadstone and found among the *Mummies*; which still retains its attraction, though probably taken out of the mine about two thousand years ago.' – Book II, Chap. VII.

The strangeness of the figure, and its being so close akin to his own nature, attracted him. He made from thin wood a large circular runner and in front of it placed the weighty god, and sent it up to the flying kite along the throbbing string.

CHAPTER XV
OOLANGA'S HALLUCINATIONS

During the last days Lady Arabella had been getting exceedingly impatient. Her debts, always pressing, were growing to an embarrassing amount. The only hope she had of comfort in life was a good marriage; but the good marriage on which she had fixed her eye did not seem to move quickly enough – indeed, it did not seem to move at all – in the right direction. Edgar Caswall was not an ardent wooer. From the very first he seemed *difficile*, but now he had been keeping to his own room ever since his struggle with Mimi Watford. On that occasion she had shown him in an unmistakable way what her feelings were; indeed, she had made it known to him, in a more overt way than pride should allow, that she wished to help and support him. The moment when she had gone across the room to stand beside him in his mesmeric struggle, had been the very limit of her voluntary action. It was quite bitter enough, she felt, that he did not come to her, but now that she had made that advance, she felt that any withdrawal on his part would, to a woman of her class, be nothing less than a flaming insult. Had she not classed herself with his nigger servant, an unreformed savage? Had she not shown her preference for him at the festival of his home-coming? Had she not ... Lady Arabella was cold-blooded, and she was prepared to go through all that might be necessary of indifference and even insult to become chatelaine of Castra Regis. In the meantime, she would show no hurry – she would wait. She would even, in an unostentatious way, come to him again. She knew him now, and could make a keen guess at his desires with regard to Lilla Watford. With that secret in her possession, she could bring pressure to bear on him which would make it no easy matter to evade her. The great difficulty she had was how to get near him. He was shut up within his Castle, and guarded by a defence of convention which she could not pass without danger of ill repute to herself. Over this question she thought and thought for days and nights. At last she thought she saw a way of getting at him. She would go to him openly at Castra Regis. Her individual rank and position would make such a thing possible if carefully done. She could explain matters afterwards if necessary. Then when they were alone – as she would manage – she would use her arts and her experience to make him commit himself. After all, he was only a man, with a man's dislike of difficult or awkward situations. She felt quite sufficient confidence in her own womanhood to carry her through any difficulty which might arise. From Diana's Grove she heard each day the luncheon-gong from Castra Regis sound, and knew the hour when the servants would be in the back of the house. She would enter the house at that hour, and, pretending that she could not make anyone hear her, would seek him in his own rooms. The tower was, she knew, away from all the usual sounds of the house, and moreover she knew that the servants had strict orders not to interrupt him when he was in the turret chamber. She had found out, partly by the aid of an opera-glass and partly by judicious questioning, that several times lately a heavy chest had been carried to and from his room, and that it rested in the room each night. She was, therefore, confident that he had some important work on hand which would keep him busy for long spells. And so she was satisfied that all was going well with her – that her designs were ripening.

Synchronously, another member of the household at Castra Regis had got ideas which he thought were working to fruition. A man in the position of a servant has plenty of opportunity of watching his betters and forming opinions regarding them. Oolanga, now living at the Castle, was in his way a clever, unscrupulous man, and he felt that with things moving round him in this great household there should be opportunities of self-advancement. Being unscrupulous and stealthy – and a savage – he looked to dishonest means. He saw plainly enough that Lady Arabella was making a dead set at his master, and he was watchful of even the slightest sign of anything which might materialise this knowledge. Like the other men in the house, he knew of the carrying to and fro of the great chest, and had got it into his head that the care exercised in its portage indicated that it was full of great treasure. He was for ever lurking around the turret-rooms on the chance of making some useful discovery. But he was as cautious as he was stealthy, and took care that no one else watched him. It was thus that he became aware of Lady Arabella's venture into the house, as she thought, unseen. He took more care than ever, since he was watching another, that the positions were not reversed. More than ever he kept his eyes and ears open and his mouth shut. Seeing Lady Arabella gliding up the stairs towards his master's room, he took it for granted that she was there for no good, and doubled his watching intentness and caution. She waited patiently, hidden in his room, till Caswall returned upstairs after his lunch. She took care not to frighten or startle him in any way. As she did not know that anyone was watching and listening, her movements were merely a part of caution. She knew that sudden surprise occasions sudden sound, and that by this, in turn, others who were listeners would almost of necessity betray themselves. Oolanga was disappointed, but he dared not exhibit any feeling on the subject lest it should betray that he was hiding. Therefore he slunk downstairs again noiselessly, and waited for a more favourable opportunity of furthering his plans. It must be borne in mind that he thought that the heavy trunk was full of valuables, and that he believed that Lady Arabella had come to try to steal it. His purpose of using for his own advantage the combination of these two ideas was seen later in the day. When, after some time, Lady Arabella had given up the idea of seeing Caswall that afternoon, she moved quietly out of the Castle, taking care not to be noticed either within the house or outside it. Oolanga secretly followed her. He was an expert at this game, and succeeded admirably on this occasion. He watched her enter the private gate of Diana's Grove and then, taking a roundabout course and keeping altogether out of her sight, by following her at last overtook her in a thick part of the Grove where no one could see the meeting. Lady Arabella was at the moment much surprised. She had not seen him for several days, and had almost forgotten his existence. Oolanga would have been surprised had he known and been capable of understanding the real value placed on him, his beauty, his worthiness, by other persons, and compared it with the value in these matters in which he held himself. But in some cases, if ignorance be bliss, bliss has a dynamic quality which later leads to destruction. Doubtless Oolanga had his dreams like other men. In such cases he doubtless saw himself – or would have done had he had the knowledge with which to make the comparison – as a young sun-god – colour not stated – as beautiful as the eye of dusky or even white womanhood had ever dwelt upon. He would have been filled with all noble and captivating qualities regarded as such in West Africa. Women would have loved him, and would have told him so in the overt and fervid manner usual in affairs of the alleged heart in the shadowy depths of the forest of the Gold Coast.[1] After all, etiquette is a valuable factor in the higher circles of even Africa in reducing chaos to social order and in avoiding mistakes properly ending in lethal violence. Had he known of such an educational influence, the ambitious Oolanga might have regretted its absence from his curriculum. But as it was, intent on his own ends, he went on in blind ignorance of offence. He came close behind Lady Arabella, and in a hushed voice suitable to the importance of his task, and in deference to the respect he had for her and the place, began to unfold the story of his love. Lady Arabella was not usually a humorous person, but no man or woman born with the usual risible faculties of the white race could have checked the laughter which rose spontaneously to her lips. The circumstances were too grotesque, the contrast too violent, for even subdued mirth. The man a debased specimen of one of the most debased races of the earth, and of an ugliness which was simply devilish; the woman of high degree, beautiful, accomplished. She thought that her first moment's consideration of the outrage – it was nothing less in her eyes – had given her the full material for thought. But every instant after threw new and varied lights on

the affront. Her indignation was too great for passion: only
irony or satire would meet the situation. And so her temper
was able to stand the test. Calmed by a few moments of irony,
she found voice. Her cold, cruel nature helped, and she did not
shrink to subject even the poor ignorant savage to the merciless
fire-lash of her scorn. Oolanga was dimly conscious, at most,
that he was being flouted in a way he least understood; but his
anger was no less keen because of the measure of his ignorance.
So he gave way to it as does a tortured beast. He ground his
great teeth together, he raved, he stamped, he swore in barbarous tongues and with barbarous imagery. Even Lady Arabella
felt that it was well she was within reach of help, or he might
have offered her brutal violence – even have killed her.

'Am I to understand,' she said with cold disdain, so much
more effective to wound than hot passion, 'that you are offering
me your love? *Your* – love?'

For reply he nodded his head. The scorn of her voice in a
sort of baleful hiss sounded – and felt – like the lash of a whip.

Then she continued, her passion rising as she spoke:

'And you dared! you – a savage – a slave – the basest thing
in the world of vermin! Take care! I don't value your worthless
life more than I do that of a rat or spider. Don't let me ever see
your hideous face here again, or I shall rid the earth of you. Have
you anything to say for yourself why I should not kill you?'

As she was speaking, she had taken out her revolver and was
pointing it at him. In the immediate presence of death his
impudence forsook him, and he made a weak effort to justify
himself. His speech was short, consisting of single words. To
Lady Arabella it sounded mere gibberish, but it was in his own
dialect, and meant love, marriage, wife. From the intonation of
the words, she guessed, with her woman's quick intuition, at
their meaning; but she quite failed to follow when, becoming
more pressing, he continued to urge his suit in a mixture of the
grossest animal passion and ridiculous threats. In the latter he
said that he knew she had tried to steal his master's treasure,
and that he had caught her in the act. So if she would be his he
would share the treasure with her, and they would live in luxury
in the African forests. But if she refused, he would tell his

master, who would flog and torture her and then give her to the police, who would kill her.

Altogether it was a fine mixture of opposing base projects, just such as a savage like him might be expected to evolve out of his passions.

CHAPTER XVI

BATTLE RENEWED

The consequences of that meeting in the dusk of Diana's Grove were acute and far-reaching, and not only to the two engaged in it. From Oolanga, this might have been expected by anyone who knew the character of the tropical African savage. To such, there are two passions that are inexhaustible and insatiable – vanity and that which they are pleased to call love. Oolanga left the Grove with an absorbing hatred in his heart. His lust and greed were afire, and his vanity had been wounded to the core. Lady Arabella's icy nature was not so deeply stirred, though she too was in a seething passion. More than ever was she set upon bringing Edgar Caswall to her feet. The obstacles she had encountered, the insults she had endured, were only as fuel to the purpose of revenge which consumed her.

As she sought her own rooms in Diana's Grove, she went over the whole subject again and again, always finding in the face of Lilla Watford a key to a problem which puzzled her – the problem of a way to turn Caswall's powers – his very existence – to aid her purpose.

When in her boudoir, she wrote a note, taking so much trouble over it that she wrote, destroyed, and rewrote, till her dainty waste-basket was half-full of torn sheets of notepaper. When quite satisfied, she copied out the last sheet afresh, and then carefully burned all the spoiled fragments. She put the copied note in an emblazoned envelope, and directed it to Edgar Caswall at Castra Regis. This she sent off by one of her grooms. The letter ran:

'DEAR MR CASWALL, – I want to have a little chat with you on a subject in which I believe you are interested. Will you kindly call for me to-day after lunch – say at three or four o'clock, and we can walk a little way together. Only as far as Mercy Farm, where I want to see Lilla and Mimi Watford. We can take a cup of tea at the Farm. Do not bring your African servant with you, as I am afraid his face frightens the girls. After all, he is not pretty, is he? I have an idea you will be pleased with your visit this time. – Yours sincerely,

'ARABELLA MARCH.'

At half-past three Edgar Caswall called at Diana's Grove. Lady Arabella met him on the roadway outside the gate. She wished to take the servants into confidence as little as possible. She turned when she saw him coming, and walked beside him towards Mercy Farm, keeping step with him as they walked. When they got near Mercy, she turned and looked around her, expecting to see Oolanga or some sign of him. He was, however, not visible. He had received from his master peremptory orders to keep out of sight – an order for which the African scored a new offence up against her. They found Lilla and Mimi at home and seemingly glad to see them, though both the girls were surprised at the visit coming so soon after the other.

The proceedings were a simple repetition of the battle of souls of the former visit. On this occasion, however, Edgar Caswall seemed as if defeated, even before the strife began. This was the more strange, as on this occasion he had only the presence of Lady Arabella to support him – Oolanga being absent. Moreover, Mimi lacked on the present occasion the support of Adam Salton, which had been of such effective service before. This time the struggle for supremacy of will was longer and more determined. Caswall felt that if on this occasion he could not achieve supremacy, he had better give up the idea of trying to settle at Castra Regis, and so all his pride was enlisted against Mimi. When they had been waiting for the door to be opened, Lady Arabella, believing in a sudden attack, had said to him in a low, stern voice which somehow carried conviction:

'This time you should win. She is, after all, only a woman. Show her no mercy. That is weakness. Fight her, beat her, trample on her, kill her if need be. She stands in your way, and I hate her. Never take your eyes off her. Never mind Lilla – she is afraid of you. You are already her master. The other, Mimi, will try to make you look at her cousin. Do not. There lies defeat. Let nothing – no, not death itself, no matter of whom – take your attention from Mimi, and you will win. If she is overcoming you, take my hand and hold it hard whilst you are looking into her eyes. If she is too strong for you, I shall interfere. I shall make a diversion, and under the shade of it you must retire unbeaten, even if not victorious. Hush! silence! they are coming. Be resolute, and still.'

The two girls came to the door together. They had been fixing up an æolian harp[1] which Adam had given Mimi. At the open door they listened for a few moments. Strange sounds were coming up over the Brow from the east. It was the rustling and crackling of the dry reeds and rushes from the low lands on the hither side of the Eastern Sea. The season had been an unusually dry one. Also the sound came from another cause: the strong east wind was helping forward enormous flocks of birds, most of them pigeons with white cowls. Not only were their wings whirring, but their cooing was plainly audible. From such a multitude of birds the mass of sound, individually small, assumed the volume of a storm. Surprised at the influx of birds, to which they had been strangers so long, they all looked towards Castra Regis, from whose high tower the great kite had been flying as usual. But even as they looked the string broke, and the great kite fell headlong in a series of sweeping dives. Its own weight and the aerial force opposed to it which caused it to rise, combined with the strong easterly breeze, had been too much for the great length of cord holding it.

Somehow, the mishap to the kite gave new hope to Mimi. It was as though the side issues had been shorn away, so that the main struggle was thenceforth on simpler lines. She had a feeling in her heart as though some religious chord had been newly touched. It may, of course, have been that with the renewal of the bird voices a fresh courage, a fresh belief in the good issue

of the struggle came too. It may also have been that the unaccustomed sounds of the æolian harp woke fresh trains of thought.
In the misery of silence, from which they had all for so long
suffered, any new train of thought was almost bound to be a
boon. As the inrush of birds continued, their wings beating
against the crackling rushes, Lady Arabella suddenly grew pale,
and almost fainted. With strained ears she listened, and suddenly asked:

'What is that?'

To Mimi, bred in Siam,[2] the sound was strangely like an
exaggeration of the sound produced by a snake-charmer. It was
doubtless the union of the crackling from the rushes and the
weird sound of the harp; but no one asked explanation, and
none offered it.

Edgar Caswall was the first to recover from the interruption
of the falling kite. After a few minutes he seemed to have quite
recovered his *sang froid*, and was able to use his brains to the
end which he had in view. Mimi too quickly recovered herself,
but from a different cause. With her it was a deep religious
conviction that the struggle round her was of the powers of
Good and Evil, and that Good was triumphing. The very
appearance of the snowy birds, with the cowls of Saint Columba, heightened the impression. With this conviction strong
upon her, it is hardly to be wondered at that she continued the
strange battle with fresh vigour. She seemed to tower over
Caswall, and he to give back before her oncoming. Once again
her vigorous passes drove him to the door. He was just going
out backward when Lady Arabella, who had been gazing at
him with fixed eyes, caught his hand and tried to stop his
retrograde movement. She was, however, unable to stop him,
and so holding hands they passed out together. As they did so,
the strange music which had so alarmed Lady Arabella suddenly
stopped. Instinctively they looked toward the tower of Castra
Regis, and saw that the workmen had refixed the kite, which
had risen again and was beginning to float out to its former
station.

As they were looking, the door opened and Michael Watford
came into the room. By that time all had recovered their

self-possession, and there was nothing out of the common to attract his attention. As he came in, seeing inquiring looks all around him, he said:

'A telegram has come from the Agricultural Department. The new influx of birds is only the annual migration of pigeons from Africa. They say it will soon be over.'

CHAPTER XVII
THE SHUTTING OF
THE DOOR

The second victory of Mimi Watford made Edgar Caswall more moody than ever. He felt thrown back on himself, and this, superadded to his absorbing interest in the hope of a victory of his will, was now a deep and settled purpose of revenge. The chief object of his animosity was, of course, Mimi, whose will had overcome his, but it was obscured in greater or lesser degree by all who had opposed him. Lilla was next to Mimi in his hate – Lilla, the harmless, tender-hearted, sweet-natured girl, whose heart was so full of love for all things that in it was no room for the passions of ordinary life – whose nature resembled those doves of St Columba, whose colour she wore, whose appearance she reflected. Adam Salton came next – after a gap; for against him Caswall had no direct animosity. He regarded him as an interference, a difficulty in the way to be got rid of or destroyed. The young Australian had been so discreet that the most he had against him was his knowledge of what had been. Caswall did not understand him, and to such a nature as his, ignorance was a cause of alarm, of dread. He resumed his habit of watching the great kite straining at its cord, varying his vigils in this way by a further examination of the mysterious treasures of his house, especially Mesmer's chest. He sat much on the roof of the tower, brooding over all his thwarted hopes. The vast extent of his possessions visible to him at that altitude might, one would have thought, have restored some of his complacency. But not so; the very extent of his ownership thus perpetually brought before him made a fresh sense of grievance. How was it, he thought, that with so much at command that others wished for, he could not achieve the dearest wishes of his

heart? It was the very cry of fallible humanity, which, because it
yearns for something as yet unattainable, looks on disappointment to his wishes as a personal and malicious wrong done to
himself by the powers that be. In this state of intellectual and
moral depravity, he found a solace in the renewal of his experiments with the mechanical powers of the kite. This study helped
to take him out of himself, to bring his esoteric woes in exoteric
thought, even in his bafflements had an element of comfort,
though a melancholy one. For quite a couple of weeks he did
not see Lady Arabella, who was always on the watch for a
chance of meeting him; neither did he see the Watford girls,
who studiously kept out of his way. Adam Salton simply
marked time, keeping himself ready to deal with anything at
his hands that might affect his friends. He heard from Mimi of
the last battle of wills, but it had only one consequence of one
kind. He got from Ross several more mongooses, including a
second king-cobra-killer, which he generally carried with him
in its box whenever he walked out.

He constantly saw Sir Nathaniel de Salis, and the two talked
over the things that happened, and they remembered all the
things that had been before these; so that the two who thought
and remembered seemed also to know what would be before it
too happened.

Mr Caswall's experiments with the kite went on successfully.
Each day he tried the lifting of greater weight, and it seemed
almost as if the machine had a sentience of its own, which was
increasing with the obstacles placed before it. All this time the
kite hung in the sky at an enormous height. The wind was
steadily from the north, so the trend of the kite was to the
south. All day long, runners of increasing magnitude were sent
up. These were only of paper or thin cardboard, or leather, or
other flexible materials. The great height at which the kite hung
made a great concave curve in the string, so that as the runners
went up they made a flapping sound. If one laid a hand or a
finger on the string, the sound answered to the flapping of the
runner in a sort of hollow intermittent murmur. Edgar Caswall,
who was now wholly obsessed by the kite and all belonging to
it, found a distinct resemblance between that intermittent rum-

ble and the snake-charming music produced by the pigeons flying through the dry reeds whilst the æolian harp was playing.

One day he made a discovery in Mesmer's chest which he thought he would utilise with regard to the runners. This was a great length of wire 'fine as human hair,' coiled round a finely made wheel, which ran to a wondrous distance freely, and as lightly. He tried this on runners, and found it worked admirably. Whether the runner was alone, or carried something much more weighty than itself, it worked equally well. Also it was strong enough and light enough to easily draw back the runner without undue strain. He tried this a good many times successfully, but it was now growing dusk and he found some difficulty in keeping the runner in sight. So he looked for something heavy enough to keep it still. He placed this, which happened to be the Egyptian image of Bes, on the fine wire which crossed the wooden ledge which protected it. Then the darkness growing, he went indoors and forgot all about it. He had a strange feeling of uneasiness that night – not sleeplessness, for he was conscious of being asleep. At daylight he rose, and as usual looked out for the kite. He did not see it in its usual position in the sky, so took a glass and looked all round the points of the compass. He was more than astonished when presently he saw the missing kite struggling as customary against the controlling string. But it had gone to the further side of the tower, and now hung and strained *against the wind* to the north. He thought it so strange that he determined to investigate the phenomenon, and to say nothing about it in the meantime. In his many travels, Edgar Caswall had been accustomed to use the sextant,[1] and was now an expert in the matter. By the aid of this and other instruments of the kind, he was able to fix the exact position of the kite and the point over which it hung. He was actually startled to find exactly under it – so far as he could ascertain – was Diana's Grove. He had an inclination to take Lady Arabella into his confidence in the matter, but he thought better of it and wisely refrained. For some reason which he did not even try to explain to himself, he was glad of his silence, when on the following morning he found, on looking out, that the point over which the kite then hovered was Mercy Farm. When he had verified this with his instruments, he sat before the window of the tower, looking out and thinking. The new locality was more to his liking than the other; but the why of it puzzled him, all the same. He spent the rest of the day in the turret-room, which he did not leave all day. It seemed to him that he was now drawn by forces which he could not control – of which, indeed, he had no knowledge – in directions which he did not understand, and which were without his own volition. In sheer helpless inability to think the problem out satisfactorily, he called up a servant and told him to tell Oolanga that he wanted to see him at once in the turret-room. The answer came back that the African had not been seen since the previous evening. He was now so irritable that even this small thing upset him. As he was distrait and wanted to talk to somebody, he sent for Simon Chester, who came at once, breathless with hurrying and upset by the unexpected summons. Caswall made him sit down, and when the old man was in a less uneasy frame of mind, he again asked him if he had ever seen what was in Mesmer's chest or heard it spoken of. Chester admitted that he had once in the time of 'the then Mr Edgar' seen the chest open, which, knowing something of its history and guessing more, so upset him that he had fainted. When he recovered, the chest was closed. From that time the then Mr Edgar had never spoken about it again.

When Caswall asked him to describe what he had seen when the chest was open, he got very agitated, and, despite all his efforts to remain calm, he suddenly went off into a dead faint. Caswall summoned servants, who applied the usual remedies. Still the old man did not recover. After the lapse of a considerable time, the doctor who had been summoned made his appearance. A glance was sufficient for him to make up his mind. Still, he knelt down by the old man, and made a careful examination. Then he rose to his feet, and in a hushed voice said:

'I grieve to say, sir, that he has passed away.'

CHAPTER XVIII
ON THE TRACK

Those who had seen Edgar Caswall familiarly since his arrival, and had already estimated his cold-blooded nature at something of its true value, were surprised that he took so to heart the death of old Chester. The fact was that not one of them had guessed correctly at his character. Good, simple souls, they had estimated it by their own. They thought, and naturally enough, that the concern which he felt was that of a master for a faithful old servant of his family. They little thought that it was merely the selfish expression of his disappointment that he had lost the only remaining clue to an interesting piece of family history – one which was now and would be for ever wrapped in mystery. Caswall knew enough of the life of his ancestor in Paris to wish to know more fully and more thoroughly all that had been. The period covered by that ancestor's life in Paris was one inviting every form of curiosity. The only one who *seemed* to believe in the sincerity of his sorrow was Lady Arabella, who had her own game to play, and who saw in the *métier* of sympathetic friend a series of meetings with the man she wanted to get hold of. She made the first use of the opportunity the day after old Chester's death; indeed, so soon as ever the news had filtered in through the back door of Diana's Grove. At that meeting, she played her part so well that even Caswall's cold nature was impressed. Oolanga was the only one who did not credit her with at least some sense of fine feeling in the matter. But this was only natural, for he was perhaps the only one who did not know what fine feeling meant. In emotional, as in other matters, Oolanga was distinctly a utilitarian, and as he could not understand anyone feeling grief except for his own suffering pain or

for the loss of money, he could not understand anyone simu-
lating such an emotion except for show intended to deceive.
He thought that she had come to Castra Regis again for the
opportunity of stealing something, and was determined that on
this occasion the chance of pressing his advantage over her
should not pass. He felt, therefore, that the occasion was one
for extra carefulness in the watching of all that went on. Ever
since he had come to the conclusion that Lady Arabella was
trying to steal the treasure-chest, he suspected nearly everyone
of the same design, and, as the night generally is friendly to
thieves, he made it a point to watch all suspicious persons and
places when night is merging into dawn and dawn into day. At
that time, too, the active faculties of the mind are not at their
best. Sleep is a factor of carelessness to be counted on, and, as
it affects both thief and guardian, may be doubly useful both
to learn and to do. The dawn, therefore, generally found him
on the watch; and as this was the period also when Adam was
engaged on his own researches regarding Lady Arabella, it was
only natural that there should be some crossing of each other's
tracks. This is what did happen. Nature is a logician, and what
does happen is generally what ought to happen if the chances
are in its favour. Adam had gone for an early morning survey
of the place in which he was interested, taking with him, as
usual, the mongoose in its box. He arrived at the gate of Diana's
Grove just as Lady Arabella was preparing to set out for Castra
Regis on what she considered her mission of comfort. And she,
seeing from her window Adam in a mysterious way going
through the shadows of the trees round the gate, thought that
he must be engaged on some purpose similar to her own. So,
quickly making her toilet, she quietly left the house without
arousing anybody, and, taking advantage of every shadow and
substance which could hide her from him, followed him on
his walk. Oolanga, the experienced tracker, followed her, but
succeeded in hiding his movements better than she did. He saw
that Adam had hung on his shoulder the mysterious box, which
he took to contain something valuable. Seeing that Lady Arabella was secretly following him, confirmed this idea. His mind
– such as it was – was fixed on her trying to steal, and he

credited her at once with making use of this new opportunity. In his walk, Adam went into the grounds of Castra Regis, and Oolanga saw her follow him with great secrecy. He feared to go closer, as now on both sides of him were enemies who might make discovery. Therefore, when he ascertained that Lady Arabella was bound for the Castle, he devoted himself to following her with singleness of purpose. He therefore missed seeing that Adam branched off the track he was following and returned to the high road, and that she, seemingly not interested in his further movements, took her course to the Castle.

That night Edgar Caswall had slept badly. The tragic occurrence of the day was on his mind, and he kept waking and thinking of it. At the early dawn he rose and, wrapping himself in a heavy dressing-gown, sat at the open window watching the kite and thinking of many things. From his room he could see all round the neighbourhood, and as the morning advanced, its revealing light showed him all the little happenings of the place. His life had not had much interest for him in the doings of other people, and he had no distinct idea of how many little things went to make up the sum of an ordinary person's daily life. This bird's-eye view of a community engaged in its ordinary avocations at even this early hour was something new to him. He set himself to watch it as a new interest. His cold nature had no place for sympathy for lesser things than himself; but this was a study to be followed just as he would have watched the movements of a colony of ants or bees or other creatures of little interest individually. He saw, as the light grew more searching, the beginnings of the day for humble people. He saw the movements which followed waking life. He even began to exercise his imagination in trying to understand the why and the wherefore of each individual movement. As soon as he was able to recognise individual houses as they emerged from the mass of darkness or obscurity, he became specially interested in all that went on around him. The two places that interested him most were Mercy Farm and Diana's Grove. At first the movements were of a humble kind – those that belonged to domestic service or agricultural needs – the opening of doors and windows, the sweeping and brushing, and generally the restoration of habitual order. Then the farm servants made preparations for the comfort of the cattle and other animals; the drawing of water, the carrying of food, the alterations of bedding, the removal of waste, and the thousand offices entailed by the needs of living things. To Caswall, self-absorbed, disdainful, selfish egotist, this bird's-eye view was a new and interesting experience of the revolution of cosmic effort. He was so interested with this new experience that the dim hours of the morning slipped by unnoticed. The day was in full flow when he bethought him of his surroundings. He could now distinguish things and people, even at a distance. He could see Lady Arabella, whose blinds had been drawn and windows opened, move about in her room, the white dress which she wore standing out against the darker furniture of her room. He saw that she was already dressed for out of doors. As he looked, he saw her suddenly rise and look out of the window, keeping herself carefully concealed behind the curtain, and, following the direction in which her face was turned, he saw Adam Salton, with a box slung on his shoulder, moving in the shadow of the clump of trees outside her gate. He noticed that she quickly left the room, and in another minute was following Salton down the road in the direction of Castra Regis, carefully avoiding observation as she went. Then he was surprised to see Oolanga's black face and rolling white eyeballs peering out from a clump of evergreens in the avenue. He too was watching.

From his high window – whose height was alone a screen from the observation of others – he saw the chain of watchers move into his own grounds, and then presently break up, Adam Salton going one way, and Lady Arabella, followed by the nigger, another. Then Oolanga disappeared amongst the trees; but Caswall could see that he was still watching. Lady Arabella, after looking around her, slipped in by the open door, and he could, of course, see her no longer.

Presently, however, he heard a light tap at his door – a tap so light that he only knew it was a tap at all when it was repeated. Then the door opened very, very slowly, and he could see the flash of Lady Arabella's white dress through the opening.

CHAPTER XIX
A VISIT OF SYMPATHY

Caswall was genuinely surprised when he saw Lady Arabella, though he need not have been surprised after what had already occurred in the same way. The look of surprise on his face was so much greater than Lady Arabella had expected – though she thought she was prepared to meet anything that might occur – that she stood still, open-eyed in sheer amazement. Cold-blooded as she was and ready for all social emergencies, she was nonplussed how to go on. She was plucky, however, and began to speak at once, although she had not the slightest idea what she was going to say. Had she been told that she was beginning to propose to a man, she would have indignantly denied it.

'I came to offer you my very, very warm sympathy with the grief you have so lately experienced.'

There was a new surprise in his voice as he replied:

'My grief? I am afraid I must be very dull; but I really do not understand.'

Already she felt at a disadvantage, and hesitated as she went on:

'I mean about the old man who died so suddenly – your old . . . retainer.'

Caswall's face relaxed something of its puzzled concentration:

'Oh, him! I hope you don't think he was any source of grief. Why, he was only a servant; and he had overstayed his three-score and ten years by something like twenty years. He must have been ninety, if he was a day!'

'Still, as an old servant . . . !'

Caswall's words were not so cold as their inflection.

'I never interfere with servants. Besides, I never saw or heard of him. He was kept on here merely because he had been so long on the premises, or for some other idiotic reason. I suppose the steward thought it might make him unpopular if he were to be dismissed. All that is nonsense. There is no sentiment in business; if he is a sentimentalist, he has no right to be a steward of another man's property!'

Somehow this tone almost appalled her. How on earth was she to proceed on such a task as hers if this was the utmost geniality she could expect? So she at once tried another tack – this time a personal one:

'I am very sorry I disturbed you. I took a great liberty in the so doing. I am really not unconventional – and certainly no slave to convention. Still there are limits . . . It is bad enough to intrude in this way, and I do not know what you can say or think of the time selected for the intrusion.'

After all, Edgar Caswall was a gentleman by custom or habit, so he rose to the occasion:

'I can only say, Lady Arabella, that you are always welcome at any time when you may deign to honour my house with your presence.'

She smiled at him sweetly as she said:

'Thank you *so* much. You *do* put one at ease. A breach of convention with you makes me glad rather than sorry. I feel that I can open my heart to you about anything.'

Caswall smiled in his turn.

'Such consideration and understanding as yours are almost prohibitive of breach of convention.'

'Try me. If I stand the test it will be another link between us.'

'That, indeed, would be a privilege. Come, I will try you.'

Forthwith she proceeded to tell him about Oolanga and his strange suspicions of her honesty. He laughed heartily and made her explain all the details. He laughed genuinely at her reading of Oolanga's designs, which he did not even dignify with the *sobriquet* of insolence. His final comment was enlightening.

'Let me give you a word of advice: If you have the slightest fault to find with that infernal nigger, shoot him on sight. A swelled-headed nigger with a bee in his bonnet is one of the worst difficulties in the world to deal with. So better make a clean job of it, and wipe him out at once!'

'But what about the law, Mr Caswall?'

'Oh, the law is all right. But even the law doesn't concern itself much about dead niggers. A few more or less of them does not matter. To my mind it's rather a relief!'

'I'm afraid of you,' was her only comment, made with a sweet smile and in a soft voice.

'All right,' he said, 'let us leave it at that. Anyhow, we shall be rid of one of them!'

'I don't love niggers more than you do,' she said, 'but I suppose one mustn't be too particular where that sort of cleaning up is concerned.'

Then she changed in voice and manner, and asked genially:

'And now tell me, am I forgiven?'

'You are, dear lady – if there be anything to forgive.'

As he spoke, seeing that she had moved to go, he came to the door with her, and in the most natural way accompanied her downstairs. He passed through the hall door with her and down the avenue. As he went back to the house, she smiled to herself and took herself into her own confidence in a whisper:

'Well, that is all right. I don't think the morning has been altogether thrown away.'

And she walked slowly back to Diana's Grove.

When Adam Salton separated from Lady Arabella he continued the walk which he had begun. He followed the line of the Brow, and refreshed his memory as to the various localities. He got home to Lesser Hill just as Sir Nathaniel was beginning breakfast. Mr Salton had gone to Walsall to keep an early appointment; so he was all alone. When breakfast was over, he, seeing in Adam's face that he had something to speak about, followed into the study and shut the door.

When the two men had lighted their pipes, Sir Nathaniel began:

'Since we talked, I have remembered an interesting fact about Diana's Grove that I intended to have mentioned earlier, only that something put it out of my head. It is about the house, not the Grove. There is, I have long understood, some strange mystery about that house. It may be of some interest, or it may be trivial, in such a tangled skein as we are trying to unravel.'

'I am listening. Please tell me all – all you know or suspect, and I shall try to form an opinion. To begin, then, of what sort is the mystery – physical, mental, moral, historical, scientific, occult? Any kind of hint will help me.'

'Well, my dear boy, the fact is, I don't know!'

'Don't know, sir?'

'That is not so strange as it may appear. It may belong to any or all of these categories. Naturally, you are incredulous of such complete ignorance –'

'Oh, sir, I would not doubt you.'

'No, of course not. But all the same, you may not be able to believe or understand. Of course I understand your reluctance to speak of a doubt. But that applies not to the fact, but to the manner of expressing it. Be quite assured. I fully accept your belief in my *bona fides*. But we have difficulties to encounter, barriers to pass; so we must trust each other to speak the truth even if we do not understand it ourselves.'

Adam was silent for a few moments, and then said, with his face brightening:

'I think, sir, the best way we can go on is to tell each other facts. Explanation may bring necessary doubt; but we shall have something to go on!'

'Quite right. I shall try to tell you what I think; but I have not put my thoughts on the subject in sequence, and so you must forgive me if due order is not observed in my narration. I suppose you have seen the house at Diana's Grove?'

'The outside of it; but I have that in my mind's eye, and I can fit into my memory whatever you may call my attention to.'

'Good! Well, I shall just tell you, to begin with, what I know, and I may happen to know more of it than you do.

'The house is very old – probably the first house of some sort that stood there was in the time of the Romans. This was probably renewed – perhaps several times at later periods. The house stands, or, rather, used to stand as it is when Mercia was a kingdom – I do not suppose that the basement was later than the Norman Conquest. Some years ago, when I was President of the Mercian Archæological Society, I went all over it very carefully. This was before it was purchased by Captain March. The house had then been done up so as to be suitable to bring the bride to. The basement is very strange – almost as strong and as heavy as if it was intended to be a fortress. There are a whole series of rooms deep underground. One of them in particular struck me. The room itself is of considerable size, but the masonry is more than massive. In the middle of the room is a sunk well, built up to floor level and evidently going to deep underground. There is no windlass or any trace of there ever having been any – no rope – nothing. Now, we know that even the Romans had wells of immense depth from which the water was lifted by the "old rag rope"; that at Woodhull used to be nearly a thousand feet. Here, then, we have simply an enormously deep well-hole. The door of the room when I saw it was massive, and was fastened with a lock nearly two feet square. It was evidently intended for some kind of protection to something or someone; but no one in those days when I made the visit had ever heard of anyone having been allowed even to see the room. All this is *à propos* of the suggestion of which I have hinted that the well-hole was a way by which the White Worm (whatever it was) went and came. At that time I would have had search made, even excavation if necessary, at my own expense, but all suggestions were met with a prompt and explicit negative. So, of course, I took no further step in the matter. Then it died out of recollection – even of mine.'

'Do you remember, sir,' asked Adam, 'what was the appearance of the room where the well-hole was? And was there furniture – in fact, any sort of thing in the room?'

'I do not remember. It was all very dark – so dark that it was impossible to distinguish anything. The only thing I do remember was a sort of green light – very clouded – very dim, which came up from the well. Not a fixed light, but intermittent and irregular. Quite unlike anything I had ever seen.'

'Do you remember how you got into that room – the well-room? Was there a separate door from outside, or was there any interior room or passage which opened into it?'

'I think there must have been some room with a way into it. I remember going up some steep steps by which I came into the well-room. They must have been worn smooth by long use or something of the kind, for I could hardly keep my feet as I went up. Once I stumbled and nearly fell into the well-hole. I was more careful after that.'

'Was there anything strange about the place – any queer smell, for instance?'

'Queer smell? – yes. Like bilge or a rank swamp.

'It was distinctly nauseating; I remember that when I came out I felt that I had been just going to be physically sick. I shall try back on my visit and see if I can recall any more of what I saw or felt.'

'Then perhaps, sir, later in the day you will kindly tell me anything you may chance to recollect.'

'I shall be delighted, Adam. If your uncle has not returned by then, I shall join you in the study after dinner, and we shall resume this interesting chat.'

CHAPTER XX

THE MYSTERY OF 'THE GROVE'

When Adam, after leaving Lady Arabella, went on his own road outside Castra Regis, Oolanga followed him in secret. Adam had at first an idea, or rather a suspicion, that he was being followed, and looked around a good many times in the hope of making discovery of his pursuer. Not being successful in any of these attempts, he gradually gave up the idea, and accepted the alternative that he had been mistaken. He wondered what had become of the nigger, whom he had certainly seen at first, so kept a sharp look-out for him as he went on his way. As he passed through the little wood outside the gate of Diana's Grove, he thought he saw the African's face for an instant. He knew it must be him; otherwise, there must be a devil wandering loose somewhere in the neighbourhood. So he went deeper into the undergrowth, and followed along parallel to the avenue to the house. He was, in a way, glad that there was no workman or servant about, for he did not care that any of Lady Arabella's people should find him wandering about her grounds at such an hour. Taking advantage of the thickness of the trees, he came close to the house and skirted round it. He was repaid for his trouble, for on the far side of the house, close to where the rocky frontage of the cliff fell away, he saw Oolanga crouched behind the irregular trunk of a great oak. The man was so intent on watching someone, or something, that he did not guard against being himself watched. This suited Adam, for he could thus make scrutiny at will. The thick wood, though the trees were mostly of small girth, threw a heavy shadow, in addition to that made by the early sun being in the east, so that the steep declension, in front of which grew the tree behind which the African lurked, was almost in darkness. Adam drew as close as he could, and was amazed to see a patch of light on the ground before him; when he realised what it was, he was determined more than ever to follow on his quest. The nigger had a dark lantern in his hand, and was throwing the light down the steep incline. The glare showed that the decline, which was in a sort of sunken way, emerged on a series of stone steps, which ended in a low-lying heavy iron door fixed against the side of the house. His mind was in a whirl. All the strange things he had heard from Sir Nathaniel, and all those, little and big, which he had himself noticed, crowded into his mind in a chaotic way, such as marks the intelligence conveyed in a nightmare. Instinctively he took refuge from the possibility of Oolanga seeing him behind a thick oak stem, and set himself down to watch what might occur.

After a very short time it was apparent that the African was trying to find out what was behind the heavy door. There was no way of looking in, for the door fitted tight into the massive stone slabs. The only opportunity for the entrance of light was through a small hole left in the building between the great stones above the door. This hole was much too high up to look through from the ground level. The nigger was so intent on his effort to see beyond this, that Adam found there was no necessity for his own careful concealment, which was a considerable help to him in his task. Oolanga, having tried standing tiptoe on the highest point near, and holding the lantern as high as he could, threw the light round the edges of the door to see if he could find anywhere a hole or a flaw in the metal through which he could obtain a glimpse. Foiled in this, he brought from the shrubbery a plank, which he leant against the top of the door and then climbed up with great dexterity. This did not bring him near enough to the window-hole to look in, or even to throw the light of the lantern through it, so he climbed down and carried the plank back to the place from which he had got it. Then he concealed himself near the iron door and waited, manifestly with the intent of remaining there till someone came near. Presently Lady Arabella, moving noiselessly through the shade, approached the door. When he saw her close enough to touch it, Oolanga stepped forward from his concealment, and said in a whisper, which through the gloom sounded like a hiss:

'I want to see you, missy – soon and secret.'

Her lip curled in scorn as she answered:

'You see me now. What do you want? What is it?'

'You know well, missy. I told you already.'

She turned on him with her eyes blazing, so that the green tint in them shone like emeralds.

'Come, none of that. If there is anything sensible which you may wish to say to me, you can see me here, just where we are, at seven o'clock.'

He made no reply in words, but, putting the backs of his hands together, bent lower and lower still till his forehead touched the earth. She stood stone-still, which seeing, he rose and went slowly away. Adam Salton, from his hiding-place, saw and wondered. In a few minutes he moved from his place and went away home to Lesser Hill, fully determined that seven o'clock would find him in some hidden place behind Diana's Grove.

When he got home he placed the box containing the mongoose in the gun-room. Not having any immediate intention of making use of the animal, it passed quite out of his mind.

At a little before seven Adam stole softly out of the house and took the back-way to the rear of Diana's Grove. The place seemed silent and deserted, so he took the opportunity of concealing himself near the spot whence he had seen Oolanga trying to investigate whatever was concealed behind the iron door. He was quite content when he found himself safely ensconced in his hiding-place. He waited, perfectly still, and at last saw a gleam of white passing soundlessly through the undergrowth. He was not surprised when he recognised the shape and colour of Lady Arabella's dress. She came close and waited, with her face to the iron door. From some place of concealment near at hand Oolanga appeared, and came close to her. Adam noticed with surprised amusement that over his shoulder was his, Adam's, box with the mongoose. Of course the African did not know that he was seen by anyone, least of all by the man whose property he had in possession. Silent-footed as he was, Lady Arabella heard him coming, and turned to meet him. It was somewhat hard to see in the gloom, for, as usual, he was all in black, only his collar and cuffs showing white. The black of his face helped with that of his clothing in eating up what faint light there was. Lady Arabella opened the conversation which ensued between the two:

'I see you are here – what do you want? To rob me, or murder me?'

'No, to lub you!'

This, getting explicit so soon, frightened her a little, and she tried to change the tone:

'Is that a coffin you have with you? If so, you are wasting your time. It would not hold me.'

When a nigger suspects he is being laughed at, all the ferocity of his nature comes to the front; and as the man was naturally of the lowest kind, the usual was to be expected:

'Dis ain't no coffin for nobody. Quite opposite. Dis box is for you. Somefin you lub. Me give him to you!'

Still anxious to keep off the subject of affection, on which she believed him to have become crazed, she made another effort to keep his mind elsewhere:

'Is this why you want to see me?'

He nodded.

She went on: 'Then come round to the other door. And be quiet. I have no particular desire to be seen so close to my own house in conversation with a – a – a nigger like you!'

She had chosen the word of dishonour deliberately. She wished to meet his passion with another kind. Such would, at all events, help to keep him quiet. In the deep gloom she could not see the anger which suffused his face. Rolling eyeballs and grinding teeth are, however, sufficient indices of anger to be decipherable in the dark. She moved round the corner of the house to her right hand. Oolanga was following her, when she stopped him by raising her hand:

'No, not that door,' she said: 'that is not for niggers. The other door will do well enough for that!'

There was such scorn in her voice – scorn carried to a positive quality with malignity added – that the African writhed. Suddenly he stopped as if turned into stone, and said in a voice, whose very quietude was dangerous:

'Gib me your gun.'

Unthinkingly, she pulled out the revolver, which was in her breast, and handed it to him:

'Do you want to kill me?' she said. 'Go on. I am not afraid of you; but, remember, you will swing for it. This is not Benin or Ashantee[1] – this is England!'

He answered in an even voice:

'Don't fear, missee. Gun no to kill nobody. Only to protect myself.'

He saw the wonder in her face, and explained:

'I heard this morning what master said in his room. You no thought I heard. He say, "If you have any fault to find with that infernal nigger" – he said that – "shoot him on sight." Now you call me nigger, speak to me like a dog. And you want me to go into your house by door which I not know. Gun safer now with me. Safer for Oolanga if gun wanted to hurt him.'

'What have you in that box?'

'That is treasure for you, missee. I take care of it, and give it to you when we get in.'

Lady Arabella took in her hand a small key which hung at the end of her watch-chain, and moved to a small door, low down, round the corner, and a little downhill from the edge of the Brow. Oolanga, in obedience to her gesture, went back to the iron door. Adam looked carefully at the mongoose box as the African went by, and was glad to see that it was locked. Unconsciously, as he looked, he fingered the key that was in his waistcoat pocket. When Oolanga was out of sight, Lady Arabella, who had waited quite still, said to him:

'Mr Salton, will you oblige me by coming with me for a few minutes? I have to see that – that coloured person – on a matter of business, and I do not care to see him alone. I shall be happier with a witness. Do you mind obliging me, and coming? It will be very kind of you.'

He bowed, and walked with her to the door round the corner.

CHAPTER XXI
EXIT OOLANGA

The moment they got out of sight of the nigger, Adam said to Lady Arabella:

'One moment whilst we are alone. You had better not trust that nigger!'

Her answer was crisp and concise:

'I don't.'

'Forewarned is forearmed. Tell me if you will – it is for your own protection. Why do you mistrust him?'

'It is an odd story, but I had better tell you, though, in truth, it is somewhat humiliating – disturbing – to my *amour propre*.[1] He is a thief – at least, so I gather from his readiness to commit a felony. Then you saw that he took my pistol practically under threat. Again he wants to blackmail me – oh I have lots of reasons to distrust him.'

'*He* blackmail *you*! The scoundrel! But how could he hope to do such a thing?'

'My friend, you have no idea of that man's impudence. Would you believe that he wants me to marry him?'

'No!' said Adam incredulously, amused in spite of himself.

'Yes, and wanted to bribe me to do it by sharing a chest of treasure – at least, he thought it was – stolen from Mr Caswall. Why do you yourself distrust him, Mr Salton?'

'I shall give you an instance. Did you notice that box he had slung on his shoulder? That belongs to me. I left it in the gun-room when I went to lunch. He must have crept in and stolen it. Doubtless he thinks that it, too, is full of treasure.'

'He does!'

'How on earth do you know?' asked Adam.

'A little while ago he offered to give it to me – another bribe to accept him. Faugh! I am ashamed to tell you such a thing. The beast!'

'You say he has an appointment to see you?' asked Adam.

'Yes, that was his reason for taking my revolver. He thought perhaps, naturally enough, that I should want to shoot him.'

'You would be all right for anything of that sort with him – if I were on the jury.'

'Oh, he isn't worth it. After all, even a bullet is of *some* little value.'

'Don't alarm yourself, Lady Arabella. You shan't have to do any dirty work. I have a gun!' As he spoke, he took from his pistol pocket a revolver carrying an ounce ball. 'I mention this now to make and keep your mind at rest. Moreover, I am a good and a quick shot.'

'Thanks!'

'By the way, in case there should be any need to know later, what revolver do you use?'

'Weiss of Paris, No. 3,' she answered. 'And you?'

'Smith and Wesson,[2] "The Ready!"'

'You noticed, I suppose, how deftly he stole it?'

Adam was astonished – with quite a new astonishment. It had been so dark that he himself had only been able to see the general movement as Oolanga had annexed the pistol. And yet, this woman had seen the smallest details. She must have wonderful eyes to see in the dark like that!

Whilst they had been speaking, she had opened the door, a narrow iron one well hung, for it had opened easily and closed tightly without any creaking or sound of any kind. Within all was dark; but she entered as freely and with as little misgiving or restraint as if it had been broad daylight. For Adam, there was just sufficient green light from somewhere to see that there was a broad flight of heavy stone steps leading upward; but Lady Arabella, after shutting the door behind her, when it closed tightly without a clang, tripped up the steps lightly and swiftly. For an instant all was dark again, but there came again the faint green light which enabled him to see the outlines of things. Another iron door, narrow like the first and fairly high, led into another large room, the walls of which were of massive stones so closely joined together as to exhibit only one smooth surface. This too presented the appearance of having at one time been polished. On the far side, also smooth like the walls, was the reverse of a great wide but not high iron door. Here there was a little more light, for the high-up aperture over the door opened to the air. Lady Arabella took from her girdle another small key, which she inserted in a tiny keyhole in the centre of a massive lock, which seemed the counterpart and reverse of the lock of some two feet square which Adam had noted on the outside of the door. The great bolt seemed wonderfully hung, for the moment the small key was turned the bolts of the great lock moved noiselessly and the iron doors swung open. On the stone steps outside stood Oolanga with the mongoose box slung over his shoulder. Lady Arabella stood a little on one side and moved back a few feet, and the African, accepting the movement as an invitation, entered in an obsequious way. The moment, however, that he was inside, he gave a quick look around him, and in an oily voice, which made Adam shudder, said with a sniff:

'Much death here – big death. Many deaths. Good, good!'

He sniffed round as if he was enjoying a scent. The matter and manner of his speech were so revolting that instinctively Adam's hand wandered to his revolver, and, with his finger on the trigger, rested satisfied that he was ready for any emergency.

Oolanga seemed more 'crawly' than ever in his movements. He unslung the box from his shoulder and put it on a stone ledge which ran along the side of the room to the right of the iron door, saying as he looked towards Adam:

'I have brought your box, master, as I thought you would want it. Also the key which I got from your servant.'

He laid this beside the box, and began to sniff again with an excellent pretence of enjoyment, raising his nose as he turned his head round as if to breathe all the fragrance he could.

There was certainly opportunity for such enjoyment, for the open well-hole was almost under his nose, sending up such a stench as almost made Adam sick, though Lady Arabella seemed not to mind it at all. It was like nothing that Adam had ever met with. He compared it with all the noxious experiences he ever had – the drainage of war hospitals, of slaughter-houses, the refuse of dissecting rooms. None of these were like it, though it had something of them all, with, added, the sourness of chemical waste and the poisonous effluvium of the bilge of a water-logged ship whereon a multitude of rats had been drowned. However, he was content not to go any further in a search for analogy; it was quite bad enough to have to endure even for a moment, without thinking of it. Besides, he was lost in wonder at a physical peculiarity of Lady Arabella. She seemed to be able to see as well in the dark as in the light. In the gloom under the trees, she had followed every movement of Oolanga. In the Cimmerian darkness[3] of the inner room she had not been for a moment at a loss. It was wonderful. He determined to watch for developments of this strange power – when such should arrive. In the meantime, he had plenty of use for his eyesight to notice what was going on around him. The movements of Oolanga alone were enough to keep his eyes employed. Since the African had laid down the box and the key, Adam had only taken his eyes off it to watch anything seemingly more pressing. He had an idea or an intuition that before long that box would be of overwhelming importance. It was by an intuition also that he grasped his revolver and held it tight. He could see that Oolanga was making up his mind to take some step of which he was at present doubtful. All in a moment it explained itself. He pulled out from his breast Lady Arabella's pistol and shot at him, happily missing. Adam was himself usually a quick shot, but this time his mind had been on something else and he was not ready. However, he was quick to carry out an intention, and he was not a coward. In another second both men were in grips. Beside them was the dark well-hole, with that horrid effluvium stealing up from its mysterious depths. Adam and Oolanga both had pistols. Lady Arabella, who had not one, was probably the most ready of them all in the theory of shooting, but that being impossible, she made her effort in another way. Gliding forward with inconceivable rapidity, she tried to seize the African; but he eluded her grasp, just missing, in doing so, falling into the mysterious hole. As he swayed back to firm foothold, he turned her own gun on her and shot. Instinctively Adam leaped at her assailant; clutching at each other, they tottered on the very brink. Lady Arabella's anger, now fully awake, was all for Oolanga. She moved forward towards him with her bare hands extended, and had just seized him when the catch of the locked box from some movement from within flew open, and the king-cobra-killer flew at her with a venomous fury impossible to describe. As it seized her throat she caught hold of it, and, with a fury superior to its own, actually tore it in two just as if it had been a sheet of paper. The strength used for such an act must have been terrific. In an instant, it seemed to spout blood and entrails, and was hurled into the well-hole. In another instant she had seized Oolanga, and with a swift rush had drawn him, her white arms encircling him, with her down into the gaping aperture. As the forms flashed by him Adam saw a medley of green and red lights blaze in a whirling circle, and as it sank down into the well a pair of blazing green eyes became fixed, sank lower and lower with frightful rapidity, and disappeared, throwing upward the green light which grew more and more vivid every second. As the light sank into the noisome depths, there came a shriek which chilled Adam's very blood – a prolonged agony of pain and terror which seemed to have no end.

Adam Salton felt that he would never be able to free his mind from the memory of those last dreadful moments. The gloom which surrounded that horrible charnel pit, which seemed to go down to the very bowels of the earth, conveyed from far down the sights and sounds of the nethermost hell. The ghastly fate of the African as he sank down to his terrible doom, his black face growing grey with terror, his white eyeballs, now like veined bloodstone,[4] rolling in the helpless extremity of fear. The mysterious green light was in itself a *milieu* of horror. And through it all the awful cry came up from that fathomless pit, whose entrance was flooded with gouts of fresh blood. Even the death of the fearless little snake-killer – so fierce, so frightful, as if stained with a ferocity which told of no living force above earth, but only of the devils of the pit – was only an incident. Adam was in a state of intellectual tumult, which had no peer

in his existence. He tried to rush away from the horrible place;
even the baleful green light thrown up through the gloomy
well-shaft was dying away as its source sank deeper into the
primeval ooze. The darkness was closing in on him in over-
whelming density. Darkness in such a place and with such a
memory of it! He made a wild rush forward – slipt on the steps
in some sticky, acrid-smelling mass that felt and smelt like
blood, and, falling forward, felt his way into the inner room,
where the well-shaft was not. A faint green light began to grow
around him until it was sufficient to see by. And then he rubbed
his eyes in sheer amazement. Up the stone steps from the narrow
door by which he had entered, glided the thin white-clad figure
of Lady Arabella, the only colour to be seen on her being
blood-marks on her face and hands and throat. Otherwise, she
was calm and unruffled, as when earlier she stood aside for him
to pass in through the narrow iron door.

CHAPTER XXII

SELF-JUSTIFICATION

Adam Salton went for a walk before returning to Lesser Hill; he felt that it might be well, not only to steady his nerves, shaken by the horrible scene, but to get his thoughts into some sort of order, so as to be ready to enter on the matter with Sir Nathaniel. He was a little embarrassed as to telling his uncle, for already affairs had so vastly progressed beyond his original view that he felt a little doubtful as to what would be the old gentleman's attitude when he should hear of the strange events for the first time. He might take umbrage that he had not been consulted or, at least, told of the earlier happenings. At first there had only been inferences from circumstances altogether outside his uncle and his household. Now there were examples of half the crimes in the calendar, of which there was already indisputable proof, together with dark and bloody mysteries, enough to shake the nerves of the whole country-side. Mr Salton would certainly not be satisfied at being treated as an outsider with regard to such things, most of which had points of contact with the interior of his own house. It was with an immense sense of relief that Adam heard that he had telegraphed to the housekeeper that he was detained by business at Walsall, where he would remain for the night; and that he would be back in the morning in time for breakfast. When Adam got home after his walk, he found Sir Nathaniel just going to bed. He did not say anything to him then of what had happened, but contented himself with arranging that they would walk together in the early morning, as he had much to say that would require serious attention.

Strangely enough he slept well, and awoke at dawn with his

mind clear and his nerves in their usual unshaken condition. The maid brought up, with his early morning cup of tea, a note which had been found in the letter-box. It was from Lady Arabella, and was evidently intended to put him on his guard as to what he should say about the previous evening. He read it over carefully several times before he was satisfied that he had taken in its full import.

'DEAR MR SALTON, – I cannot go to bed until I have written to you, so you must forgive me if I disturb you, and at an unseemly time. Indeed, you must also forgive me if, in trying to do what is right, I err in saying too much or too little. The fact is that I am quite upset and unnerved by all that has happened in this terrible night. I find it difficult even to write; my hands shake so that they are not under control, and I am trembling all over with memory of the horrors we saw enacted before our eyes. I am grieved beyond measure that I should be, however partially or remotely, a cause of this shock and horror coming on you. Forgive me if you can, and do not think too hardly of me. This I ask with confidence, for since we shared together the danger – the very pangs – of death, I feel that we should be to one another something more than mere friends, that I may lean on you and trust you, assured that your sympathy and pity are for me. A common danger draws, they say, even men together. How close, then, must be the grasp of a poor, weak woman to you, a brave, strong man, and we have together looked into the eyes of Death. You really must let me thank you for the friendliness, the help, the confidence, the real aid at a time of deadly danger and deadly fear which you showed me. That awful man – I shall see him for ever in my dreams. His black, malignant face will shut out all memory of sunshine and happiness. I shall eternally see his evil eyes as he threw himself into that well-hole in a vain effort to escape from the inevitable consequences of his own misdoing. The more I think of it, the more apparent it seems to me that he had premeditated the whole thing – of course, except his own horrible death. He must have intended to murder me, else why did he take away from me my pistol, the only weapon I had? He probably intended to murder you too. If he had known you had a revolver, he would have tried to get that also, I am sure. You know that women do not reason – we know – that he meant to seize that occasion also for stealing my emeralds.'

When next Adam saw her he asked:
'How did it all come about?'
She explained simply, sweetly, and seeming to say what she could in the man's favour, but doubly damning him whilst she did so.

'Perhaps you have noticed – of course, I do not blame if you have not; men are not supposed to remember such trivial things – a fur collar I occasionally wear – or rather wore, it is now. It is one of my most valued treasures – an ermine collar studded with emeralds. They are very fine ones, if that is any justification to anything. It is an old collar, with hanging pieces as well as those of the collar proper. I had often seen the nigger's eyes gleam covetously when he looked at it. Unhappily, I wore it yesterday. That may have been the last cause that lured the poor man to his doom. I hope you do not think me altogether hard-hearted. Of course, as a Christian, I ought to forgive my enemies, and this individual was my enemy – he tried to murder me, and did rob me; but it is above my nature to forgive him stealing my emeralds, which were an heirloom, and, though valuable, in themselves of greater value to me from historical association. I mention these things now, for I may not have an opportunity of referring to them again.'
The letter went on:

'I saw a look on your face as the nigger sank into that terrible pit which I – probably wrongly – mistook; but it seemed to me you were surprised at seeing what seemed to be my arms round his neck. The fact is, on the very brink of the abyss he tore the collar from my neck and threw it over his own shoulder. That was the last thing of him that I saw. When he sank into the hole, I was rushing from the iron door, which I pulled behind me. I am glad to say I did, for it shut out from me the awful sight. When I heard that soul-sickening yell, which marked his disappearance in the deep, darkling chasm, I was more glad than I can say that my eyes were spared the pain and horror which my ears had to endure. Even with the fear and horror which I had so recently endured, and the last awful moments which, although it was through his own act, he had to suffer, I could not forgive him – I have prayed ever since, and will ever pray, for forgiveness of my unchristian spirit. And it may one day come in God's mercy. I have endured the punishment; the sweetness of forgiveness of such an error may come in time. Won't you pray for me too?

'When I tore myself out of the villain's grasp as he sank into the well-hole, I flew upstairs to be safe with you again. But it was not till I was out in the night, and saw the blessed stars gleaming and flashing above me in their myriad beauty, that I could realise what freedom meant. Freedom! Freedom! Not only from that noisome prison-house, which has now such a memory, but from the more noisome embrace of that hideous monster. Whilst I live I shall always thank you for my freedom. You must let me. A woman must sometimes express her gratitude; otherwise it is too great to bear. I am not a sentimental girl who merely likes to thank a man. I am a woman who knows all, of bad as well as good, that life can give. I have known what it is to love and to lose. But there, you must not let me bring any unhappiness into your life. I must live on – as I have lived – alone, and, in addition, bear with other woes the memory of this latest insult and horror. I hardly know which is greatest or worst. In the meantime, I must get away as quickly as possible from Diana's Grove. In the morning I shall go up to town, where I shall remain for a week – I cannot stay longer, as certain business affairs demand my presence here after that time. I think, however, that a week in the rush of busy London, surrounded with multitudes of busy, commonplace people, will help to wear out – I cannot expect total obliteration – the terrible images of the bygone night. When I can sleep easily – which will be, I expect, after a day or two – I shall be fit to return home and take up again the burden which will, I suppose, be always with me.

'I shall be most happy to see you on my return – or earlier, if my good fortune sends you on any errand to London. I shall be in the Great Eastern Hotel. In that busy spot we may forget some of the dangers and horrors we have already shared together. Adieu, and thank you, again and again, for all your kindness and consideration to me.'

Adam was naturally somewhat surprised by this effusive epistle, but he determined to say nothing of it to Sir Nathaniel until he should have thought it well over.

CHAPTER XXIII
AN ENEMY IN THE DARK

When Adam Salton met Sir Nathaniel de Salis at breakfast, he was glad that he had taken the time to turn things over in his mind. The result had been that not only was he familiar with the facts of everything, but he had already so far differentiated them that he was now able to arrange them in his own mind according to their values. Thus he was in a position to form his own opinions, and to accept any fact or any reading of it if at all credible; whatever was mysterious, or seemed to be mysterious, he frankly accepted as such, and held it apart in his own mind for future investigation and discussion. The utility of this course was apparent to him when he began to talk to Sir Nathaniel, which was so soon as breakfast was over and they had withdrawn to the study. They were alone, for Mr Salton was not expected home till noon. Breakfast had been a silent function, so it did not interfere in any way with the process of thought.

So soon as the door was closed, Sir Nathaniel began:

'I see, Adam, that much has occurred, and that you have much to tell me and to consult about.'

'That is so, sir. I suppose I had better begin by telling you all I know – all that has happened since I left you last evening?'

'Quite right. Tell me *all*. It will be time enough to look for meanings when we know facts – that is, know them as we understand them to be.'

Accordingly Adam began, and gave him details of all that had been during the previous evening. He confined himself rigidly to the narration of circumstances, taking care not to colour events, even impliedly, by any comment of his own, or any opinion of the meaning of things which he did not fully understand. At first, Sir Nathaniel seemed disposed to ask some questions, but shortly gave this over when he recognised that the narration was well thought over, concise and self-explanatory. Thenceforth, he contented himself with quick looks and glances, easily interpreted or by some acquiescent motions of his hands, when such could be convenient, to emphasise his idea of the correctness of inference. He was so evidently *en rapport*[1] with Adam, that the latter was helped and emboldened when the time came for his statement of beliefs or inferences as to the meanings of things. This suited Adam exactly – and also Sir Nathaniel came to a quicker, more concise, and more thorough understanding than he could otherwise have done. Until Adam ceased speaking, having evidently come to an end of what he had to say with regard to this section of his story, the elder man made absolutely no comment whatever, remaining silent, except on a very few occasions asking an elucidatory question now and then. Even when Adam, having finished the purely narrative part of what he had seen and heard, took from his pocket Lady Arabella's letter, with manifest intention of reading it, he did not make any comment. Finally, when Adam folded up the letter and put it, in its envelope, back in his pocket, as an intimation that he had now quite finished, the old diplomatist carefully made a few notes in his pocket-book. After a careful reconsideration of these, he spoke:

'That, my dear Adam, is altogether admirable. It is a pity that your duty in life does not call for your writing either political or military despatches or judicial reports. For in all of these branches of work you would probably make a name for yourself. I think I may now take it that we are both well versed in the actual facts, and that our further conference had better take the shape of mutual exchange of ideas. Let us both ask questions as they may arise; and I do not doubt that we shall arrive at some enlightening conclusions.'

'Carried *nem. con.*[2] Will you kindly begin, sir? and then we shall have all in order. I do not doubt that with your experience you will be able to dissipate some of the fog which envelops certain of the things which we have to consider.'

'I hope so, my dear boy. For the beginning, then, let me say that Lady Arabella's letter makes clear some things which she intended – and also some things which she did not intend. But, before I begin to comment and draw deductions, let me ask you a few, a very few questions. I know that this is not necessary; but as two men of full age, talking of matters of a peculiarly intimate kind and which may bring in considerations of other persons, it will be as well to have a thorough understanding, leaving nothing to chance or accident!'

'Good again, sir! Please ask away what you will. I shall keep nothing back.'

'Right, my boy. That is the spirit in which to begin a true conference, if it is to have any result.'

The old man pondered a few moments, and then asked a question which had manifestly been troubling him all along, and which he had made up his mind to ask:

'Adam, are you heart-whole, quite heart-whole, in the matter of Lady Arabella?'

He answered at once, each looking the other straight in the eyes during question and answer:

'Lady Arabella, sir, is a very charming woman, and I have hitherto deemed it a privilege to meet her – to talk to her – even – since I am in the confessional – to flirt a little with her. But if you mean to ask if my affections are in any way engaged, I can emphatically answer "No!" – as indeed you will understand when presently I give you the reason.'

'Could you – would you mind giving me the reason now? It will help us to understand what is before us in the way of difficulty, and what to rely on.'

'Certainly, sir. I can speak at once – should like to. My reason, on which I can fully depend, is that I love another woman!'

'That clinches it. May I offer my good wishes, and, I hope, my congratulations?'

'I am proud of your good wishes, sir, and I thank you for them. But, it is too soon for congratulations – the lady does not even know my wishes yet. Indeed, I hardly knew them myself, as definite, till this moment. Under the circumstances, it may be wiser to wait a little.'

'Quite so. A very wise precaution. There can never be any harm in such delay. It is not a check, remember, but only wise forethought. I take it then, Adam, that at the right time I may be allowed to know who the lady is?'

Adam laughed a low, sweet laugh, such as ripples from a happy heart.

'In the matter there need not be an hour's, a minute's delay. I shall be glad to share my little secret with you, sir. We two are, I take it, tiled.[3] So that there come no wrong or harm to anyone else in the enlargement of the bounds of our confidence!'

'None. As for me, I promise absolute discretion and, unless with your own consent, silence.'

Both men smiled and bowed.

'The lady, sir, whom I am so happy as to love and in whom my dreams of life-long happiness are centred, is Mimi Watford!'

'Then, my dear Adam, I need not wait to offer hopes and congratulations. She is indeed a very charming lady. I do not think I ever saw a girl who united in such perfection the qualities of strength of character and sweetness of disposition. With all my heart, I congratulate you. Then I may take it that my question as to your heart-wholeness is answered in the affirmative?'

'Yes; and now, sir, may I ask in turn why the question?'

'Certainly! I asked because it seems to me that we are coming to a point where such questions would be painful – impossible, no matter how great friends we may be.'

Adam smiled.

'You will now understand why I spoke so positively. It is not merely that I love Mimi, but I have reason to look on Lady Arabella as her enemy!'

'Her enemy?'

'Yes. A rank and unscrupulous enemy who is bent on her destruction.'

Sir Nathaniel paused.

'Adam, this grows worse and worse. I do not contradict you; do not doubt. I only want to be sure.'

He went on with an infinite sadness in his tone. 'I wish to God, my dear young friend, that I could disagree with you.

I wish also that she or you – if not both – could be kept completely outside this question. But that, I fear, is impossible. Now for a moment let me hark back to your story of last night. It is better that we clear up an important matter right here; we can then get on more easily.'

Adam said nothing, but he looked interrogatively.

The other went on: 'It is about Lady Arabella's letter in connection with last night. And indeed, I almost fear to approach it – not on her account, but on yours and Mimi's.' Adam, when his friend mentioned Mimi so familiarly, felt his heart warm at once from the chill that accompanied the ominous opening of his speech. Sir Nathaniel saw the look and smiled. Then he went over to the door, looked outside it and returned, locking it carefully behind him.

CHAPTER XXIV

METABOLISM

'Am I looking grave?' asked Sir Nathaniel inconsequently when he re-entered the room.

'You certainly are, sir.'

'Yes. I ought to be. I feel as if I had on the Black Cap!' Then he went on more calmly: he felt that he should remain calm if he could. Calmness was a necessary condition of what he had to say. 'This is in reality a black-cap affair. We little thought the day we met, only a few days ago, that we should be drawn into such a vortex. Already we are mixed up in robbery, manslaughter, and probably murder, but, a thousand times worse than all the crimes in the calendar, in an affair of gloom and mystery which has no bottom and no end – with magic and demonology, and even with forces of the most unnerving kind, which had their origin in an age when the world was different from the world which we know. We are going back to the origin of superstition – to the age when dragons of the prime tore each other in their slime.[1] I shall come back to all these things presently. We must fear nothing – no conclusion, however improbable, almost impossible it may be. Life and death is at the present moment hanging on our judgment. Life and death not only for ourselves, but for others whom we love. Therefore we must think accurately, go warily, and act boldly. Remember, I count on you as I hope you count on me.'

'I do, with all confidence.'

'Then,' said Sir Nathaniel, 'let us think justly and boldly and fear nothing, however terrifying it may seem. I suppose I am to take as exact in every detail your account of all the strange things which happened whilst you were in Diana's Grove?'

'So far as I know, yes. Of course I may be mistaken in recollection or appreciation, at the time, of some detail or another, but I am certain that in the main what I have said is correct.'

'Then you will not be offended if I ask you, if occasion demands it, to reiterate?'

'I am altogether at your service, sir, and proud to serve.'

'We have one account of what happened from an eye-witness whom we do believe and trust – that is you. We have also another account written by Lady Arabella under her own hand. These two accounts do not agree. Therefore we must take it that one of the two is lying.'

'Apparently, sir.'

'And Lady Arabella is the liar!'

'Apparently – as I am not.'

'We must, therefore, try to find a reason for her lying. She has nothing to fear from Oolanga, who is dead. Therefore the only reason which could actuate her would be to convince someone else that she was blameless. This "someone" could not be you, for you had the evidence of your own eyes. There was no one else present; therefore it must have been an absent person.'

'That seems beyond dispute, sir.'

'There is only one other person whose good opinion she could wish to keep – that person we know to be Edgar Caswall. He is the only one who fills the bill.'

The old man smiled and went on:

'Her lies point to other things besides the death of the African. She evidently wanted it to be accepted that Oolanga had killed the mongoose, but that his falling into the well was his own act. I cannot suppose that she expected to convince you, the eye-witness; but if she wished later on to spread the story, it was at least wise of her to try to get your acceptance of it.'

'That is so!'

Again Sir Nathaniel smiled. He felt that his argument was convincing.

'Then there were other matters of untruth. That, for instance, of the ermine collar embroidered with emeralds. If an understandable reason be required for this, it would be to draw attention away from the green lights which were seen in the room, and especially in the well-hole. Any unprejudiced person would accept the green lights to be the eyes of a great snake such as tradition pointed to living in the well-hole. In fine,[2] therefore, Lady Arabella wanted the general belief to be that there was no snake of the kind in Diana's Grove. Let us consider this. For my own part, I don't believe in a partial liar. This art does not deal in veneer; a liar is a liar right through. Self-interest may prompt falsity of the tongue; but if one prove to be a liar, nothing that he says can ever be believed. This leads us to the conclusion that because she said or inferred that there was no snake, we should look for one – and expect to find it, too.

'Now let me here digress. I live, and have for many years lived, in Derbyshire, a county more celebrated for its caves than any other county in England. I have been through them all, and am familiar with every turn of them; as also with other great caves in Kentucky,[3] in France, in Germany, and a host of places – with all, in fact, of these very deep caves of narrow aperture which are so valued by intrepid explorers, who descend narrow gullets of abysmal depth and sometimes never return. In many of the caverns in the Peak I am convinced that some of the smaller passages were used in primeval times as the lairs of some of the great serpents of legend and tradition. It may have been that such caverns were formed in the usual geologic way – bubbles or flaws in the earth's crust – which were later used by the monsters of the period of the young world. It may have been, of course, that some of them at least were worn originally by water; but in time they all found a use when suitable for living monsters. Such may be – I only give it as a suggestion for thought.

'This brings us to another point more difficult to accept and understand than any other requiring belief in a base not usually accepted or indeed entered on: whether such abnormal growths, as must have been in the case of the earlier inhabitants, could have ever changed in their nature. Some day the study of metabolism may progress so far as to enable us to accept structural changes proceeding from an intellectual or moral base. If such ever be probable, we may lean towards a belief that great animal strength may be a sound base for changes of all sorts. If this be so, what could be a more fitting subject than primeval monsters whose strength was such as to allow a survival of thousands of years? Mind, I do not assert, but only suggest it as a subject for thought. We do not know yet if brain can increase and develop independently of other parts of living structure. This again I only suggest as a subject for thought. My reason for doing so will be presently touched on.

'After all, the mediæval belief in the Philosopher's Stone which could transmute metals has its counterpart in the accepted theory of metabolism which changes living tissue. Why, the theory has been put forward by a great scientist that the existence of radium and its products proves the truth of the theory of transmutation of metal.[4] In an age of investigation like our own, when we are returning to science as the base of wonders – almost of miracles, – we should be slow to refuse to accept facts, however impossible they may seem to be. We are apt to be hide-bound as to theory when we begin to learn. In a more enlightened age, when the base of knowledge has not only been tested but broadened, perhaps we shall come to an understanding of that marvellous definition of "faith" by St Paul: "the substance of things hoped for; the evidence of things unseen."[5]

'Now, my dear Adam, pardon these digressions into matters which are as far from that with which we are concerned as are the Poles from each other; but even these may help us to accept, even if they cannot help to elucidate. We are in a quagmire, my boy, as vast and as deep as that in which the monsters of the geologic age found shelter and perhaps advance.

'Now, I think we have talked enough for the present of many things hard to understand. It will be better, perhaps, if we lay them aside for the present. When you and I resume this chat we shall be more clear-headed to accept evident deductions, more resolute and better satisfied to act on them. Let us adjourn till to-morrow.'

CHAPTER XXV
THE DECREE

When after breakfast the next morning Sir Nathaniel and Adam met, the elder man, after inquiring how his companion had slept, and satisfying him as to his own experiences in the same matter, said:

'I think we may take it that we are both calm of nerve and brain, and that we are fit to resume so momentous a subject as that deferred. Suppose we begin by taking a problematical case of fact based on our conclusions of yesterday. Let us suppose a monster of the early days of the world – a dragon of the prime – of vast age running into thousands of years, to whom had been conveyed in some way – it matters not – a brain of even the most rudimentary kind – some commencement, however small, just sufficient for the beginning of growth. Suppose the monster to be of incalculable size and of a strength quite abnormal – a veritable incarnation of animal strength. Suppose this animal was allowed to remain in one place, thus being removed from accidents of interrupted development: might not, would not this creature in process of time – ages, if necessary – have that rudimentary intelligence developed? There is no impossibility in all this. It is only the natural process of evolution; not taken from genii and species,[1] but from individual instances. Atmosphere, which is the condition of life – vegetable and animal, – is an immediate product of size. In the beginning, the instincts of animals are confined to alimentation, self-protection, and the multiplication of their species. As time goes on and the needs of life become more complex, power follows need. Here let me make another digression. We are prepared already for abnormal growth – it is the corollary of normal growth. We have been long accustomed to consider growth as applied almost exclusively to size in its various aspects. But Nature, who has no doctrinaire ideas, may equally apply it to concentration. A developing thing may expand in any given way or form. Now, it is a scientific law that increase implies gain and loss of various kinds; what a thing gains in one direction it may lose in another. In mechanics direction is a condition of the increase or limitation of speed or force. Why not apply this more widely? May it not be that Mother Nature may deliberately encourage decrease as well as increase – that it may be an axiom that what is gained in concentration is lost in size? Take, for instance, monsters tradition has accepted and localised, such as the Worm of Lambton or that of Spindleston Heugh. If such a one were, by its own process of metabolism, to change much of its bulk for a little intellectual growth, we should at once arrive at a new class of creature, more dangerous, perhaps, than the world has ever had any experience of – a force which can think, which has no soul and no morals, and therefore no acceptance of responsibility. A worm or snake would be a good illustration of this, for it is cold-blooded[2] and therefore removed from the temptations which often weaken or restrict warm-blooded creatures. If, for instance, the Worm of Lambton – if such ever existed – were guided to its own ends by an organised intelligence capable of expansion, what form of creature could we imagine which would equal it in potentialities of evil? Why, such a being would devastate a whole country. Now, all these things require much thought, and we want to apply the knowledge usefully, and we should therefore be exact. Would it not be well to have another "easy," and resume the subject later in the day?'

'I quite agree, sir. I am all in a whirl already; and I want to attend carefully to what you say; so that I may try to digest it.'

Both men seemed fresher and better for the 'easy,' and when they met in the afternoon each of them had, out of his thought, something to contribute to the general stock of information. Adam, who was by nature of a more militant disposition than his elderly friend, was glad to see that the conference at once assumed a practical trend. Sir Nathaniel recognised this, and, like an old diplomatist, turned it to present use.

'Tell me now, Adam, what is the outcome, in your own mind, of our previous conversations?'

He answered at once:

'That the whole difficulty already assumes practical shape; but with added dangers that at first I did not dream of.'

'What is the practical shape, and what are the added dangers? I am not disputing, but only trying to clear my own ideas by the consideration of yours –'

Sir Nathaniel waited, so he went on:

'Will it bore you, sir, if I put in order of an argument your own ideas as seen by me?'

'Not at all; I should like it if it will help to clear my own mind.'

'Then I will begin with your argument – only in general, not in detail. And please bear in mind, sir, that I am trying to state not so much what you said as the ideas conveyed to my mind – possibly erroneously, – but in the honest belief to comprehend thoroughly.'

'Go on, my dear boy, do not fear. I shall understand and, if necessary, make allowance.'

So Adam went on:

'In the past, in early days of the world, there were monsters who were so vast that they could exist thousands of years. Some of them must have overlapped the Christian era. They may have progressed intellectually in process of time. If they had in any way so progressed, or got even the most rudimentary form of brain, they would be the most dangerous things that ever were in the world. Tradition says that one of these monsters lived in the Marsh of the East and came up to a cave in Diana's Grove which was also called the Lair of the White Worm. Such creatures may have grown down (small) as well as up (long). They *may* have grown into, or something like, human beings. Lady Arabella March is of snake nature. She has committed crimes to our knowledge. She retains something of the vast strength of her primal being – can see in the dark – has eyes of a snake. She used the nigger, and then dragged him through the snake's hole down to the swamp; she is intent on evil, and hates some we love. Result . . .'

'Yes, the result you arrive at?'

'First, Mimi Watford should be taken away at once – I should suggest West Australia. And then –'

'Yes?'

'The monster must be destroyed.'

'Bravo! That is a true and fearless conclusion. At whatever cost, it must be carried out.'

'At once?'

'Soon, at all events. That creature's very existence is a danger. Her presence in this neighbourhood makes the danger immediate.'

As he spoke, Sir Nathaniel's mouth hardened and his eyebrows came down till they met. There was no doubting his concurrence in the resolution, or his readiness to help in carrying it out. But he was an elderly man with much experience and knowledge of law and diplomacy. It seemed to him to be a stern duty to prevent anything irrevocable taking place till it had been thought out and all was ready. There were all sorts of legal cruxes to be thought out, not only regarding the taking of life, even of a monstrosity in human form, but also of property. Lady Arabella, be she woman or snake or devil, owned the ground she moved in, according to British law, and the law is jealous and swift to avenge wrongs done within its ken. Within three hundred years the law has accepted facts and evidence that would not be received in later years by school children. All such difficulties should be – must be – avoided for Mr Salton's sake, for Adam's own sake, and, most of all, for Mimi Watford's sake. Before he spoke again, Sir Nathaniel had made up his mind that he must try to postpone decisive action until the circumstances depended on – which, after all, were only problematical – should have been tested satisfactorily, one way or another. When he did speak, Adam at first thought that his friend was wavering in his intention, or 'funking' the responsibility. He could have no such thought regarding Adam. That young man's strong, mobile face was now as set as flint. His eyes were full of fire, non-blazing fire, but slumbrous, which is much more indicative of danger. His brows were in a straight line across his face, and his eyes in parallel course. As to purpose, he was fixed; the only question with him was – when!

However, his respect for Sir Nathaniel was so great that he
would not act or even come to a conclusion on a vital point
without his sanction.

He came close and almost whispered in his ear:

'Will you speak with me of this again – say, when my uncle
has gone to bed, and we shall be undisturbed?'

Sir Nathaniel nodded. They had both determined to wait.

CHAPTER XXVI
A LIVING BARBETTE[1]

When Mr Salton had retired for the night, Adam and Sir Nath-aniel with one accord moved to the study. Things went with great regularity at Lesser Hill, so they knew that there would be no interruption to their talk.

When their cigars were lighted, Sir Nathaniel said:

'I hope, Adam, that you do not think me either slack or changeable of purpose. I really am not so, and I mean to go through this business to the bitter end – whatever it may be. Be satisfied that my first care is, and shall be, the protection of Mimi Watford. To that I am pledged; my dear boy, we who are interested are all in some form of the same danger. That monster out of the pit hates and means to destroy us all – you and me certainly, and probably your uncle. We are just on the verge of stormy times for us all. I wanted especially to talk with you to-night, for I cannot help thinking that the time is fast coming – if it has not come already – when we must take your uncle into confidence. It was one thing when fancied evils threatened, but now he as well as the rest of us is marked for death; and it is only right that he should know all.'

'I am with you, sir. Things have changed since we agreed to keep him out of the trouble. Now we dare not; consideration for his feelings might cost him his life. It is a duty we have – and no light or pleasant one, either. I have not a shadow of doubt that he will want to be one with us in this. But remember, we are his guests, in his house; and his name, his honour have to be thought of as well as his safety.

'I am still with you – to the death. Only, if there be any special danger to him, let me bear, or at any rate share it.'

'All shall be as you wish, Adam. We need say no more of that. We are at one. And now as to practicability. What are we to do? We cannot manifestly take and murder Lady Arabella off-hand. Therefore we shall have to put things in order for the killing, and in such a way that we may not be taxed with a base crime. That is why I suggested waiting till we have some definite and complete proof.'

Adam stood up, and his voice rang as he said heartily:

'You are quite right, sir, as usual. We must be at least as exact as if we were in a law court. I see that.'

Sir Nathaniel acquiesced in such a hearty way as to set his young companion's mind at rest.

Adam sat down again and resumed the conversation, using an even, reflective tone which made the deliberation altogether useful:

'It seems to me, sir, that we are in an exceedingly tight place. Our first difficulty is to know where to begin. Our opponent has pretty well all the trumps. I never thought this fighting an antediluvian monster was such a complicated job. This one is a woman, with all a woman's wisdom and wit, combined with the heartlessness of a *cocotte*[2] and the want of principle of a suffragette. She has the reserved strength and impregnability of a diplodocus. We may be sure that in the fight that is before us there will be no semblance of fair-play. Also that our unscrupulous opponent will not betray herself!'

Sir Nathaniel commented on this:

'That is so. But being of feminine species, she probably will over-reach herself. That is much more likely – more in woman's way. Now, Adam, it strikes me that, as we have to protect ourselves and others against feminine nature, our strong game will be to play our masculine against her feminine. Men can wait better than women.'

He laughed a mirthless laugh that was all from the brain and had no heart at all, and went on:

'You must remember that this female has had thousands of years' experience in waiting. As she stands, she will beat us at that game.'

For answer Adam began preparing his revolver, which was at half-cock:

'There is always a quick way of settling differences of that kind!' was all he said; but Sir Nathaniel understood and again uttered a warning:

'How are differences to be settled with a creature of that kind? We might as well fight with a barbette; she is invulnerable so far as physical harm at our hands is concerned.'

'Even barbettes get occasionally blown up!' said Adam.

'Ah! barbettes aren't alive all over and, so far as we know, self-recuperative. No! we must think out some plan to have ready if all else should fail. We had better sleep on it. She is a thing of the night; and the night may give us some ideas.'

So they both turned in.

Adam knocked at Sir Nathaniel's door in the gray of the morning, and, on being bidden, came into the room. He had several letters unclosed in his hand. Sir Nathaniel sat up in bed.

'Well!'

'I should like to read you a few letters, but, of course, shall not send them unless you approve. In fact' – this with a smile and a blush – 'there are several things which I want to do; but I hold my hand and my tongue till I have your approval.'

'Go on!' said the other kindly. 'Tell me all, and count at any rate on my sympathy and on my approval and help if I can see my way.'

Accordingly Adam proceeded:

'When I told you the conclusions I had arrived at, I put in the foreground that Mimi Watford should for the sake of her own safety be removed – to West Australia, I suggested, – and that the monster which had wrought all the harm should be destroyed.'

'Yes, I remember.'

'To carry this into practice, sir, one preliminary is required – unless harm of another kind is to be faced.'

Sir Nathaniel looked as if he had on his reflecting cap. Then he proceeded, taking up the other's argument:

'Before she goes to West Australia, or indeed to anywhere else, Mimi should have some protector which all the world would recognise. The only form of this safety recognised by convention is marriage!'

'Yes, sir. I see you realise!'

Sir Nathaniel smiled in a fatherly way.

'To marry, a husband is required. And that husband should be you.'

'Yes, yes.'

'And that marriage should be immediate and secret – or, at least, not spoken of outside ourselves . . . And now I must ask you a somewhat delicate question! Would the young lady be agreeable to that proceeding?'

'I do not know, sir!'

'You do not know? Then how are we to proceed?'

'I suppose we – or one of us – must ask her. That one must be myself – and I am ready.'

'Is this a sudden idea, Adam, a sudden resolution?'

'A sudden resolution, sir, but not a sudden idea. The resolution is sudden because the need is sudden and imperative. If I were to speak in hyperbole, I could say that the idea is as old as Fate, and that the resolution was waiting before the beginning of the world!'

'I am glad to hear it. I hope it will turn out that the coming of the White Worm has been a blessing in disguise. But now, if things have to be hurried on like this, what is to be the sequence of events?'

'First, that Mimi should be asked to marry me. If she agrees, all is well and good. The sequence is obvious.'

'And is to be kept a secret amongst ourselves?'

Adam answered at once:

'I want no secret, sir, except for Mimi's good. For myself, I should like to go and shout it out on the house-tops! But I see that we must be discreet. Untimely knowledge to our enemy might work incalculable harm.'

'And how would you suggest, Adam, that we could combine the momentous question with secrecy?'

Here Adam grew red and moved uneasily. Then with a sudden rush he spoke:

'Someone must ask her – as soon as possible!'

'And that someone?'

'I have been thinking the matter over, sir, since we have been here. It requires expedition to achieve safety, and we shall all have to do as duty requires.'

'Certainly. And I trust that none of us shall shirk such a duty. But this is a concrete thing. We may consider and propose in the abstract, but the action is concrete – who, again, is to be the "someone"? Who is to ask her?'

'I thought that you, sir, would be so good!'

'God bless my soul! This is a new kind of duty to take on one – at my time of life. Adam, I hope you know that you can count on me to help in any way I can!'

'I have counted on you, sir, when I ventured to make such a suggestion. I can only ask, sir,' he added, 'that you will be more than ever kind to me – to us, and look on the painful duty as a voluntary act of grace prompted by kindness and affection.'

Sir Nathaniel said in a meek but not a doubting voice:

'Painful duty!'

'Yes,' said Adam boldly. 'Painful to you, though to me it would be all joyful.'

'Yes, I understand!' said the other kindly.

Then he went on: 'It is a strange job for an early morning! Well, we all live and learn. I suppose the sooner I go the better. Remember, I am in your hands and shall do just what you wish, and shall try to do it just as you wish. Now you had better write a line for me to take with me. For, you see, this is to be a somewhat unusual transaction, and it may be embarrassing to the lady, even to myself. So we ought to have some sort of warrant, something to show on after-thought, that we have been all along mindful of her feelings. It will not do to take acquiescence for granted – although we act for her good. You had better write the letter to have ready, and I had better not know what is in it – except the main purpose of the introducing the subject. I shall explain fully as we go along anything that she may wish.'

'Sir Nathaniel, you are a true friend; and I am right sure that both Mimi and I shall be grateful to you for all our lives – however long or however short they may be!'

So the two talked it over and agreed as to points to be borne in mind by the ambassador. It was striking six when Sir Nathaniel left the house, Adam seeing him quietly off.

As the young man followed him with wistful eyes – almost jealous of the privilege which his kind deed was about to bring him, he felt that his own heart was in his friend's breast.

CHAPTER XXVII

GREEN LIGHT

The memory of that morning was like a dream to all those concerned in it. Sir Nathaniel had a confused recollection of detail and sequence, though the main facts stood out in his memory boldly and clearly. Adam Salton's recollection was of an illimitable time filled with anxiety, hope, and chagrin, all unified and dominated by a sense of the slow passage of time and accompanied by vague nebulous fears. Mimi could not for a long time think at all or recollect anything, except that Adam loved her and was saving her from a terrible danger. In the bitter time itself, whilst she was learning those truths she found her own heart. When she had time to think, later on, she wondered how or when she had any ignorance of the facts that Adam loved her and that she loved him with all her heart. Everything, every recollection however small, every feeling, seemed to fit into those elemental facts as though they had all been moulded together. The main and crowning recollection was her saying goodbye to Sir Nathaniel and entrusting to him loving messages straight from her heart to Adam Salton, and of his bearing when with an impulse which she could not check – and did not want to – she put her lips to his and kissed him. Later, when she was alone and had time to think, it was a passing grief to her that she would have to be silent, for a time, to Lilla on the happy events of that strange early morning mission.

She had, of course, agreed to keep all secret until Adam should give her leave to speak.

The advice and assistance of Sir Nathaniel de Salis was a great help to Adam Salton in carrying out his idea of marrying Mimi Watford without publicity. He went with him to London, and, with his knowledge and influence, the young man got the licence of the Archbishop of Canterbury for a private marriage. Sir Nathaniel then took him to live in his own house till the marriage should have been solemnised. All this was duly done, and, the formalities having been fixed, Adam and Mimi were married at Doom.

Adam had tried to arrange that he and his wife should start for Australia at once; but the first ship to suit them did not start for ten days. So he took his bride off to the Isle of Man[1] for the interim. He wished to place a stretch of sea between Mimi and the White Worm, that being the only way to ensure protection for his wife. When the day for departure arrived, they went from Douglas in the *King Orrey* to Liverpool. On arrival at the landing-stage, they drove to Congleton, where Sir Nathaniel met them and drove them at once to Doom, taking care to avoid any one that he knew on the journey. They travelled at a great pace and arrived before dusk at Doom Tower.

Sir Nathaniel had taken care to have the doors and windows shut and locked – all but the door used for their entry. The shutters were up and the blinds down. Moreover, heavy curtains were drawn across the windows. When Adam commented on this, Sir Nathaniel said in a whisper:

'Wait till we are alone, and I shall tell you why this is done; in the meantime not a word or a sign. You will approve when we have had a talk together.'

They said no more on the subject till, when after dinner, they were ensconced alone in Sir Nathaniel's study, which was on the top story of the tower. Doom Tower was a lofty structure, seated on an eminence high up in the Peak. The top of the tower commanded a wide prospect ranging from the hills above the Ribble[2] to the near side of the Brow, which marked the northern bound of ancient Mercia. It was of the early Norman period, less than a century younger than Castra Regis. The windows of the study were barred and locked, and heavy dark curtains closed them in. When this was done not a gleam of light from the tower was seen from outside.

When they were alone Sir Nathaniel spoke, keeping his voice to just above a whisper:

'It is well to be more than careful. In spite of the fact that your marriage was kept secret, as also your temporary absence, both are known.'

'How? To whom?'

'How, I know not; but I am beginning to have an idea. To whom is it the worst? Where it is most dangerous.'

'To her?' asked Adam in momentary consternation.

Sir Nathaniel shivered perceptibly as he answered:

'The White Worm – yes!'

Adam noticed that from thence on he never spoke amongst themselves of Lady Arabella otherwise, except when he wished to divert the suspicion of others or cover up his own. Then, having opened the door, looked outside it and closed it again, he put his lips to Adam's ear and whispered even more softly:

'Not a word, not a sound to disturb your wife. Her ignorance may be yet her protection. You and I know all and shall watch. At all costs, she must have no suspicion!'

Adam hardly dared to breathe. He put his finger to his lips and at last said under his breath:

'I shall do whatever you tell me to, and all the thanks of my heart are to you!'

Sir Nathaniel switched off the electric light, and when the room was pitch dark he came to Adam, took him by the hand, and led him to a seat set in the southern window. Then he softly drew back a piece of the curtain and motioned his companion to look out.

Adam did so, and immediately shrank back as though his eyes had opened on pressing danger. His companion set his mind at rest by saying in a low voice, not a whisper:

'It is all right; you may speak, but speak low. There is no danger here – at present!'

Adam leaned forward, taking care, however, not to press his face against the glass. What he saw would not under ordinary circumstances have caused concern to anybody but to him. With his knowledge, it was simply appalling – though the night was now so dark that in reality there was little to be seen.

On the western side of the tower stood a grove of old trees of forest dimensions. They were not grouped closely, but stood a little apart from each other, producing the effect of a row widely planted. Over the tops of them was seen a green light, something like the danger signal at a railway-crossing. At the height of the tower, the light was not enough to see anything even close to it. It seemed at first quite still; but presently, when Adam's eye became accustomed to it, he could see that it moved a little as if trembling. This at once recalled to Adam's mind all that had been. He seemed to see again the same duplicate light quivering above the well-hole in the darkness of that inner room at Diana's Grove – to hear again Oolanga's prolonged shriek, and to see the hideous black face, now grown gray with terror, disappear into the impenetrable gloom of the mysterious orifice. Instinctively he laid his hand on his revolver, and stood up ready to protect his wife. Then, seeing that nothing happened, and that the light and all outside the tower remained the same, he softly pulled the curtain over the window, and, rising up, came and sat down beside Sir Nathaniel who looked up for a moment with a sharp glance, and said in an even voice:

'I see you understand. I need say nothing.'

'I understand!' he replied in the same quiet tone.

Sir Nathaniel switched on the light again, and in its comforting glow they began to talk freely.

CHAPTER XXVIII

AT CLOSE QUARTERS

'She has diabolical cunning,' said Sir Nathaniel. 'Ever since you left, she has ranged along the Brow and wherever you were accustomed to frequent. I have not heard whence the knowledge of your movements came to her, nor have I been able to learn any data whereon I have been able to found an opinion. She seems to have heard both of your marriage and your absence; but I gather, by inference, that she does not know where you and your wife are, or of your return. So soon as the dusk falls, she goes out on her rounds, and before dawn covers the whole ground round the Brow, and away up into the heart of the Peak. I presume she doesn't condescend to rest or to eat. This is not to be wondered at in a lady who has been in the habit of sleeping for a thousand years at a time, and of consuming an amount of food at a sitting which would make a moderate-sized elephant kick the beam.[1] However, be all that as it may, her ladyship is now nightly on the prowl, and in her own proper shape that she used before the time of the Romans. It certainly has great facilities for the business on which she is now engaged. She can look into windows of any ordinary kind. Happily, this house is beyond her reach, especially if she wishes – as she manifestly does – to remain unrecognised. But, even at this height, it is wise to show no lights, lest she might learn something of even our presence or absence.'

Here Adam stood up again and spoke out.

'Would it not be well, sir, if some one of us should see this monster in her real shape at close quarters? I am willing to run the risk – for I take it there would be no slight risk in the doing.

I don't suppose anyone of our time has seen her close and lived to tell the tale.'[2]

Sir Nathaniel rose and held up an expostulatory hand as he said:

'Good God, lad! what are you suggesting? Think of your wife and all that is at stake.'

Adam interrupted:

'It is of my wife that I think, for her sake that I am willing to risk whatever is to be risked. But be assured I shall not drag her into it – or even tell her anything to frighten her. When I go out she shall not know of it.'

'But if you mention the matter at all she will suspect.'

'The fact of the snake being on the look-out must be told to her to warn her, but I will do it in such a way as not to create any undue suspicion regarding herself. Indeed, I had made up my mind as to what to say some time ago, when it was borne in on me to warn her about keeping the place dark. With your permission, I shall go now and tell her of that, and then when I return here you might lend me a key so that I can let myself in.'

'But do you mean to go alone?'

'Certainly. It is surely enough for one person to run the risk.'

'That may be, Adam, but there will be two.'

'How so! You surely don't mean that Mimi should come with me?'

'Lord, no! But if she knew you were going she would be sure to want to go too; so be careful not to give her a hint.'

'Be sure I shall not. Then who is to be the other?'

'Myself! You do not know the ground; and so would be sure to get into trouble. Now, I know every inch of it, and can guide you how to go safely to any place you want. Adam, this is an exceptional thing – yielding to no law of action that any of us ever heard of. As to danger! what of that to you and me when your wife's safety is concerned! I tell you, no forlorn hope that either of us ever heard of has a hundredth part of the danger we are running into. Yet I do it with all my heart – even as you do.'

Adam made a low bow as to one worthy of all honour, but he said no word more on the subject. After he had switched off the light he then peeped out again through the window and saw where the green light still hung tremblingly above the trees. Before the curtain was drawn and the lights put up again, Sir Nathaniel said:

'So long as her ladyship does not know whereabout we are, we shall have as much safety as remains to us; so, then, bear in mind that we cannot be too careful.'

When the two men slipped out by the back door of the house, they walked cautiously along the avenue which trended towards the west. Everything was pitch dark – so dark that at times they had to feel their way by the borders and palings and tree-trunks. They could still see, seemingly far in front of them and high up, the baleful dual light which at the height and distance seemed like a faint line. As they were now on the level of the ground, the light seemed infinitely higher than it had looked from the top of the tower; it actually seemed now, when it trembled, to move amongst the stars. At the sight Adam's heart fell; the whole danger of the desperate enterprise which he had undertaken burst upon him. But shortly this feeling was followed by another which restored him to himself – a fierce hate and loathing, and a desire to kill, such as he had never experienced or even dreamt of.

They went on for some distance on a level road fairly wide, from which the green light was still visible. Here Sir Nathaniel spoke softly again, placing his lips to Adam's ear for safety:

'We must be very silent. We know nothing whatever of this creature's power of either hearing or smelling, though we presume that both are of no great strength. As to seeing, we may presume the opposite, but in any case we must try to keep in the shade or hidden behind the tree-trunks. The slightest error would be fatal to us.'

Adam made no answer. He only nodded, in case there should be any chance of the monster seeing the movement.

After a time, that seemed interminable, they emerged from the circling wood. It was like coming out into sunlight by comparison with the misty blackness which had been around them. There was actually some light – enough to see by, though not sufficient to distinguish things at a distance or minutely. Naturally Adam's eyes sought the green light in the sky. It was still in about the same place, but its surroundings were more visible. It now was at the summit of what seemed to be a long white pole, near the top of which were two pendant white masses like rudimentary arms. The green light, strangely enough, did not seem lessened by the surrounding starlight, but had a clearer effect and a deeper green. Whilst they were carefully regarding this – Adam with the aid of a folding opera-glass – their nostrils were assailed by a horrid stench – something like that which rose from the well-hole in Diana's Grove. This put them in mind of the White Worm, and they tried to examine its position as seen against the sky in the faint starlight. By degrees, as their eyes got and held the right focus, they saw an immense towering mass that seemed snowy white. It was tall and wonderfully thin. The lower part was hidden by the trees which lay between, but they could follow the tall white shaft and the duplicate green lights which topped it. As they looked there was a movement: the shaft seemed to bend and the line of green light descended amongst the trees. They could see the green light twinkle as it passed through the obstructing branches. Seeing where the head of the monster was, the two men ventured a little further forward, and, a propitious ray of moonlight helping, saw that the hidden mass at the base of the shaft was composed of vast coils of the great serpent's body, forming a substratum or base from which the upright mass rose. As still they looked, this lower mass moved, the glistening folds catching the moonlight, and they could see the monster's progress was along the ground. It was coming towards them at a swift pace, so instinctively they both turned and ran, taking care as they went to make as little noise as possible, either by their footfalls or by disturbing the undergrowth close to them. They never stopped or paused till they saw before them the high dark tower of Doom. Quickly they entered, locking the door behind them. They did not need to talk, with such a horrid memory behind them and still accompanying them. So in the dark they found their separate rooms and went to bed.

CHAPTER XXIX
IN THE ENEMY'S HOUSE

Sir Nathaniel was in the library next morning after breakfast when Adam came to him carrying a letter. As he entered the room he said:

'Her ladyship doesn't lose any time. She has begun work already!'

Sir Nathaniel, who was writing at a table near the window, looked up.

'What is it?' said he.

Adam held out to him the letter he was carrying. It was in a blazoned envelope.

'Ha!' said Sir Nathaniel, 'from Lady Arabella! I expected something of the kind.'

'But, sir,' said Adam, 'how could she have known we were here? She didn't know last night.'

'I don't think we need trouble about that, Adam. There is much we do not and cannot understand. This is only another mystery. Suffice it that she does not know. It is all the better and safer for us.'

'Better and safer?' replied Adam, amazed.

'Certainly. It is better to know the danger before us; and this is a warning, though it was not intended so. Let me see it. Addressed to Mr Adam Salton! Then she knows everything. All the better.'

'How,' said Adam with a puzzled look. 'How is it all the better?'

'General process of reasoning, my boy; and the experience of some years in the diplomatic world. Just that we are all the safer with a creature that follows its own instincts. This creature is a monster without heart or consideration for anything or anyone. She is not nearly so dangerous in the open as when she has the dark to protect her. Besides, we know, by our own experience of her movements, that for some reason she shuns publicity. Perhaps it is that she knows it won't interfere in her designs on Caswall – or rather, on Caswall's estate. In spite of her vast bulk and abnormal strength, she is afraid to attack openly. After all, vast as she is, she is only a snake and with a snake's nature, which is to keep low and squirm and proceed by stealth and cunning.[1] She will never attack when she can run away, although she knows well that running away would probably be fatal to her. What is the letter about?'

Sir Nathaniel's voice was calm and self-possessed. When he was engaged in any struggle of wits he was all diplomatist.

'It is asking Mimi and me to tea this afternoon at Diana's Grove, and hoping that you also will favour her.'

Sir Nathaniel smiled as he answered directly:

'Please ask Mrs Salton to accept for us all.'

'Accept? To go there? She means some deadly mischief. Surely – surely it would be wiser not.'

'It is an old trick that we learn early in diplomacy, Adam: to fight on ground of your own choice. It is true that she initiated the place on this occasion; but by accepting it we make it ours. Moreover, she will not be able to understand our reason or any reason for our doing so, and her own bad conscience – if she has any bad or good – and her own fears and doubts will play our game for us. No, my dear boy, let us accept, by all means.'

'Must we accept for you too, sir? I am loth that you should run such a risk. Surely you are better out of it.'

'No! It is better that I should be with you. In the first place, it will be less suspicious – you know you are my guests, and it will be better to preserve convention than to break it. In the next place, and the main reason for my going, there will be two of us to protect your wife in case of necessity. As to fear for me, do not count that. In any case, I am not a timorous man. And in this case I should accept all the danger that could be heaped on me.'

Adam said nothing, but he silently held out his hand, which the other shook: no words were necessary.

When it was getting near tea-time, Mimi asked Sir Nathaniel: 'Shall we walk over? It is only a step.'

'No, my dear,' he answered. 'We must make a point of going in state. We want all publicity.' She looked at him inquiringly. 'Certainly, my dear. In the present circumstances publicity is a part of safety. Do not be surprised if, whilst we are at Diana's Grove, occasional messages come for you – for all or any of us.'

'I see!' said Mrs Salton. 'You are taking no chances.'

'None, my dear. All I have learned at foreign courts and amongst civilised and uncivilised people is going to be utilised within the next couple of hours.'

'I shall gladly learn,' she said: 'it may help me on other occasions.'

'I hope to God it will not!'

Sir Nathaniel's voice was full of seriousness, which made the look grave also. Somehow it brought to her in a convincing way the awful gravity of the occasion. Before they came to the gate, Sir Nathaniel said to her:

'I have arranged with Adam certain signals which may be necessary if certain eventualities occur. These need be nothing to do with you directly. Only bear in mind that if I ask you or Adam to do anything, please do not lose a second in the doing of it. We shall all try to pass off such moments with an appearance of unconcern. In all probability nothing requiring such care shall occur. She will not try force though she has so much of it to spare. Whatever she may attempt to-day of harm to any of us will be in the way of secret plot. Some other time she may try force, but – if I am able to prognosticate such a thing – not to-day. The messengers who may ask for you or any of us shall not be witnesses only: they may help to stave off danger.' Seeing query in her face he went on. 'Of what kind the danger may be I know not, and cannot guess. It will doubtless be some ordinary circumstance of triviality; but none the less dangerous on that account. Here we are at the gate. Now, be self-possessed and careful in all matters, however small. To keep your head is half the battle.'

There were quite a lot of servant men in livery in the hall. The doors of the green drawing-room were thrown open, and

Lady Arabella came forth and offered them cordial welcome. This having been got over, Lady Arabella went into the other room, where a servant was holding a salver on which was laid a large letter sealed. The instant her back was turned, Sir Nathaniel whispered to Adam:

'Careful! I remember just such a cloud of servants at the Summer Palace in the Kremlin the day the Grand Duke Alexipof was assassinated at the reception given to the Khan of Bokhara.'[2]

With a slight motion of his left hand, he put the matter aside, enjoining silence. At that moment a servant in plain clothes came and bowed to Lady Arabella, saying:

'Tea is served, your ladyship, in the atrium.'

The doors of a suite of rooms were thrown partially open, the farthest of them showing the lines and colours of a Roman villa. Adam, who was acutely watchful and was suspicious of everything, saw on the far side of this newly disclosed room a panelled iron door of the same colour and configuration as the outer door of the inner room where was the well-hole wherein Oolanga had disappeared. Something in the sight alarmed him, and he quietly went forward and stood near the door. He made no movement even of his eyes, but he could see that Sir Nathaniel was watching him intently and, he fancied, with approval.

They all sat near the table spread for tea, Adam still keeping near the door. Lady Arabella had taken Mimi with her, the two men following, and sat facing the iron door. She fanned herself, impressively complaining of heat, and told one of the footmen to throw all the outer doors open. Tea was in progress when Mimi suddenly started up with a look of fright on her face; at the same moment, the men became cognisant of a thick smoke which began to spread through the room – a smoke which made those who experienced it gasp and choke. The men – even the footmen – began to edge uneasily towards the inner door. Lady Arabella alone was unmoved. She sat still in her seat at the table, with a look of unconcern on her face which disturbed all present, except Sir Nathaniel – and later, Adam, so soon as he caught Sir Nathaniel's eye. Denser and denser grew the smoke, and more acrid its smell. Presently, Mimi, towards whom the draught from the open door wafted the smoke, rose up choking, and ran to the door, which she threw open to its fullest extent, disclosing on the outside of it a curtain of thin silk fixed not to the door but the doorposts. As the door opened more freely the draught from the open door swayed the thin silk towards her, enveloping her in a sort of cloud. In her fright, she tore down the curtain, which enveloped her from head to foot. Then she ran towards the open outer door, unconscious or heedless of the fact that she could not see where she was going. At this moment, Adam, followed by Sir Nathaniel, rushed forward and joined her – Adam catching her by the upper arm and holding her tight. It was well that he did so, for just before her lay the black orifice of the well-hole, which, of course, she could not see with the silk curtain round her head. The floor was extremely slippery; something like thick oil had been spilled where she had to pass; and close to the edge of the hole her feet shot from under her, and she stumbled forward towards the well-hole.

CHAPTER XXX

A RACE FOR LIFE

When Adam saw Mimi slip, he sprang forward, still holding her arm, so, as they both moved forward at equal rate of speed, there was no unnecessary shock. Instinctively he flung himself backward, still holding her. His weight here told, and, as his grip held her fast, he dragged her up from the hole and they fell together on the floor outside the zone of slipperiness. In a moment he had sprung to his feet and raised her up, so that together they rushed out through the open door into the sunlight, Sir Nathaniel coming close behind them. They were all pale except the old diplomatist, who looked both calm and cool. It sustained and cheered both Adam and his wife to see him thus master of himself. Both Mr and Mrs Salton managed to follow his example, to the wonderment of the footmen, who saw the three who had just escaped a terrible danger walking together gaily, as under the guiding pressure of Sir Nathaniel's hand they turned to re-enter the house. When they were out of earshot of the servants, Sir Nathaniel whispered softly:

'Hush – not a sound. Do not appear to notice that anything has happened. We are not safe yet – not out of this ordeal.'

And so chatting and laughing they re-entered the atrium where Lady Arabella still sat in her place as motionless as a statue of marble. In fact, all those in the room remained so still as to give the newcomers the impression that they were looking at an instantaneous photograph. In a few seconds, however, normal sound and movement were renewed. Lady Arabella, whose face had blanched to a deadly white, now appeared to be in great spirits, and resumed her ministrations at the tea-

board as though nothing unusual had happened. The slop-
basin[1] was full of half-burned brown paper over which tea had
been poured.

Sir Nathaniel, who had been narrowly observing his hostess,
took the first opportunity afforded him of whispering to Adam:

'More than ever be careful. The real attack is to come yet.
She is too quiet for reality. When I give my hand to your wife
to lead her out – by whatever door, – I don't know which yet,
– come with us – quick, and caution her to hurry. Don't lose a
second, even if you have to make a scene. Hs-s-s-h!'

Then they resumed their places close to the table, and the
servants, in obedience to Lady Arabella's order, brought in
fresh tea.

Thence on, that tea-party seemed to Adam, whose faculties
were at their utmost intensity, like a terrible dream. As for poor
Mimi, she was so overwrought both with present and future
fear, and with horror at the danger she had escaped, that her
faculties were numb. However, she was braced up for a trial,
and she felt assured that whatever might come she would be
able to go through with it. Sir Nathaniel seemed just as usual –
suave, dignified, and thoughtful – perfect master of himself and
his intentions. To her husband it was evident that Mimi was ill
at ease. The mere way she kept constantly turning her head to
look around her, the quick coming and going of the colour of
her face, her hurried breathing, alternating with periods of
suspicious calm, were to those who had power to discern subtle
evidence of mental perturbation. To her, the attitude of Lady
Arabella seemed compounded of social sweetness and personal
consideration. It would be hard to imagine any more thoughtful
and tender kindness towards an honoured guest. Even Adam
seemed touched with it, though he never relaxed his vigilance
or took his eyes off the lady's movements. When tea was over
and the servants had come to clear away the cups, Lady Arabella, putting her arms round Mimi's waist, strolled with her
into the adjoining room, where she collected a number of photographs which were scattered about, and, sitting down beside
her guest, began to show them to her. While she was doing this,
the servants closed all the doors of the suite of rooms and that

which opened from the room outside, – that of the well-hole into the avenue. Presently she came back to the room where Adam and Sir Nathaniel were, and sat on a sofa on which Mimi had already taken her seat. Suddenly, without any seeming cause, the light in the room began to grow dim. The light outside seemed to become similarly affected, even the glass of the window becoming obscure. Sir Nathaniel, who was sitting close to Mimi, rose to his feet, and, crying, 'Quick!' caught hold of her right hand and began to drag her from the room. Adam caught her other hand, and between them they drew her through the outer door which the servants were beginning to close. It was difficult at first to find the way, the darkness was so great; but to their relief a multitude of the cowled birds rushed through the open door, and then, falling back, formed a lane-way through the air which there was no mistaking. In seemingly frantic haste they rushed through the avenue towards the gate, Adam whistling shrilly. Mr Salton's double carriage with the four horses and two postillions, which had been wait-ing quite still in the angle of the avenue, dashed up. Her husband and Sir Nathaniel lifted – almost threw – Mimi into the carriage. The postillions plied whip and spur, and the vehicle, rocking with its speed, swept through the gate and tore up the road. Behind them was a hubbub – servants rushing about, orders being called out, doors shutting, and somewhere, seemingly far back in the house, a strange noise like a lumbering cart moving on thin ice. There was no slackening of pace. Every nerve of the men, and even of the horses, was strained as they dashed recklessly along the road. The two men held Mimi between them, the arms of both of them round her as though protectingly. As they went, there was a sudden rise in the ground; but the horses, breathing heavily as if mad, dashed up it at racing speed, not even slackening their pace when the hill fell away again leaving them to hurry along the downgrade. At the utmost speed of which the horses were capable, they made for Macclesfield. Thence on to Congleton. Having passed the latter place, as they looked back they saw a great shapeless mass behind them, its white showing through the creeping dusk, all form lost in its swift passage. From Congleton they headed for Runcorn, where there were clusters of lights at the bridge and a stream of single lights, or small groups of lights, along by the ship canal. The horses tore madly on, seemingly in the extremity of terror, and followed in their course by a sickening smell such as had arisen through the well-hole. At Runcorn they headed for Liverpool, joyous, even in the midst of their terror, when they saw the blaze of lights at the landing-stage and extending down the river till they disappeared in the line of the piers and floating buoys. As they drew near they heard with glad ears the hooting of a great steamer, ablaze with many lights from stem to stern.

'We are in time!' said Adam, but made no other remark. At Runcorn they saw a white mass slip down the slope from the roadway to the Mersey, and heard the wash of a great body that slid into the tide-way. The postillions, with their goal in sight, redoubled their exertions, and they tore along the streets at reckless pace, careless of the shouted warnings and threats of the police and the many drivers of various vehicles. They tore down the steep movable way to the landing-stage – just in time to see the great vessel move into the river, and to hear the throb of the engines.

The hearts of Adam and his wife grew cold, for their last chance seemed gone. But at the foot of the movable bridge stood Davenport, watch in hand. The moment the carriage drove up he raised his hand in signal to the captain of a great Isle of Man steamer, who was evidently looking out for him. When he saw the hand raised, he worked the engine telegraph, and the great paddle-wheels began to revolve. The *Manx Maid* was the fastest boat sailing from Liverpool; and from the instant the flanges to her paddles struck the water, she began to over-haul the Australian boat. They had not got far down the river when she overtook the latter and ranged alongside without slackening speed. Affairs had already been arranged between the two boats with a time to be reckoned by seconds. Adam and his wife, Sir Nathaniel, and Davenport were transferred to the ocean steamship whilst going at as full speed as was allow-able at this point of the river, and the latter swept on her way. Davenport went down to his cabin with Adam, telling him on the way what arrangements had been made and how he had received the message from Diana's Grove; and that the voyagers would be able to get off at Queenstown[2] as they might desire.

CHAPTER XXXI
BACK TO DOOM

There seemed to be a great and unusual excitement on the river and along both banks as the *Manx Maid* swept on her way. From the tops of the lighthouses and the pleasure towers; from the yards of every big ship going out or coming in, spy-glasses were projected and binoculars in use; there was rushing to and fro on all the docks, and many shots were heard. Sir Nathaniel went about the deck trying to find the cause; at last a quarter-master told him that, so far as they could make out from semaphore signals,[1] a great whale had come down the river and was heading out to sea. It had been first noticed at Runcorn, he said, going downstream; but where it had come from no one knew, for it had been unnoticed before that time. For Sir Nathaniel and his friends this was quite sufficient. The danger was not over yet. Adam went straight to the captain and made a request that the search-light with which the ship was equipped should be kept on the alleged whale day and night, as long as it might be within sight. This was attended to at once, and so long as there was anything to be seen there were constant reports. Adam and his friends had many opportunities of seeing the monster, and more than once recognised the contours of its head and the green flash of its eyes. Just before midnight the report came that the whale had been seen to turn, and was now heading towards the Mersey. Then all was darkness, and reports ceased. The pursuit had been given over.

Adam and Mimi and Sir Nathaniel slept sound that night.

Refreshed with sleep, which had for many nights been a stranger to them all, the party rose with renewed courage and the brave intentions which come with it.

When Queenstown was in sight, Adam, leaving his wife in their cabin, took Sir Nathaniel to the saloon, then empty, and astonished him by telling him that he was going off when the ship stopped, and was returning to the Brow at once.

'But what about your wife?' the latter asked. 'Does she go on alone?'

'No, sir; she comes back with me,' was the startling reply.

Sir Nathaniel walked back and forwards several times before he spoke:

'I presume, my dear boy, that you have thought well over what you are about to do, and weighed up the possible consequences. I am not given to interfere with my neighbour's affairs, and such a thing as this is a man's own responsibility to be decided entirely by himself. Of course when he has a wife her wishes are paramount. What does she say?'

'We are quite agreed, Sir Nathaniel. We both see it as a duty which we owe to other people to be on the spot and do what we can.'

'But,' expostulated Sir Nathaniel, 'with the terrible experiences you have had – the recollection of the terrible dangers which you have escaped – is it wise to place such an awful burden as a possible repetition, or even extension of these things, on the shoulders of a young girl just entering – and happily entering – life? Forgive my interference. I shall not press my views unduly on either of you; but to bring the view before your notice is also a duty, a very sacred duty which I must not forgo.'

'I know that, sir, and with all our heart Mimi and I thank you for your kindness. But it is just because of that experience which is already had, and perhaps paid for, that our power to help others has grown – and our responsibility in equal proportion.'

Sir Nathaniel said solemnly:

'God forbid that I should come between any man – or woman – and a duty. Remember that I am with you, heart and soul. I shared the trouble and the risk with you at the beginning, and, please God, I shall do so to the end – whatever that may be!'

Sir Nathaniel said no more, but he was helpful in all ways,

loyally accepting the wishes of his friends and supporting them. Mimi thanked him in the warmth of her handclasp, for his sharing the risk, and for his devoted friendship. Then they three settled all matters so far as they could foresee.

When the ship arrived in the roads at Queenstown they debarked in the tender and set out in the first train towards Liverpool. There, in obedience to instructions telegraphed to him by Davenport, they were met with the carriage with four horses and the postillions just as when they had left Diana's Grove. The postillions, who were well-plucked men, had volunteered to come though they knew the terrible risk they ran. But the horses had been changed – wisely – for they could not easily get over the fright in the prolonged race against the monster.

Mr Salton had been advised that they were not returning to Lesser Hill, so did not expect to see them. All was prepared at Doom with locks and bolts and curtains as when they left.

It would be foolish to say that neither Adam nor Mimi had fears in returning. On the contrary, the road from Liverpool and Congleton was a *via dolorosa*.[2] Of course Mimi felt it more keenly than her husband, whose nerves were harder, and who was more inured to danger. Still she bore up bravely, and as usual the effort was helpful to her. When once she was in the study in the top of the turret, she almost forgot the terrors which lay outside in the dark. She did not attempt even a peep out of the window; but Adam did – and saw nothing. The full moonlight showed all the surrounding country, but nowhere was to be observed that tremulous line of green light or the thin white tower rising up beyond the woods.

The peaceful night had good effect on them all; danger, being unseen, seemed afar off. At times it was hard to realise that it had ever been. With courage quite restored, Adam rose early and walked all along the Brow, seeing no change in the signs of life in Castra Regis. What he did see, to his wonder and concern, on his returning homeward, was Lady Arabella in her tight-fitting white dress and ermine collar, but without her emeralds, emerging from the gate of Diana's Grove and walking towards the Castle. Pondering on this and trying to find some meaning in it, occupied his thoughts till he joined Mimi and Sir

Nathaniel at breakfast. They were all silent during the meal, simply because none of them had anything to say. What had been had been, and was known to them all. Moreover, it was not a pleasant topic. One experience they had – at least Adam and Mimi had, for Sir Nathaniel had long ago learned all that it could teach – that is, that memory of even the most stirring or exciting or mournful time soon passes; the humdrum of life is beyond all episodes, and swamps them. A fillip was given to the conversation when Adam told of his seeing Lady Arabella, and her being on her way to Castra Regis. They each had something to say of her, and of what her wishes or intentions were towards Edgar Caswall. Mimi spoke bitterly of her in every aspect. She had not forgotten – and never would – never could – the occasion when to Lilla's harm she consorted even with the nigger. As a social matter, she was disgusted with her over following up of the rich landowner – 'throwing herself at his head so shamelessly,' was how she expressed it. She was interested to know that the great kite still flew from Caswall's tower. But beyond such matters she did not try to go. Indeed, for such she had no data. She was really surprised – in a quiet way – to hear how fully the old order of things had been already restored. The only comments she made in this connection were of strongly expressed surprise at her ladyship's 'cheek' in ignoring her own criminal acts, and her impudence in taking it for granted that others had overlooked them also. Adam had tried unsuccessfully to find any report of the alleged whale in the Mersey, so he remained silent on that subject. Perhaps he had a vague hope that the monster had been unable to sustain her maritime adventures, and had perished. He was well content that this should be so, though he had already made up his mind that he would spare neither time nor effort, or indeed life itself, to root out Diana's Grove and all it contained. He had already expressed his intention to Sir Nathaniel and to Mimi. The former thoroughly approved his intention and pledged himself to support him in his efforts. Mimi agreed with him, but woman-like advised caution.

CHAPTER XXXII

A STARTLING
PROPOSITION

The more Mimi thought over the late events, the more puzzled she was. Adam had actually seen Lady Arabella coming from her own house on the Brow, yet he – and she too – had last seen the monster in the guise in which she had occasionally appeared wallowing in the Irish Sea. What did it all mean – what could it mean? except that there was an error of fact somewhere. Could it be possible that some of them – all of them had been mistaken? That there had been no White Worm at all? That the eyes of Adam and Sir Nathaniel had deceived them? She was all at sea! On either side of her was a belief impossible of reception. Not to believe in what seemed apparent was to destroy the very foundations of belief ... And yet ... and yet in old days there had been monsters on the earth, and certainly some people had believed in just such mysterious changes of identity ... It was all very strange. Perhaps, indeed, it was that she herself was mad. Yes, that must be it! Something had upset her brain. She was dreaming untruths based on reality. Just fancy how any stranger – say a doctor – would regard her if she were to calmly tell him that she had been to a tea-party with an antediluvian monster, and that they had been waited on by up-to-date men-servants. From this she went into all sorts of wild fancies. What sort of tea did dragons prefer? What was it that essentially tickled their palates? Who did the washing for dragons' servants? Did they use starch? If, in the privacy of their houses – homes – lairs, were dragons accustomed to use knives and forks and teaspoons? Yes, that at any rate was true; she had seen them used herself. Here she got into such a state of intellectual confusion that even the upside-down reasoning of the border-land between waking and sleeping would not account for it. She set herself to thinking deeply. Here she was in her own bed in the house of Sir Nathaniel de Salis, Doom Tower – that at any rate was a fact; and to that she would hold on. She would keep quiet and think of nothing – certainly not of any of these strange things – till Adam was with her. He would tell her the truth. She could believe all that he would say. Therefore, till he came she would remain quiet and try not to think at all. This was a wise and dutiful resolution; and it had its reward. Gradually thoughts, true or false, ceased to trouble her. The warmth and peace of her body began to have effect; and after she had left a message for Adam to come up to her when he returned, she sank into a deep sleep.

Adam returned, exhilarated by his walk, and more settled in his mind than he had been for some time. He, too, had been feeling the reaction from the high pressure which he had been experiencing ever since the intentions of Lady Arabella had been manifested. Like Mimi, he had gone through the phase of doubt and inability to believe in the reality of things, though it had not affected him to the same extent. The idea, however, that his wife was suffering ill-effects from her terrible ordeal braced him up, and when he came into her room and waked her, he was at his intellectual and nervous best. He remained with her till she had quite recovered her nerve, and in this condition had gone again into a peaceful sleep. Then he sought Sir Nathaniel in order to talk over the matter with him. He knew that the calm commonsense and self-reliance of the old man, as well as his experience, would be helpful to them all. Sir Nathaniel had by now come to the conclusion that for some reason which he did not understand, or indeed try to, Lady Arabella had entirely changed her plans, and, for the present at all events, was entirely pacific. Later on, when the ideas of the morning were in farther perspective, he was inclined to attribute her changed demeanour to the fact that her influence over Edgar Caswall was so far increased as to justify a more fixed belief in his submission to her charms. She had seen him that morning when she visited Castra Regis, and they had had a long talk together, during which the possibility of their union had been discussed. Caswall, without being enthusiastic on the subject, had been courteous and attentive; as she had walked back to Diana's Grove she almost congratulated herself on her new settlement in life. That the idea was becoming fixed in her mind, and was even beginning to materialise, was shown by a letter which she wrote later in the day to Adam Salton and had sent to him by hand. It ran as follows:

'DEAR MR SALTON, – I wonder if you would kindly advise and, if possible, help me in a matter of business. I have no aptitude or experience in such matters, and am inclined to lean on a friend. Briefly, it is this. I have been for some time trying to make up my mind to sell this place (Diana's Grove), but so many difficulties have been suggested about so doing, that I have put off and put off the doing of it till now. The place is entirely my own property, and no one has to be consulted with regard to what I may wish to do about it. It was bought by my late husband, Captain Adolphus Ranger March, who then had a residence, The Crest, Appleby. He acquired all rights of all kinds, including mining and sporting. When he died he left his whole property to me. Now my father wants me to live with him, and I feel it a call of duty to do so. I am his only child, and he is beginning to be an old, a very old man. Moreover, he has certain official duties to perform and dignities to support. He is, as perhaps you know, Lord Lieutenant of the County, and he feels the want of a female relative to take the head of the table. I am, he says, the only one for the post. He is too old to marry again, and, besides help in the duties named, he wants the comfort of a companion. I shall feel the leaving this place, which has become endeared to me by many sacred memories and affections – the recollection of many happy days of my young married life and the more than happy memories of the man I loved and who loved me so much. I should be glad to sell the place for any kind of fair price – so long, of course, as the purchaser was one I liked and of whom I approved. May I say that you yourself would be the ideal person. But I dare not hope for so much. It strikes me, however, that among your Australian friends may be someone who wishes to make a settlement in the Old Country, and would, in such case, care to fix the spot in one of the most historic regions in England, full of romance and legend, and with a never-ending vista of historical interest – an estate which, though small, is in perfect condition and with illimitable possibilities of development, and many doubtful – or unsettled – rights which have existed before the time of the Romans or even Celts, who were the original possessors. In addition, the house is one of the oldest in England, and kept up to the *dernier cri*[1] for the last two thousand years. Of all this, immediate possession is to be had. My lawyers can provide you, or whoever you may suggest, with all business and historical details. A word from you of acceptance or refusal is all that is necessary, and we can leave details to be thrashed out by our agents. Forgive me, won't you, for troubling you in the matter, and believe me, yours very sincerely,

'ARABELLA MARCH.'

Adam read this over several times, and then, his mind being made up – though not with inflexible finality, – he went to Mimi and asked if she had any objection. She answered – though after a shudder – that she was in this, as in all things, willing to do whatever he might wish. She added as he was leaving the room:

'Dear, I am willing you should judge what is best for us both. Be quite free to act as you see your duty, and as your inclination calls. We are in the hands of God, and He has hitherto guided us, and will to His own end.'

CHAPTER XXXIII
WAR À L'OUTRANCE

From his wife's room Adam Salton went straight to the study in the tower, where he knew Sir Nathaniel would be at that hour. The old man was alone, so, when he had entered in obedience to the 'Come in,' which answered his query, he closed the door and came and sat down beside him. He began at once:

'Do you think, sir, it would be well for me to buy Diana's Grove?'

'God bless my soul!' said the old man, startled, 'what on earth would you want to do that for?'

'Well, sir, I have vowed to destroy that White Worm, and my being able to do whatever I may choose with the Lair would facilitate matters and avoid complications.'

Sir Nathaniel hesitated longer than usual before speaking. He was thinking deeply.

'Thank you, Adam, for telling me – though, indeed, I had almost taken so much for granted. But it is well to have accurate knowledge if one is going to advise. I think that, for all reasons, you would do well to buy the property and to have the convey-ance settled at once. If you should want more money than is immediately convenient, let me know, so that I may be your banker.'

'Thank you, sir, most heartily; but, indeed, I have more money at immediate call than I can want. I am glad you approve.'

'More than approve. You are doing a wise thing in a financial way. The property is historic, and as time goes on it will increase in value. Moreover, I may tell you something which indeed is only a surmise, but which, if I am right, will add great value to the place.'

Adam listened. He went on:

'Has it ever struck you why the old name, "The Lair of the White Worm," was given? Imagine the word "white" in italics. We know now that there was a snake which in early days was called a worm; but why white?'

'I really don't know, sir; I never thought of it. I simply took it for granted.'

'So did I at first – long ago. But later I puzzled my brain for a reason.'

'And what was the reason, sir?'

'Simply and solely because the snake or worm *was* white.'

'How was that? There must have been a reason. Tradition did not give it a colour without *some* reason.'

'Evidently what people saw was white. I puzzled over it till I saw some light on the subject.'

'Won't you let me follow your reasoning, sir?'

'Certainly. We are in the county of Stafford, where the great industry of china-burning was originated and grew. Stafford owes much of its wealth to the large deposits of the rare china clay found in it from time to time.[1] These deposits became in time pretty well exhausted; but for centuries Stafford adventurers looked for the special clay as Ohio and Pennsylvania farmers and explorers looked for oil. Anyone owning real estate on which clay can be discovered strikes a sort of gold mine.'

'Yes, and then – ?' The young man looked puzzled.

The old man continued:

'The original "Worm" so-called, from which the name of the place came, had to find a direct way down to the marshes and the mud-holes. Now, the clay is easily penetrable, and the original hole probably pierced the bed of china clay. When once the way was made it became a sort of highway for the Worm. But as much movement was necessary to ascend such a great and steep height, some of the clay got attached to his rough skin by attrition. The downway must have been easy work, and there was little attrition; but the ascent was different, and when the monster came to view in the upper world, he was fresh from contact with the white clay. Hence the name, which has no cryptic significance but only fact. Now, if that surmise be true

– and I do not see why it is not – there must be a deposit of valuable clay of immense depth. And there is no reason why it is not of equally large superficies.'

Adam's comment pleased the old gentleman.

'I have it in my bones, sir, that you have struck – or rather reasoned out – a great truth.'

Sir Nathaniel went on cheerfully. 'When the world of commerce and manufacture wakes up to the value of your find, it will be as well that your title to ownership has been perfectly secured. If anyone ever deserved such a gain, it is you.'

With his friend's aid, Adam secured the property without loss of time. Then he went to see his uncle, and told him about it. Mr Salton was delighted to find his young relative already constructively the owner of so fine an estate – and one which gave him an important status in the county.

The next morning, when Adam went in to his host in the smoking-room, the latter asked him how he purposed to proceed with regard to keeping his vow.

'It is a difficult matter which you have undertaken. To destroy such a monster is something like one of the labours of Hercules,[2] in that not only its size and weight and power of using them in little-known ways are against you, but the occult side is alone an unsurpassable difficulty. The Worm is already master of all the elements except fire. And I do not see how fire can be used for the attack. It has only to sink into the earth in its charted way, and you could not overtake it if you had the resources of the biggest coal-mine in existence. But I daresay you have mapped out some plan in your mind,' he added courteously.

'I have, sir. But, of course, it is purely theoretical and may not stand the test of practice.'

'May I know the idea you formed?'

'Well, sir, this was my argument: This old lady is fairly experienced. I suppose, by the way, that there is no offence in calling her an old lady, considering that she has been disporting herself in her own way for some thousands of years. So there is no use in trying means that were familiar to her at the time of the Flood. I have been turning my brain inside out and upside down to hit on a new scheme. We hear in Ecclesiastes that there

is nothing new under the sun,[3] and as she antedated that work,
I daresay she is up to everything which has been popularly
known ever since. So at last I decided to try a new adaptation
of an old scheme. It is about a century old. But what is a century
to her? At the time of the Chartist trouble[4] an idea spread
amongst financial circles that an attack was going to be made
on the Bank of England. Accordingly, the directors of that
institution consulted many persons who were supposed to
know what steps should be taken, and it was finally decided
that the best protection against fire – which is what was feared
– was not water but sand. To carry the scheme into practice
great store of fine sea-sand – the kind that blows about and is
used to fill hour-glasses – was provided throughout the building,
especially at the points liable to attack, from which it could be
brought into use.

'I propose to follow the example. I shall provide at Diana's
Grove, as soon as it comes into my possession, an enormous
amount of such sand, and shall take an early occasion of pouring it into the well-hole, which it will in time choke. Thus Lady
Arabella, in her guise of the White Worm, will find herself cut
off from her refuge. The hole is a narrow one, and is some
hundreds of feet deep. The weight of the sand this can contain
would not in itself be sufficient to obstruct; but the friction of
such a body working up against it would be tremendous.'

'One moment. What use, then, would the sand there be for
destruction?'

'None, directly; but it would hold the struggling body in
place till the rest of the scheme came into practice.'

'And what is the rest?'

'As the sand is being poured into the well-hole at intervals,
large quantities of dynamite can also be thrown in!'

'Good. But how would the dynamite explode – for, of course,
that is what you intend. Would not some sort of wire or fuse
be required for each parcel of dynamite?'

Adam smiled.

'Not in these days, sir. That was proved in the second and
greater explosion at Hell Gate in New York.[5] Before the
explosion a hundred thousand pounds of dynamite in sealed

canisters was placed about the miles of workings. At the last a charge of gunpowder was fired – a ton or so. And the concussion exploded all the dynamite. It was most successful. Those who were non-experts in high explosives expected that every pane of glass in New York would be shattered. But, in reality, the explosive did no harm outside the area intended, although sixteen acres of rock had been mined and only the supporting walls and pillars had been left intact. The whole of the rocks which made the whirlpool in East River were simply shattered into the size of matches.'

Sir Nathaniel nodded approval.

'That seems a good plan – a very excellent one. But if it has to tear down so many feet of precipice it may wreck the whole neighbourhood.'

'And free it for ever from a monster,' added Adam, as he left the room to find his wife.

CHAPTER XXXIV
APPREHENSION

Lady Arabella had instructed her solicitors to hurry on with the conveyance of Diana's Grove, so no time was lost in letting Adam Salton have formal possession of the estate. After his interview with Sir Nathaniel, he had taken steps to begin putting his plan into action. In order to accumulate the necessary amount of fine sea-sand, he had ordered the steward to prepare for an elaborate system of top-dressing all the grounds. A great heap of the chosen sand, which Mr Salton's carts had brought from bays on the Welsh coast, began to grow at the back of the Grove. No one seemed to suspect that it was there for any purpose other than what had been given out. Lady Arabella, who alone could have guessed, was now so absorbed in her matrimonial pursuit of Edgar Caswall, that she had neither time nor inclination for thought extraneous to this. Adam, as a member of the Australian Committee for Defence and a crack gunner in the West Australian Volunteer Artillery, had, of course, plenty of opportunities for purchasing and storing war material; so he put up a rough corrugated-iron shed behind the Grove, in which he had stored his explosives and also a couple of field pieces which he thought it well to have near him in case of emergency. Even the White Worm would have to yield to the explosive shells which they could carry. All being ready for his great attempt whenever the time should come, he was now content to wait, and, in order to pass the time, was content to interest himself in other things – even in Caswall's great kite, which still flew from the high tower of Castra Regis. Strange to say, he took a real interest, beyond the advantage to his own schemes, in Caswall's childish play with the runners. It may, of course, have been that in such puerile matters, which in reality did not matter how they eventuated, he found a solace, or at any rate a relief, from things which were naturally more trying. At any rate, however intended, the effect was there, and the time passed without any harm being done by its passage. The mount of fine sand grew to proportions so vast as to puzzle the bailiffs and farmers round the Brow. The hour of the intended cataclysm was approaching apace. Adam wished – but in vain – for an opportunity, which would appear to be natural, of visiting Caswall in the turret of Castra Regis. At last he got up early one morning, and when he saw Lady Arabella moving towards the Castle, took his courage *à deux mains* and asked to be allowed to accompany her. She was glad, for her own purposes, to comply with his wishes. So together they entered, unobserved at that early hour, and found their way to the turret-room. Caswall was much surprised to see Adam come to his house in such a way, but lent himself to the task of seeming to be pleased. He played the host so well as to deceive even Adam. They all went out on the turret roof, where he explained to his guests the mechanism for raising and lowering the kite, taking also the opportunity of testing the movements of the multitudes of birds, how they answered almost instantaneously to the lowering or raising of the kite. After a little while, Adam's stock of knowledge of this was so increased that he was glad that he had ventured on the visit.

As Lady Arabella walked home with Adam from Castra Regis, she asked him if she might make a request. Permission having been accorded, she explained that before she finally left Diana's Grove, where she had lived so long, she had a desire to know the depth of the well-hole. Adam was really happy to meet her wishes, not from any sentiment, but because he wished to give some valid and ostensible reason for examining the passage of the Worm, which would obviate any suspicion resulting from his being on the premises. This exactly suited him, and he made full use of his opportunities. He brought from London a Kelvin sounding apparatus[1] with an adequate length of piano-wire for testing any depth, however great. The wire passed over the easily-running wheel, and when this was once fixed over the hole, he was satisfied to wait till the most advantageous time to make his final experiment. He was absolutely satisfied with the way things were going. It seemed to him almost an impossibility that there should be any hitch or disturbance in his carefully arranged plans. It often amazed Adam to see how thoroughly Lady Arabella seemed to enjoy the sounding of the well-hole, despite the sickening stench exhaled by the fissure. Sometimes he would have to go out into the outer air to get free from it for a little while. It really was not merely an evil smell; it rather seemed to partake of some of the qualities of some noxious chemical waste. But she seemed never to tire in the work, but went on as though unconscious that anything disagreeable at all existed. Adam tried to find relief by interesting her in the experiments with the kite. The top of the Castle, at any rate, was free from the foul breath of the pit, and whilst he was engaged there he did not feel as if his actual life was being imperilled by the noxious smell. One thing he longed for, a little artillery practice, though indeed there was a solace to him in the thought that he was the crack shot in the West Australian Artillery.

In the meantime, affairs had been going quietly at Mercy Farm. Lilla, of course, felt lonely at the absence of her cousin, but the even tenor of life went on for her as for others. After the first shock of parting was over, things went back to their accustomed routine. In one respect, however, there was a marked difference. So long as home conditions had remained unchanged, Lilla was content to put ambition far from her and to settle down to the life which had been hers as long as she could remember. But Mimi's marriage set her thinking; naturally, she came to the conclusion that she too might have a mate. There was not for her much choice – there was little movement in the matrimonial direction at the farmhouse. But there was a counter-balancing advantage that one man had already shown his preference for her in an unmistakable way. True, she did not approve of the personality of Edgar Caswall, and his struggle with Mimi had frightened her; but he was unmistakably an excellent *parti*,[2] much better than she could ever have any right to expect. This weighs much with a woman, and more particularly one of her class. So, on the whole, she was content to let things take their course, and to abide by the issue. As time had gone on, she had reason to secretly believe that things did not point to happiness. But here again was a state of things purely feminine, which was easily got over. The happiness which is, so to speak, 'in the bush,' is at best vague, and the opposite is more vague still. It is hard for a young person, specially of the female sex, to believe that things may not turn out eventually as well as they had originally promised. She could not shut her eyes to certain disturbing facts, amongst which were the existence of Lady Arabella and her growing intimacy with Edgar Caswall; his own cold and haughty nature, so little in accord with the love which is the foundation of a young maid's dreams of happiness; and, finally, that the companion of her youth – her life – would, by her marriage to Adam, be taken away to the other side of the earth, where she was to make her home. How things would of necessity alter if she were to marry herself, she was afraid to think. All told, the prospect was not happy for her, and she had a secret longing that *something* might occur to upset the order of things as at present arranged. She had a feeling that she would be happy to accept whatever might happen in consequence of the change. She had also a sort of foreknowledge that the time was coming with startling rapidity when Mr Caswall would come to pay another visit at the farm – a thing which she was quite unable to contemplate with any unmixed pleasure, more especially as Mimi would not be with her to help her in bearing the trial. She dreaded lest there should be another struggle of wills in which she would have to be the shuttlecock. The result of her pondering over the subject was that she saw the beginning of the end of her happy life, and felt as if she was looking into a cold fog in which everything was concealed from her. And so she was filled with many unrelieved apprehensions.

CHAPTER XXXV
THE LAST BATTLE

When Lilla Watford got Edgar Caswall's note asking if he might come to tea on the following afternoon, her heart sank within her. If it was only for her father's sake, she must not refuse him or show any disinclination which he might construe into incivility. She missed Mimi more than she could say or even dared to think. Hitherto, she had always looked to her for sympathy, for understanding, for loyal support. Now she and all these things, and a thousand others – gentle, assuring, supporting – were gone. And instead there was a horrible aching void. In matters of affection for both sexes, and overcoming timorousness for woman, want ceases to be a negative and becomes positive. For the whole afternoon and evening, and for the following forenoon, poor Lilla's loneliness grew to be a positive agony. For the first time she began to realise the sense of her loss as though all the previous suffering had been merely a preparation. Everything she looked at, everything she remembered or thought of, became laden with poignant memory. Then on the top of all was a new sense of dread. The reaction from the sense of security, which had surrounded her all her life, to a never-quieted apprehension was at times almost more than she could bear. It so filled her with fear that she had a haunting feeling that she would as soon die as live. However, whatever might be her own feelings, duty had to be done. And as she had been brought up to consider duty as first, she braced herself to go through, to the very best of her ability, what was before her. Still, the severe and prolonged struggle for self-control told upon her. She looked as she felt, ill and weak. She was really in a nerveless and prostrate condition, with

black circles round her eyes, pale even to her lips, and with an
instinctive trembling which she was quite unable to repress. It
was for her a sad mischance that Mimi was away, for her
love would have seen through all obscuring causes, and have
brought to light the girl's unhappy condition of health. Lilla
was utterly unable to do anything to escape from the ordeal
before her; but her cousin, with the experience of her former
struggles with Mr Caswall and of the condition in which these
left her, would have taken steps – even peremptory ones, if
necessary – to prevent a repetition.

Edgar arrived punctually to the time appointed by herself.
When Lilla, through the great window, saw him approaching
the house, her condition of nervous upset was pitiable. She
braced herself up, however, and managed to meet and go on
with the interview in its preliminary stages without any percep-
tible change in her normal appearance and bearing. It had been
to her an added terror that the black shadow of Oolanga, whom
she dreaded, should follow hard on his master. A load was
lifted from her mind when he did not make his usual stealthy
approach. She had also feared, though in lesser degree, lest
Lady Arabella should be present to make trouble for her as
before. The absence of her, too, made at least the beginning of
the interview less intolerable. With a woman's natural fore-
thought in a difficult position, she had provided the furnishing
of the tea-table as a subtle indication of the social difference
between her and her guest. She had chosen the implements of
service, as well as all the provender set forth, of the humblest
kind. Instead of arranging the silver teapot and china cups, she
had set out an earthen teapot such as was in common use in
the farm kitchen. The same idea was carried out in the cups
and saucers of thick homely delft, and in the cream-jug of
similar kind. The bread was of simple whole-meal, home-baked.
The butter was of course good, since she had made it herself,
and the preserves and honey came from her own garden. Her
face beamed with satisfaction when the guest eyed the appoint-
ments with a supercilious glance. It was all a shock to the
poor girl herself, who enjoyed offering to a guest the little
hospitalities possible to her; but that had to be sacrificed with

other pleasures. Caswall's face was more set and iron-clad than ever – his piercing eyes seemed from the very beginning to look her through and through. Her heart quailed when she thought of what would follow – of what would be the end, when this was only the beginning. As some protection, though it could be only of a sentimental kind, she brought from her own room the photographs of Mimi, of her grandfather, and of Adam Salton, whom by now she had grown to look on with reliance, as a brother whom she could trust. She kept the pictures near her heart, to which her hand naturally strayed when her feelings of constraint, distrust, or fear became so poignant as to interfere with the calm which she felt was necessary to help her through her ordeal. At first Edgar Caswall was courteous and polite, even thoughtful; but after a little while, when he found her resistance to his domination grow, he abandoned all forms of self-control and appeared in the same dominance as he had previously shown. She was prepared, however, for this, both by her former experience and the natural fighting instinct within her. By this means, as the minutes went on, both developed the power and preserved the equality in which they had begun.

Without warning or any cogent cause, the psychic battle between the two individualities began afresh. This time both the positive and negative causes were all in the favour of the man. The woman was alone and in bad spirits, unsupported; and nothing at all was in her favour except the memory of the two victorious contests; whereas the man, though unaided, as before, by either Lady Arabella or Oolanga, was in full strength, well rested, and in flourishing circumstances. It was not, therefore, to be wondered at that his native dominance of character had full opportunity of asserting itself. He began his preliminary stare with a conscious sense of power, and, as it appeared to have immediate effect on the girl, he felt an ever-growing conviction of ultimate victory. After a little Lilla's resolution began to flag. She felt that the contest was unequal – that she was unable to put forth her best efforts. As she was an unselfish, unegotistical person, she could not fight so well in her own battle as in that of someone whom she loved and to whom she was devoted. Edgar saw the relaxing of the muscles of face and brow, and the almost collapse of the heavy eyelids which seemed tumbling downward in sleep. She made gallant efforts to brace her dwindling powers, but for a time unsuccessfully. At length there came an interruption, which seemed like a powerful stimulant. Through the wide window she saw Lady Arabella enter the plain gateway of the farm and advance towards the hall door. She was clad as usual in tight-fitting white, which accentuated her thin, sinuous figure. The sight did for Lilla what no voluntary effort could. Her eyes flashed, and in an instant she felt as though a new life had suddenly developed within her. Lady Arabella's entry, in her usual unconcerned, haughty, supercilious way, heightened the effect, so that when the two stood close to each other battle was joined. Mr Caswall, too, took new courage from her coming, and all his masterfulness and power came back to him. His looks, intensified, had more obvious effect than had been noticeable that day. Lilla seemed at last overcome by his dominance. Her face became red and pale – violently red and ghastly pale by rapid turns. Her strength seemed gone. Her knees collapsed, and she was actually sinking on the floor, when to her surprise and joy Mimi came into the room, running hurriedly and breathing heavily. Lilla rushed to her, and the two clasped hands. With that, a new sense of power, greater than Lilla had ever seen in her, seemed to quicken her cousin. Her further hand swept the air in front of Edgar Caswall, seeming to drive him backward more and more by each movement, till at last he seemed to be actually hurled through the door which Mimi's entrance had left open, and fell on his back at full length on the gravel path without. Then came the final and complete collapse of Lilla, who, without a sound, sank down pale as death on the floor.

CHAPTER XXXVI
FACE TO FACE

Mimi was greatly distressed when she saw her cousin lying prone. She had a few times in her life seen Lilla on the verge of fainting, but never senseless; and now she was frightened. She threw herself on her knees beside Lilla, and tried, by rubbing her hands and such measures commonly known, to restore her. But all her efforts were unavailing. Lilla still lay white and senseless. In fact, each moment she looked worse; her breast, that had been heaving with the stress, became still, and the pallor of her face grew like marble. At these succeeding changes Mimi's fright grew, till it altogether mastered her. She succeeded in controlling herself only to the extent that she did not scream. Lady Arabella followed Caswall, when he had recovered sufficiently to get up and walk – though stumblingly – in the direction of Castra Regis. When Mimi was quite alone with Lilla and the need for effort had ceased, she felt weak and trembled. In her own mind, she attributed it to a sudden change in the weather. It was momentarily becoming apparent that a storm was coming on. The sky was covered with flying clouds. The silence was so marked as to become a positive quality. There was in the air that creaking sound that shows that electricity is gathering. For a little while she noticed that though the great kite still flew from the turret, the birds were beginning to gather as they had done when the kite had fallen. But now they began to disappear in some mysterious way: first singly, and then in increasing numbers till the whole world without seemed a widespread desolation. Something struck her when she had become cognizant of this, and with wild affright in her face she again stooped over Lilla.

And then came a wild cry of despair. She raised Lilla's white face and laid it on her warm young breast, but all in vain. The cold of the white face thrilled through her, and she utterly collapsed when it was borne in on her that Lilla had passed away.

The dusk gradually deepened and the shades of evening closed in, but she did not seem to notice or to care. She sat still on the floor with her arms round the body of the girl whom she loved. Darker and blacker grew the sky as the coming storm and the closing night joined forces. Still she sat on – alone – tearless – unable to think. Slowly the evening merged in night. Mimi did not know how long she sat there. Though it seemed to her that ages had passed, it could not have been more than a few minutes. She suddenly came to herself, and was surprised to find herself in almost absolute darkness. For a while she lay quiet, thinking of the immediate past. Lilla's hand was still in hers, and to her surprise it was still warm. Somehow this helped her consciousness, and without any special act of will she stood up. She lit a lamp and looked at her cousin. There was no doubt that Lilla was dead; but the death must have been recent. Though her face was of set white, the flesh was still soft to the touch. When the lamplight fell on her eyes, they seemed to look at her with intent – with meaning. She put out the light and sat still in the darkness, feeling as though she were seeing with Lilla's eyes. The blackness which surrounded her allowed of no disturbing influence on her own consciousness: the gloom of the sky, of which there was an occasional glimpse as some flying cloud seemed to carry light with it, was in a way tuned to her own gloomy thoughts. For her all was dark, both within and without. Her hope seemed as dead as her cousin's body. And over and behind all was a sense of unutterable loneliness and sorrow. She felt that nothing in the world could ever come right again. In this state of dark isolation a new resolution came to her, and grew and grew until it became a fixed definite purpose. She would face Caswall and call him to account for his murder of Lilla – that was what she called it to herself. She would also take steps – she knew not what or how – to avenge the part taken by Lady Arabella. In this frame of mind she lit all the lamps in the room, got water and linen from her room, and set about the decent ordering of Lilla's body. This took some time; but when it was finished, she put on her hat and cloak, put out the light, and, locking the door behind her, set out quietly and at even pace for Castra Regis. As she drew near the Castle, she saw no lights except those in and around the tower room. The lights showed her that Mr Caswall was there, and so she entered by the hall door, which as usual was open, and felt her way in the darkness up the staircase to the lobby of the room. The door was ajar, and the light from within showed brilliantly through the opening. She saw Edgar Caswall walking restlessly to and fro in the room with his hands clasped behind his back. She opened the door without knocking, and walked right into the room. As she entered, he ceased walking, and stared at her in surprise. She made no remark, no comment, but continued the fixed look which he had seen on her entrance.

For a time silence reigned, and the two stood looking fixedly at each other. Caswall was the first to speak.

'I had the pleasure of seeing your cousin, Miss Watford, to-day.'

'Yes,' she answered, her head up, looking him straight between the eyes, which made even him flinch. 'It was an ill day for her that you did see her.'

'Why so?' he asked in a weak way.

'Because it cost her her life. She is dead!'

'Dead! Good God! When did she die? What of?'

'She died this evening just after you left her.'

'Are you sure?'

'Yes – and so are you – or you ought to be. You killed her!'

'I killed her! Be careful what you say! Why do you say such a thing?'

'Because, as God sees us, it is true; and you know it. You came to Mercy Farm on purpose to kill her – if you could. And the accomplice of your guilt, Lady Arabella March, came for the same purpose.'

'Be careful, woman,' he said hotly. 'Do not use such names in that way, or you shall suffer for it.'

'I am suffering for it – have suffered for it – shall suffer for it. Not for speaking the truth as I have done, but because you two with devilish malignity did my darling to death. It is you and your accomplice who have to dread punishment, not I.'

'Take care!' he said again.

'Oh, I am not afraid of you or your accomplice,' she answered spiritedly. 'I am content to stand by every word I have said, every act I have done. Moreover, I believe in God's justice. I fear not the grinding of His mills. If needed, I shall set the wheels in motion myself. But you don't care even for God, or believe in Him. Your god is your great kite, which cows the birds of a whole district. But be sure that His hand, when it rises, always falls at the appointed time. His voice speaks in thunder, and not only for the rich who scorn their poorer neighbours. The voices that call on Him come from the furrow and the workshop, from grinding toil and unrelieved stress and strain. Those voices He always hears, however frail and feeble they may be. His thunder is their echo, His lightning the menace that is borne. Be careful! I say even as you have spoken. It may be that your name is being called even at this very moment at the Great Assize. Repent while there is still time. Happy you if you may be allowed to enter those mighty halls in the company of the pure-souled angel whose voice has only to whisper one word of justice and you thenceforth disappear for ever into everlasting torment.'

CHAPTER XXXVII

ERITIS SICUT DEUS[1]

For the last two days most of those concerned had been especially busy. Adam, leaving his wife free to follow her own desires with regard to Lilla and her grandfather, had busied himself with filling the well-hole with the fine sand prepared for the purpose, taking care to have lowered at stated intervals quantities of the store of dynamite so as to be ready for the final explosion. He had under his immediate supervision a corps of workmen, and was assisted in their superintendency by Sir Nathaniel, who had come over for the purpose and was staying at Lesser Hill. Mr Salton, too, showed much interest in the job, and was eternally coming in and out, nothing escaping his observation. Lady Arabella was staying at her father's place in the Peak. Her visit to Mercy Farm was unknown to any one but herself and Mimi, and she had kept her own counsel with regard to its unhappy conclusion. She had, in fact, been at some pains to keep the knowledge from Edgar. The Kelvin sounding apparatus was in good working order, and it seemed to be a perpetual pleasure to her, despite the horrible effluvium, to measure again and again the depth of the well-hole. This appeared to have some strange fascination for her which no one employed in the work shared. When any of the workmen made complaint of the stench to which they were subjected, she did not hesitate to tell them roundly that she believed it was a 'try on' on their part to get an immoderate quantity of strong drink. Naturally, Adam did not hear of Lilla's death. There was no one to tell him except Mimi, who did not wish to give him pain, and who, in addition, was so thoroughly occupied with many affairs, some of which we are aware of, that she lacked the opportunity of broaching the matter – even to her husband.

When Mimi returned to Sir Nathaniel's after her interview with Edgar Caswall, she felt the new freedom as to her movements. Since her marriage to Adam and their coming to stay at Doom Tower, she had been always fettered by fear of the horrible monster at Diana's Grove. But now she dreaded it no longer. She had accepted the fact of its assuming at will the form of Lady Arabella and *vice versa*, and had been perhaps equally afraid whichever form it took. But now she did not concern herself about one or the other. True, she wanted to meet Lady Arabella, but this was for militant purposes. She had still to tax and upbraid her for her part in the unhappiness which had been wrought on Lilla and for her share in her death. As for the monster, it had been last seen in the channel, forging a way out to sea, and, so far as she knew or cared, had not been seen since and might never be seen again. Now she could once more wander at will along the breezy heights of the Brow or under the spreading oaks of Diana's Grove unfearful of the hateful presence of either the Lady or her *alter ego*, the Worm. She dared not compare what the place had been to her before the hateful revelation, but she could – and she thanked God for that – enjoy the beauties as they were, what they had been, and might be again were they once free. When she left Castra Regis after her interview with Edgar Caswall, she walked home to Doom, making a long detour along the top of the Brow. She wanted time to get calm and be once more master of herself before she should meet her husband. Her nerves were in a raw condition, and she felt more even than at first the shock of her cousin's death, which still completely overwhelmed her. The walk did her good. In the many changes of scene and the bracing exercise, she felt her nervous strength as well as her spirits restored. She was almost her old self again when she had entered the gates of Doom and saw the lights of her own room shining out into the gloom.

When she entered her own room, her first act was to run to the window and throw an eager look round the whole circle of sight. This was instructive – an unconscious effort to clear her mind of any apprehension that the Worm was still at hand rearing its vast height above the trees. A single glance satisfied her that at any rate the Worm *in propria persona* was not visible. So she sat down for a little in the window-seat and enjoyed the pleasure of full view from which she had been so long cut off. The maid who waited on her had told her that Mr Salton had not yet returned home, so that she felt free to enjoy the luxury of peace and quiet.

As she looked out of the window of the high tower, which she had opened, she saw something thin and white move along the avenue far below her. She thought she recognised the figure of Lady Arabella, and instinctively drew back behind the drawn curtain. When she had ascertained by peeping out several times that the Lady did not see her, she watched more carefully, all her instinctive hatred of Lady Arabella flooding back at the sight of her. Lady Arabella was moving swiftly and stealthily, looking back and around her at intervals as if she feared to be followed. This opportunity of seeing her, as she did not wish to be seen, gave Mimi an idea that she was up to no good, and so she determined to seize the occasion of watching her in more detail. Hastily putting on a dark cloak and hat, she ran downstairs and out into the avenue. Lady Arabella had moved, but the sheen of her white dress was still to be seen among the young oaks around the gateway. Keeping herself in shadow, Mimi followed, taking care not to come so close as to awake the other's suspicion. The abnormal blackness of the sky aided her, and, herself unnoticed and unnoticeable, she watched her quarry pass along the road in the direction of Castra Regis.

She followed on steadily through the gloom of the trees, depending on the glint of the white dress to keep her right. The little wood began to thicken, and presently, when the road widened and the trees grew closer to each other though they stood farther back, she lost sight of any indication of her where-abouts. Under the present conditions it was impossible for her to do any more, so, after waiting for a while, still hidden in the shadow to see if she could catch another glimpse of the white frock, she determined to go on slowly towards Castra Regis and trust to the chapter of accidents to pick up the trail again. She went on slowly, taking advantage of every obstacle and shadow to keep herself concealed. At last she entered on the grounds of the Castle at a spot from which the windows of the turret were dimly visible, without having seen again any sign of Lady Arabella. In the exceeding blackness of the night, the light in the turret chamber seemed by comparison bright, though it was indeed dim, for Edgar Caswall had only a couple of candles alight. The gloom seemed to suit his own state of mind.

All the time that she, Mimi Salton, had been coming from Doom, following as she thought Lady Arabella March, she was in reality being followed by Lady Arabella, who, having the power of seeing in the darkness, had caught sight of her leaving Doom Tower and had never again lost sight of her. It was a rarely complete case of the hunter being hunted, and, strange to say, in a manner true of both parties to the chase. For a time Mimi's many turnings, with the natural obstacles that were perpetually intervening, kept Mimi disappearing and reappearing; but when she was close to Castra Regis there was no more possibility of concealment, and the strange double following went swiftly on. At this period of the chase, the disposition of those concerned was this: Mimi, still searching in vain for Lady Arabella, was ahead; and close behind her, though herself keeping well concealed, came the other, who saw everything as well as though it were daylight. The natural darkness of the night and the blackness of the storm-laden sky had no difficulties for her. When she saw Mimi come close to the hall door of Castra Regis and ascend the steps, she followed. When Mimi entered the dark hall and felt her way up the still darker staircase, still, as she believed, following Lady Arabella, the latter still kept on her way. When they had reached the lobby of the turret-rooms, neither searched actively for the other, each being content to go on, believing that the object of her search was ahead of her.

Edgar Caswall sat thinking in the gloom of the great room, occasionally stirred to curiosity when the drifting clouds allowed a little light to fall from the storm-swept sky. But nothing really interested him now. Since he had heard of Lilla's death, the gloom of his poignant remorse, emphasised by

Mimi's upbraiding, had made more hopeless even the darkness of his own cruel, selfish, saturnine nature. He heard no sound. In the first place, his normal faculties seemed benumbed by his inward thought. Then the sounds made by the two women were in themselves difficult to hear. Mimi was light of weight, and in the full tide of her youth and strength her movements were as light and as well measured and without waste as an animal of the forest.

As to Lady Arabella, her movements were at all times as stealthy and as silent as those of her pristine race, the first thousands of whose years was occupied, not in direct going to and fro, but on crawling on their bellies without notice and without noise.

Mimi, when she came to the door, still a little ajar, gave with the instinct of decorum a light tap. So light it was that it did not reach Caswall's ears. Then, taking her courage in both hands, she boldly but noiselessly pushed the door and entered. As she did so, her heart sank, for now she was face to face with a difficulty which had not, in her state of mental perturbation, occurred to her.

CHAPTER XXXVIII
ON THE TURRET ROOF

The storm which was coming was already making itself manifest, not only in the wide scope of nature, but in the hearts and
natures of human beings. Electrical disturbance in the sky and
the air is reproduced in animals of all kinds, and particularly
in the highest type of them all – the most receptive – the most
electrical themselves – the most recuperative of their natural
qualities, the widest sweeping with their net of interests. So it
was with Edgar Caswall, despite his selfish nature and coldness
of blood. So it was with Mimi Salton, despite her unselfish,
unchanging devotion for those she loved. So it was even with
Lady Arabella, who, under the instincts of a primeval serpent,
carried the ever-varying indestructible wishes and customs of
womanhood, which is always old – and always new. Edgar,
after he had once turned his eyes on Mimi, resumed his apa-
thetic position and sullen silence. Mimi quietly took a seat a
little way apart from Edgar, whence she could look on the
progress of the coming storm and study its appearance throughout the whole visible circle of the neighbourhood. She was in
brighter and better spirits than she had been all day – or for
many days past. Lady Arabella tried to efface herself behind
the now open door. At every movement she appeared as if
trying to squeeze herself into each little irregularity in the flooring beside her. Without, the clouds grew thicker and blacker as
the storm-centre came closer. As yet the forces, from whose
linking the lightning springs, were held apart, and the silence
of nature proclaimed the calm before the storm. Caswall felt
the effect of the gathering electric force. A sort of wild exultation grew upon him such as he had sometimes felt just before

the breaking of a tropical storm. As he became conscious of this he instinctively raised his head and caught the eye of Mimi. He was in the grip of an emotion greater than himself; in the mood in which he was he felt the need upon him of doing some desperate deed. He was now absolutely reckless, and as Mimi was associated with him in the memory which drove him on, he wished that she too should be engaged in this enterprise. Of course, he had no knowledge of the proximity of Lady Arabella. He thought that he was alone, far removed from all he knew and whose interests he shared – alone with the wild elements, which were being lashed to fury, and with the woman who had struggled with him and vanquished him, and on whom he would shower, though in secret, the full measure of his hate.

The fact was that Edgar Caswall was, if not mad, something akin to it. His always eccentric nature, fed by the dominance possible to one in his condition in life, had made him oblivious to the relative proportions of things. That way madness lies.[1] A person who is either unable or unwilling to distinguish true proportions is apt to get further afield intellectually with each new experience. From inability to realise the true proportions of many things, there is but one step to a fatal confusion. Madness in its first stage – monomania – is a lack of proportion. So long as this is general, it is not always noticeable, for the uninspired onlooker is without the necessary base of comparison. The realisation only comes with an occasion, when the person in the seat of judgment has some recognised standard with which to compare the chimerical ideas of the disordered brain. Monomania gives the opportunity. Men do not usually have at hand a number, or even a choice of standards. It is the one thing which is contrary to our experience which sets us thinking; and when once the process of thought is established it becomes applicable to all the ordinary things of life; and then discovery of the truth is only a matter of time. It is because imperfections of the brain are usually of a character or scope which in itself makes difficult a differentiation of irregularities that discovery is not usually made quickly. But in monomania the errant faculty protrudes itself in a way that may not be denied. It puts aside, obscures, or takes the place of something else – just as the head of a pin placed before the centre of the iris will block out the whole scope of vision. The most usual form of monomania has commonly the same beginning as that from which Edgar Caswall suffered – an overlarge idea of self-importance. Alienists, who study the matter exactly, probably know more of human vanity and its effects than do ordinary men. Their knowledge of the intellectual weakness of an individual seldom comes quickly. It is in itself an intellectual process, and, if the beginnings can at all be traced, the cure – if cure be possible – has already begun. Caswall's mental disturbance was not hard to identify. Every asylum is full of such cases – men and women who, naturally selfish and egotistical, so appraise to themselves their own importance that every other circumstance in life becomes subservient to it. The declension is rapid. The disease supplies in itself the material for self-magnification. The same often modest, religious, unselfish individual who has walked perhaps for years in all good ways, passing stainless through temptations which wreck most persons of abilities superior to his own, develops – by a process so gradual that at its first recognition it appears almost to be sudden – into a self-engrossed, lawless, dishonest, cruel, unfaithful person who cannot be trusted any more than he can be restrained. When the same decadence attacks a nature naturally proud and selfish and vain, and lacking both the aptitude and habit of self-restraint, the development of the disease is more swift, and ranges to farther limits. It is such persons who become imbued with the idea that they have the attributes of the Almighty – even that they themselves are the Almighty. Vanity, the beginning, is also the disintegrating process and also the melancholy end. A close investigation shows that there is no new factor in this chaos. It is all exact and logical. It is only a development and not a re-creation: the germs were there already; all that has happened is that they have ripened and perhaps fructified. Caswall's was just such a case. He did not become cruel or lawless or dishonest or unfaithful; those qualities were there already, wrapped up in one or other of the many disguises of selfishness.

Character – of whatever kind it be, of whatever measure,

either good or bad – is bound in the long run to justify itself according to its lights. The whole measure of drama is in the development of character. Grapes do not grow on thorns nor figs on thistles. This is true of every phase of nature, and, above all, true of character which is simply logic in episodical form. The hand that fashioned Edgar Caswall's physiognomy in aquiline form, and the mind that ordained it, did not err. Up to the last he maintained the strength and the weakness of aquiline nature. And in this final hour, when the sands were running low, he, his intentions, and his acts – the whole variations and complexities of his individuality – were in essence the very same as those which marked him in his earliest days. He had ripened; that was all.

Mimi had a suspicion – or rather, perhaps, an intuition – of the true state of things when she heard him speak, and at the same time noticed the abnormal flush on his face, and his rolling eyes. There was a certain want of fixedness of purpose which she had certainly not noticed before – a quick, spasmodic utterance which belongs rather to the insane than to those of intellectual equilibrium. She was a little astonished, not only by his thoughts but by his staccato way of expressing them. The manner remained almost longer in her memory than the words. When, later, thinking the matter over, she took into account certain matters of which at the time she had not borne in mind: the odd hour of her visit – it was now after midnight – close on dawn; the wild storm which was now close at hand; the previous nervous upset, of her own struggle with him, of his hearing the news of Lilla's death, of her own untimely visit so fraught with unpleasant experiences and memories. When in a calmer state she weighed all these things in the balance, the doing so not only made for toleration of errors and excesses, but also for that serener mental condition in which correctness of judgment is alone attainable.

As Caswall rose up and began to move to the door leading to the turret stair by which the roof was reached, he said in a peremptory way, whose tone alone made her feel defiant:

'Come! I want you.'

She instinctively drew back – she was not accustomed to such words, more especially to such tone. Her answer was indicative of a new contest:

'Where to? Why should I go? What for?'

He did not at once reply – another indication of his over-whelming egotism. He was now fast approaching the attitude of conscious Final Cause. She repeated her questions. He seemed a little startled; but habit reasserted itself, and he spoke without thinking the words which were in his heart.

'I want you, if you will be so good, to come with me to the turret roof. I know I have no right to ask you, or to expect you to come. It would be a kindness to me. I am much interested in certain experiments with the kite which would be, if not a pleasure, at least a novel experience to you. You would see something not easily seen otherwise. The experience *may* be of use some time, though I cannot guarantee that.'

'I will come,' she answered simply; Edgar moved in the direction of the stair, she following close behind him.

She did not like to be left alone at such a height, in such a place, in the darkness, with a storm about to break. Of himself she had no fear; all that had been seemed to have passed away with her two victories over him in the struggle of wills. More-over, the more recent apprehension – that of his madness – had also ceased. In the conversation of the last few minutes he seemed so rational, so clear, so unaggressive, that she no longer saw reason even for doubt. So satisfied was she that even when he put out a hand to guide her to the steep, narrow stairway, she took it without thought in the most conventional way. Lady Arabella, crouching in the lobby behind the door, heard every word that had been said, and formed her own opinion of it. It was evident to her that there had been some *rapprochement* between the two, who had so lately been hostile to each other, and that made her furiously angry. It was not jealousy, but only that Mimi was interfering with her plans. She had by now made certain of her capture of Edgar Caswall, and she could not tolerate even the lightest and most contemptuous fancy on his part which might divert him from the main issue. When she became aware that he wished Mimi to come with him to the roof and that she had acquiesced, her rage got beyond bounds.

She became oblivious to any danger that might be in the visit to such an exposed place at such a time, and to all lesser considerations, and made up her mind to forestall them. By now she knew well the turns and difficulties of the turret stair, and could use it in darkness as well as in light, – this, independent of her inherited ophidian power of seeing without light. When she had come to the lobby this evening, she had seen that the steel wicket, usually kept locked, that forbade entrance on the stairway, had been left open. So, when she was aware of the visit of the two others to the roof, she stealthily and noiselessly crept through the wicket, and, ascending the stair, stepped out on the roof. It was bitterly cold, for the fierce gusts of the storm which swept round the turret drove in through every unimpeded way, whistling at the sharp corners and singing round the trembling flagstaff. The kite-string and the wire which controlled the runners made a concourse of weird sounds which somehow, perhaps from the violence which surrounded them, acting on their length, resolved themselves into some kind of harmony – a fitting accompaniment to the tragedy which seemed about to begin.

Lady Arabella scorned all such thoughts, putting them behind her as she did fear. Still moving swiftly and stealthily, she glided across the stone roof and concealed herself behind one of the machicolations of the tower. She was already safely ensconced when the heads of Edgar and Mimi, whom he guided, appeared against the distant sky-line as they came up the steep stair. Mimi's heart beat heavily. Just before leaving the turret-chamber she had got a fright which she could not shake off. The lights of the room had momentarily revealed to her, as they passed out, Edgar's face concentrated as it did whenever he intended to use his mesmeric power. Now the black eyebrows made a thick line across his face, under which his eyes shone and glittered ominously. Mimi recognised the danger, and assumed the defiance that had twice already served her so well. She had a fear that the circumstances and the place were against her, and she wanted to be forearmed.

The sky was now somewhat lighter than it had been. Either there was lightning afar off, whose reflections were carried by the rolling clouds, or else the gathered force, though not yet breaking into lightning, had an incipient power of light. It seemed to affect both the man and the woman. Edgar seemed altogether under its influence. His spirits were boisterous, his mind exalted. He was now at his worst; madder even than he had been earlier in the night. Mimi, trying to keep as far from him as possible, moved across the stone floor of the turret roof, and found a niche which concealed her. It was not far from Lady Arabella's place of hiding, but the angle of the machicolation stood between them, separating them. It was fortunate for Mimi that she could not see the other's face. Those burning eyes concentrated in deadly hate would have certainly unnerved her just as she wanted the full of her will power to help her in extremity.

Edgar, left thus alone on the centre of the turret roof, found himself altogether his own master in a way which tended to increase his madness. He knew that Mimi was close at hand, though he had lost sight of her. He spoke loudly, and the sound of his own voice, though it was carried from him on the sweeping wind as fast as the words were spoken, seemed to exalt him still more. Even the raging of the elements round him seemed to add to his exaltation. To him it seemed that these manifestations were obedient to his own will. He had reached the sublime of his madness; he was now in his own mind actually the Almighty, and whatever might happen would be the direct carrying out of his own commands. As he could not see Mimi nor fix whereabout she was, he shouted loudly:

'Come to me. You shall see now what you are despising, what you are warring against. All that you see is mine – the darkness as well as the light. I tell you that I am greater than any other who is, or was, or shall be. Look you now and learn. When the Master of Evil took Him up on a high place and showed Him all the kingdoms of the earth,[2] he was doing what he thought no other could do. He was wrong. He forgot *Me*. You shall see. I shall send you light to see by. I shall send it up to the very ramparts of heaven. A light so great that it shall dissipate those black clouds that are rushing up and piling around us. Look! Look! At the very touch of my hand that light springs into being and mounts up – and up – and up!'

He made his way whilst he was speaking to the corner of the
turret whence flew the giant kite, and from which the runners
ascended. Mimi looked on, appalled and afraid to speak lest
she should precipitate some calamity. Within the machicolated
niche Lady Arabella, quiet and still as death, cowered in a
paroxysm of fear. Edgar took from his pocket a small wooden
box, through a hole in which the wire of the runner ran. This
evidently set some machinery in motion, for a sound as of
whirring came. From one side of the box floated what looked
like a piece of stiff ribbon, which snapped and crackled as the
wind took it. For a few seconds Mimi saw it as it rushed along
the sagging line to the kite. When close to it, there was a loud
crack, like a minor explosion, and a sudden light appeared to
issue from every chink in the box. Then a quick flame flashed
along the snapping ribbon, which glowed with an intense light
– a light so great that the whole of the countryside around
stood out against the background of black driving clouds. For
a few seconds the light remained, then suddenly disappeared in
the blackness around. That light had no mystery for either
Mimi or Lady Arabella, both of whom had often seen manifestations of the same thing. It was simply a magnesium light[3]
which had been fired by the mechanism within the box carried
up to the kite. Edgar was in a state of tumultuous excitement,
shouting and yelling at the top of his voice and dancing about
like a violent lunatic. But the others were quiet, Mimi nestling
in her niche and avoiding observation as well as she could.
Once the sagging string, caught in a wind-flurry, was thrown
across the back of her hand. Its trembling had an extraordinary
effect on her, bracing her up to the full of her emotional power.
She felt, on the instant, that the spirit of Lilla was beside her,
and that it was Lilla's touch which she had felt. Lady Arabella
had evidently made up her mind what to do; the inspiration
how to do it came to her with the sight of Mimi's look of power
evident to her ophidian sight. On the instant she glided through
the darkness to the wheel whereon the string of the kite was
wound. With deft fingers she found where the wheel of the
Kelvin sounding apparatus was fixed to it, and, unshipping this,
took it with her, reeling out the wire as she went, and so

keeping, in a way, in touch with the kite. Then she glided swiftly to the wicket, through which she passed, locking the gate behind her as she went. Down the turret stair she flew quickly, letting the wire run from the wheel which she carried carefully, and, passing out of the hall door, ran down the avenue with all her speed. She soon reached her own gate, ran down the avenue, and with her small key opened the iron door leading to the atrium. The fine wire passed easily under the door. In the room beside the atrium, where was the well-hole, she sat down panting, unknown to all, for in the coming she had escaped observation. She felt that she was excited, and in order to calm herself began a new form of experiment with regard to her observation of the hole. She fastened the lamp which was ready for lowering to the end of the wire, whose end came into the room. Then she began quietly and methodically lowering the two by means of the Kelvin sounding apparatus, intending to fire at the right time the new supply of magnesium ribbon which she had brought from the turret. She felt well satisfied with herself. All her plans were maturing, or had already matured. Castra Regis was within her grasp. The woman whose interference she feared, Lilla Watford, was dead. Diana's Grove and all its hideous secrets was now in other hands, an accident to whom would cause her no concern. Truly, all was well, and she felt that she might pause a while and rest. She lay down on a sofa close to the well-hole so that she could see it without moving when she had lit the lamp. In a state of blissful content she sank into a gentle sleep.

CHAPTER XXXIX

THE BREAKING OF THE STORM

When Lady Arabella had gone away in her usual noiseless fashion, the two others remained for a while quite still in their places on the turret roof: Caswall because he had nothing to say and could not think of anything; Mimi because she had much to say and wished to put her thoughts in order. For quite a while – which seemed interminable – silence reigned between them. At last Mimi made a beginning – she had made up her mind how to act.

'Mr Caswall,' she said loudly, so as to make sure of being heard through the blustering of the wind and the perpetual cracking of the electricity.

Caswall said something in reply which she understood to be: 'I am listening.'

His words were carried away on the storm as they came from his mouth. However, one of her objects was effected: she knew now exactly whereabout on the roof he was. So she moved close to the spot before she spoke again, raising her voice almost to a shout:

'The wicket is shut. Please to open it. I can't get out.'

As she spoke she was quietly fingering the revolver which Adam had given to her when she got back to Liverpool, and which now lay in her breast. She felt that she was caged like a rat in a trap, but did not mean to be taken at a disadvantage, whatever happened. By this time Caswall also was making up his mind what his own attitude would be. He, too, felt trapped, and all the brute in him rose to the emergency. He never had been counted – even by himself – as chivalrous; but now, when he was at a loss, even decency of thought had no appeal for

him. In a voice which was raucous and brutal – much like that
which is heard when a wife is being beaten by her husband in
a slum – he hissed out, his syllables cutting through the roaring
of the storm:

'I didn't let you in here. You came of your own accord –
without permission, or even asking it. Now you stay or go as
you choose. But you must manage it for yourself; I'll have
nothing to do with it.'

She answered, woman-like, with a query:

'It was Lady Arabella who shut and locked it. Was it by your
wish?'

'I had no wish one way or the other. I didn't even know that
she was here.'

Then suddenly he added: 'How did you know it?'

'By her white dress and the green gleam of her eyes. Her
figure is not hard to distinguish, even in the dark.'

He gave some kind of snort of disagreement. Taking
additional umbrage at this, she went on in words which she
thought would annoy him most:

'When a woman is gifted with a figure like hers, it is easy to
tell her even in a rope-walk or a bundle of hop-poles.'[1]

He even improved on her affronting speech:

'Every woman in the eastern counties seems to think that she
has a right to walk into my house at any hour of the day or
night, and into every room in the house whether I am there or
not. I suppose I'll have to get watch-dogs and police to keep
them out, and spring guns[2] and man-traps to deal with them if
they get in.' He went on more roughly as if he had been wound
up to it.

'Well, why don't you go?'

Her answer was spoken with dangerous suavity:

'I am going. Blame yourself if you do not like the time and
manner of it. I daresay Adam – my husband – Mr Salton, will
have a word to say to you about it!'

'Let him say, and be damned to him, and to you too! I'll
show you a light. You shan't be able to say that you could not
see what you were doing.'

As he spoke he was lighting another piece of the magnesium

ribbon, which made a blinding glare in which everything was plainly discernible, down to the smallest detail. This exactly suited her. She took accurate note of the wicket and its fastening before the glare had died away. She took her revolver out and had fired into the lock, which was shivered on the instant, the pieces flying round in all directions, but happily without causing hurt to anyone. Then she pushed the wicket open and ran down the narrow stair and so to the hall door. Opening this also, she ran down the avenue, never lessening her speed till she stood outside the door of Doom Tower. The household was all awake, and the door was opened at once on her ringing.

She asked: 'Is Mr Salton in?'

'He has just come in, a few minutes ago. He has gone up to the study.'

She ran upstairs at once and joined him. He seemed relieved when he saw her, but scrutinised her face keenly. He saw that she had been in some concern, so led her over to the sofa in the window and sat down beside her.

'Now, dear, tell me all about it!' he said.

She rushed breathlessly through all the details of her adventure on the turret roof. Adam listened attentively, helping her all he could, both positively and negatively, nor embarrassing her by any questioning or surprise. His thoughtful silence was a great help to her, for it allowed her to collect and organise her thoughts. When she had done he gave her his story without unnecessary delay:

'I kept out of your way so as to leave you unhampered in anything you might wish to attend to. But when the dark came and you were still out, I was a little frightened about you. So I went to where I thought you might be. First to Mercy; but no one there knew where you were. Then to Diana's Grove. There, too, no one could tell me anything. But when the footman who opened the door went to the atrium, looking if you were about, I caught a glimpse of the room where the well-hole is. Beside the hole, and almost over it, was a sofa on which lay Lady Arabella quietly sleeping. So I went on to Castra Regis, but no one there had seen you either. When that magnesium light flared out from close to the kite, I thought I saw you on the turret. I tried to ascend, and actually got to the wicket at foot of the turret stair. But that was locked, so I turned back and went round the Brow on the chance of meeting or seeing you; then I came on here. I only knew you had come home when Braithwait came up to the study to tell me. I must go and see Caswall to-morrow or next day to hear what he has to say on the subject. You won't mind, will you?'

She answered quickly, a new fear in her heart:

'Oh no, dear, I wouldn't and won't mind anything you think it right to do. But, dear, for my sake, don't have any quarrel with Mr Caswall. I have had too much trial and pain lately to wish it increased by any anxiety regarding you.'

'You shall not, dear – if I can help it – please God,' he said solemnly, and he kissed her.

Then, in order to keep her interested so that she might forget the fears and anxieties that had disturbed her, he began to talk over details of her adventure, making shrewd comments which attracted and held her attention. Presently, *inter alia*,[3] he said:

'That's a dangerous game Caswall is up to. It seems to me that that young man – though he doesn't appear to know it – is riding for a fall!'

'How, dear? I don't understand.'

'Kite flying on a night like this from a place like the tower of Castra Regis is, to say the least of it, dangerous. It is not merely courting death or other accident from lightning, but it is bringing the lightning into where he lives.'

'Oh, do explain to me, Adam. I am very ignorant on such subjects.'

'Well, you see, Mimi, the air all around is charged and impregnated with electricity, which is simply undeveloped lightning. Every cloud that is blowing up here – and they all make for the highest point – is bound to develop into a flash of lightning. That kite is up in the air about a mile high and is bound to attract the lightning. Its very string makes a road for it on which to travel to earth. When it does come, it will strike the top of the tower with a weight a hundred times greater than a whole park of artillery. It will knock Castra Regis into matches. Where it will go after that, no one can tell. If there be any metal by which it can travel, such will not only point the road, but be the road itself. If anything of that sort *should* happen, it may – probably will – wreck the whole neighbourhood!'

'Would it be dangerous to be out in the open air when such a thing is taking place?' she asked.

'No, little girl. It would be the safest possible place – so long as one was not in the line of the electric current.'

'Then, do let us go outside. I don't want to run into any foolish danger – or, far more, to ask you to do so. But surely if the open is safest, that is the place to be. We can easily keep out of electric currents – if we know where they are. By the way, I suppose these are carried and marked by wires, or by something which can attract? If so, we can look for such. I had my electric torch that you gave me recharged the day I was in Wolverhampton with Sir Nathaniel.'

'I have my torch too, all fit,' interposed Adam.

Without another word, she put on again the cloak she had thrown off, and a small, tight-fitting cap. Adam too put on his cap, and, after looking that his revolver was all right, gave her his hand, and they left the house together. When they had come to the door, which lay quite open, Adam said:

'I think the best thing we can do will be to go round all the places which are mixed up in this affair.'

'All right, dear, I am ready. But, if you don't mind, we might go first to Mercy. I am anxious about grandfather, and we might see that – as yet, at all events – nothing has happened there.'

'Good idea. Let us go at once, Mimi.'

So they went on the high-hung road along the top of the Brow. The wind here was of great force, and made a strange booming noise as it swept high overhead; though not the sound of cracking and tearing as it passed through woods of high slender trees which grew on either side of the road. Mimi could hardly keep her feet. She was not afraid; but the force to which she was opposed gave her a good excuse to hold on to her husband extra tight.

At Mercy there was no one up. At least, all the lights were out. But to Mimi, accustomed to the nightly routine of the house, there were manifest signs that all was well, except in the little room on the first floor, where the blinds were down. Mimi could not bear to look at that, to think of it. Adam understood her pain. He bent over and kissed her, and then took her hand and held it hard. And thus they passed on together, returning to the high road towards Castra Regis. They had now got ready their electric torches, depressing the lens of each towards the ground so that henceforth on their journey two little circles of bright light ran ahead of them, and, moving from side to side as they went, kept the ground in front of them and at either side well disclosed.

At the gate of Castra Regis they were, if possible, extra careful. When drawing near, Adam had asked his wife several questions as to what signs, if any, had been left of Lady Arabella's presence in the tower. So she told him, but with greater detail, of the wire from the Kelvin sounder, which, taking its origin from the spot whence the kite flew, marked the way through the wicket, down the stairs and along the avenue.

Adam drew his breath at this, and said in a low, earnest whisper:

'I don't want to frighten you, Mimi, dear, but wherever that wire is there is danger.'

'Danger! How?'

'That is the track where the lightning will go; any moment, even now whilst we are speaking and searching, a fearful force may be loosed upon us. You run on, dear; you know the way down to where the avenue joins the high road. Keep your torch moving, and if you see any sign of the wire keep away from it, for God's sake. I shall join you at the gateway.'

She said in a low voice:

'Are you going to find or to follow that wire alone?'

'Yes, dear. One is sufficient for that work. I shall not lose a moment till I am with you.'

'Adam, when I came with you into the open, when we both feared what might happen, my main wish was that we should be together when the end came. You wouldn't deny me that right, would you, dear?'

'No, dear, not that or any right. Thank God that my wife

has such a wish. Come; we will go together. We are in the hands of God. If He wishes, we shall be together at the end, whenever or wherever that may be. Kiss me, dear – even if it be for the last time. Give me your hand. Now, I am ready.'

And so, hand in hand, they went to find the new danger together. They picked up the trail of the wire on the steps of the entrance and followed it down the avenue, taking especial care not to touch it with their feet. It was easy enough to follow, for the wire, if not bright, was self-coloured, and showed at once when the roving lights of the electric torches exposed it. They followed it out of the gateway and into the avenue of Diana's Grove. Here a new gravity clouded over Adam's face, though Mimi saw no cause for fresh concern. This was easily enough explained. Adam knew of the explosive works in progress regarding the well-hole, but the matter had been studiously kept from his wife. As they came near the house, Adam sent back his wife to the road, ostensibly to watch the course of the wire, telling her that there might be a branch wire leading to somewhere else. She was to search the undergrowth which the wire went through, and, if she found it, was to warn him by the Australian native 'Coo-ee!' which had been arranged between them as the means of signalling. When Mimi had disappeared in the avenue, Adam examined the wire inch by inch, taking special note of where it disappeared under the iron door at the back of the house. When he was satisfied that he was quite alone, he went round to the front of the house and gently shoved the hall door, thinking that perhaps it was unlocked and unbolted, after the usual custom. It yielded, so he stole into the hall, keeping his torch playing the light all over the floor, both to avoid danger and to try to pick the wire up again. When he came to the iron door he saw the glint of the wire as it passed under it. He traced it into the room with the well-hole, taking care to move as noiselessly as possible. He saw Lady Arabella sleeping on the sofa close to the hole into which the continuation of the wire disappeared. As he did so he heard a whispered 'H-ss-h!' at the door, and, looking up, saw Mimi, who signalled him to come out. He joined her, and together they passed into the avenue.

Mimi whispered to him:

'Would it not be possible to give someone here warning? They are in danger.'

He put his lips close to her ear and whispered his reply:

'We could, but it would not be safe. Lady Arabella has brought the wire here herself for some purpose of her own. If she were to suspect that we knew or guessed her reason, she would take other steps which might be still more dangerous. It is not our doing, any of it. We had better not interfere.'

Mimi, who had spoken from duty, far from any wish or fear of her own, was only too glad to be silent, and to get away, both safe. So her husband, taking her by the hand, led her away from the wire.

When they were in the wide part of the avenue, he whispered again:

'We must be careful, Mimi, what we do. We are surrounded with unknown dangers on every side, and we may, in trying to do good in some way, do the very thing which we should most avoid.'

Under the trees, which cracked as the puff of wind clashed their branches and the slender shafts swayed to and from the upright, he went on:

'We know that if the lightning comes it will take the course of the kite string. We also know that if it strikes Castra Regis it will still follow the wire, which we have just seen running along the avenue. But we don't know to where else that wire may lead the danger. It may be to *Mercy* – or to *Lesser Hill*; in fact, to anywhere in the neighbourhood. Moreover, we do not know when the stroke may fall. There will be no warning, be sure of that. It will, or may, come when we least expect it. If we cut off the possibilities of the lightning finding its own course, we may do irreparable harm where we should least wish. In fact, the Doom is probably spoken already. We can only wait in what safety, or possibility of safety, we can achieve till the moment sounds.'

Mimi was silent, but she stood very close to him and held his hand tight. After a few moments she spoke:

'Then let the Doom fall when it may. We are ready. At least, we shall die together!'

With the belief that death was hovering over them, as was shown in the resignation which they expressed to each other, it was little wonder that Adam and Mimi were restless and practically unable to remain quiet or even in one place. They spent the dark hours of the night wandering along the top of the Brow, and waiting for – they knew not what. Strange to say, they both enjoyed, or thought they did, the tumult of Nature's forces around them. Had their nervous strain been less, the sense of æstheticism which they shared would have had more scope. Even as it was, the dark beauties of sky and landscape appealed to them; the careering of the inky-black clouds; the glimpses of the wind-swept sky; the rush and roar of the tempest amongst the trees; the never-ceasing crackle of electricity; the distant booming of the storm as it rushed over the Mercian highlands, and ever mingling its roar with the scream of the waves on the pebble beaches of the eastern sea; the round, big waves breaking on the iron-bound marge of the ocean; the distant lights, which grew bright as the storm swept past, and now and again seemed to melt into the driving mist – all these things claimed their interest and admiration, forming, as it were, a background of fitting grandeur and sublimity to the great tragedy of life which was being enacted in their very midst. When such a thought crossed Mimi's mind, it seemed to restore in an instant her nerve and courage. In the wild elemental warfare, such surface passions as fear and anger and greed seemed equally unworthy to the persons within their scope and to the occasion of their being. In those flying minutes, Adam and Mimi found themselves, and learned – did they not know it already? – to value personal worthiness.

As the dawn grew nearer, the violence of the storm increased. The wind raged even more tumultuously. The flying clouds grew denser and blacker, and occasionally flashes of lightning, though yet far-distant, cut through the oppressive gloom. The tentative growling of thunder changed, at instants, to the rolling majesty of heaven's artillery. Then came a time when not seconds elapsed between the white flash and the thunder-burst, which ended in a prolonged roll which seemed to shake the whole structure of the world.

But still through all the great kite, though assailed by all the forces of air, tugged strenuously but unconquered against its controlling string.

At length, when the sky to the east began to quicken there seemed a lull in the storm. Adam and Mimi had gone the whole length of the Brow, and had come so far on the return towards Castra Regis as to be level with Diana's Grove. The comparative silence of the lull gave both Adam and his wife the idea of coming again close to the house. In his secret heart Adam was somewhat impatient of the delay of the kite drawing down the lightning – and he was also not too well pleased at it. He had been so long thinking of the destruction of the Lair of the White Worm that the prolongation seemed undue and excessive – indeed, unfair. Nevertheless, he waited with an outward appearance of patience and even calm; but his heart was all the while raging. He wanted to know and to feel that he had seen the last of the White Worm. With the coming of the day the storm *seemed* less violent, simply because the eyes of the onlookers came to the aid of their ears. The black clouds seemed less black because the rest of the landscape was not swathed in impenetrable gloom. When any of our usual organs of sense are for any cause temporarily useless, we are deprived of the help of perspective in addition to any special deprivation. To both Adam and Mimi the promise of the dawn was of both help and comfort. Not only was the lifting of the pall of blackness – even if light only came through rents in the wind-torn sky – hopeful, but the hope that came along with light brought consolation and renewing of spirit. Together they moved on the road to Diana's Grove. Adam had taken his wife's arm in that familiar way which a woman loves when she loves the man, and, without speaking, guided her down the avenue towards the house.

The top of the hill on which Diana's Grove was seated had, from time immemorial, been kept free from trees or other obstruction which might hide the view. In early days this was not for any æsthetic reason, but simply to guard against the unseen approach of enemies. However, the result was the same; an uninterrupted view all round was obtained or preserved.

Now, as the young people stood out in the open they could see most of the places in which for the time they were interested. Higher up on the Brow and crowning it rose Castra Regis, massive and stern – the very moral of a grey, massive frowning Norman fortress. Down the hill, half way to the level of the plain where lay the deep streams and marsh-ringed pools, Mercy Farm nestled among protecting woods. Half hidden among stately forest trees, and so seeming far away, Lesser Hill reared its look-out tower. Adam took Mimi's hand, and instinctively they moved down close to the house of Diana's Grove, noticing, as they went, its inhospitable appearance. Never a window, a door, or chimney seemed to have any living force behind it. It was all cold and massive as a Roman temple, with neither prospect nor promise of welcome or comfort. Adam could not help recalling to his mind the last glimpse he had of its mistress – looking thinner even than usual in her white frock, drawn tight to her as it had been to resist the wind pressure. Calmly sleeping, she lay on the sofa close to the horrible well-hole – so close to it that it seemed as if the slightest shock or even shake would hurl her into the abyss. The idea seemed to get hold of him; he could not shake it off. For a few moments it seemed to him as if the walls had faded away like mist, and as if, in a vision of second sight, there was a dim adumbration of a phase of the future – a kind of prophecy. Mimi's touch on his arm as if to suggest moving from the spot, recalled him to himself. Together they moved round to the back of the house, and stood where the wind was less fierce in the shelter of the iron door.

Whilst they were standing there, there came a blinding flash of lightning which lit up for several seconds the whole area of earth and sky. It was only the first note of the celestial prelude, for it was followed in quick succession by numerous flashes, whilst the crash and roll of thunder seemed continuous. Adam, appalled, drew his wife to him and held her close. As far as he could estimate by the interval between lightning and thunder-clap, the heart of the storm was still some distance off, and so he felt no present concern for their safety. Still, it was apparent that the course of the storm was moving swiftly in their direction. The lightning flashes came faster and faster and closer together; the thunder-roll was almost continuous, not stopping for a moment – a new crash beginning before the old one had ceased. Adam kept looking up in the direction where the kite strained and struggled at its detaining cord, but, of course, the dawn was not yet sufficiently advanced to permit of his seeing it in a glance.

At length there came a flash so appallingly bright that in its glare nature seemed to be standing still. So long did it last that there was time to distinguish its configuration. It seemed like a mighty tree inverted, pendent from the sky. The roots overhead were articulated. The whole country around within the angle of vision was lit up till it seemed to glow. Then a broad ribbon of fire seemed to drop on the tower of Castra Regis just as the thunder crashed. By the glare of the lightning he could see the tower shake and tremble and finally fall to pieces like a house of cards. The passing of the lightning left the sky again dark, but a blue flame fell downward from the tower and, with inconceivable rapidity running along the ground in the direction of Diana's Grove, reached the dark silent house, which in the instant burst into flame at a hundred different points. At the same moment rose from the house a rending, crashing sound of woodwork, broken or thrown about, mixed with a quick yell so appalling that Adam, stout of heart as he undoubtedly was, felt his blood turned into ice. Instinctively, despite the danger and their consciousness of it, husband and wife took hands and listened, trembling. *Something* was going on close to them, mysterious, terrible, deadly. The shrieks continued, though less sharp in sound, as though muffled. In the midst of them was a terrific explosion, seemingly sounding from deep in the earth. They looked around. The flames from Castra Regis and also from Diana's Grove made all around almost as light as day, and now that the lightning had ceased to flash, their eyes, unblinded, were able to judge both perspective and detail. The heat of the burning house caused the iron doors either to warp and collapse or to force the hinges. Seemingly of their own accord, they flew or fell open, and exposed the interior. The Saltons could now look through the atrium and the room beyond where the well-hole yawned, a deep narrow circular chasm. From this the agonised shrieks were rising, growing even more terrible with each second that passed. But it was not only the heart-rending sound that almost paralysed poor Mimi with terror. What she saw was alone sufficient to fill her with evil dreams for the remainder of her life. The whole place looked as if a sea of blood had been beating against it. Each of the explosions from below had thrown out from the well-hole, as if it had been the mouth of a cannon, a mass of fine sand mixed with blood, and a horrible repulsive slime in which were great red masses of rent and torn flesh and fat. As the explosions kept on, more and more of this repulsive mass was shot up, the great bulk of it falling back again. The mere amount of this mass was horrible to contemplate. Many of the awful fragments were of something which had lately been alive. They quivered and trembled and writhed as though they were still in torment, a supposition to which the unending scream gave a horrible credence. At moments some mountainous mass of flesh surged up through the narrow orifice as though it were forced by a measureless power through an opening infinitely smaller than itself. Some of these fragments were covered or partially covered with white skin as of a human being, and others – the largest and most numerous – with scaled skin as of a gigantic lizard or serpent. And now and again to these clung masses of long black hair which reminded Adam of a chest full of scalps which he had seen seized from a marauding party of Comanche Indians. Once, in a sort of lull or pause, the seething contents of the hole rose after the manner of a bubbling spring, and Adam saw part of the thin form of Lady Arabella forced up to the top amid a mass of blood and slime and what looked as if it had been the entrails of a monster torn in shreds. Several times some masses of enormous bulk were forced up through the well-hole with inconceivable violence, and, suddenly expanding as they came into larger space, disclosed great sections of the White Worm which Adam and Sir Nathaniel had seen looking over the great trees with its enormous eyes of emerald-green flickering like great lamps in a gale.

At last the explosive power, which was not yet exhausted,

evidently reached the main store of dynamite which had been lowered into the worm hole. The result was appalling. The ground for far around quivered and opened in long deep chasms, whose edges shook and fell in, throwing up clouds of sand which fell back and hissed amongst the rising water. The heavily built house shook to its foundations. Great stones were thrown up as from a volcano, some of them, great masses of hard stone squared and grooved with implements wrought by human hands, breaking up and splitting in mid air as though riven by some infernal power. Trees near the house, and therefore presumably in some way above the hole, which sent up clouds of dust and steam and fine sand mingled, and which carried an appalling stench which sickened the spectators, were torn up by the roots and hurled into the air. By now, flames were bursting violently from all over the ruins, so dangerously that Adam caught up his wife in his arms and ran with her from the proximity of the flames.

Then almost as quickly as it had begun, the whole cataclysm ceased. A deep-down rumbling continued intermittently for some time. And then silence brooded over all – silence so complete that it seemed in itself a sentient thing – silence which seemed like incarnate darkness, and conveyed the same idea to all who came within its radius. To the young people who had suffered the long horror of that awful night, it brought relief – relief from the presence or the fear of all that was horrible – relief which seemed perfected when the red rays of sunrise shot up over the far eastern sea, bringing a promise of a new order of things with the coming day.

CHAPTER XL
WRECKAGE

His bed saw little of Adam Salton for the remainder of that night. He and Mimi walked hand in hand in the brightening dawn round by the Brow to Castra Regis and on to Doom Tower. They did so deliberately in an attempt to think as little as possible of the terrible experiences of the night. They both tried loyally to maintain the other's courage, and in helping the other to distract attention from the recollections of horror. The morning was bright and cheerful, as a morning sometimes is after a devastating storm. The air was full of sunshine. The clouds, of which there were plenty in evidence, brought no lingering idea of gloom. All nature was bright and joyous, being in striking contrast to the scenes of wreck and devastation, of the effects of obliterating fire and lasting ruin.

The only evidence of the once stately pile of Castra Regis was a shapeless huddle of shattered architecture dimly seen at moments as the sea-breeze swept aside the cloud of thin, bluish, acrid smoke which presently marked the site of the once lordly castle. As for Diana's Grove, they looked in vain for a sign which had a suggestion of permanence. The oak trees of the Grove were still to be seen – some of them – emerging from a haze of smoke, the great trunks solid and erect as ever, but the larger branches broken and twisted and rent, with bark stripped and chipped, and the smaller branches broken and dishevelled looking from the constant stress and threshing of the storm. Of the house as such, there was, even at the little distance from which they looked, no trace. With the resolution to which he had come – to keep from his wife as well as he could all sights which might cause her pain or horror or leave unpleasant memories – Adam resolutely turned his back on the area of the devastation and hurried on to Doom Tower. This, with the strength and cosiness of the place, its sense of welcome and the perfection of its thoughtful ordering, gave Mimi the best sense of security and peace which she had had since, on last evening, she had left its shelter. She was not only upset and shocked in many ways, but she was physically 'dog tired' and falling asleep on her feet. Adam took her to her room and made her undress and get into bed, taking care that the room was well lighted both by sunshine and lamps. The only obstruction was from a silk curtain drawn across the window to keep out the glare. When she was feeling sleep steal over her, he sat beside her holding her hand, well knowing that the comfort of his presence was the best restorative for her. He stayed with her in that way till sleep had overmastered her wearied body. Then he went softly away. He found Sir Nathaniel in the study having an early cup of tea, amplified to the dimensions of possible breakfast. After a little chat, the two agreed to go together to look at the ruins of Diana's Grove and Castra Regis. Adam explained that he had not told his wife that he was going over the horrible places again, lest it would frighten her, whilst the rest and sleep in ignorance would help her and make a gap of peacefulness between the horrors. Sir Nathaniel agreed in the wisdom of the proceeding, and the two went off together.

They visited Diana's Grove first, not only because it was nearer, but that it was the place where most description was required, and Adam felt that he could tell his story best on the spot. The absolute destruction of the place and everything in it seen in the broad daylight was almost inconceivable. To Sir Nathaniel it was as a story of horror full and complete. But to Adam it was, as it were, only on the fringes. He knew what was still to be seen when his friend had got over the knowledge of externals. As yet, Sir Nathaniel had only seen the outside of the house – or rather, where the outside of the house had been. The great horror lay within. However, age – and the experience of age – counts. Sir Nathaniel in his long and eventful life had seen too many terrible and horrible sights to be dismayed at a new one, even of the kind which lay close before him, though

just beyond his vision. A strange, almost elemental, change in
the aspect had taken place in the time which had elapsed since
the dawn. It would almost seem as if Nature herself had tried
to obliterate the evil signs of what had occurred, and to restore
something of the æsthetic significance of the place. True, the
utter ruin and destruction of the house was made even more
manifest in the searching daylight; but the more appalling
destruction which lay beneath was not visible. The rent, torn,
and dislocated stonework looked worse than before; the
upheaved foundations, the piled-up fragments of masonry, the
fissures in the torn earth – all were at the worst. The Worm's
hole was still evident, a round fissure seemingly leading down
into the very bowels of the earth. But all the horrid mass of
blood and slime, of torn, evil-smelling flesh and the sickening
remnants of violent death, were gone. Either some of the later
explosions had thrown up from the deep quantities of water
which, though foul and corrupt itself, had still some cleansing
power left, or else the writhing mass which stirred from far
down below had helped to drag down and obliterate the items
of horror. A gray dust, partly of fine sand, partly of the waste
of the falling ruin, covered everything, and, though ghastly
itself, helped to mask in something still worse. After a few
minutes of watching, it became apparent to both men that the
turmoil far below had not yet quite ceased. At short irregular
intervals the hell-broth in the hole seemed as if boiling up. It
rose and fell again and turned over, showing in fresh form
much of the nauseous detail which had been visible earlier. The
worst parts to see were the great masses of the flesh of the
monstrous Worm in all its red and sickening aspect. Such fragments had been naturally bad enough before, but now they
were infinitely worse. Corruption comes with startling rapidity
to beings whose destruction has been due wholly or in part to
lightning. Now the whole mass seemed to have become all at
once corrupt. But that corruption was not all. It seemed to have
attracted every natural organism which was in itself obnoxious.
The whole surface of the fragments, once alive, was covered
with insects, worms, and vermin of all kinds. The sight was
horrible enough, but, with the awful smell added, was simply

unbearable. The Worm's hole appeared to breathe forth death in its most repulsive forms. Both Adam and Sir Nathaniel, with one impulse, turned and ran to the top of the Brow, where a fresh breeze from the eastern sea was blowing up.

At the top of the Brow, beneath them as they looked down, they saw a shining mass of white, which looked strangely out of place amongst such wreckage as they had been viewing. It appeared so strange that Adam suggested trying to find a way down so that they might see it closely.

Sir Nathaniel suddenly stopped and said:

'We need not go down. I know what it is. The explosions of last night have blown off the outside of the cliffs. That which we see is the vast bed of china clay through which the Worm originally found its way down to its lair. See, there is the hole going right down through it. We can catch the glint of the water of the deep quags far down below. Well, her ladyship didn't deserve such a funeral, or such a monument. But all's well that ends well. We had better hurry home. Your wife may be waking by now, and is sure to be frightened at first. Come home as soon as you can. I shall see that breakfast is ready. I think we all want it.'

Appendix I
Florence Stoker's Preface to *Dracula's Guest and Other Weird Stories* (1914)

Following Bram Stoker's death on 20 April 1912 his widow, Florence
Ann Lemon Stoker (née Balcombe, 1844–1935), collected to-
gether the stories which were subsequently published as *Dracula's
Guest and Other Weird Stories* (1914). A number of them had
previously appeared in periodicals during Stoker's lifetime. 'The
Judge's House' was originally published on 5 December 1891 in the
Christmas edition of *The Illustrated Sporting and Dramatic News*,
'The Squaw' and 'Crooken Sands' appearing in the 1893 and 1894
Christmas editions respectively. 'The Secret of the Growing Gold' first
appeared on 23 January 1892 in *Black and White* and 'A Dream of
Red Hands' on 11 July 1894 in *The Sketch*. 'A Gipsy Prophecy', 'The
Coming of Abel Behenna' and 'The Burial of the Rats', meanwhile,
were all published for the first time in 1914. Although Florence
Stoker's claim that 'Dracula's Guest' was an 'unpublished episode'
from *Dracula* is certainly accurate, it is unlikely that the version
published in this collection was the same that Stoker intended for
inclusion in his novel.

PREFACE

A few months before the lamented death of my husband – I might say
even as the shadow of death was over him – he planned three series
of short stories for publication, and the present volume is one of them.
To his original list of stories in this book, I have added an hitherto
unpublished episode from 'Dracula.' It was originally excised owing
to the length of the book, and may prove of interest to the many
readers of what is considered my husband's most remarkable work.
The other stories have already been published in English and American
periodicals. Had my husband lived longer, he might have seen fit to
revise this work, which is mainly from the earlier years of his strenuous

life. But, as fate has entrusted to me the issuing of it, I consider it fitting and proper to let it go forth practically as it was left by him.

FLORENCE A. L. BRAM STOKER.

Appendix II
The Laidly Worm of Spindleston Heugh (1890) and *The Lambton Worm* (1890)

The care which Bram Stoker took in rooting his stories in a relevant historical or mythological framework is particularly evident in *The Lair of the White Worm*. Entrenched in the environment of England's legendary past, whilst playing to the social concerns of the early twentieth century, *The Lair of the White Worm's* citation of the legends of the Laidly Worm of Spindleston Heugh and the Lambton Worm underscore its multivalent concerns about aggressive femininity, male gallantry and the classification of humanity, transposing them from author-centred anxieties to fundamental issues. Whilst providing a solid mythological backdrop to reinforce the 'longstanding' nature of such anxieties, in using them Stoker simultaneously elevates his own story into a modern myth for the contemporary reader.

As is the nature of folk-tales, the stories themselves exist in a variety of forms, from poetry to prose. The versions given here are those most contemporary with Stoker's own novel; 'The Laidly Worm of Spindleston Heugh' is taken from Joseph Jacobs's edited collection *English Fairy Tales* (London: David Nutt, 1890), pp. 183–7 and 'The Lambton Worm' from Edwin Sidney Hartland's edited collection *English Fairy and Other Folk Tales* (London: Walter Scott, 1890), pp. 78–82.

THE LAIDLY WORM OF SPINDLESTON HEUGH

In Bamborough Castle once lived a king who had a fair wife and two children, a son named Childe Wynd and a daughter named Margaret. Childe Wynd went forth to seek his fortune, and soon after he had gone his mother died. The king mourned her long and faithfully, but one day while he was hunting he came across a lady of great beauty, and became so much in love with her that he determined to marry her. So he sent word home that he was going to bring a new queen to Bamborough Castle.

Princess Margaret was not very glad to hear of her mother's place being taken, but she did not repine but did her father's bidding. And at the appointed day came down to the castle gate with the keys all ready to hand over to her stepmother. Soon the procession drew near, and the new queen came towards Margaret who bowed low and handed her the keys of the castle. She stood there with blushing cheeks and eyes on ground, and said: 'O welcome, father dear, to your halls and bowers, and welcome to you my new mother, for all that's here is yours,' and again she offered the keys. One of the king's knights who had escorted the new queen cried out in admiration: 'Surely this northern Princess is the loveliest of her kind.' At that the new queen flushed up and cried out: 'At least your courtesy might have excepted me,' and then she muttered below her breath: 'I'll soon put an end to her beauty.'

That same night the queen, who was a noted witch, stole down to a lonely dungeon wherein she did her magic and with spells three times three, and with passes nine times nine she cast Princess Margaret under her spell. And this was her spell:

> 'I weird ye to be a Laidly Worm,
> And borrowed shall ye never be,
> Until Childe Wynd, the King's own son
> Come to the Heugh and thrice kiss thee;
> Until the world comes to an end,
> Borrowed shall ye never be.'

So Lady Margaret went to bed a beauteous maiden, and rose up a Laidly Worm. And when her maidens came in to dress her in the morning they found coiled up on the bed a dreadful dragon, which uncoiled itself and came towards them. But they ran away shrieking, and the Laidly Worm crawled and crept, and crept and crawled till it reached the Heugh or rock of the Spindleston, round which it coiled itself, and lay there basking with its terrible snout in the air.

Soon the country round about had reason to know of the Laidly Worm of Spindleston Heugh. For hunger drove the monster out from its cave and it used to devour everything it could come across. So at last they went to a mighty warlock and asked him what they should do. Then he consulted his works and his familiar, and told them: 'The Laidly Worm is really the Princess Margaret and it is hunger that drives her forth to do such deeds. Put aside for her seven kine,[1] and each day as the sun goes down, carry every drop of milk they yield to the stone trough at the foot of the Heugh, and the Laidly Worm will trouble the country no longer. But if ye would that she be borrowed to her natural shape, and that she who bespelled her be rightly punished, send over the seas for her brother, Childe Wynd.'

All was done as the warlock advised, and the Laidly Worm lived on the milk of the seven kine, and the country was troubled no longer. But when Childe Wynd heard the news, he swore a mighty oath to rescue his sister and revenge her on her cruel stepmother. And three-and-thirty of his men took the oath with him. Then they set to work and built a long ship, and its keel they made of the rowan tree.[2] And when all was ready, they out with their oars and pulled sheer for Bamborough Keep.

But as they got near the keep, the stepmother felt by her magic power that something was being wrought against her, so she summoned her familiar imps and said: 'Childe Wynd is coming over the seas; he must never land. Raise storms, or bore the hull, but nohow must he touch shore.' Then the imps went forth to meet Childe Wynd's ship, but when they got near, they found they had no power over the ship, for its keel was made of the rowan tree. So back they came to the queen witch, who knew not what to do. She ordered her men-at-arms to resist Childe Wynd if he should land near them, and by her spells she caused the Laidly Worm to wait by the entrance of the harbour.

As the ship came near, the Worm unfolded its coils, and dipping into the sea, caught hold of the ship of Childe Wynd, and banged it off the shore. Three times Childe Wynd urged his men on to row bravely and strong, but each time the Laidly Worm kept it off the shore. Then Childe Wynd ordered the ship to be put about, and the witch-queen thought he had given up the attempt. But instead of that, he only rounded the next point and landed safe and sound in Budle Creek, and then, with sword drawn and bow bent, rushed up followed by his men, to fight the terrible Worm that had kept him from landing.

But the moment Childe Wynd had landed, the witch-queen's power over the Laidly Worm had gone, and she went back to her bower all alone, not an imp, nor a man-at-arms to help her, for she knew her hour was come. So when Childe Wynd came rushing up to the Laidly Worm it made no attempt to stop him or hurt him, but just as he was going to raise his sword to slay it, the voice of his own sister Margaret came from its jaws saying:

> 'O quit your sword, unbend your bow,
> And give me kisses three;
> For though I am a poisonous worm,
> No harm I'll do to thee.'

Childe Wynd stayed his hand, but he did not know what to think if some witchery were not in it. Then said the Laidly Worm again:

> 'O quit your sword, unbend your bow,
> And give me kisses three,
> If I'm not won ere set of sun,
> Won never shall I be.'

Then Childe Wynd went up to the Laidly Worm and kissed it once; but no change came over it. Then Childe Wynd kissed it once more; but yet no change came over it. For a third time he kissed the loathsome thing, and with a hiss and a roar the Laidly Worm reared back and before Childe Wynd stood his sister Margaret. He wrapped his cloak about her, and then went up to the castle with her. When he reached the keep, he went off to the witch queen's bower, and when he saw her, he touched her with a twig of rowan tree. No sooner had he touched her than she shrivelled up and shrivelled up, till she became a huge ugly toad, with bold staring eyes and a horrible hiss. She croaked and she hissed, and then hopped away down the castle steps, and Childe Wynd took his father's place as king, and they all lived happy afterwards.

But to this day, the loathsome toad is seen at times, haunting the neighbourhood of Bamborough Keep, and the wicked witch-queen is a Laidly Toad.

THE LAMBTON WORM

The park and manor-house of Lambton, belonging to a family of the same name, lie on the banks of the Wear, to the north of Lumley. The family is a very ancient one, much older, it is believed, than the twelfth century, to which date its pedigree extends. The old castle was dismantled in 1797, when a site was adopted for the present mansion on the north bank of the swiftly-flowing Wear, in a situation of exceeding beauty. The park also contains the ruins of a chapel, called Brugeford or Bridgeford, close to one of the bridges which span the Wear.

Long, long ago – some say about the fourteenth century – the young heir of Lambton led a careless, profane life, regardless alike of his duties to God and man, and in particular neglecting to attend mass, that he might spend his Sunday mornings in fishing. One Sunday, while thus engaged, having cast his line into the Wear many times without success, he vented his disappointment in curses loud and deep, to the great scandal of the servants and tenantry as they passed by to the chapel at Brugeford.

Soon afterwards he felt something tugging at his line, and trusting he had at last secured a fine fish, he exerted all his skill and strength to bring his prey to land. But what were his horror and dismay on finding that, instead of a fish, he had only caught a worm of most unsightly appearance! He hastily tore the thing from his hook, and flung it into a well close by, which is still known by the name of the Worm Well.

The young heir had scarcely thrown his line again into the stream when a stranger of venerable appearance, passing by, asked him what sport he had met with; to which he replied: 'Why, truly, I think I have caught the devil himself. Look in and judge.' The stranger looked, and remarked that he had never seen the like of it before; that it resembled an eft,[3] only it had nine holes on each side of its mouth; and, finally, that he thought it boded no good.

The worm remained unheeded in the well till it outgrew so confined a dwelling-place. It then emerged, and betook itself by day to the river, where it lay coiled round a rock in the middle of the stream, and by night to a neighbouring hill, round whose base it would twine itself, while it continued to grow so fast that it soon could encircle the hill three times. This eminence is still called the Worm Hill. It is oval in shape, on the north side of the Wear, and about a mile and a half from old Lambton Hall.

The monster now became the terror of the whole countryside. It sucked the cows' milk, worried the cattle, devoured the lambs and committed every sort of depredation on the helpless peasantry. Having laid waste the district on the north side of the river, it crossed the stream and approached Lambton Hall, where the old lord was living alone and desolate. His son had repented of his evil life, and had gone to wars in a distant country. Some authorities tell us he had embarked as a crusader for the Holy Land.

On hearing of their enemy's approach, the terrified household assembled in council. Much was said, but to little purpose, till the steward, a man of age and experience, advised that the large trough which stood in the courtyard should immediately be filled with milk. This was done without delay; the monster approached, drank the milk, and, without doing further harm, returned across the Wear to wrap his giant form around his favourite hill. The next day he was seen recrossing the river; the trough was hastily filled again, and with the same results. It was found that the milk of 'nine kye' was needed to fill the trough; and if this quantity was not placed there every day, regularly and in full measure, the worm would break out into a violent rage, lashing its tail round the trees in the park, and tearing them up by the roots.

The Lambton Worm was now, in fact, the terror of the North County. It had not been left altogether unopposed. Many a gallant knight had come out to fight with the monster, but all to no purpose; for it possessed the marvellous power of reuniting itself after being cut asunder, and thus was more than a match for the chivalry of the North. So, after many conflicts, and much loss of life and limb, the creature was left in possession of its favourite hill.

After seven long years, however, the heir of Lambton returned home, a sadder and wiser man – returned to find the broad lands of his ancestors waste and desolate, his people oppressed and well-nigh exterminated, his father sinking into the grave overwhelmed with care and anxiety. He took no rest, we are told, till he had crossed the river and surveyed the Worm as it lay coiled round the foot of the hill; then, hearing how its former opponents had failed, he took counsel in the matter from a sibyl or wise woman.

At first the sibyl did nothing but upbraid him for having brought this scourge upon his house and neighbourhood; but when she perceived that he was indeed penitent, and desirous at any cost to remove the evil he had caused, she gave him her advice and instructions. He was to get his best suit of mail studded thickly with spear-heads, to put it on, and thus armed to take his stand on the rock in the middle of the river, there to meet his enemy, trusting the issue to Providence and his good sword. But she charged him before going to the encounter to take a vow that, if successful, he would slay the first living thing that met him on his way homewards. Should he fail to fulfil this vow, she warned him that for nine generations no lord of Lambton would die in his bed.

The heir, now a belted knight, made the vow in Brugeford chapel. He studded the armour with the sharpest spear-heads, and unsheathing his trusty sword took his stand on the rock in the middle of the Wear. At the accustomed hour the Worm uncoiled its 'snaky twine', and wound its way towards the hall, crossing the river close by the rock on which the knight was standing eager for the combat. He struck a violent blow upon the monster's head as it passed, on which the creature, 'irritated and vexed', though apparently not injured, flung its tail round him, as if to strangle him in its coils.

In the words of a local poet –
'The worm shot down the middle stream
Like a flash of living light,
And the waters kindled round his path
In rainbow colours bright.
But when he saw the armoured knight
He gathered all his pride,
And, coiled in many a radiant spire,
Rode buoyant o'er the tide.
When he darted at length his dragon strength
An earthquake shook the rock,
And the fireflakes bright fell round the knight
As unmoved he met the shock.
Though his heart was stout it quailed no doubt,
His very life-blood ran cold,
As round and round the wild Worm wound
In many a grappling fold.'

Now was seen the value of the sibyl's advice. The closer the Worm wrapped him in its folds the more deadly were its self-inflicted wounds, till at last the river ran crimson with its gore. Its strength thus diminished, the knight was able at last with his good sword to cut the serpent in two; the severed part was immediately borne away by the swiftness of the current, and the Worm, unable to reunite itself, was utterly destroyed.

During this long and desperate conflict the household of Lambton had shut themselves within-doors to pray for their young lord, he having promised them that when it was over he would, if conqueror, blow a blast on his bugle. This would assure his father of his safety, and warn them to let loose the favourite hound, which they had destined as the sacrifice on the occasion, according to the sibyl's requirements and the young lord's vow. When, however, the bugle-notes were heard within the hall, the old man forgot everything but his son's safety, and rushing out of doors, ran to meet the hero and embrace him.

The heir of Lambton was thunderstruck: what could he do? It was impossible to lift his hand against his father; yet how else to fulfil his vow? In his perplexity he blew another blast; the hound was let loose, it bounded to its master; the sword, yet reeking with the monster's gore, was plunged into its heart; but all in vain. The vow was broken, the sibyl's prediction fulfilled, and the curse lay upon the house of Lambton for nine generations.

NOTES

1. *kine*: Cows.
2. *rowan tree*: The European rowan tree was thought to possess magical properties, in particular, protection against malevolent beings.
3. *eft*: A newt, or lizard-like animal.

Notes

DRACULA'S GUEST AND OTHER WEIRD STORIES

DRACULA'S GUEST

1. *Munich*: Harker recalls having travelled through Germany in the opening sentence of *Dracula*: '3 May. Bistritz. – Left Munich at 8.35 p.m. on 1st May, arriving at Vienna early next morning' (Bram Stoker, *Dracula*, ed. Maurice Hindle (London: Penguin Books, 2003), p. 7).

2. *Walpurgis nacht*: In German folklore, a feast of the powers of darkness or witches' sabbath celebrated on the night of 30 April.

3. *the horses . . . suspiciously*: Compare this with the reaction of the horses to the arrival of Count Dracula: 'Whilst he was speaking the horses began to neigh and snort and plunge wildly, so the driver had to hold them up' (Stoker, *Dracula*, p. 16). Similar textual and stylistic comparisons with *Dracula* can be made throughout this story.

4. *burying suicides at cross-roads*: To take one's life was considered a sin by Christians, and suicides were buried at crossroads with a stake through their bodies and their property confiscated by the State.

5. *men and women . . . red with blood*: Whilst the Eastern Orthodox Church believed that incorrupt corpses denoted sainthood, the Roman Catholics held them to be a sign of vampirism.

6. *yew and cypress*: Whilst yew is commonly planted in graveyards and is regarded as a symbol of sadness, branches or sprigs of cypress are often used at funerals as a symbol of mourning.

7. *a beautiful woman . . . sleeping on a bier*: The image of the 'undead' women is a frequent feature of Stoker's stories, from Lucy Westenra in *Dracula* to Queen Tera in *The Jewel of Seven*

Stars (1903) and Lady Teuta in *The Lady of the Shroud* (1909).

8. *the sacred bullet*: It was believed that a werewolf was immune to damage caused by ordinary weapons, being vulnerable only to silver objects (usually a bullet or a blade), although this is more a reflection of nineteenth-century fiction than folk legends.

THE JUDGE'S HOUSE

1. *Jacobean style*: An English art, architectural and furniture style dominant during the reign of James I (1603–25), Jacobean design followed the general lines of Elizabethan design, but used classical features with greater complexity and with more extravagant ornamentation.

2. *a judge . . . Assizes*: Bram Stoker probably found inspiration for his malicious protagonist in the figure of Judge George Jeffreys (1648–89), Lord Chancellor under King James II (r. 1685–1701), who was perhaps the most notorious 'hanging judge' in English history. Henry Irving's son, Henry Brodribb, wrote a biography of him, *The Life of Judge Jeffreys* (London: William Heinemann, 1898).

3. *Tripos*: The final honours examinations for university degree subjects at Oxford and Cambridge. The name derives from the three-legged stool on which the examinee would sit.

4. *Harmonical Progression . . . Elliptic Functions*: The listing of such mathematical terminology, continued in later pages of the story, highlights the battle between rational logic and the supernatural threat of the Judge.

5. *a Senior Wrangler*: The head of the 'wranglers', i.e. of the first class of those who are successful in the Mathematical Tripos at Cambridge University.

6. *Greenhow's Charity*: Stoker could possibly be referring to Dr Edwin Headlam Greenhow (1814–88), physician, sanitarian, clinician and lecturer, whose academic studies and negotiations with the government led to the environmental clean-up in the later nineteenth century and the end of cholera and typhoid epidemics.

7. *Saint Anthony . . . the point*: Born about the middle of the third century at Coma, Egypt, Anthony disposed of his worldly possessions at an early age to devote himself exclusively to an ascetic life, abnegating human contact for twenty years. St Anthony is frequently hailed as the founder of Christian monasticism, and

is also the patron saint of gravediggers – an ominous indicator, perhaps, of this ascetic student's fate.

8.   *Laplace*: Pierre-Simon Laplace (1749–1827) was a gifted French mathematician and astronomer who established the stability of planetary motion. He also excelled at, and made considerable advances in, integral calculus, finite differences and differential equations.

9.   *the diamond-paned bay window*: The earliest glass was extremely expensive and only available without severe distortions in relatively small panes. As a result almost all windows of the Tudor and Jacobean periods were made up of leaded light panels, often with diamond shapes, called 'quarries'. The quarries were joined together to form the window light using strips of lead, called 'cames', which were soldered together to make up one large glazed area.

10. *Shake! as they say in America*: Throughout his stories, Stoker displays a fondness for the colloquial dialect and aphorisms of his foreign or provincial characters. Subsequent reviewers have taken a less enthusiastic stance to this, one review of *The Watters Mou* (1895) remarking: 'Conscious of his weakness in the manner of Scottish dialect, Mr Stoker has indulged in that luxury as little as possible, but the little that he does introduce is truly awful' ('New Books', *The Dundee Advertiser*, 10 January 1895).

11. *he trembled like an aspen*: The aspen tree is characterized by elongated, flexible leaves that give it the appearance of 'shivering' in the slightest breeze. The aspen's idiosyncrasy was immortalized in 'Binsey Poplars' (1879), by Gerald Manley Hopkins (1844–89), who moved to Dublin in 1884.

12. *a black cap*: A square of black cloth that was part of English judges' full dress. It was traditionally donned when passing a death sentence.

THE SQUAW

In the summer of 1885 Bram Stoker, Henry Irving and Ellen Terry journeyed to Nuremberg and Rothberg in southern Germany in preparation for the Lyceum Company's production of *Faust*. In Nuremberg's castle they visited a torture tower, in which the Iron Virgin was displayed.

1.   *Irving ... Faust*: Mephistopheles was one of Henry Irving's most celebrated roles and *Faust* the Lyceum Company's greatest

success. Written by William Gorman Wills, *Faust* opened on
19 December 1885 and was performed 792 times.

2.   *Methuselah ... Yurrup*: Cf. Genesis 5:27: 'Thus all the days of
Methuselah were nine hundred and sixty-nine years; and he died.'
Methuselah is thus used as a means by which to ascribe great
age. *Yurrup*: Europe (slang).

3.   *the Burg*: A fortress or walled town of early or medieval times.

4.   *Claude Lorraine*: The artist Claude Gené (1604–82) was better
known as Lorraine after the place of his birth. Chiefly concerned
with the picturesque, Lorraine often depicted romantic old castles
or ruins set against the rough textures of wild nature.

5.   *the Torture Tower*: Nuremberg's Max Tower was the location
of the offices of the Nuremberg Inquisition during the period
when Duke Albert V of Bavaria (1550–79) attempted the forcible
restoration of Roman Catholicism. The Iron Virgin was the final
destination of those prisoners who refused to recant their hereti-
cal beliefs.

6.   *tender as a Maine cherry-tree*: The American north-eastern state
of Maine is famous for its fruit orchards, particularly blueberries
and apples. Possibly Stoker is here referring to the native Pin
Cherry (*Prunus pensylvanica*), a rapidly growing cherry tree with
soft and light wood, most commonly used as a grafting and
budding stock for the sour cherry.

7.   *the Gothic restorers of forty years ago*: In the late eighteenth
century there was a revival of Gothic styles of architecture, with
the emphasis on a romantic interest in the medieval. This was
followed in the nineteenth century by a more scholarly style of
Gothic, the architectural proponents of which included A. W.
Pugin (1812–52) and Gilbert Scott (1811–78). The widespread
adoption of the Gothic style transformed the appearance of English towns and cities. Buildings of this later style of Gothic architecture include the Palace of Westminster and St Pancras Station,
London.

8.   *the Pantheistic souls of Philo or Spinoza*: Pantheism is the philosophy that God is immanent in or identical with the universe.
Philo Judaeus (*c.*25 BC – AD *c.*50), a Hellenized Jewish philosopher, was born in Alexandria, Egypt. Born in Amsterdam to
Sephardic Jews, Benedict De Spinoza (1632–77) is best known
for his five books of *Ethica Ordine Geometrico Demonstrata*
(1677), which worked towards the conclusion that 'God' and
'Nature' are two names for the same reality that underlies the
universe, of which all lesser entities are made.

9. *implements of torture . . . to man*: Stoker may have gained inspiration for his descriptions of the instruments of torture from James A. Wylie's *The History of Protestantism* (1874–7), which contains a chapter on the Inquisition of Nuremberg and the methods of torture used.

10. *a rude birthmark . . . Nurnberg Virgin*: Stoker was much taken with the notion that birthmarks were either a direct result of 'maternal impression' (the representation of an event experienced by a mother during pregnancy) or a physical manifestation of a past-life memory, often corresponding to a fatal wound from that life. In *The Jewel of Seven Stars* Margaret Trelawny's birthmark on her wrist replicates the wound-line of Queen Tera's severed hand. Margaret herself, it is later revealed, is the reincarnation of Tera.

11. *Montana Territory*: Montana lies in the north-west of the United States. It was first explored by white colonizers in the early nineteenth century, eventually becoming a state in its own right in 1889. Gold was discovered there in the late 1850s, and in 1876 it was the scene of the Battle of the Little Bighorn, in which the Sioux and Cheyenne famously defeated the United States' army: it is perhaps to these conflicts between white settlers and Native Americans that Hutcheson is referring.

12. *Idaho territory*: Bordered on its eastern side by Montana, Idaho experienced similar events subsequent to its settlement by white colonials, including the mid-nineteenth-century gold rush and Native American uprisings. Idaho became a state in its own right in 1890.

13. *Wapping*: Wapping's proximity to the sea gave it a strong maritime character for centuries. Located on the north bank of the Thames, to the east of London, it was the site of 'Execution Dock', where pirates and other water-borne criminals faced execution by hanging from a gibbet constructed close to the low water mark. Bodies were left hanging until they had been submerged three times by the tide.

14. *euchered*: In the nineteenth century the trick-taking card game euchre was highly popular in the United States. To be 'euchered' thus implies being outwitted, tricked or deceived.

THE SECRET OF THE GROWING GOLD

Bram Stoker explored the Zermatt valley in southern Switzerland on a visit to his parents, who had emigrated to the continent in the summer of 1872. The story's fatal climax may have been inspired by Stoker's familiarity with the macabre tale of the exhumation of Dante Gabriel Rossetti's wife, Elizabeth Siddal. Although Siddal was disinterred seven years after her death, when the coffin was opened it was said that her hair was still golden and growing.

1. *the causes of decadence ... plebeian forms*: In Stoker's stories the threat to middle-class stability emanates both from the aristocracy and the lower classes. Stoker here makes reference to the *fin-de-siècle* theory of Degeneration, notably expounded in Max Nordau's *Degeneration* (1892), which held that certain supposed retrograde changes in the social and cultural fabric were symptomatic of a wholesale deterioration of the human race. Stoker's concern for the racial deterioration of England's stock is countered in his novels by an assertive promotion of national regeneration through hybridization. In *The Lair of the White Worm*, for example, the half-Australian Adam Salton marries the half-Burmese Mimi Watford.

2. *splenetic humour*: In ancient and medieval philosophy it was believed the body was composed of four fluids, or humours: blood, phlegm, choler and melancholy, or black choler. The relative mental qualities and dispositions of a person were determined by the proportion of these humours in the body. Black choler was held to be secreted by the spleen and associated with a melancholic or irritable nature.

3. *lime*: Apart from being a building material, in its most pure form (which is also known as quicklime) lime was widely used to dispose of corpses in mass graves, due to its highly corrosive alkalinity.

A GIPSY PROPHECY

1. *La Tour*: Château-Latour is situated in the Médoc region of France, near Bordeaux. A creator of high-quality wine, it is one of the only five châteaux in the region to be classified as a 'premier grand cru classé' – a prestigious position in the French wine-growing industry.

2. *the young barrister*: Stoker himself was called to the bar on 30 April 1890, although he never practised as a lawyer.

3. *Mendelssohn*: The German composer Felix Mendelssohn (1809–47) is probably most popularly recognized for his 'Wedding March' from *A Midsummer Night's Dream* (1826).

4. *Bohemia*: An historical region in central Europe, Bohemia was an independent kingdom until 1743, when it was annexed into the Hapsburg Empire. After the First World War Bohemia became the cornerstone of the newly formed country of Czechoslovakia. It now occupies the western and middle thirds of the Czech Republic.

5. *Madame Tussaud's*: Born Marie Grosholtz, Madame Tussaud (1761–1850) established her first permanent wax museum on Baker Street in 1835. It was later moved to its current location on Marylebone Road in 1884.

6. *Ghourka knife . . . the mutiny*: Part of the regimental weaponry and heraldry of Ghurkha fighters, the Kukri or Khukuri is a heavy, curved Nepalese knife used as both a tool and a weapon. The 1857 mutiny by the Indian army led to civil and military insurrections throughout northern and central India against British Imperial authority. Although order was restored by 1858, the upheaval enabled the British to impose direct rule (the British Raj) on the Indian subcontinent until 1947.

THE COMING OF ABEL BEHENNA

In 1892 Stoker holidayed in the small fishing village of Boscastle on the west coast of Cornwall, which he had discovered earlier that year on a walking tour. A medieval harbour village in the folds of high steep cliffs situated between Tintagel and Bude, Boscastle was a working port up until the end of the nineteenth century and the arrival of the railway at nearby Camelford. Both Boscastle's location and its blowhole, Devil's Bellows, served as inspiration for Stoker's fictional village of Pencastle.

1. *yellow-hammer*: The male yellow-hammer bird has a bright yellow head, a yellow underbelly and a heavily streaked brown back.

2. *stonecrop*: The common name of *Sedum acre*, a herb with bright yellow flowers and small cylindrical fleshy sessile leaves, which grows in masses on rocks, old walls, etc.

3. *Phoenician . . . Norseman*: An ancient civilization in the north

of ancient Canaan, central Phoenicia lay along the coastal plain of what is now Lebanon and Syria. The Phoenicians were an enterprising maritime people, and their trading culture spread right across the Mediterranean Sea and beyond during the first millennium BC. 'Norseman' was a name for the native people of ancient or medieval Scandinavia, including the Vikings.

4.   *cast sheep's eyes*: To look lovingly, amorously or longingly.

5.   *Damon . . . Pythias*: In Greek mythology, the legend of Damon and Pythias symbolizes trust, loyalty and true friendship. Pythias was accused of plotting against the tyrant of Syracuse, Dionysius I, and sentenced to death. Damon was allowed to stand bail for his friend, who wished to return home to say farewell to his family, under the condition that if Pythias did not return Damon would be executed in his place. Both were saved from execution when Pythias eventually returned to Syracuse, thus overwhelming Dionysius with his display of loyalty to his friend.

6.   *the wreckers' fire basket*: Cornwall's rugged coastline was a haven for wreckers and smugglers, whose activities reached a peak in the eighteenth century. Booty from shipwrecked vessels was often considered fair game by local inhabitants, whilst more sinister wreckers actively lured ships to their destruction with false lights.

7.   *Pahang . . . Chersonese*: Although 'chersonese' technically indicates any peninsula, Stoker seems to be referring to the Malay Peninsula at the southern extremity of the Asian continent lying between the Andaman Sea of the Indian Ocean and the Strait of Malacca on the west, and the Gulf of Thailand and the South China Sea on the east. The important British role on the peninsula began with the founding of settlements at Pinang (1786) and Singapore (1819). Located in the east coast region of the peninsula, Pahang is the Malay Peninsula's largest state.

8.   *the old Berserker fury*: Berserkers (or Berserks) were Norse warriors who had sworn allegiance to Odin, the god of war, and who worked themselves into a murderous fury before a battle. In *Dracula*, Chapter XI, the wolf that escapes from London Zoo is named Bersicker.

9.   *a 'ketch' . . . only a jib*: A ketch is a sailing craft with two masts (main and mizzen) whilst a jib is the triangular stay-sail that is set ahead of the foremost mast.

10. *the hatred of Cain*: The first-born of Adam and Eve, Cain killed his younger brother, Abel, in jealousy of God's preference for him. Cain was subsequently cursed by God and became a fugitive wanderer.

11. *Canton*: Officially renamed Guangzhou in 1918, the city of
     Canton lies toward the south of China's coast, approximately
     180 kilometres north-west of Hong Kong.

THE BURIAL OF THE RATS

Bram Stoker visited Paris in 1875, staying with his close friend the
actress Geneviève Ward and her mother. Following a letter in which
Stoker professed admiration for a 'Miss Henry' (possibly Geneviève
Ward herself), his father wrote back advising against forming close
acquaintanceship with actresses. The narrator's 'forbidden love' for a
girl may well be a reference to Stoker's father's disapproval.

1. *Enceinte*: A fortification enclosing a fortress or town.
2. *ad absurdum . . . devil fish*: *Ad absurdum*: literally 'to the absurd'
    (Latin). A devil fish is an octopus, cuttle-fish, or other cephalopod.
3. *Messrs Cook or Gaze*: Thomas Cook (1808–92) founded his
    travel business in the mid nineteenth century. Henry Gaze's com-
    pany was Cook's closest rival travel agent operator. Henry Gaze
    & Sons travel agency went bankrupt in 1903, whilst Thomas
    Cook's empire still operates to the present day.
4. *chiffonier*: Rag picker. The rag pickers of Paris were traditionally
    despised and marginalized as the lowest caste, subjected to social
    exclusion and held responsible for the ills of society, including
    epidemics, thefts and urban insecurity in general. Relegated to
    areas outside the city walls, they were nevertheless organized into
    a hierarchical, disciplined system. At the bottom was the night
    'collector' who did not have his own patch or tools and roamed
    over a wide area; the 'runner' was equipped with a basket, a
    lantern and a hook to sift through refuse; the 'placer' had his
    own patch and had first pick of the refuse in that area. At the
    top of the social scale were the master rag pickers, genuine
    merchants with storage sheds and weighing scales.
5. *Napoleon . . . Baron Hausseman*: Under the orders of Charles
    Louis Napoleon Bonaparte (1808–73) and the direction of civic
    planner Georges-Eugène, Baron Haussmann (1809–91), Paris
    was largely redesigned and redeveloped. Large sections of the
    city were razed and the old narrow streets replaced with broad
    avenues with the intent of allowing both cavalry and cannon easy
    access, and also of reducing the ability of future revolutionaries to
    challenge the government.
6. *'hope deferred maketh the heart sick'*: Cf. Proverbs 13:12: 'Hope

deferred maketh the heart sick, but when the desire cometh, it is a tree of life.'

7.   *Ultima Thule*: The highest or uttermost point or degree attained or attainable (Latin).

8.   Bog of Allan: A large peat bog in the centre of Ireland. The Bog of Allen, as it is usually known, features prominently in Stoker's first novel, *The Snake's Pass* (1890).

9.   *Charles VII . . . Henry II*: Charles VII of France (1403–61); Henry II of France (1519–59).

10. *First Republic*: The French people proclaimed the country's First Republic and the abolition of the monarchy on 21 September 1792 as a result of the French Revolution (1789–99), itself triggered by the storming of the Bastille prison, a potent symbol of autocratic cruelty, by the people of Paris. This presaged a new era of republican governments in Europe.

11. *mauvais sujet . . . absinthe*: A *mauvais sujet* (French) is a worthless person, a bad lot. Allegedly invented in 1797 by Dr Pierre Ordinaire, absinthe was originally distilled from wine mixed with wormwood and typically contains between 45 and 85 per cent alcohol. A feature of the bohemian lifestyle in the latter decades of the nineteenth century, *la fée verte* (the green fairy), as it became commonly known, found particularly fashionable status in France, until its prohibition in 1915. Vincent Van Gogh (1853–90), Henri de Toulouse-Lautrec (1864–1901), and Ernest Hemingway (1899–1961) were among the drink's devotees.

12. *Dutch roll*: A roll in ice-skating, executed by gliding with the feet parallel and pressing alternately on the edges of each foot.

13. *the ceteuces . . . in the revolution*: Synonymous with the French Revolution, the guillotine was the favoured execution method of insurgents. A quick, reliable and 'entertaining' means of disposing of adversaries, it became the only legal execution method in France until the abolition of the death penalty in 1981. The image of women avidly witnessing and celebrating such executions, particularly the infamous 'tricoteuses' ('ceteuces' is most likely Stoker's misspelling) who would knit at the foot of the guillotine, was regarded with horror by contemporary reporters who condemned them as unnatural examples of their sex.

14. '*Oh! To see or hear her singing! Scarce I know which is the divinest*': Elizabeth Barrett Browning (1806–61), 'Lady Geraldine's Courtship: A Romance of the Age' (1844), 'Oh, to see or hear her singing! Scarce I know which is divinest', line 173.

15. *the rabble*: Horror of mob violence is a recurrent theme in the Gothic genre, from the vengeful, mindless mob that tears apart the prioress in Matthew Lewis's *The Monk* (1796) to James Whale's film version of *Frankenstein* (1931) in which a hollering throng sets fire to the windmill in which the monster is trapped.

16. *bridge of Arcola . . . Old Guard at Waterloo*: The Battle of Arcola (15–17 November 1796) was notable for Napoleon Bonaparte grabbing a flag and personally leading an assault across the Arcola bridge. At the Battle of Waterloo (18 June 1815), the Old Guard fought to the end to enable the Emperor Napoleon to escape from the battlefield as the Allied troops closed in. General Cambronne is reputed to have answered a call to surrender with the words 'The Guard dies but does not surrender.'

17. *Hobson's choice*: An apparently free choice that is really no choice at all.

A DREAM OF RED HANDS

1. *a flaming sword*: According to the Bible, a Cherub with a rotating flaming sword was placed by God at the gates of Paradise after Adam and Eve were banished from it (Genesis 3:24).

2. *a soul is typified by a butterfly*: Many ancient civilizations believed that butterflies were symbols of the human soul. The Greek goddess Psyche, for example, the personification of the human soul, was often represented in the shape of a butterfly, and the Greek word *Psykhē* can be translated either 'soul' or 'butterfly'.

CROOKEN SANDS

In the 1890s Bram Stoker took numerous holidays to the Scottish east-coast village of Cruden Bay. The village itself was overlooked by Slaines Castle, ancestral home of the Errolls, from where it was said the elderly nineteenth Earl was in the habit of walking around Cruden Bay in a tweed suit of antique cut and high Glengarry bonnet with the family's falcon crest pinned upon it. Certainly, the story lampoons the late eighteenth and nineteenth centuries' nostalgic romanticizing of a powerful yet largely inchoate idea of Celticism.

1. *the Goodwins*: The Goodwin sands, a stretch of shoals and sandbars about fifteen kilometres long, lie off the east coast of

Kent. They are a notorious hazard to shipping and are littered with wrecks.

2. *Copthall-court*: Copthall Court lies near to the Bank of England and the Stock Exchange in central London.

3. *cairngorm brooches . . . sporran*: A precious stone of a yellow or wine-colour, cairngorm stone was commonly used for brooches, seals and for ornamenting the handles of dirks (a kind of dagger). A sporran is a large purse made of animal skin, usually with the hair left on, that is worn in front of the kilt (or philibeg) by Scottish Highlanders.

4. *Royal Stuart dress tartan . . . Balmoral*: The Royal Stewart is the tartan of the British Royal House of Stewart and the personal tartan of Her Majesty the Queen. The Balmoral Estate, situated in Royal Deeside, Aberdeenshire, was purchased by Queen Victoria in 1848 and has been the Scottish home of the British Royal Family ever since.

5. *claymore*: The two-edged broadsword of the ancient Scottish Highlanders.

6. *Girdle Ness lighthouse*: Situated at the south entrance to Aberdeen harbour, Girdle Ness lighthouse was designed by Robert Stevenson and built in 1833.

7. *Glengarry cap*: Invented by Alasdair Ranaldson MacDonell of Glengarry, a Glengarry cap (or bonnet) is a boat-shaped cap without a peak made of thick-milled woollen material with a *toorie*, or bobble, on top and ribbons hanging down behind.

8. *mulls*: Snuffboxes.

9. *'Vanity of vanities . . . one of these'*: Cf. Ecclesiastes (Qoheleth) 1:2: 'Vanity of vanities, saith the Preacher, vanity of vanities; all is vanity' and Matthew 6:28–9: 'Consider the lilies of the field, how they grow; they toil not, neither do they spin: and yet I say unto you, that even Solomon in all his glory was not arrayed like one of these.'

10. *döppleganger*: Traditionally, seeing one's double was an omen of ill-luck, ill-health or death. The theme of the doppelgänger was popular in nineteenth-century literature, especially Gothic fiction, examples including James Hogg's *The Private Memoirs and Confessions of a Justified Sinner* (1824), Robert Louis Stevenson's *The Strange Case of Dr Jekyll and Mr Hyde* (1886) and Oscar Wilde's *The Picture of Dorian Gray* (1890).

THE LAIR OF THE WHITE WORM

DEDICATION

1. *Bertha Nicoll*: A friend of Bram Stoker's who first made him aware of the 'Bisley Boy' legend attached to Overcourt manor house in Bisley, Gloucestershire. The legend held that the young Queen Elizabeth had died in infancy there, and had been replaced by a male child. The episode formed a section in Stoker's penultimate book, *Famous Impostors* (1910).

CHAPTER I
ADAM SALTON ARRIVES

1. *the Great Eastern Hotel*: Large hotel adjacent to Liverpool Street railway station. Opened in May 1884, the Great Eastern was for many years pre-eminent among London's elegant railway hotels. It also features in *Dracula* as Abraham Van Helsing's hotel of choice when staying in London: 'Have then rooms for me at the Great Eastern Hotel' (p. 123).

2. *West Australia*: James Cook (1728–79) 'discovered' Australia in 1770, claiming possession in the name of George III (1738–1820). On 26 January 1788 the British government assumed control over the eastern half of the country, exploiting its potential as a trading, whaling and penal colony. In the nineteenth century, with a rapidly expanding and diversifying immigrant population, Australia underwent a transition from penal colony to free and self-governing dominion, and finally became a nation in its own right on 1 January 1901.

3. *Mercia*: After the end of Roman rule in 409, the British Isles became a patchwork of territories founded by both indigenous and immigrant communities and led by chieftains and kings. Mercia emerged as one of the most powerful of these kingdoms, between the sixth and eighth centuries fiercely maintaining its independence and often waging war with other major kingdoms to preserve, or expand, its area of control. At the height of its power Mercia stretched from the River Thames to the borders of Yorkshire and Lancashire, and from the coast of Lincolnshire and the borders of East Anglia to the Welsh border. After a series of strong warrior kings, most notably Offa, who ruled from 757 to his death in 796, Mercian hegemony declined in the ninth

century, the kingdom losing much of its territory to its neighbours. It was finally and irrevocably annexed by King Edward
the Elder of Wessex (c. 874/7–924) in 919.

4.   *Stafford*: In 913 Stafford was fortified by Queen Æthelflaed
     (r. 911–18) and became the new capital of Mercia. It was also
     home to a royal mint for 250 years from 924 to 1189.

5.   *William IV*: William IV of England (1765–1837).

6.   *ribbons*: Reins.

CHAPTER II

THE CASWALLS OF CASTRA REGIS

1.   *the 'donkey' engine*: A small steam-engine, usually for subsidiary
     operations on board ship, for instance feeding the boilers of the
     propelling engines.

2.   *Salisbury . . . Stafford*: All of these towns and cities are ancient
     settlements dating back to Anglo-Saxon, Roman or pre-Roman
     times. Stoker's reference to these locations reinforces the sense
     of Adam Salton's journey into the heart of ancient Britain.

3.   *the British Romans*: Following Julius Caesar's reconnaissance
     expeditions to Britain in 55 and 54 BC, Emperor Claudius
     (10 BC – AD 54) ordered its forcible invasion in 43 BC. Despite
     meeting with fierce resistance from British tribes, by AD 47 the
     Claudian armies occupied Britain as far as the Severn and the
     Trent and by AD 84 Roman control had extended to the far
     north of Scotland with garrisons to the edge of the Highlands.

4.   *all the various nationalities . . . became Britain*: Britain only
     became so-called after the 1707 Act of Union which created the
     United Kingdom of Great Britain. The early history of the country
     is dominated both by foreign invasion (Roman, Anglo-Saxon,
     Viking and Norman) and the division of the country itself into
     tribal territories.

5.   *Salisbury Cathedral*: Relocated from its original position in Old
     Sarum, Salisbury Cathedral was started in 1220 and finally conse-
     crated in 1258. The spire, the tallest in England (123m), was
     added in the middle of the fourteenth century. Although it
     escaped relatively unscathed from the religious architectural
     purging of the Commonwealth, in 1790 permission was granted
     for the architect James Wyatt (1746–1813) to 'restore' the
     interior of the cathedral. Porches, chapels, screens and stained
     glass were destroyed and the interior was white-washed. The
     campanile, which rose almost 61 metres over the north side of

the churchyard and housed the original bells which rang at Old Sarum, were also destroyed at this time.

6.   *The aquiline features . . . close and curly*: Dracula's face, too, is described as: 'very strong – aquiline . . . His eyebrows were massive, almost meeting over the nose, and with bushy hair that seemed to curl in its own profusion' (Stoker, *Dracula*, p. 24). Many of Stoker's stories pay homage to the late eighteenth- and nineteenth-century pseudo-science of physiognomy, pioneered by Johann Caspar Lavater (1741–1801), which held that the true character of an individual could be deduced by the structure of the head and body, and from facial expressions and physical gestures.

7.   *partly hypnotic, partly mesmeric*: Mesmerism was first popularized by Franz Anton Mesmer (1734–1815), who claimed that all animal life was underpinned by a 'magnetic' fluid which, in illness, became unbalanced. Mesmer maintained that he could realign a patient's magnetic field through the influence of his own 'animal magnetism'. Although mesmerism was discredited by a scientific commission established by Louis XVI of France in 1784, Mesmer's techniques had great popular appeal and were variously developed by other practitioners in the late eighteenth and early nineteenth centuries, ultimately forming the basis of the modern practice of hypnosis, itself first developed by Dr James Braid (1795–1860).

8.   *in propria persona*: 'In proper person' (Latin).

CHAPTER III
DIANA'S GROVE

1.   *the coup d'œil*: A comprehensive glance (French).

2.   *Welsh Marches . . . Humber to the Wash*: The term 'march' is derived from the Anglo-Saxon *mearc* meaning 'boundary', the Welsh Marches thus roughly encompassing the area between the Welsh mountains and English river beds that divide the two nations.

3.   *seriatim*: OED: 'One after the other; one by one in succession' (Latin).

4.   *Druidical*: Belonging to the Celtic tribes of Gaul and Britain, the Druids, according to Julius Caesar's *Gallic Wars*, were priests and teachers. Their name is synonymous in native Irish and Welsh legend with magician and sorcerer, however. Druidism was suppressed after the Roman conquests of Britain and Gaul, but retained its influence in Ireland until the coming of Christianity.

5. *Vilula Misericordiæ*: Literally 'House of Mercy' (Latin).
6. *Queen Bertha ... King Penda ... St Augustine*: Augustine arrived from Rome in Kent in May 597, under the direction of Pope Gregory the Great (*c.*540–604), and he and his mission were received hospitably by Kent's pagan king, Ethelbert, whose Frankish queen, Bertha, was already a Christian. The account of Augustine's mission suggests that English Christianity began in the year 597, but the English had been exposed to Christianity from more than one direction throughout the sixth century. Kent was the first kingdom to convert in the late 590s/early 600s, East Anglia followed in the early seventh century and Wessex set up a bishopric at Dorchester-on-Thames in 634. The Mercians held out against outright conversion for most of Penda's reign (633–53) and it was only under King Wulfhere (r. 658–75) that official sanction was given to Christianity.
7. *savage Wales*: Welsh military might ensured that the country resisted capitulation to Roman, Anglo-Saxon and Norman invasion. It was only finally conquered in 1282 when Edward I (1272–1307) defeated Llywelyn the Last (*c.*1228–82).
8. *each fresh wave ... the Normans*: The traditional dates applied to these various invasions of Britain are: Anglo-Saxons, *c.*450; Danes, 865 (with smaller raids on Lindisfarne in 793, Jarrow in 794 and Iona in 795); Normans, 1066. This history of invasion roots the novel in a culture of national conflict, making it a tale of physical *and* spiritual boundary disruption.
9. *Henry I*: Henry I of England (1068–1135).

CHAPTER IV
THE LADY ARABELLA MARCH

1. *Stone*: Located in Staffordshire, about seven miles north of Stafford and seven miles south of Stoke-on-Trent, Stone was the early capital of Mercia before Stafford and then Tamworth.
2. *Wulfere ... Christianity*: Contrary to Stoker's interpretation, King Wulfhere in reality embraced Christianity and married a Christian Kentish princess, Eormenhild, in about 660. The Mercian king gave every assistance to Christianity, providing much land for the founding of monasteries and seeing to it that they were richly endowed. Wulfhere was also father of a saintly daughter, St Waerburh.
3. *My father is Lord Lieutenant of the County*: The Lord-lieutenant of a county acted as the chief executive authority and head of

the magistracy. First introduced in the sixteenth century, his role was the active defence of the realm, and up until 1871 he had extensive powers with regard to the militia. Although the position is now mainly ceremonial, the position of Lord-lieutenant retains some of its former powers, including the recommendation of persons for appointment as justices of the peace.

4. *several black snakes*: There are no wholly black snakes indigenous to Britain. Stoker could, however, have been alluding to the black racer or black rat snakes of America, both constrictor snakes, or perhaps the poisonous Australian hooded black snake, *Pseudechis*, of the cobra family.

5. *She was clad . . . her sinuous figure*: In an article entitled 'Character Note: The New Woman', published in *Cornhill Magazine* 23 (1894), the New Woman is depicted thus: 'She dresses simply in close-fitting garments, technically known as tailor-made. She wears her elbows well away from her side. It has been hinted that this habit serves to diminish the apparent size of her waist . . . It certainly adds to a somewhat aggressive air of independence which finds its birth in the length of her stride . . . Her attitudes are strong and independent, indicative of a self-reliant spirit.'

CHAPTER V
HOME-COMING

1. *so brutal as to be hardly human*: The mid-nineteenth-century theory of polygenism posited the theory that the human races are separate biological species. Non-white races were held to be essentially another – lesser – form of life, closer to the animals, thus 'justifying' their inferior status.

2. *he treated her . . . a deity*: If Oolanga is a practitioner of Voodoo, then his adoration of Lady Arabella and her snakiness correlates to the voodoo worship of Dan, the great snake. Often depicted as a snake biting its own tail (and also represented in the form of a rainbow circling the earth) who creates a bridge between heaven and earth, Dan is symbolic of unity in the world, and is also responsible for the control of all the activities of the numerous nature gods. The snake is a very important figure and symbol in Voodoo rites and worship, whilst (like Lady Arabella) the Voodoo *hounon* (priest) traditionally wears white.

3. *the local Jamrach*: Johann Christian Jamrach (1815–91) was an importer of wild animals for zoos and circuses, and a well-known East End personality. Having moved to England in 1843,

Jamrach eventually established his business on the Ratcliffe High-way. Jamrach's business is also mentioned in *Dracula* as the place where Bersicker, the grey wolf which escapes from the London Zoological Gardens, was purchased.

4.   *the coigns of vantage*: A position affording facility for observa-tion or action. Cf. William Shakespeare, *Macbeth* (I, vi, 7–9): 'No jutty frieze,/Buttress, nor coign of vantage, but this bird/Hath made her pendent bed and procreant cradle.'

5.   *dacoits in Burmah*: Derived from the Hindi word *dakait* ('a robber'), dacoits were a class of robbers in India and Burmah who plundered in armed bands. Previously an independent kingdom, Burma (Myanmar) was invaded by the British in 1824–6, 1851–2 and 1885–6 and became a part of India. It regained indepen-dence from Indian administration in 1937, becoming a sovereign state on 4 January 1948.

6.   *Lilla all fair … her mother's race*: Such physiological contrasts between two characters are a common feature in Stoker's work. See also Mina Harker and Lucy Westenra in *Dracula*, and Abel Behenna and Eric Sanson in 'The Coming of Abel Behenna'.

CHAPTER VI
THE WHITE WORM

1.   '*Advance, Australia!*': 'Advance Australia Fair' was composed by Glasgow-born Peter Dodds McCormick (*c.*1834–1916), under the pseudonym 'Amicus'. The first public performance is thought to have been given in Sydney on 30 November 1878. On 19 April 1984 it was proclaimed Australia's national anthem, to be played at all official and ceremonial occasions. 'God Save the Queen' subsequently became the 'royal anthem', to be played when the Queen or members of the Royal Family are present.

2.   '*They stumble that run fast*': Cf. William Shakespeare, *Romeo and Juliet* (II, iii, 94): 'Wisely and slow; they stumble that run fast.'

3.   *legend of the 'Worm Well' … near Bamborough*: See Appendix II.

4.   *shikaree*: A hunter or sportsman.

5.   *The condition of things … possibility of survival*: Evolution theory's emotive principle of a 'struggle for survival' inspired many writers from Thomas Hardy to H. G. Wells. The premise of large primeval creatures, existing in vast subterranean caves, who challenged the hegemony of *Homo sapiens* was an enduring

concept in fiction, appearing in such works as Charles John Cutcliffe Hyne's 'The Lizard' (1898) and Sir Arthur Conan Doyle's 'The Terror of the Blue John Gap' (1910) and *The Lost World* (1912).

CHAPTER VII
HAWK AND PIGEON

1. *the Christy Minstrel*: Minstrelsy was a form of music that began in the United States in the 1820s. It was often staged by white performers who used cork to make themselves up in blackface, although there were many black groups also. While not, as he claimed, the leader of the first blackface minstrel troupe, Edwin P. Christy (1815–62) indisputably led one of the most renowned. Formed in New York in 1842, Christy's Minstrels crystallized the pattern of the minstrel show. For over ten years Christy and his troupe had great success all over the United States (including Broadway), most notably performing the works of Stephen Collins Foster (1826–64). E. P. Christy himself eventually retired in 1854 and committed suicide in 1862. Minstrelsy continued as a part of the American music scene until the 1950s.

2. *à l'outrance*: Literally 'at outrageousness' (French); to the bitter end.

CHAPTER VIII
OOLANGA

1. *an Obi-man . . . a user of Voodoo*: Voodoo is a set of religious practices deeply rooted in African culture whose adherents believe that nature and natural forces are animated by divinities and spirits, and that in ecstatic states, such as trance, it is possible to establish direct contact with them. In Jamaica, the faith brought from Africa continues to flourish as Obeah, hence an Obeah man is one that practises the rituals of Voodoo.

CHAPTER IX
SURVIVALS

1. *the scheme of a First Cause*: Cf. Revelations 22:13: 'Christ is the First and Last Cause.'

2. *'the effectual fervent prayer . . . availeth much'*: James 5:16.

3. *the dove became . . . the nunnery*: In Christian iconography the

dove is a traditional symbol of love and peace. A dove was supposed to have been released by Noah after the flood in order to find land, returning with an olive branch. A dove also symbolizes the Holy Spirit in reference to Matthew 3:16 and Luke 3:22 where the Holy Spirit appears as a dove at the Baptism of Jesus.

4.   *Penda*: Penda, pagan king of Mercia (r. 626–55), consolidated and enlarged the Kingdom of Mercia. His military achievements ensured the emergence of Mercia as one of the most important kingdoms of the Anglo-Saxon era.

5.   *King Offa . . . restored Christianity*: Although supporting Christianity, Offa actually sought to control it in England by maintaining effective political control over the Kingdom of Kent, and so over the Archbishop of Canterbury.

CHAPTER XI
THE FIRST ENCOUNTER

1.   *a comparative anatomist*: Comparative anatomy is the study of similarities and differences in organisms.

2.   *a new Berserker fury*: see *Dracula's Guest and Other Weird Stories*, 'The Coming of Abel Behenna', note 8.

CHAPTER XII
THE KITE

1.   *the Yang-tze-kiang*: At 6300 kilometres long, the Yangtze Kiang is the longest river in Asia, flowing eastward from Tibet into the East China Sea near Shanghai.

2.   *which who might read*: Cf. Habakkuk 2:2: 'Write the vision, and make it plain upon tables that he may run that readeth it.' The inference is that the depression is so obvious that anyone on two legs would notice it.

3.   *the universal darkness . . . with pain*: Cf. Revelations 16:10: 'And the fifth angel poured out his vial upon the seat of the beast; and his kingdom was full of darkness; and they gnawed their tongues for pain.'

CHAPTER XIII
MESMER'S CHEST

1.   *decadence*: Decadence was a highly emotive term in the later nineteenth century, referring to the supposed decline of society due to moral weakness.

2. *ancient Egyptian relics . . . mummies*: Stoker's interest in Egyptian history manifested itself in his 1903 novel, *The Jewel of Seven Stars*. His enthusiasm for Egyptology may have been fired during his Dublin years by his frequent visits to 1 Merrion Square, the home of Sir William and Lady Jane Wilde, the parents of Oscar Wilde. Sir William Wilde had been a keen archaeologist and explorer in Egypt, and was a tireless campaigner for the transportation of Cleopatra's Needle to England (finally accomplished in 1878, two years after his death).

CHAPTER XIV
THE CHEST OPENED

1. *Bes . . . destructive power of nature*: Bes was a dwarf god protecting against evil with his tambourine or harp, swords, maces and knives. He is usually depicted with somewhat leonine facial features, tongue sticking out, standing on bow legs, his genitals prominent, and often with a lion's tail. He was also thought to be able to strangle bears, lions, antelopes and snakes with his bare hands and as such was held to be able to protect people from dangerous creatures of all types. In this role, despite being thought of as a demon, he was seen as a supporter of the god Ra, helping to defeat his serpent enemies.

2. *Sir Thomas Brown's Popular Errors*: Sir Thomas Browne, *Pseudodoxia Epidemica, or Enquiries into Very Many Received Tenents, and Commonly Presumed Truths* (1646). The quotation Stoker gives here is actually taken from Book 2, Chapter 3: 'A Rejection of sundry opinions and Relations thereof, Naturall, Medicall, Historicall, Magicall'.

3. *Mr Graves*: John Greaves, *Pyramidographia: or a Description of the Pyramids in Ægypt* (1646).

CHAPTER XV
OOLANGA'S HALLUCINATIONS

1. *the Gold Coast*: The Gold Coast was a British colony, formed in 1821, on the west coast of Africa. It became the independent nation of Ghana in 1957.

CHAPTER XVI
BATTLE RENEWED

1.   *an æolian harp*: A stringed instrument adapted to produce musical sounds on exposure to a current of air. So named from Aeolus, the Greek god of the winds.
2.   *Siam*: Siam first changed its name to Thailand in 1939, and definitively in 1949 after reverting to the old name post Second World War.

CHAPTER XVII
THE SHUTTING OF THE DOOR

1.   *the sextant*: An astronomical instrument resembling a quadrant used for measuring angular distances between objects, and specially for observing altitudes of celestial bodies, thus calculating latitude at sea.

CHAPTER XX
THE MYSTERY OF 'THE GROVE'

1.   *Benin or Ashantee*: Benin and Ashanti (now an administrative region in central Ghana) lie on the west coast of Africa. Both states participated in the African slave trade with Europe until its abolition in the nineteenth century. Ashanti's wealth was based primarily on the region's substantial deposits of gold, whilst Benin is notable for being the country from which Voodoo worship originates.

CHAPTER XXI
EXIT OOLANGA

1.   *amour propre*: Self-esteem (French).
2.   *Smith and Wesson*: Founded in 1856, the gun manufacturer Smith & Wesson (first established by Horace Smith and Daniel B. Wesson) is now America's largest producer of handguns.
3.   *the Cimmerian darkness*: The Cimmerii were a nomadic people, the earliest known inhabitants of the Crimea, who overran Asia Minor in the 7th century BC. As described in Homer's *Odyssey* (Book XI, 12–19) they were fabled to live in a state of perpetual darkness.
4.   *veined bloodstone*: A precious stone spotted or streaked with

red, bloodstone was supposed to have the power of staunching bleeding when worn as an amulet.

CHAPTER XXIII
AN ENEMY IN THE DARK

1. *en rapport*: In sympathy (French).
2. *nem. con.*: OED: 'Especially with reference to a motion carried: (with) no one speaking (or voting) against.' From *nemine contradicente* (Latin).
3. *tiled*: OED: 'Tile: *Freemasonry*. (Usually 'tyle'). To protect (a lodge or meeting) from interruption and intrusion, so as to keep its proceedings secret, by placing a 'tiler' before the door. Also *transf.* to bind (a person) to secrecy; to keep (any meeting or proceeding) strictly secret.'

CHAPTER XXIV
METABOLISM

1. *dragons . . . in their slime*: Cf. Alfred, Lord Tennyson (1809–92), *In Memoriam* (1854):

    > No more? A monster then, a dream,
    > A discord. Dragons of the prime,
    > That tare each other in their slime,
    > Were mellow music matched with him. (56: 21–4)

2. *In fine*: To conclude or sum up, finally (Latin).
3. *Derbyshire . . . Kentucky*: Some of the deepest caves in Britain are found in Derbyshire, including the Blue John Cavern (worked by the Romans for its deposits of the mineral Blue John); Treak Cliff Cavern (containing some of Britain's finest stalactite and stalagmite formations); and Speedwell Cavern (mined for its rich lead deposits). The Mammoth caves in Kentucky remain the longest recorded cave system in the world with more than 360 miles explored and mapped. It is the second-oldest tourist attraction in America after Niagara Falls, with guided tours offered since 1816.
4. *Philosopher's Stone . . . transmutation of metal*: The Philosopher's Stone was reputed by alchemists to possess the property of changing other metals into gold or silver. Commonly identified with the *elixir vitae* (elixir of life), it was also supposed to heal

wounds and prolong life indefinitely. Although scientifically discredited by the twentieth century, the metaphors and imagery of the Philosopher's Stone persisted. In 1901, atomic scientists Ernest Rutherford (1871–1937) and Frederick Soddy (1877–1956) discovered that radioactivity was a sign of fundamental changes (transmutation) within elements. Soddy, an alchemical hobbyist, quickly made the connection between this and the ancient search for the Philosopher's Stone, and the process was subsequently named the 'Disintegration Theory of Atomic Transmutation'. Radium itself had been discovered in 1898 by the Polish-born French chemist Marie Sklodowska Curie (1867–1934) and her husband, Pierre (1859–1906). Awarding their Nobel Prize in 1911, Dr E. W. Dahlgren declared: 'The theory of transmutation, dear to the alchemists, has been unexpectedly restored to life, this time in an exact form, deprived of any mystical element; and the Philosopher's Stone with the property of inducing such transmutations is no longer a mysterious, elusive elixir but is something which modern science calls energy.'

5.   'the substance . . . things unseen': Cf. Hebrews 11:1: 'Now faith is the substance of things hoped for, the evidence of things not seen.'

CHAPTER XXV
THE DECREE

1.   genii and species: In 1735 Swedish biologist Carl Linnaeus (1707–78) published the first volume of his Systema Naturae, in which he established his scheme for classifying all known and yet to be discovered organisms according to the greater or lesser extent of their structural similarity. Linnaeus used a binomial nomenclature system, according all organisms two Latin name categories, genus and species. In total, Linnaeus' classification hierarchy consisted of five levels: kingdom, class, order, genus and species. The Linnaean system of classification was widely accepted by the early nineteenth century and remains the basic framework for all categorization in the biological sciences, although the modern taxonomical system now includes seven levels of classification: kingdom, phylum, class, order, family, genus, species.

2.   it is cold-blooded: Arabella herself is referred to as being cold-blooded in Chapters XV and XIX.

CHAPTER XXVI
A LIVING BARBETTE

1. *Barbette*: A platform or mound of earth within a fortification, on which the guns are raised so that they can be fired over the parapet.
2. *a cocotte*: A prostitute (French).

CHAPTER XXVII
GREEN LIGHT

1. *the Isle of Man*: Stoker's links with the Isle of Man (of which Douglas is the capital) were through his friendship with Thomas Henry Hall Caine (1853–1931), to whom *Dracula* was dedicated. Of Manx parentage, Caine was the highly successful author of such melodramatic novels as *The Deemster* (1887), *The Bondman* (1890) and *The Manxman* (1894).
2. *the Ribble*: The River Ribble, which runs through North Yorkshire and Lancashire in the north of England, marked the ancient northern boundary of Mercia, and at the time of the Domesday Book (1086) was the northern boundary of Cheshire.

CHAPTER XXVIII
AT CLOSE QUARTERS

1. *kick the beam*: To die; to be of inferior consequence.
2. *seen her close and lived to tell the tale*: Links can be made here between Lady Arabella's avatar as serpent and the Greek mythological character of Medusa, a monstrous female with hair of living venomous serpents whose glance would turn all living creatures to stone.

CHAPTER XXIX
IN THE ENEMY'S HOUSE

1. *a snake . . . stealth and cunning*: Compare this with Van Helsing's assessment of Dracula: 'he too have child-brain, and it is of the child to do what he have done' (*Dracula*, p. 363). Contemporary criminal anthropologists such as Cesare Lombroso (1836–1909) and Max Nordau (1849–1923) postulated the existence of a criminal type, physically distinguishable and 'lower' in the evolutionary scale than the 'normal' human being.

In her animality, Lady Arabella thus reveals her abnormality and criminality.

2.   *I remember ... the Khan of Bokhara*: Stoker may possibly be referring here to the assassination of Alexander II of Russia (1818–81) who, whilst driving through the streets of St Petersburg near the Winter Palace on 13 March 1881, was mortally wounded in a grenade ambush organized by a gang of revolutionaries.

CHAPTER XXX
A RACE FOR LIFE

1.   *The slop-basin*: Properly equipped, a tea-tray would comprise a teapot and stand, teacups and saucers, sugar bowl, milk jug and slop basin for discarding used tea leaves.

2.   *Queenstown*: It is possible that Stoker here is referring to the sea port in County Cork (Ireland) now called Cobh. The locality was renamed Queenstown in 1849 to commemorate a visit by Queen Victoria. One of the major transatlantic Irish ports, Cobh was the last port of call for the RMS *Titanic* on 11 April 1911 before she set out across the Atlantic.

CHAPTER XXXI
BACK TO DOOM

1.   *semaphore signals*: The semaphore system is an alphabet-signalling method based on the waving of hand-held flags in a particular pattern. The flags are usually square, red and yellow, with the red portion in the upper hoist.

2.   *a via dolorosa*: Literally 'way of grief' (Latin), the Via Dolorosa is the route in Jerusalem that Christ is believed to have followed from Pilate's judgement hall to Calvary.

CHAPTER XXXII
A STARTLING PROPOSITION

1.   *dernier cri*: Latest fashion (literally 'last cry') (French).

CHAPTER XXXIII
WAR À L'OUTRANCE

1. *Stafford owes much ... time to time*: A fine white potter's clay, also called kaolin, china clay was employed in the manufacture of china or porcelain. North Staffordshire became the centre of ceramic and porcelain production in Britain in the seventeenth century, due to the ready availability of clay, salt, lead and coal.

2. *the labours of Hercules*: To atone for the killing of his wife and children, executed in a fit of madness, Hercules was sentenced by the Oracle to serve King Eurystheus. As part of his sentence, Hercules had to perform twelve seemingly impossible Labours. These were: procuring the skin of the Nemean Lion; killing the Lernean Hydra; acquiring the Hind of Ceryneia and the Erymanthian Boar; cleaning the Augean Stables in a single day; driving away the Stymphalian Birds; killing the Cretan Bull; acquiring the Man-Eating Horses of Diomedes, Hippolyte's Girdle, the Cattle of Geryon and the Apples of the Hesperides; and finally, journeying into the Underworld to kidnap the beast Cerberus.

3. *there is nothing new under the sun*: Cf. Ecclesiastes 1:9: 'The thing that hath been, is that which shall be; and that which is done is that which shall be done: and there is no new thing under the sun.'

4. *the Chartist trouble*: Chartism was a movement for social and political reform in Britain during the mid nineteenth century which took its name from the *People's Charter* of 1838, a document calling for radical reform of the electoral and enfranchisement system.

5. *greater explosion at Hell Gate in New York*: Hell Gate is a narrow tidal channel in the East River in New York City separating Ward's Island and Astoria, Queens. Navigation in the strait was extremely hazardous due to the submerged rocks and converging tide-currents and by the late nineteenth century hundreds of ships had sunk in the channel. In 1876 the US Army Corps of Engineers blasted the dangerous rocks – one explosion of which was the largest man-made blast in history up until the Atomic Age.

CHAPTER XXXIV
APPREHENSION

1. *a Kelvin sounding apparatus*: The Kelvin Sounding Machine, invented by the mathematical physicist and engineer William Thomson, 1st Baron Kelvin (1824–1907), was a device used to calculate water depth in fathoms. A lead weight was lowered on a wire and the depth recorded by the apparatus.
2. *parti*: A person considered in terms of eligibility for marriage on grounds of wealth, social status, etc. (French).

CHAPTER XXXVII
ERITIS SICUT DEUS

1. *Eritis Sicut Deus*: 'Ye shall be as gods' (Latin), from Genesis 3:5: 'For God doth know that in the day ye eat thereof, then your eyes shall be opened, and ye shall be as gods, knowing good and evil.'

CHAPTER XXXVIII
ON THE TURRET ROOF

1. *That way madness lies*: Cf. William Shakespeare, *King Lear* (III, iv, 21): 'O, that way madness lies. Let me shun that.'
2. *When the Master of Evil . . . kingdoms of the earth*: Cf. Luke 4:5: 'And the devil, taking him up into an high mountain, shewed unto him all the kingdoms of the world in a moment of time.'
3. *a magnesium light*: When burnt, magnesium produces a blinding white light, commonly used in signalling, in pyrotechnics or in photography where a strong illumination is required.

CHAPTER XXXIX
THE BREAKING OF THE STORM

1. *a rope-walk or a bundle of hop-poles*: A rope-walk is a stretch of ground appropriated to the making of ropes. A hop-pole is a tall pole on which hop-plants are trained.
2. *spring guns*: A gun rigged to fire when a string or other triggering device is tripped by contact with the string of sufficient force to 'spring' the trigger.
3. *inter alia*: 'Amongst other things' (Latin).

PENGUIN CLASSICS

THE MOONSTONE   WILKIE COLLINS

'When you looked down into the stone, you looked into a yellow deep that drew your eyes into it so that they saw nothing else'

The Moonstone, a yellow diamond looted from an Indian temple and believed to bring bad luck to its owner, is bequeathed to Rachel Verinder on her eighteenth birthday. That very night the priceless stone is stolen again and when Sergeant Cuff is brought in to investigate the crime, he soon realizes that no one in Rachel's household is above suspicion. Hailed by T. S. Eliot as 'the first, the longest, and the best of modern English detective novels', *The Moonstone* is a marvellously taut and intricate tale of mystery, in which facts and memory can prove treacherous and not everyone is as they first appear.

Sandra Kemp's introduction examines *The Moonstone* as a work of Victorian sensation fiction and an early example of the detective genre, and discusses the technique of multiple narrators, the role of opium, and Collins's sources and autobiographical references.

'Enthralling and believable . . . evokes in vivid language the spirit of a place' P. D. James, *Sunday Times*

Edited with an introduction and notes by Sandra Kemp

PENGUIN CLASSICS

THE PRIVATE MEMOIRS AND CONFESSIONS OF A JUSTIFIED SINNER   JAMES HOGG

'My life has been a life of trouble and turmoil; of change and vicissitude; of anger and exultation; of sorrow and of vengeance'

Robert Colwan, a clergyman's son, is so confident of his salvation as one of the Lord's elect that he comes to look on himself as a man apart, unhindered by considerations of mere earthly law. Through Robert's own unforgettable account, we follow the strange and sinful life into which he is led by a devilish doppelgänger – a life that will finally lead him to murder. Steeped in the folkloric superstitions and theological traditions of eighteenth-century Scotland, this macabre and haunting novel is a devastating portrayal of the stages by which the human spirit can descend into darkness.

Based on the first edition of 1824, John Wain's text incorporates key revisions from the 1837 edition to provide the most accurate possible version of this complex and rewarding work. In his introduction, he illuminates the novel's historical background of religious and political controversy.

'Astounding' André Gide

Edited with an introduction by John Wain

CONFESSIONS OF AN ENGLISH OPIUM EATER
THOMAS DE QUINCEY

'Thou hast the keys of Paradise, oh just, subtle, and mighty opium!'

Confessions is a remarkable account of the pleasures and pains of worshipping at the 'Church of Opium'. Thomas De Quincey consumed large daily quantities of laudanum (at the time a legal painkiller), and this autobiography of addiction hauntingly describes his surreal visions and hallucinatory nocturnal wanderings though London, along with the nightmares, despair and paranoia to which he became prey. The result is a work in which the effects of drugs and the nature of dreams, memory and imagination are seamlessly interwoven. *Confessions* forged a link between artistic self-expression and addiction, paving the way for later generations of literary drug-users from Baudelaire to Burroughs, and anticipating psychoanalysis with its insights into the subconscious.

This edition is based on the original serial version of 1821, and reproduces the two 'sequels', 'Suspiria De Profundis' (1845) and 'The English Mail-Coach' (1849). It also includes a critical introduction discussing the romantic figure of the addict and the tradition of confessional literature, and an appendix on opium in the nineteenth century.

Edited with an introduction by Barry Milligan

PENGUIN CLASSICS

FRANKENSTEIN MARY SHELLEY

'Now that I had finished, the beauty of my dream vanished, and breathless horror and disgust filled my heart . . .'

Obsessed by creating life itself, Victor Frankenstein plunders graveyards for the material to fashion a new being, which he shocks into life by electricity. But his botched creature, rejected by Frankenstein and denied human companionship, sets out to destroy his maker and all that he holds dear. Mary Shelley's chilling gothic tale was conceived when she was only eighteen, living with her lover Percy Shelley near Byron's villa on Lake Geneva. It would become the world's most famous work of horror fiction, and remains a devastating exploration of the limits of human creativity.

Based on the third edition of 1831, this contains all the revisions Mary Shelley made to her story, as well as her 1831 introduction and Percy Bysshe Shelley's preface to the first edition. It also includes as appendices a select collation of the texts of 1818 and 1831 together with 'A Fragment' by Lord Byron and Dr John Polidori's 'The Vampyre: A Tale'.

Edited with an introduction by Maurice Hindle

PENGUIN CLASSICS

KIDNAPPED   ROBERT LOUIS STEVENSON

'There was no doubt about my uncle's enmity . . . and he would leave no stone unturned that might compass my destruction'

Orphaned and left penniless, David Balfour sets out to find his last living relative, miserly and reclusive Uncle Ebenezer. But Ebenezer is far from welcoming, and David narrowly escapes being murdered before he is kidnapped and imprisoned on a ship bound for Carolina. When the ship is wrecked, David, along with fiery Alan Breck, makes his way back across the treacherous Highland terrain on a quest to see that justice is done. Through his powerful depiction of the contrasting personalities of his two central characters – the romantic Jacobite Breck and the rationalist Whig David – Stevenson dramatized a conflict that was at the heart of Scottish culture in the aftermath of the Jacobite rebellion, as well as creating an unforgettable adventure story.

This edition contains an introduction and historical note to illuminate the social and political background of the novel, and also includes notes and a glossary.

Edited with an introduction and notes by Donald McFarlan

PENGUIN CLASSICS

DRACULA BRAM STOKER

'Alone with the dead! I dare not go out, for I can hear the low howl of the wolf through the broken window'

When Jonathan Harker visits Transylvania to help Count Dracula with the purchase of a London house, he makes horrifying discoveries about his client and his castle. Soon afterwards, a number of disturbing incidents unfold in England: an unmanned ship is wrecked at Whitby; strange puncture marks appear on a young woman's neck; and the inmate of a lunatic asylum raves about the imminent arrival of his 'Master'. In the ensuing battle of wits between the sinister Count Dracula and a determined group of adversaries, Bram Stoker created a masterpiece of the horror genre, probing deeply into questions of human identity and sanity, and illuminating dark corners of Victorian sexuality and desire.

For this completely updated edition, Maurice Hindle has revised his introduction, list of further reading and textual notes, and added two new appendices: Stoker's essay on censorship and his interview with Winston Churchill, both published in 1908.

'One of the most powerful horror tales ever written'
Malcolm Bradbury, *Mail on Sunday*

Edited with an introduction and notes by Maurice Hindle and with a preface by Christopher Frayling

PENGUIN CLASSICS

THE FALL OF THE HOUSE OF USHER AND OTHER WRITINGS   EDGAR ALLAN POE

'And much of Madness and more of Sin
And Horror the Soul of the Plot'

This selection of Poe's critical writings, short fiction and poetry demonstrates an intense interest in aesthetic issues and the astonishing power and imagination with which he probed the darkest corners of the human mind. 'The Fall of the House of Usher' describes the final hours of a family tormented by tragedy and the legacy of the past. In 'The Tell Tale Heart', a murderer's insane delusions threaten to betray him, while stories such as 'The Pit and the Pendulum' and 'The Cask of Amontillado' explore extreme states of decadence, fear and hate. These works display Poe's startling ability to build suspense with almost nightmarish intensity.

David Galloway's introduction re-examines the myths surrounding Poe's life and reputation. This edition includes a new chronology and further reading.

'The most original genius that America has produced'
Alfred, Lord Tennyson

'Poe has entered our popular consciousness as no other American writer'
The New York Times Book Review

Originally published under the title *Selected Writings*
Edited with an introduction and notes by David Galloway

PENGUIN CLASSICS

THE WAR OF THE WORLDS H. G. WELLS

'For countless centuries Mars has been the star of war'

The night after a shooting star is seen streaking through the sky from Mars, a cylinder is discovered on Horsell Common in London. At first, naïve locals approach the cylinder armed just with a white flag – only to be quickly killed by an all-destroying heat-ray, as terrifying tentacled invaders emerge. Soon the whole of human civilisation is under threat, as powerful Martians build gigantic killing machines, destroy all in their path with black gas and burning rays, and feast on the warm blood of trapped, still-living human prey. The forces of the Earth, however, may prove harder to beat than they at first appear.

The first modern tale of alien invasion, *The War of the Worlds* remains one of the most influential of all science fiction works. Part of a brand new Penguin series of H. G. Wells's works, this edition includes a newly-established text, a full biographical essay on Wells, a further reading list and detailed notes. The introduction, by Brian Aldiss, considers the novel's view of religion and society.

Introduced by Brian Aldiss

Textual Editing by Patrick Parrinder

Notes by Andy Sawyer

THE STORY OF PENGUIN CLASSICS

Before 1946 ...'Classics' are mainly the domain of academics and students, without readable editions for everyone else. This all changes when a little-known classicist, E. V. Rieu, presents Penguin founder Allen Lane with the translation of Homer's *Odyssey* that he has been working on and reading to his wife Nelly in his spare time.

1946 *The Odyssey* becomes the first Penguin Classic published, and promptly sells three million copies. Suddenly, classic books are no longer for the privileged few.

1950s Rieu, now series editor, turns to professional writers for the best modern, readable translations, including Dorothy L. Sayers's *Inferno* and Robert Graves's *The Twelve Caesars*, which revives the salacious original.

1960s The Classics are given the distinctive black jackets that have remained a constant throughout the series's various looks. Rieu retires in 1964, hailing the Penguin Classics list as 'the greatest educative force of the 20th century'.

1970s A new generation of translators arrives to swell the Penguin Classics ranks, and the list grows to encompass more philosophy, religion, science, history and politics.

1980s The Penguin American Library joins the Classics stable, with titles such as *The Last of the Mohicans* safeguarded. Penguin Classics now offers the most comprehensive library of world literature available.

1990s The launch of Penguin Audiobooks brings the classics to a listening audience for the first time, and in 1999 the launch of the Penguin Classics website takes them online to a larger global readership than ever before.

The 21st Century Penguin Classics are rejacketed for the first time in nearly twenty years. This world famous series now consists of more than 1300 titles, making the widest range of the best books ever written available to millions – and constantly redefining the meaning of what makes a 'classic'.

The Odyssey continues ...

The best books ever written

PENGUIN CLASSICS

SINCE 1946